CRITICS RAV[...]

"To say that Jennifer [...] [...]st understatement."
—*Romance Reviews Today*

"Ashley sprinkles in the perfect amount of humor…to keep the story sprightly."
—*Romantic Times*

"Ms. Ashley has a serious sense of humor, which comes out in her writing."
—*Rakehell*

PENELOPE & PRINCE CHARMING

"Ashley's latest sinfully sexy historical Regency will delight and charm readers with its enchanting mix of fantasy and fairy-tale romance."
—*Booklist*

"The magic of Ashley's latest is in not only the spellbinding plotline but also her impressive writing style and engaging characters involved in a grand adventure. This is a very special, highly satisfying read."
—*RT BOOKreviews*

"*Penelope & Prince Charming* gives readers a sexy, magical read."
—*Fresh Fiction*

"*Penelope & Prince Charming* is not only romance at its best, but celebrates fairy tales and folklore…. Jennifer Ashley has another winner that will entertain fans and new readers alike."
—*Romance Reviews Today*

"Along with magic, peril, and a fairy tale romance, Jennifer Ashley fills the pages with sensuality…. *Penelope & Prince Charming* marks the wonderful beginning of a captivating Regency series!"
—*Romance Junkies*

MORE PRAISE FOR JENNIFER ASHLEY!

CONFESSIONS OF A LINGERIE ADDICT

"Ashley brilliantly blends a generous bit of chick-lit sass with a dash of contemporary romance...in a tale that is surprisingly thoughtful, often quite sexy, and always entertaining."

—*Booklist*

"Entertaining...amusing and often engaging."

—*RT BOOKreviews*

"*Confessions of a Lingerie Addict* is a truly addicting book; I could not put it down. It has humor, romance, and scenes so HOT that I had to turn on the air conditioner."

—Romance Junkies

THE CARE & FEEDING OF PIRATES

"More witty, sexy, and swashbuckling fun from the always entertaining Ashley."

—*Booklist*

"Wit combines perfectly with sizzling sensuality and exhilarating adventure. ...Ashley has fine-tuned the pirate romance with her rapier storytelling talents."

—*RT BOOKreviews*

THE PIRATE HUNTER

"Readers who relish deliciously tortured heroes and spirited heroines who can give as good as they get will find much to savor in the latest bracing mix of sexy romance and treacherous intrigue from the consistently satisfying Ashley."

—*Booklist*

THE PIRATE NEXT DOOR

"A witty and splendidly magical romance."

—*Booklist*

MAD HOT BALLROOM

Alexander, his eyes hot and blue, snaked his arm around Meagan's waist and dragged her to the dance floor. This was not the stately Nvengarian dance she'd learned. This dance was crazed, Alexander's arm rock-solid against her abdomen, his sword held out to his side. Whenever they passed another whirling couple, Alexander's and the man's swords met in a ringing clash.

"You're mad," she shouted, and she started to laugh. "You are completely mad."

He grinned, the wild and feral Nvengarian loose at last. It was as though without his medal-bedecked coat and sash of office, he could let free the being inside him. His face shone with perspiration, as did his muscled chest bared by the open V of his shirt. He looked like his barbarian ancestors, the gypsies and the nomads in tents under the stars who lived and loved with great passion.

"I love you," she said beneath the stamping and shouting and clanging and clapping. "I love you, Alexander."

Alexander jerked her close, and there in front of their five hundred guests, he scooped her to him and kissed her.

His sword clanged Nikolai's, and the valet laughed out loud. Meagan joined the laughter, tasting the frenzy of Alexander's bruising kiss.

A loud crash sounded even over the riot of dancing and shouting, and the two tall windows at the end of the ballroom broke and fell in sheets of shimmering glass. The night rain and wind tumbled in, along with five men carrying pistols cocked and ready.

Other books by Jennifer Ashley:

The Mad, Bad Duke

⊱⊰⊱⊰

JENNIFER ASHLEY

LEISURE BOOKS   NEW YORK CITY

A LEISURE BOOK®

December 2006

Published by

Dorchester Publishing Co., Inc.
200 Madison Avenue
New York, NY 10016

If you purchased this book without a cover you should be aware that this book is stolen property. It was reported as "unsold and destroyed" to the publisher and neither the author nor the publisher has received any payment for this "stripped book."

Copyright © 2006 by Jennifer Ashley

All rights reserved. No part of this book may be reproduced or transmitted in any form or by any electronic or mechanical means, including photocopying, recording or by any information storage and retrieval system, without the written permission of the publisher, except where permitted by law.

ISBN 0-8439-5607-0

The name "Leisure Books" and the stylized "L" with design are trademarks of Dorchester Publishing Co., Inc.

Printed in the United States of America.

Visit us on the web at www.dorchesterpub.com.

ACKNOWLEDGMENTS

Thanks go to my editor, Leah Hultenschmidt, as well as the art, production, and marketing departments at Dorchester; my agent, Bob Mecoy; and to Glenda Garland for tirelessly reading and critiquing the drafts of this book.

The Mad,
Bad Duke

CHAPTER ONE

March 1820

Alexander woke suddenly in the middle of his garish sitting room, naked and alone. The pointed arches nailed over rectangular windows and the pillars carved to resemble palm trees seemed to mock him. False things, covering the real.

Alexander, Grand Duke of Nvengaria, exiled to rainy England to watch over its new portly king, was slowly going insane.

This was the dozenth time he'd had the memory lapse—this one, he realized as he glanced at the carved ivory clock, the longest. The last thing he remembered was sitting in his study upstairs three hours ago. He stretched out his scratched and bloody hands, more determined than ever to discover what was happening to him and why.

It wasn't drink that caused the lapses, because Alexander drank only small amounts of wine and brandy and never became inebriated. He'd already ruled out poison as well. His valet Nikolai, fanatically devoted to keeping Alexander alive, had insisted on hiring a food taster and supervising the preparation of every dish.

Nikolai was the only one of the staff in on the secret of Alexander's lapses. The rest of the servants, both English and Nvengarian, so far had not noticed a thing. Most of the lapses had lasted a half hour, some only minutes, but this one would surely have caused questions.

He gave a mirthless laugh, imagining his worried staff carting him off to Bedlam. Not enough that Alexander was darkly lonely, far from a home he fiercely loved, and irritated in his task of keeping England on the side of Nvengaria. Alexander was like a ruthless sword, honed and fixed for one purpose. These memory lapses and the strange new awareness inside him distracted him, and Alexander hated to be distracted.

As he turned to leave the room, he caught sight of himself in an overly gilded mirror, his naked skin gleaming in the moonlight. His black hair, mussed from whatever had happened in the last three hours, touched wide shoulders on his tall frame, his blue eyes wide.

Alexander was the second most powerful man in Nvengaria, and that power wrapped him like a second skin. He knew how to find things out, how to bend others to his will, how to open them to him. He would learn who was doing this, and then he would show them just what happened when someone tried to manipulate Grand Duke Alexander of Nvengaria. The result would not be pretty.

He left the room, his blood burning with determination. His fantastically decorated house was silent as he crossed to the stairs. He hoped to reach his bedroom before one of his efficient Nvengarian staff saw him, or, God forbid, the English staff who still did not know quite what to make of him. He'd escape into his chamber, clean himself up, and ring for Nikolai to dress him.

Before he could start up the stairs, he spied a figure lurking behind one of the arched pillars that skirted the hall.

"Myn?" he called softly.

Myn stepped out from the shadows as though he'd been waiting to be summoned.

Myn was a logosh, one of the legendary shape-shifting creatures that roamed the high mountains of Nvengaria. He stood Alexander's height, six and a half feet tall, broad of shoulder, rippling with muscle, his face wide at the eyes and pointed at the chin. His eyes were blue, a strange, almost glowing blue that seemed to take in everything and give away nothing.

"Did it happen again?" Myn asked in slow Nvengarian. Myn never addressed Alexander as *Your Grace*, the only person who dared not to.

"What do you know about this?"

Myn gave him a cryptic look. "It is beginning."

"What is? Tell me what you know."

"It is inside you." Myn tilted his head, his strange eyes fixed on Alexander. "When you embrace it, these troubles will leave you."

"That is not an answer."

Myn looked at him quietly another moment, then the leader of the logosh walked away. Alexander started to call him back, but the word choked in his throat. Myn moved into the shadows and then, in the uncanny way of his people, he simply disappeared.

Cursing under his breath, Alexander mounted the stairs, making for his rooms. Myn's cryptic hints meant there was magic in this, and Alexander would find it and find out who wielded it, no matter what ruthless methods he had to employ.

* * *

"Do hurry," Deirdre Braithwaite hissed, grabbing Meagan's arm and dragging her into the house.

From all she had heard of the witch called Black Annie, Meagan expected to step into a dark and smoky abode with herbs and dried reptile carcasses hanging from the beamed ceiling. Instead they found a narrow, white-painted front hall trimmed with black and an ordinary mob-capped maid who curtseyed and led them to a sunny sitting room to wait.

Meagan hid her excited curiosity by sitting haughtily on the sofa, pretending she consulted with witches for potions and the like every day. Her father would be livid if he'd known her "outing" with Deirdre included a call on this witch to whom ladies of the *ton* hurried with their problems. But Meagan hadn't been able to resist the opportunity, even though Deirdre, since her marriage, had become quite indecorous.

Deirdre's husband was a wealthy nabob, a fact that she flaunted with costly frocks and as many jewels as she could cram onto her person at once. Even for this clandestine outing she wore an impractical velvet ensemble of dark blue trimmed with brilliant scarlet, carried a gold silk shawl, and had pushed diamond rings onto all ten fingers.

Meagan Tavistock, daughter of a gentleman without excessive means, wore a silver ring, a gift from her father, on her left hand, and a gold ring dusted with Nvengarian sapphires, a gift from her dearest friend Penelope, on her right. Meagan's dress was plain broadcloth, a rust color that went well with her dark red hair and did not make her complexion too sallow.

"Do sit down, Deirdre," she said. "You make me fidgety with all your pacing."

Deirdre regarded her with large, slightly protuding brown eyes. Meagan's new stepmother, with her usual lack of tact, always said Deirdre reminded her of a large, overeager rabbit.

"This is a very important transaction, Meagan darling," Deirdre said. "After tonight, you will be proud to be my best friend."

Meagan did not point out that her best friend was Penelope, who had married last summer and gone to the far-off kingdom of Nvengaria to be its princess. "Are you certain you wish to do this? Your husband is a kind man; I cannot fathom why you rush to cuckold him."

"All married women take lovers, and their husbands take mistresses. I've given Braithwaite an heir and a spare, and now I am taking my reward for being tied to a tedious and frumpy old man."

Mr. Braithwaite was middle-aged, and a little portly, but Meagan had never considered him frumpy.

"Who is this gentleman you want to ensnare with a love spell?" Meagan asked for the dozenth time.

Deirdre looked mysterious. "Shan't tell you."

"I am risking my father locking me in the cellar for the entire Season to be here, you know. You might at least tell me whom you are chasing."

Deirdre opened her mouth, then looked wise and shut it again. "You'll know soon enough."

Meagan rolled her eyes. "I vow, Deirdre, it is a great trial being your friend."

"You shall laugh when you find out. He is a very powerful man. Oh my, he is powerful. All gentlemen of the *ton* fear him, and he has the new king of England eating out of his hand. Perhaps I will convince him to introduce you to one of his colleagues and make a good marriage for you."

"That would be a fine trick," Meagan said.

Deirdre's reply was cut off as the door opened to admit the lady for whom they so anxiously waited.

Again, Meagan felt vague disappointment. Black Annie—
in truth Mrs. Arabella Reese—was not a crone with a
mass of wrinkles and a hunched back, but a tall, graceful
woman with dark hair. She might have been fifty at most,
with a touch of gray at her temples and faint lines about
her dark blue eyes. She wore a simple gown of gray serge
that made overdressed Deirdre appear ridiculous.

Deirdre nearly sprang at Black Annie, her hand out,
every diamond flashing. "Mrs. Reese, how delightful to
see you again. This is my friend, Miss Meagan Tavistock.
Have you got it ready?"

Black Annie shook Deirdre's hand, her expression
neutral, then moved her gaze to Meagan. She held out a
smooth hand adorned with one gold ring. "Miss Tavistock. How nice to meet you."

"Mrs. Reese," Meagan said politely.

As their hands clasped, a strange pressure stole
through Meagan's body. Black Annie looked into Meagan's eyes a moment, assessing her, and then she gave a
slight nod and smile. She moved away, and Meagan
rubbed her hand, wondering what had just transpired.

Deirdre, impatient, chattered. "I have brought my fifty
guineas; may I have it?"

Meagan's eyes widened. "Fifty guineas? Good heavens, Deirdre."

"It is almost finished," Black Annie said smoothly.
"Did you bring the final piece?"

"What? Oh, yes, I almost forgot." Deirdre yanked
open her reticule and withdrew something wrapped in a
handkerchief. "I got it from my maid, who got it from
one of *his* maids. Was that not clever?"

"Oh, yes, you are very clever, Mrs. Braithwaite."

Black Annie carried the handkerchief to a table in the
corner and rang a silver bell that rested there. A moment
later, the mob-capped maid entered, carrying a wide,

shallow basket. Meagan craned her head in fascination as Black Annie picked over its contents. She chose various things—a twist of cloth, a length of gold wire, and several feathers of different shades and sizes. Once she had a pile of odds and ends assembled on the table, she dismissed the maid, who curtseyed and sped away.

"She will bring tea when she returns," Black Annie said, as though apologizing for her lack as a hostess. "You may be seated if you like."

"What are you going to do?" Meagan asked curiously.

"Make the talisman that will transmit the spell." Black Annie opened the drawer of the table and added scissors, a small knife, and a length of twine to the pile. "You are welcome to watch me. I have no secrets."

Meagan approached the table with Deirdre. For fifty guineas, she thought, they ought to get a good show.

Black Annie lit a spill at the fireplace and touched it to the wick of a fat candle on the table. Then she seated herself and spread out her accoutrements. As the candle warmed, the faint scent of wax mixed with spice wafted to Meagan, filling her with sweet lassitude.

Black Annie lifted the feathers and twists of cloth and began to bind them into the length of gold wire with deft fingers. All the while she murmured under her breath, just beyond Meagan's hearing. The words were not English, but Meagan could not decipher enough to identify them.

Deirdre leaned closer, eyes bright. "Are you doing magic?"

Black Annie ignored her. Meagan clasped her hands, her body relaxing, mesmerized by Annie's smooth words and the tiny flame of the candle. She felt herself swaying, as if in rhythm with Black Annie's chant.

Annie unwrapped Deirdre's handkerchief to reveal a narrow braid of black hair. "This is his?" she asked. "You are certain? It would never do for the spell to work on the wrong person."

"Certain enough," Deirdre answered impatiently. "My maid swore it."

Annie shrugged as though that were ample proof. Resuming her murmuring, she wove the wire around the braid, binding it to the feathers and cloth. She continued to weave and add feathers until she had an oblong bundle about the length of Meagan's thumb. It looked like nothing more than a jumble of oddities held in place with the glittering wire.

"That is all?" Deirdre asked, sounding disappointed.

"Nearly. Miss Tavistock, would you put your finger there?" Annie tapped a place where the wire crossed itself.

Still in the grip of the lassitude, Meagan readily put her forefinger where Annie indicated. Annie tied the wire off in a neat knot and withdrew it from Meagan's finger. The wire scraped a tiny drop of blood from Meagan's finger to smear the feathers.

Black Annie blew out the candle. Acrid smoke filled Meagan's nose, and she sneezed. As she did so, the sweet relaxation went away.

"That will be fifty guineas, Mrs. Braithwaite," Black Annie said briskly.

Deirdre's eyes narrowed, as though belatedly sharing Meagan's father's views about young ladies visiting charlatans. "I will pay you when I see whether the spell works."

Black Annie quickly closed her hand over the talisman. "No, Mrs. Braithwaite. Cash on receipt of goods. If the spell does not work, you may of course request your money returned."

Deirdre opened her mouth to argue. Black Annie gazed at her in quiet confidence, a much stronger woman than silly Deirdre could ever hope to be.

Deirdre sighed. "Oh, very well. But it had better work."

"It will. Just have it with you when you next see the man for whom it is intended."

Deirdre opened her reticule and removed a bank draft. "For fifty guineas."

Black Annie took the draft calmly, folded it, and placed it in the drawer of the table. She wrapped the talisman in Deirdre's handkerchief and held it out.

Deirdre glanced at it, then said, "Keep it for me, Meagan. Bring it to Lady Featherstone's ball tonight. I dare not take the chance my husband will not find it if I take it home."

Meagan stared at her. "It is only a bit of wire and feathers. Your husband would not tumble to what it is, surely."

"He will ask me. He always tasks me when I come home with what I've bought and how much I've spent. So tedious. He will find it, and whatever would I say to him?"

"I do not know. Tell him it is for spots."

Deirdre gave her a disparaging look. "As if I have trouble with my complexion, thank you very much. My maid is too stupid to hide it—my husband's valet will find it and try to give her the sack. He loves to lord it over my servants. You must keep it for me."

Black Annie held out the handkerchief to Meagan. "It seems the only way, Miss Tavistock."

Meagan took the small bundle, resisting the urge to open it and study the talisman. "Very well. But only until tonight. And if my father or stepmother finds it, I will tell them truthfully that it's yours."

"Then make certain they do not find it," Deirdre said. "Now where is that maid with my wraps? I must get home."

Black Annie rang her bell and the maid reappeared, carrying their cloaks. In a sudden hurry Deirdre snatched

hers up and flung out of the room without saying good-
bye. Meagan tucked the handkerchief-wrapped talisman
into her reticule, wondering if she should apologize for
Deirdre or simply slip away.

"Miss Tavistock."

Meagan turned back. Black Annie watched her, hands
folded, her eyes wise and even kind.

"I am sorry for Deirdre's abruptness," Meagan began.

Black Annie made a small shrug. "She paid me well; I
am not interested in her manners. But I wanted to tell
you, Miss Tavistock, that I knew your mother."

Meagan stopped, her excitement at the illicit outing
fading. "My mother?"

"You look much like her, my dear. You must have been
a very young child when she died, were you not?"

"I was eight." Meagan remembered little about her
mother except for her warm smile and lovely brown
eyes. She also remembered her comforting hugs and the
fact that she'd loved Meagan's father to distraction.

"Indeed, she was taken from us far too soon. She was a
sweet woman and a dear friend."

Meagan glanced at the table with the candles and the
wire twine and thought of her father's disparaging
words about Black Annie and tricksters like her. "You
and my mother were friends?" she asked doubtfully.

Black Annie's eyes twinkled. "We were, my dear, though
I was years older than she. She'd lost her own mother, you
see, and looked to me as a sort of a substitute. And yes, before you ask, I made a spell for her. How do you think your
mother and father fell in love in the first place?"

"You gave my mother a love spell?"

Black Annie looked amused. "I did indeed. Your
mama came to me soon after she'd made her debut, distracted because the handsome Michael Tavistock would
not look her way. She was far gone in love with him, and

I had the feeling that once Mr. Tavistock noticed her he'd be easily smitten. I simply gave her something that nudged him in the right direction."

Meagan treasured a vivid memory of her father and mother standing in each other's arms in the hall of their Oxfordshire house, unaware that Meagan watched from the stairs. Meagan's father had caressed her mother's cheek and kissed her. Her mother closed her eyes and returned the kiss, looking oh so happy. It was one of the last memories she had of her mother.

"Are you claiming what they felt for each other was a spell? That it was false?"

"No, indeed, Miss Tavistock, do not distress yourself. I am saying the spell brought them together, and what if it did? It turned out well for them, did it not?"

Meagan grew indignant. "You had no right . . ." She stopped. "Goodness, what am I saying? This is all chicanery, isn't it? You are not really a witch; you only make talismans to give to silly women at fifty guineas a go. You had nothing to do with my mother and father falling in love; it is all a trick I risked my father's wrath to observe this afternoon."

Black Annie regarded her in silence.

Of course it was all foolishness and trickery, except . . . Except last year, the devastatingly handsome Prince Damien of Nvengaria had swept into Little Marching in Oxfordshire, claiming that Meagan's friend Penelope must follow a magical prophecy to save his kingdom. Around Prince Damien and his Nvengarians, magic seemed to work. Meagan would never have believed in enchanted sleeps, shape-shifting logosh, prophecies, and healing magic if she hadn't witnessed it all herself.

And now Black Annie was explaining that the strong love between Meagan's father and mother was a bit of magic, as simple as the trick Black Annie had made for

Deirdre. Meagan's mother had come here and stood in this very room and begged for a spell to make a man fall in love with her, just as Deirdre had today.

"You are very amusing, Mrs. Reese," Meagan said with an uncertain smile. "You almost took me in."

"Believe as you please, Miss Tavistock," Black Annie said, brisk once more. "But they were terribly happy, were they not? A more loving couple I never knew. And I only charged her a bob."

CHAPTER TWO

"You cannot possibly be magic," Meagan told the talisman

She sat in chemise and stockings at her dressing table and stared at the twist of feathers and wire that lay on top of Deirdre's handkerchief. The braid of black hair glistened in the candlelight, the smooth lock of the man whom Deirdre was so anxious to ensnare.

"Poor fellow," Meagan murmured. "Whoever he is."

Meagan was dressing to attend Lady Featherstone's seasonal ball, an annual event popular throughout the *ton*, to which Meagan's stepmother had finagled invitations. Simone Tavistock had once been a baronet's wife and had no compunction against using former connections to mingle in society. And more importantly, to find Meagan a husband.

Simone had decided after marrying Michael Tavistock that her raison d'être was to get Meagan married. In Simone's opinion, Meagan at twenty was far past the age when she should have been betrothed and was now in danger of being firmly on the shelf. Simone and Michael wanted to see Meagan marry well. The dear girl deserved nothing less, and after all, Simone's own daughter Penelope had married a *prince*.

Simone bent all her efforts to getting Meagan engaged, with the ruthlessness of one of the new steam-powered engines. She'd persuaded Michael to hire a house near Portman Square for the Season and dragged Meagan to every ball, soiree, musicale and outing she possibly could. Meagan suspected that Simone had another motive—once Meagan was out of the house, Simone would have Michael Tavistock all to herself with no stepdaughter underfoot.

As Meagan waited for their lady's maid, Rose, to come and dress her hair, she studied the talisman. It lay innocently on the handkerchief, nothing but cloth and wire and a braid of black hair. It had nothing to do with love and everything to do with Black Annie beguiling foolish women like Deirdre out of fifty guineas.

"I ought to go into business," Meagan declared. "I will become Madame Meagan, telling ladies what they want to hear for a guinea a turn. I shall become quite rich." She picked up the talisman, turning it toward the light.

A sudden wave of dizziness swamped her, and the small bedroom with its light yellow and white wallpaper, the comfortable chair on which she sat, and her dressing table and mirror—went away.

She opened her eyes and found herself in the arms of a brutally handsome man, their entwined bodies making love in the warm water of a sunken bath. Deep, satisfying love. Meagan sensed the imprint of his fingers in her skin, the heat of his breath on her face, the scent of lavender in the bathwater. And she could feel the exact shape and length of every inch of him inside her.

His lips opened hers without permission, his tongue

scraping into her mouth. "That's it, love." His voice was deep and melodious, the words slightly accented.

Meagan drew a sharp breath. He lifted his head, his eyes clearing as though just becoming aware he held her in his arms.

They stared at each other, his eyes hot blue under a slash of black brows. He had swarthy skin, darker than an Englishman's, reminiscent of gypsies or the wild Magyar tribes on the eastern edge of Europe. His black hair was slicked back from a broad forehead and square face, and an intricate, interlaced tattoo snaked around his right bicep.

She recognized that he was Grand Duke Alexander Octavien Laurent Maximilien, ambassador to England for Prince Damien of Nvengaria. She'd seen pictures of him in the newspapers and noticed him at opera houses and theatres, but she'd never met him in person.

As his lips formed the words *Who are you?* the vision tore away, and Meagan was sitting again in her chemise in front of her dressing table, shaking all over. The gold wire of the love charm shone in the candlelight.

Meagan was not soaking wet, in a marble bath chamber, or making love to a wildly handsome man with sinful eyes. She stared at the talisman, still able to feel his hands on her body and his vast hardness pressing her open.

She'd never been with a man—had only experienced innocent and rather chaste kisses from one or two gentlemen she'd let corner her on ballroom terraces. The sheer carnality of the vision with Alexander of Nvengaria shook her from head to foot.

Her maid popped her head around the door. "Ready for your hair, miss?" Rose asked cheerily.

Meagan gasped and jumped. She thrust the talisman back into her reticule as Rose bustled inside, smiling and ready to serve her young miss.

* * *

When Lord Featherstone's major domo intoned, "Lady
Anastasia Dimitri and Grand Duke Alexander Octavien
Laurent Maximilien of Nvengaria," Meagan swore the
temperature in the ballroom jumped twenty degrees.

She thrust her painted Chinese fan over her scalding
face and peeped over the slats as the man from her vision glided down the ballroom stairs, a beautiful woman
on his arm.

Oh, dear lord.

Meagan thanked heaven that, as usual, she was a
wallflower. She sat in a corner of the vast ballroom behind potted palms, with plump matrons chattering in
chairs nearby. She also had her wide fan with which she
could cover half her face, under the pretense that she
was too warm.

Which she was. The memory of the vision flooded
back to her so vividly that her skin flushed and sweat
beaded on her forehead.

A dream. She'd fallen asleep waiting for Rose and had
a dream, for heaven's sake. It had nothing to do with
Deirdre and her talisman and Deirdre's wishful thinking. It had to do with Meagan being overly tired and dis-
traught by Black Annie's pronouncements.

She must have remembered seeing Grand Duke
Alexander in the newspaper and about town and con-
jured him in her dream, that was all. She had never been
in a lavender-scented bath chamber with him, letting the
wildly handsome man with sinful eyes make love to her.

But it had felt so real that seeing him now made her
doubt her own common sense. She remembered his lips
hard on hers, his tongue scraping her mouth like he
wanted to scoop up every bit of her. The room had
smelled of steam and sex, and the sensation of him so

deep inside her had awakened feelings she'd never known she had.

She watched over the top of her fan as the Grand Duke and his companion moved across the polished parquet under the scrutiny of every quizzing glass and lorgnette in the *ton*. The Grand Duke was tall and so broad of shoulder that lesser men had to get out of his way. His back was ramrod straight, his unfashionably long hair caught in a tail at the nape of his neck. His severe military blue frock coat glittered with medals, and a gold and blue sash stretched from his right shoulder to cup his firm left hip.

He walked with the wary grace of a prowling panther, his careful gaze taking in every person in the room. Female heads turned as he walked by and no wonder. Meagan wagered that more than one lady wondered what he'd look like sauntering naked across her boudoir while she watched from the bed. The way he moved promised that his body would be just as elegant when he danced, and when he made love.

Oh, yes, when he made love . . .

Meagan tore her gaze from Alexander to examine the poised, black-haired beauty on his arm. She was not English, nor did she look Nvengarian. She had a tall, willowy body that made Meagan conscious of her own plumpness, creamy skin and sleek hair, and was dressed in the most elegant, understated, shoulder-baring frock money could buy.

She walked confidently beside Alexander as though she belonged there, her hand lightly on his arm. This lady knew that every woman in the room coveted her position at his side and the fact amused her.

The palms beside Meagan crashed as though a tropical storm tore through them, and Deirdre plopped into an empty chair in a cloud of perfume and satin.

"That's him," Deirdre said breathlessly. She glittered from head to foot with diamonds, wearing every single jewel she owned and a gold satin gown that bared plenty of bosom. "Grand Duke Alexander of Nvengaria. The Mad, Bad Duke, they call him."

"Who calls him?" Meagan asked absently, her gaze fixed on his dark blue back and broad shoulders.

"Oh, everybody. My husband told me the most delicious story about him—apparently young Lord Mortinson got it into his head to challenge the Grand Duke to a duel over who knows what. The Grand Duke refused, and Mortinson claimed he was a coward. The next day, the Grand Duke took Mortinson and his friends to a green near Islington and held a shooting competition. The Grand Duke shot his target three times in the bull's-eye, each shot dead center of the last. My husband was there—he says Mortinson put his finger on the bullet holes in a kind of shock, realizing the bull's-eye could have been his heart. Then the Grand Duke took him for a drink, and Mortinson has worshipped him ever since."

Meagan imagined Alexander's sharp blue eyes narrowed over the pistol, his body turned to the side, his long arm steady as a rock as he potted his target with unerring ease. She had met Lord Mortinson, a somewhat vapid young man, and suspected he'd stared at Alexander's shots with his plump mouth hanging open.

Deirdre leaned closer in a wave of patchouli. "I intend to unbutton that Nvengarian coat tonight and discover everything beneath it. You did bring the spell, did you not?"

Meagan lifted her gloved wrist, from which dangled a silk reticule embroidered with tiny roses. The talisman, still wrapped in the handkerchief, lay inside. Meagan's first instinct upon emerging from her vision had been to put it on the fire, but then she had admonished herself not to be silly. And anyway, Deirdre would demand the cost of it, and Meagan had nowhere near fifty guineas.

"He seems to be with someone," Meagan remarked.

Deirdre made an airy gesture. "Oh, *her*. She is an Austrian countess or some such. I am not afraid of her."

"They make a beautiful couple." They did, the tall man and tall woman matching each other in attractiveness, coolly self-confident against the *ton*'s scrutiny. "Are they lovers?"

"Well, of course they are, rumor is rife with it. Look at the way she drapes herself all over him."

Just then the countess moved her fingers on Alexander's arm in a possessive way and slanted a lovely smile up at him. The gesture sent a small hurt into Meagan's heart, though she could not for the life of her fathom why.

"How do you propose to cut him away from her?" she asked. "If they are lovers, and she is so beautiful?"

"Because you will help me, my friend."

Meagan dragged her gaze back to Deirdre. "I will not. Going with you to buy the talisman was one thing, but I draw the line at helping you betray your husband. He is too kind for that."

"He is a bore and never pays me any attention. And you will do it, or I will tell your father that you went with me to Black Annie's, and we both know what he'd say about that."

Meagan's anger rose. She knew Deirdre would make good on the threat, and while Meagan might have sheepishly confessed to her father and borne his disapproval, Black Annie's claim to have made a spell for her mother made her sensitive on the subject. She wanted to think things through before she endured a lecture from her father about why innocent young ladies should stay away from women like Black Annie.

"You will say nothing to my father," she hissed.

Deirdre gloated. "Excellent. Then you will help me."

"Oh, botheration, do be quiet."

Meagan flapped her fan and tried not to follow the Grand Duke with her gaze as he and the Austrian woman made their way across the room. People watched him in fascination and fear, and he regarded them coolly, as though he knew their reaction and damn well wanted it to stay that way.

She sensed him size up each person he met and categorize them—*inconsequential, possible ally, enemy*. There were no categories, she noticed, for *friend, acquaintance, would like to know him better*.

Meagan did not know how she knew this, but she did. The vision seemed to have given her the strange insight that Alexander saw each person as either a threat or someone to stand with him against a threat. That was all. It struck her as ruthlessly efficient and incredibly lonely at the same time.

Meagan wondered into what category he'd placed the Austrian woman. She seemed to have many friends and acquaintances, though Meagan noticed that most of them were male. The ladies, on the other hand, regarded her with jealous and even hostile eyes.

Seeing the lady so comfortable with him made Meagan feel odd. In the vision in the steam-fogged room, Alexander had been hers and hers alone. Thinking of the Austrian lady or, God forbid, Deirdre, sliding her hands inside his shirt and stroking his muscular chest made Meagan feel wretched.

What the devil is the matter with me? It was only a dream, for heaven's sake. I am nothing to him and he is nothing to me.

Meagan flicked her attention back to Alexander and found his gaze directly on her.

She jumped and thrust the fan in front of her face, but too late. He was staring at her with harsh intensity, his eyes sharp and blue, penetrating all the way across the room. That gaze was for her, not for Deirdre preening herself next to Meagan, not for the dowagers chatting together on Meagan's other side. Grand Duke Alexander assessed Meagan, his gaze like the edge of a razor.

He knew.

But good lord, how could he? She'd had a ridiculous dream, a waking vision—it had not been real. No one could know, thank heavens, what lurid thoughts went on inside Meagan's head.

She remembered the way he'd looked down at her in the bath chamber when he'd come out of his sexual languor, his gaze as intense as it was now. *"Who are you?"* he'd started to say before the vision ended.

Across the ballroom, Alexander leaned to the Austrian countess, murmuring to her while keeping his gaze on Meagan, obviously asking who Meagan was. The woman glanced at Meagan in eager curiosity, her eyes bright, her red-lipped mouth moving in answer. Meagan imagined her saying in her rich Austrian voice, *"That little one? She is nothing. The nobody daughter of a nobody. Do not waste a second thought on her."*

Deirdre pinched Meagan hard. "Oh, do you see? He is looking at me!"

Meagan knew differently, but she held her tongue. The Grand Duke murmured back to his companion, as they strolled toward Meagan and Deirdre.

"Lud, he is coming this way," Deirdre gasped. "I knew it. When he asks me to dance, you run up to the sitting room on the third floor, the one two doors from the top of the stairs, and wait for me. I'll entice him up, and then you slip the talisman into his pocket while I chat with him."

Deirdre was a fool, and Meagan was suddenly sick to death of her. She'd put up with Deirdre's clinging friendship this Season for old time's sake—they'd grown up near each other in Oxfordshire and Deirdre had often joined Meagan and Penelope in their games or dreaming talks of the future.

"They will hardly speak to either of us, as we have not been introduced," she said churlishly.

"Oh, bother that. They are foreign. Perhaps they will speak to us anyway, not knowing English manners."

Meagan had found that non-English Europeans often had even more scrupulous codes of politeness than Englishmen, but she said nothing.

Alexander's lovely countess solved the problem by intercepting their hostess Lady Featherstone on their way across the room and conferring with her. Lady Featherstone, a graying, slim matron, brightened and joined them on their promenade.

Meagan and Deirdre scrambled to their feet as the group approached, Deirdre swaying in excited anticipation, her diamonds rattling. Meagan edged behind Deirdre and lifted her fan to cover her face.

Lady Featherstone began chattering before the three even reached them. "Ah, girls, our distinguished guests were curious about you." She stopped, all smiles, her rouge staining her high cheekbones brilliant red. Lady Featherstone loved gossip and social gatherings and was a kind and caring woman, genuinely interested in giving all young ladies a chance, not just the titled and wealthy ones. She was even more sought out after her dearest friend Lady Stoke had married a pirate turned viscount ten years ago.

"Miss Tavistock and Mrs. Braithwaite are childhood friends," Lady Featherstone rattled on. "It is pleasant to see them together in London. Miss Tavistock's father recently married Lady Trask, the mother of Miss Tavistock's dearest friend, Penelope, who became Princess of

Nvengaria. But of course you'd know that, being the Grand Duke." She tittered.

"Indeed."

The single word was rich and pleasantly accented. His voice matched that of the man in Meagan's vision, down to the exact way he formed the brief vowels and slurred the consonants.

"Ah, yes, well," Lady Featherstone burbled. "Your Grace and Lady Anastasia, may I present Mrs. Braithwaite, wife of Hector Braithwaite, a prominent MP. Mrs. Braithwaite, Lady Anastasia Dimitri of Nvengaria and Grand Duke Alexander—er . . . I am so sorry, Your Grace, the rest of the name escapes me."

Alexander, his eyes on Meagan, did not seem to notice. Into the awkward silence, Lady Anastasia extended a slim gloved hand. "How do you do, Mrs. Braithwaite?"

Deirdre shook her hand, but her rabbit-brown eyes remained solidly on Alexander, examining his gold and blue sash, the multiple medals that dangled from his chest, and the ruby glittering in his ear. "Your Grace." She disengaged from Lady Anastasia and moved her hand toward his in hint.

Alexander, his eyes cool, lifted her hand to his lips, clicked his heels, and made a military bow. "Mrs. Braithwaite."

"And Miss Meagan Tavistock," Lady Featherstone went on. She took Meagan's arm and nearly dragged her out from behind Deirdre.

Lady Anastasia held out her hand, amusement dancing in her dark eyes. "I am pleased to meet you, Miss Tavistock."

"Likewise," Meagan choked.

She knew she was expected to acknowledge Grand Duke Alexander, but she clung to Lady Anastasia's hand almost in desperation.

In the vision, Alexander had been overwhelming enough. In person, this close, he was impossible to look at. His presence pushed aside that of the other four women, Lady Anastasia included, demanding every inch of space.

He was a foot taller than Meagan, his broad shoulders at her eye level. His masculinity, the scent of his cashmere coat and the male musk behind it, the large, strong hand in the black glove that he wrenched away from Deirdre, all made her weak in the knees. She could not take him in. She had to sit down, or run away somewhere, or maybe swoon.

No, then he might carry her out of the room, and she'd awaken to find herself again in his strong arms, his heart beating swiftly against hers.

Then again, from the look he gave her, he might simply let her lie there on the floor, perhaps signal someone to come and sweep up the mess.

His hair was dark, almost black, but shot through with streaks lightened by the sun. His skin was tan, even browner than Prince Damien's had been. Where Prince Damien had a charming grace that could make a girl smile and giggle without knowing why, Grand Duke Alexander wanted you on your knees, and only social politeness made him let you stay standing.

He executed another click of heels, another bow, and nearly snatched her hand from Anastasia's. "Miss Tavistock."

He lifted her fingers to his mouth and impressed them with one hard kiss, lips burning through her silk gloves. She slid her slippered feet together, trying to stop the trickle of heat that moved between her legs.

He raised his head and his gaze caught her like a bird in a snare, a cruel snare she would have to beat against to escape, and then she'd only get away wounded. His eyes were hard and fierce, intensely blue, Nvengarian blue.

She'd come to like Nvengarians and their wild ways and enjoyment of life. They loved nothing greater than dance and revelry, unless it was fighting a dire enemy or making love to a beautiful woman. The women, Penelope said in her letters, were just as intense as the men and saw no shame in discussing the handsomeness of their lovers or various techniques of pleasure and erotic bed games.

Not that Penelope described any of these bed games, but Meagan had an imagination and was no fool. She wondered suddenly what it would be like to have Alexander stretched full length beside her while he taught her various games.

His eyes flickered slightly, the pupils spreading black through the blue. And she knew, in that moment, he could see what she thought. Perhaps not her specific thoughts, but the gist of them. He knew about her vision, because he'd experienced it too.

She did not understand how she knew that, but his anger washed over her like floodwater. She dragged in a breath and tried to disengage her hand, but his fingers clamped hers like an iron vise.

"Miss Tavistock," he said, his voice vicious and low. "There is a waltz beginning. Will you dance it with me?"

No, I would rather struggle to the top of a mountain in Scotland in the snow, thank you.

Then again, the thought of dancing in his arms, whirling with his hand on her waist, looking deep into his eyes . . .

Oh, dear, what was happening to her?

"I do not waltz," she babbled.

"Nonsense," Lady Featherstone said helpfully. "You

have been out three Seasons and you waltz beautifully. I have seen you. Your step-mama would not mind."

Indeed, Simone Tavistock, thankfully across the room and buried in gossip with her cronies, would not. She'd practically shove Meagan at any gentleman who wanted to dance with her. In Simone's opinion, Meagan simply was not *trying*.

"I am feeling unwell," Meagan began.

"Do not be silly, you look lovely," Lady Featherstone said. "Go on, do. I will keep Deirdre company."

"As will I," Lady Anastasia announced. "Do not worry, Miss Tavistock, we will keep Mrs. Braithwaite quite entertained."

Deirdre was breathing hard, her color high, bosom straining at her tight bodice until Meagan fancied she heard the seams ripping.

"Of course," Deirdre said through her teeth. "I would be enchanted."

Lady Anastasia laid her long fingers on Deirdre's arm. "Shall we sit? Your tiara is lovely, my dear."

"Yes, isn't it?" Deirdre thumped to a chair. "My husband can afford to give me as many diamonds as I want."

"How lucky for you," Lady Anastasia said, and gracefully sank into the chair Meagan had vacated. Lady Featherstone, looking motherly and very pleased with herself, made a shooing motion at Meagan.

Alexander made no sign he even noticed this exchange. He took Meagan's hand and unceremoniously dragged her to the middle of the room where couples were forming. Short of screaming, kicking his shins, and fleeing, Meagan had no choice but to go with him.

CHAPTER THREE

If Alexander spread his fingers along Miss Tavistock's waist, the tip of his smallest finger would brush her hip while his thumb would rest just below her bosom. He felt her hand light on his, her arm a graceful arc. Her face was flushed, her eyes starry, but she would not look at him.

The music took them into the waltz. Couples whirled around them, ladies holding skirts to the side, going round and round like butterflies. Miss Tavistock held her skirt as well, but more like she'd seen a rat on the floor and didn't want it running across her train.

She was absolutely and stunningly beautiful. Her red hair had been severely tamed into a tight bun surrounded by ridiculous, unnatural ringlets. He knew that unbound, her hair would be long and thick and lush with unruly waves of its own.

He wanted it flowing over his hands, over his face, over his naked body. He wanted to cup her pointed little face in his hands, tilt it upward, and lean to kiss it. He wanted to lay her on a bed and hover over her on hands and knees, parting her legs and drawing his fingers through the fiery tangle between her thighs. She'd be wet for him, and he'd withdraw his fingers and lick her honey from them.

She'd gripped him good and hard in this spell and was not letting go. The proximity of her only made it worse.

"Who are you?" he asked, his voice harsh.

Miss Tavistock at last looked up at him. Her eyes were brown-gold, surrounded by thick, dark lashes.

"I am Miss Tavistock, as Lady Featherstone told you."

A nice, evasive answer. "You know what I mean. *Who* are you? What are your connections, and why have you come here?"

Her gaze raked him from forehead to waist, giving him thorough scrutiny. But while ladies like Lady Featherstone and Mrs. Braithwaite hungrily took in his medals and sash and the outward trappings of the Grand Duke, Meagan Tavistock looked at Alexander the man.

She examined the black hair that swept back from his forehead, the bronzed skin of his face, the black of his lowered brows, the ruby earring he always wore. She took her time studying his mouth, then examined his throat where it disappeared into the high collar of his coat. Her gaze drifted down his chest, skimming his medals, but he had the feeling she looked at what was beneath, his dark skin over pectorals, the tight points of his nipples as they responded to her scrutiny.

"Answer the question, Miss Tavistock," he said sharply.

She raised her gaze to him, her eyes wary yet holding a resilience he'd never beheld in any person, male or female. "I have come here to dance, this being a ball. My stepmother brought me here to get a husband, if you must know, because I am rather on the shelf."

He clamped his fingers on hers, and she flinched. "Your banter is amusing, but the effort is lost on me. I want to know who employed you to use a love spell, and why."

Her eyes widened the slightest bit, and her slim throat moved in a swallow. Alexander had recognized right away that this woman held no guile and was likely not a conspirator herself. She was an innocent tool, a means to an end, and he would make her lead him to whoever had manipulated her.

"You are quite mad, Your Grace. I have no idea what you are talking about."

"You do," he returned. "This is a dangerous game, Miss Tavistock, and you would be wise to inform me of everything. Who do you work for, and what did they promise you if you ensnared me?"

Her red ringlets trembled, her face turning pink enough to highlight the freckles on her nose. "I work for no one. This is a silliness, Your Grace, that is all. Not worth bothering about, I vow to you."

She was giving her word. In Nvengaria, giving a word was binding even unto death, but he had no way of knowing whether an English miss regarded things in the same fashion.

"Tell me," he said, "and I will decide whether it is worth dismissing."

Miss Tavistock looked away. He read in the set of her mouth that not only did she not want to reveal the name of the person who'd put her up to this but that she was not afraid of Alexander. That only betrayed her ignorance, and her innocence. Alexander did not hurt pawns to prove he could, but he had to know who was using her, and he would employ any method he could.

"You dance quite well, Your Grace," she said suddenly, as though trying to change the subject. "Not like I thought Nvengarians danced at all. I thought you grabbed each others' waists and snaked around in a line."

"That is a peasant dance. The dances of Nvengarian aristocrats are far more intimate."

Her lips parted, her body swaying toward him a little at the word *intimate*.

He had a sudden vision of himself and this beautiful red-haired woman dancing alone in the fantastic ballroom in his Berkeley Square house, drifting round and round under the arched, red-painted and gilded ceiling. He'd hold her much closer than this, of course. The room would be lit by sunlight from the windows on the far end, and there would be no music, just the pair of them dancing and dancing and dancing.

He was extremely aware of her waist beneath his palm, of her legs pressing at her gown as she glided in time with him, their feet a mere whisper of distance apart.

Miss Tavistock's eyes were soft, her gaze no longer wary or evasive. She was looking at him, at Alexander, as though she saw past his cold façade to all his flaws.

"The vision we shared came from a spell, Miss Tavistock," he said, reminding himself of the danger.

"Yes, I thought it must have done."

"At least you acknowledge that. Where is the talisman?"

She hesitated a moment, then she silently raised her hand. A small silk bag embroidered with roses dangled from her wrist.

And then, instantly, he was back in the marble-pillared bath chamber of his house in Berkeley Square.

Candles burned in sconces along the walls, light dancing on the water that obscured her sweet body. She sat on the far end of the Roman bath, staring at him with brown eyes in a pale, round face. Her lips were full and lush, wanting kisses, her bare shoulders brushed with a line of freckles. She stared as though surprised to see him there. Then her gaze drifted down his unclothed body, regarding him with flattering interest.

He wanted her with a suddenness that took his breath away. He could already feel his hands on her body, imagined himself opening her thighs and pushing inside her. She'd welcome him into her slick warmth and she'd move beneath him, making soft noises of pleasure. His erection lifted at the need to make his longings truth.

Hot water bit his skin as he descended into the bath. Steam rose to engulf them both, curling the wisps of red hair on Meagan's forehead. He smiled, enjoying the pretty picture she made.

"Love," he asked softly. "Would you wash my back?"

Her eyes widened, her chest rising with an intake of breath. He glided the few steps across the bath and stood over her before bracing himself on the lip of the tub and sliding his knees to each side of her on the hard marble bench. His arousal, thick with need, fell against her thighs.

He drew his fingers along her cheek, then leaned down and tasted her lips from one corner to the other.

Beneath him, she gasped, and with the suddenness of a slap, the bath dropped away, and he was standing in the glittering ballroom, her in his arms, both of them having come to a dead stop. Another couple danced into them and stared in amazement at the two standing motionless on the dance floor.

Alexander glanced swiftly down at her. By the wideness of her eyes, the way her bosom lifted with her breath, he knew Miss Tavistock had experienced every moment of the vision with him.

He seized her by the elbow, murmured, "Miss Tavistock, you seem unwell, let us get some air," and pulled her out the nearest door.

Meagan shook all over, fighting nausea. Grand Duke Alexander's gloved fingers bit into her flesh and he all but shoved her out the French door to the marble-tiled terrace.

She could barely breathe. Like the last vision, this one had been so vivid that for an instant Meagan had felt the heated damp of the steam, the hard marble under her bare backside and the racing of her heart as he came to her. Closer and closer, while the water rippled away from him and the steam swirled and danced, until he stood above her.

When he'd brushed his tongue across her lips, the touch had been so real she'd gasped aloud, and the vision had dissolved. But he'd felt it too, he'd seen, and his eyes blazed with fury.

The terrace was deserted, the March night too cold and breezy for thin ballroom finery. Alexander dragged Meagan to the far corner near the stone balustrade, right into the blustery wind. "Give me the talisman."

Meagan slid her reticule from her shaking wrist. Alexander snatched it from her and drew out the bundle of wire-wrapped feathers. He examined it while she poised on her toes, agonized. His expression changed to one of disgust.

"Hearth witchery, that is all. This hair is mine?"

"I believe so."

"And how did you obtain it?" His voice was a purr of anger.

"I did not. Please give it back."

She ought to let him have it. Let him destroy it, and

Deirdre could be out fifty guineas. But for some reason, she lunged for it. "No."

He was much taller than she and easily held it out of her reach. "If the hair is mine, then there has been a betrayal within my house, and I must know by whom."

"If I tell you, you'll give back the spell?"

"No."

She lunged again, and he caught her arm.

"Give it to me, please," she begged. "I'll destroy it, I promise."

"Not until you tell me who prepared this spell and who inside my house helped you." His hand clamped down on her arm, bruising the flesh.

"Let go of me," she cried over the wind.

She tried to squirm away and grab the talisman at the same time, but she slipped on the marble tiles and nearly pitched herself over the balustrade. He caught her heavily, and her hand closed over the talisman at the same time his did.

A bright light flashed around them, then just as suddenly was gone.

"What was that?" she asked.

"Hell," he said, then snarled words in Nvengarian that sounded violent and frightening.

A sudden flood of longing poured over her, the same as in her visions but a hundred times stronger. She fought for breath as warmth filled her body, completely erasing the chill bite of the wind.

She gazed at the black-flecked blue of his eyes and the line of his mouth. In their struggle, his cravat knot had loosened slightly, giving her a glimpse of his brown throat beneath. Oh, to have him lying under her where she could lick his skin and breathe his warmth!

He moved his hands to the small of her back and she

landed against his chest. He smelled like warm wool and musk and the fresh scent of the outdoor wind. She'd felt infatuation for handsome gentlemen before, but that faint excited flutter was nothing to the need that took hold of her now. The space between her legs was hot and wet, and because of her earlier visions, she knew what she wanted—him, inside her.

"Alexander," she said, desperate.

"Not here." He slid his arm around her waist and pulled her with him to another door in the terrace, this one leading to a small corridor that ran alongside the ballroom. "We will find a place."

They made it along the hall without encountering anyone, and Alexander pushed his way into a tiny anteroom. The room contained two low chairs and a Turkish sofa positioned near a semicircular table that held a tray of goblets. The walls were covered with gilded curlicues that snaked around busy paintings of gods pursuing naked goddesses and nymphs. The excess of gilding and clashing colors was a bit nauseating, but Meagan only noticed it distractedly.

Alexander closed the door at the same time he dragged Meagan into his arms. His mouth came down on hers, rough and brutal. He thrust his tongue into her mouth and instead of resisting, which dimly she thought she should, she played her tongue along his, learning his heady and exciting taste.

He slid his hands to her elbows, the thin silk sleeves tearing to make way for his fingers. He pushed his hands all the way to her bare shoulders and pulled the torn bodice down.

She braced herself against his broad chest as he licked her neck in one long stroke. She flicked her tongue over his jaw, tasting sharp stubble. She licked again, liking the raw, masculine taste of his sweaty skin.

Deep in the back of her mind, the sensible side of Meagan Tavistock shouted for attention. *What on earth are you doing? You are compromised, you ninny of a girl!*

It scarce mattered. All that mattered was Alexander touching her.

He nipped her, and when she made a faint noise at the small hurt, he bit harder. His hair broke loose from its bond and flowed over her neck, smelling of cologne and spice. She crumpled his sash of office beneath her fingers, the gold-laced cloth stiff and cool.

"Do you want that off, love?" he murmured.

"Yes."

She helped him push the sash from his shoulder, and he lifted it over his head and let it flutter to the floor. Then he stripped off his gloves and sat on an armless gilded chair, unfastening the cording that held his coat. Underneath he wore a lawn shirt that hugged his body, the hard muscles of his chest shadowing the opening beneath his collar.

"Turn around," he said. "I want to unlace you."

Willingly, Meagan turned her back, as if it were the most natural thing in the world to let him unfasten the catches that held her bodice closed. Lost in the moment, she saw no reason not to let him undress her. They seemed to be caught in a strange, wild feeling, dragged to a place where they were lovers. Being as intimate as man and wife felt perfectly natural to her.

His fingers played and the silk bodice parted. He ran his hand down the placket of her short stays, drawing the stays apart, unbinding her. Last he untied the drawstrings of her chemise, pushing the garment down her arms, baring her back and bosom with hot, callused hands.

She faced the door, bare to the waist, her breasts heavy and her nipples tightening. When she felt his tongue on her back, she groaned, closing her eyes.

He traced her spine to her hips, pushing fabric aside until the gown and chemise slithered to a pool at her feet. He danced his tongue over the small of her back, then pressed warm lips to the hollow there, breath scalding.

"Part your legs," he commanded in a soft voice.

She obeyed, sliding her feet apart, never minding she was standing naked except for stockings and slippers in front of a man she'd met a mere quarter of an hour ago. His tongue moved to her buttocks, swirling around each one, then to the backs of her thighs.

She moved her legs apart still more, quivering for him, wanting him, ready to beg for him. Her mind was clouded with strange thoughts that tumbled one over the other and laced with the visions she'd had in her bedroom and the ballroom.

He'd slid from the chair and was on his knees now, hands pressing her legs apart so he could find her with his tongue. He touched the curls between her thighs and she squeaked at the new sensation.

"What is happening to me?" She moaned, lifting on her toes. "Alexander, what are you doing to me?"

"Loving you," he said against her skin. He withdrew and placed his hands on her buttocks. "Turn around. I want to see you."

Meagan swallowed hard and pivoted in a slow half circle, stepping out of the pile of her dress. He looked up at her, his eyes a heated blue, the ruby glittering among the dark strands of his hair.

He slid his hands from her hips up her waist to her breasts, his thumbs caressing the aureoles. "You are beautiful." His voice was thick and low, his accent deepening, as though he had to struggle to say English words. "You are glorious, lush, like a goddess."

She laughed lightly, though it sounded a bit hysterical. "Is there a goddess Meagan?"

"We will invent one. I will have you sculpted by an artist, just as you are now, so beautiful for me. Or I will hire a portrait painter and have him paint you lying on a couch, waiting for me in nothing but your stockings and slippers."

She shook all over but tried to make a jest of it. "I should look silly covered in paint."

His gaze turned feral, his smile telling her he'd not think her naked body streaked with paint silly at all. He took her hands and guided them to hold her breasts. "Stay like that," he said. "Rub the tips for me. Feel the pleasure of it."

He leaned forward and kissed her abdomen, warming her skin with his breath, trailing little kisses to her navel, into which he flicked his tongue. Meagan tentatively squeezed the tips of her aureoles, gasping at the little tingle that sped from them.

Alexander rubbed his fingers over the coil of hair at her thighs, his voice admiring. "Beautiful." He splayed his hands on her thighs and moved his thumbs across her mound. He kissed her where his thumbs played.

"Alexander," she whispered.

He dipped his tongue to the part of her that ached most of all. He licked her, rubbing the little nub of skin, his tongue expertly understanding how to make the rasping feel she craved without knowing she craved it.

She wanted to push her hips on to him, and at the same time stand still so he could continue. She kneaded and stroked her own breasts, wanting to touch him instead, but having a strange, crazed need to obey him. They were caught in this madness together, she and he, magic that swirled around them and pulled them to each other.

She wanted to scream. She was going to cry her dark pleasure up to the gaudy gods and goddesses writhing above her. It was building, she could feel it in her throat and in her lungs, and best of all, in the fiery friction of his tongue on her.

But just then, behind her, the door handle rattled. Gasping, Meagan stumbled back from Alexander and half turned, nearly losing her balance.

She clearly heard the voice of some lord or other saying to one of his cronies, "Let us step in here, and you can tell me what those damn fools in the cabinet are saying."

The door opened an inch, then another man said, "No, let us escape to Mount Street and my man will cook a chop for us. The suppers at these balls are thin and my blood needs warming with good port."

The first man pronounced it an excellent idea and closed the door with a thump.

Meagan let out her breath. She swung back to Alexander, ready to frantically point out that they'd almost been caught.

The look on his face stunned her. He was smiling, his eyes hot and animal-like. Nearly being found out had excited him. He rose in one sinuous movement, lacing his arm behind her back, and kissed her deeply. His tongue stroked the inside of her mouth, opening her wide for him, the rings on his fingers like bands of ice across her skin.

He broke the kiss and crossed to the door to turn the key in the lock. On his way back, he loosened his cravat and untied his shirt. Then he unbuttoned his trousers, calmly pulling open the fly. He pushed his trousers down to his ankles without shame as he sat down on the chair.

She stared, eyes wide, at the erection that stood long and stiff between his legs. His thighs were brawny with muscle, sinews working as he pulled his loose shirt off over his head, tossed it away, and held out his arms to her. "Come to me."

"What are you going to do?"

"Love you, Meagan. Come to me; I'll do the rest."

It seemed wrong not to do as he said. Somewhere inside her, the sensible Meagan protested, but her voice was faint and far away and of little importance here.

She moved to the chair and carefully straddled his legs. He caught her hips and lowered her to him, pulling her forward to skim his body.

"Will it hurt?" she whispered.

"It might. I will try to make it gentle for you. You are wet for me; that is good."

She knew what he meant. Her opening was full of warm liquid, which excited her, and the more excited she became, the more it filled. She remembered from the vision the feel of him inside her, and knew she was going to experience it in truth.

"Spread your legs a little more," he instructed.

She complied. He slid his hand between her thighs and parted her petals with his fingers. His erection moved into her as he slowly and gently lowered her down to him.

Her head went back as he stretched her, filling her unbelievably. She clutched his shoulders, her nails biting his flesh, and he smiled against her mouth, taking her lips in a series of kisses.

"You are *mine*," he growled, voice fierce.

"If you insist."

He laughed, low and dark. The tightness inside her hurt, and it did not.

Meagan knew the moment her maidenhead broke— her entire body squeezed itself to one point, then suddenly opened, snapping a string that had kept her tethered, setting her free.

"Yes," she whispered. "I belong to you."

He spoke a string of Nvengarian, low and muttered, as

though his mind could no longer conjure English words. He filled her fully, thighs tight against hers, the feeling astonishing and strange. It was not pleasure that flooded her, or pain, but a *rightness*, as though she'd been born for the moment she would couple with this man.

He slid his fingers to her buttocks, dipping slightly between them, and then sensation took over her and thoughts went to the wind. She screamed aloud, but he caught the screams in his mouth. She writhed, his erection straight up inside her, knowing she'd never feel anything else as wonderful as this.

Never let this end. His mouth was all over hers, his eyes closed tight in his own world of pleasure. He smelled of sweat and sex, tasted of brandy and his own hard spice. His shoulders moved beneath her hands, solid muscle under tight flesh that she wanted to touch forever.

He was a beautiful man, and if anyone should be painted, it should be him, standing hard and upright and naked, half turned to the viewer perhaps, in a room with a tumbled bed where he'd waited for her.

I need this man. I need him inside me and to love me and to teach me.

She fancied she felt something click inside her like a clasp closing, and she also fancied for some reason that she heard Black Annie's soft laughter.

Alexander released her mouth to babble more Nvengarian against her skin. *"Shengen dem, me coura sel."*

"What do you mean? Tell me what you are saying."

He dragged his eyes open, cheekbones flushed, and focused on her with effort. "I want you, my heart."

Her own heart banged in her chest with ferocity. "I want you too."

His brows drew together as though in concern. "I'm

coming," he murmured, then his head dropped back, and he thrust and thrust into her, his hot seed spilling into her. She wriggled and writhed, loving the feel of him, laughing.

"Meagan," he breathed, then he lifted his head. "Damnation."

"Do not say you are sorry. Please, do not."

He kissed her, hard and possessive, nothing apologetic about it. "My heart," he whispered again, and wound his arms around her.

"Say it in Nvengarian. I like to hear you say it."

"Me coura sel."

As his tongue formed the *l*, she wrapped hers around it. He completed the kiss, then pulled her close and let her rest her head on his shoulder while he smoothed his hand down her back.

"I feel blessed," she whispered, inhaling the salty scent of him. "My Alexander."

"Meagan," he murmured, his fingers continuing the slow dance on her spine. "Red is a beautiful color. Warm, like fire."

She smiled, happy. Nothing existed but her, and him, and this room, and that was just fine with her.

The sensible young woman deep inside her put her hands over her face and groaned. *Oh, Meagan. What have you done?*

CHAPTER FOUR

Alexander held Meagan on his lap, still buried deep inside her, wanting to stay there forever. He knew the love spell—a lust spell, to be more accurate—made him feel this way, but wrapped in its tendrils he did not care.

Dangerous things, love spells. They rendered the victims completely unable to do anything but seek pleasure in each other. Outside this room a ball raged on, and Lady Anastasia awaited him. He had been meant to question von Hohenzahl about a secret weapon he claimed would make Austria powerful against Nvengaria, and Alexander was already late for the appointment.

He skimmed his fingers across Meagan's flesh, enjoying her softness. His own wife had been very slender, like Anastasia, and neither woman had been the delight to hold that Meagan was.

Alexander's wife had never loved him, nor he her, though he'd trusted her and viewed her as a partner. The Grand Duchess of Nvengaria had been a fashionable, beautiful woman and his most staunch supporter before the wasting disease had taken her. But she'd had her own lovers, and tender affection had not reigned between husband and wife.

He felt tender affection for the woman presently in his arms. "Meagan." He repeated her name just to hear the sound of it.

"Alexander," she said into his shoulder.

He kissed her red hair, loving the taste of her. He was dimly aware that he'd taken her virginity and he'd have to do something about that, but the feel of her naked body against his was most satisfying for now.

Behind his initial sated comfort, his razor-sharp mind worked, listing the myriad things he'd have to do. Everything would have to be right, from the jewels to the legal documents to the ceremony itself, done beforehand so if he'd given her a child this night, no one would count his next son or daughter a bastard.

The English had such peculiar rules for bastardy, such as the child never being able to inherit his father's lands, whereas in Nvengaria, illegitimate children were treasured, and inherited what was their due. Also, a Nvengarian child conceived while the parents were betrothed was not considered illegitimate, unlike in England.

And who, *who*, his mind cried, wanted me to drop my seed into this innocent girl?

It had been cruel to use her, and when Alexander found the man, or woman, he'd make them pay. He knew, even in the lassitude of afterglow, that he'd ruined her in the eyes of her world, and he determined that someone would make recompense for that.

But all would be well. He had a solicitor and a team of people at his disposal who could make this situation only a small snag in the fabric of his life. It would be smoothed out, and they'd go on.

"Alexander." She raised her head and gave him a sleepy smile, and he knew he loved her.

Then, suddenly, the love spell faded. He saw the languorousness leave her at the same time the warm contentment drained from his own limbs. They sat face to face, returning to sanity together, cool worry entering Meagan's brown-gold eyes.

"Did I hurt you?" he asked softly.

She shook her head. "I thought it would, but it felt— strange."

"The spell helped with the pain." He put his hands on her hips and gently eased her to her feet. "Likely so we would not turn back."

She stepped away from him, shaking, her face flushed with embarrassment. There was a dabble of blood on his half erection and some spattered on her thighs. He lifted his cravat from the floor, using the linen to gently clean her.

"You will not be able to return to the ball," he told her.

She shook her head, her loosened hair dancing enticingly on her shoulders. She could not understand how erotic she looked clad in only her silk stockings and slippers, the stockings tied with gold lace garters.

"I will tell Stepmama I am sick and must go home," she said.

She was strong, this English girl. She did not break down or fling accusations at him but only looked sad, as though something beautiful had been taken from her, and she regretted its loss.

"You will go nowhere." Alexander rose from the chair and refastened his trousers. "I will send the appropriate messages, and you will go home without seeing anyone. I will take care of things."

"You are no doubt right." Her voice was quiet and controlled.

She retrieved her chemise from the floor, her backside half turned toward him, and Alexander's semi-erection became a full one again. The love spell was powerful, but even without it the beauty of Meagan, like a goddess casual in her nakedness, would be an intoxicating sight. The fool who'd wasted money on the spell need only have paraded Meagan before him, and Alexander would have become randy and willing.

No, in truth he would never have taken an innocent. That had been planned most carefully by some enemy.

Silent tears streaked Meagan's face as she pulled the chemise over her body. She wiped them away, but they continued to flow. Her shaking fingers could not do up the ribbon that held the chemise closed.

"Let me." Alexander tied the tape of her chemise, then picked up the stiff stays and put them around her body, gently rethreading the laces he'd so eagerly untied. He helped her pull the cream silk gown on and buttoned the cloth-covered buttons up the back.

All the while, tears streamed down Meagan's cheeks, although she did not sob or sniffle as she realized she'd lost her maidenhead to a stranger and what the consequences could be.

He'd heard of plenty of callous English dandies who ruined girls and left them by the wayside, promising them marriage and then abandoning them. Some of these dandies were shot by brothers and fathers, and rightly so, but the vengeance never truly helped the woman.

But Meagan would never know the pain of abandonment, Alexander would make damn sure of that. She was as much a victim as he in this.

Alexander quietly donned his shirt and pulled on his coat, fastening it and settling it at his throat so it would not look odd without his cravat. He wrapped the linen cravat into a ball, which he thrust into the lit fireplace, letting fire consume the evidence of their first coupling. He settled the sash of office on his shoulders, looking in the mirror over the sideboard to adjust it correctly.

He found the ribbon for his hair, smoothed the unruly black mess into something resembling order, and tied it again. Then he poured Meagan brandy from the decanter on the table.

"You stay here and drink this," he ordered, closing her hand over the glass. "Lock the door and let no one in but me. My servants will put it about that you are ill and had to leave, and my man will get you home without anyone seeing. Do you understand?"

She looked up at him with brown-gold eyes that held too much sadness.

He smoothed her hair, loving the softness of it. "I swear to you on my honor, you'll not be wronged by this. Now, lock the door as I go."

The last thing in the world he wanted to do was leave her. The love spell clamped down on him as he tried to turn away, and he leaned down and kissed her lips, tasting tears on them.

She pressed him away, the sharp smell of the brandy cutting through his daze. "You'd better go."

He touched her cheek, then made himself turn around, cross the room, and walk out the door.

He heard the click of the key in the lock as he walked away, the cold sound shutting him out. The love spell wanted him to go back and beg her to let him back in, even if he had to pound on the door and shout for her to do so. The spell wanted him to stay close to her, to hear her voice, touch her skin, breathe her scent.

Damn what the spell wanted. Alexander's Nvengarian blood raged through him, newly aroused instincts making him want to rush back to Meagan and have her until they both were exhausted.

Let the fierceness of your father be yours, a voice inside him urged. *Damien's father turned you into cold-blooded viciousness—do not let him take your fire.*

Alexander tamped down his Nvengarian barbarity. The ice coldness he'd adopted after being forced to witness the execution of his own father by firing squad had allowed him to survive and take his vengeance. If Alexander had not quelled his hot bloodedness, he would have died that day at age thirteen.

His famous disciplined control helped him now. By the time he found Nikolai, calm had replaced the madness, and he was able to tell the valet in clipped tones what needed to be done.

Meagan sat numbly after Alexander departed, the glass of brandy untouched on the table next to her. Some part of her was horrified at what had just happened. She'd allowed a man to make love to her as though she were his wife—more accurately, his courtesan.

Foremost in Meagan's mind, however, was wonder. She'd been with a beautiful man, Alexander the Mad, Bad Duke, and he'd touched her and kissed her and called her *beautiful* and *his.*

Meagan was not a fool. She'd heard plenty of stories of seductive rakes who lured innocent misses into their arms, only to bring about said misses' downfalls. Alexander was a Nvengarian, and she'd learned from Penelope that Nvengarians played by different rules. Prince Damien had thought nothing of coupling with Penelope after they'd been betrothed, and by the laws of his people, there had been nothing sinful about it.

But Alexander had not asked Meagan to marry him, or

even to perform the betrothal ritual as Penelope and Damien had. No, he'd danced with her and kissed her, and the love spell meant for Deirdre had ignited her instead.

Meagan put her hand over her limp reticule, wondering where the talisman had got to. She did not find it in the room after a hasty search, and concluded that Alexander must have taken it away with him.

She stared a moment at the glass of brandy resting on the marble-topped table where she'd left it. Drawing a ragged breath, she lifted the glass to her lips, dumped the contents into her mouth, and swallowed.

She winced as the spirits burned her tongue and trailed fire down her throat. "Lud," she gasped. "How can men love this?"

A knock on the door made her jump. "Miss?" someone said in a low voice. "His Grace, the Grand Duke, he has sent me to you."

The accent was Nvengarian, the voice deep like Alexander's. Meagan hastened across the room and unlocked the door. Before she could pull it open, a tall, thin young man opened it mere inches, slipped through, and closed it again. He carried Meagan's hooded mantle over his arm.

"I am Nikolai, valet to His Grace," the young man said, bowing. He was Nvengarian, with high cheekbones, swarthy skin, and deep blue eyes. "If you follow my instructions precisely, we will get you home without, as you English say, anyone being the wiser."

Meagan flushed. Alexander must have told him exactly what had happened and given him instructions to help clean up the mess. How embarrassing. But in her half panic and sudden inebriation, she felt relieved that someone knew what to do.

"You will not become hysterical, will you?" Nikolai

asked. "If you do, I will have to slap your cheek or pour water on your face to keep you quiet, and His Grace will be very angry." He grimaced and shook his head. "You do not want to see His Grace angry."

Meagan hiccoughed. "Why? Is he so very terrible?"

"My God, yes. One time that His Grace was angry, half of Nvengaria's capital was flattened, with people running from their homes and screaming in the streets. The river was a flotilla of makeshift barges of people trying to get away from him. It is terrible indeed, the wrath of Grand Duke Alexander."

Meagan eyed him skeptically. "He flattened half the city? Just like that?"

"I do not lie, miss. I was there. He sent in his men, and . . ." He flourished his hand. "Horrible days. I am Prince Damien's man, miss, and glad I am Prince Damien has come home at last." Meagan knew from experience that Nvengarians liked dramatics, the more sturm and drang, the better. Nikolai was probably exaggerating, but the core of truth would still be there—that Alexander, for whatever his reason, had sent in men to rout part of the city.

"But do not worry, miss, I am here to look after you." He draped the mantel over her shoulders. "You wrap up in this and keep your face hidden. I have already put it about that you are ill and a friend has taken you home. I suggested several names of your acquaintance as possibilities, one of whom has already departed, so that by the time all have unraveled that you were not with this one or that one, the incident will long be over."

Meagan fastened the mantel and pulled up the hood. "And how will I truly get home?"

"His Grace's carriage, miss, which is waiting a few steps down the street. When you reach your house, do not rouse your servants, creep upstairs ever so softly, and undress by yourself. Wash yourself all over before you go to bed. Then you should call the servant and pretend to be ill. Groaning, I believe, helps. Let them make a fuss over you and do not look too well the following morning."

Meagan's head was pounding, and she imagined she would not have to feign illness. "You seem to know much about this, Nikolai. I suppose His Grace has you help a young miss home every week?"

Her heart burned when she spoke the words. She knew her intimacy with Alexander was false, but she hated to think of him holding any other young woman in his arms while he uttered tender Nvengarian phrases.

"No, indeed. His Grace has ice water in his veins, so what has happened tonight is very unusual. But I worked for a baron in Nvengaria, and *ay . . .*" Nikolai put a pained hand to his forehead. "Every night a different lady, and he was never discreet. I slept not at all in his service, and then he expected me to protect him with my body when his wife came at him with a knife. No, indeed, I stepped aside and let her do as she pleased."

Meagan gasped. "Did she kill him?"

"No, no, but she slashed his clothes to ribbons while she cursed him something horrible. It was a joy to watch. We passed wine around in the servants' hall that day. But it was a relief to find a position in the palace. Prince Damien, he is a true gentleman and treats his wife so tenderly. She is a beautiful and a fine princess. It is a joy to serve her."

Emotion gripped Meagan, and her eyes stung. "Penelope is my dearest friend."

"Which is why I am honored to be at your service, miss. If there is anything you need, at any time, in any place, I, Nikolai, will be at your side. It is the least I can do, for *her* sake."

He pressed his hand to his chest and made another bow, his face serious. Meagan remembered how Prince Damien's entourage had become fanatically devoted to Penelope and wondered if Penelope had experienced the same sense of disorientation and dismay.

"That is kind of you, Nikolai," Meagan breathed. "For now, please get me home."

"As you wish." He gestured her toward the door. "Follow me, keep your face covered, and all will be well. Trust me, miss; I am expert at this."

"Alexander," Lady Anastasia hissed from behind a gold and white pillar in an upper hall. "Where on earth have you been? You had an appointment with von Hohenzahl at midnight."

Alexander halted his determined steps as Lady Anastasia swept toward him. Anastasia was a lovely woman with a face that had Europe swooning at her feet. He knew the *ton* supposed that her gown and tiara would adorn his floor tonight while he entertained her in his bed, but they supposed wrong.

Lady Anastasia Dimitri was the best information collector he knew, and at present, she was feeding him important intelligence about the Austrian empire, which he in turn passed to Damien, at least the bits Damien needed to know. Alexander used her to keep his eye on Austria, and she used Alexander's mistrust of the Austrians to fuel her games of revenge.

Anastasia had spoken in Nvengarian, and Alexander answered her in the same language. "I had something to take care of."

"What, for heaven's sake? It took you weeks to convince von Hohenzahl to meet you informally, and now it has gone for nothing."

"Not if you spoke to him. What did he tell you?"

She took his arm and fell into step beside him. "Nothing very useful, although he did try to woo me to his bed." She looked disgusted. "He babbled a bit about there being more dangers in the Nvengarian mountains than we could possibly imagine and about something only he knew. He was gloating, and I did not like it."

"I will question him," Alexander said. "If he is hard to crack, we will use other means to crack him, but crack him we will."

Otto von Hohenzahl, an Austrian toady of Prince Metternich, had lately been making noise that he had information Alexander needed to know. Von Hohenzahl was a minor official and likely wanted nothing more than money from Alexander, but Alexander knew from experience to investigate every rumor and source of information in case they bore a grain of truth. He'd been trying to pin down von Hohenzahl for weeks, and was to have met him tonight, the entire reason he'd chosen to come to this ball and bring Anastasia with him.

"I am happy to hear you say so, but what happened to you? It is not like you to miss an appointment." She stopped, her shrewd gaze going to his absent cravat, the faint finger marks on his neck, and his half-mussed hair. "Good lord, you had a liaison. With whom? What did you learn?"

Typical of Anastasia to think of lovemaking only in terms of gaining information. Before tonight, her assumption would not have annoyed him, but it did now. "Not that sort of liaison."

"What then? A dalliance with a maid? Alexander, what on earth were you thinking?"

He'd been thinking of a red-haired lady whose lips

were curved and warm, whose thighs were soft under his fingers, whose broken cries of passion had aroused him like nothing had in ages. She'd smashed through Alexander's aloof shell and touched the volatile man inside him, the one he'd suppressed for years.

It startled him, but at the same time he relished the awakening. Violent Nvengarian emotions could be inconvenient, but Meagan had tapped ones he'd forgotten—joy, elation, happiness.

"I would ask a favor of you, Anastasia," he began. "Come home with me tonight and make it obvious that you are doing so."

She studied him with a frown, and then her eyes widened in shock. "Dear God, you were with the Tavistock girl. Alexander, have you run mad? She is an innocent miss, untouchable. Or are you playing some sort of game against Damien, since she is Princess Penelope's friend?"

"I am playing no games. I have fallen in love with her."

She stared at him, mouth open. "Love? You *have* run mad."

"It was a spell," Alexander explained. "Someone is using her to get to me. I do not know who. I do not believe she knows either, but she knew about the spell."

He withdrew the talisman from his pocket. Anastasia's gaze moved to it, and she nodded. She'd seen spell talismans before.

"Would you like me to destroy it for you?" she asked.

Alexander stroked it absently, then dropped it back into his pocket. "No. I wish to discover who had it made. I doubt Meagan did it herself. I cannot see her plucking feathers and chanting over candles."

"How do you know? You've only just met her."

"I know."

Anastasia's gaze was piercing. "You are too used to

political intrigue, Alexander. Perhaps she simply wanted to catch herself a husband."

"A dangerous way to land a proposal. Love spells create only physical attraction, and most gentlemen walk away at the end of them, forgetting about the woman as soon as the magic has gone."

"Yes, but you are not most gentlemen."

Alexander shrugged. "She had no way of knowing that. Tomorrow, I will approach her father. The English have a habit of tearing to pieces any who break their rules, and I do not wish that to happen to her."

"I see. Hence, I go home with you tonight so people talk about me and you, not her."

He nodded, his mind still turning over the procedures he needed to follow, while another part wondered about von Hohenzahl and his secret and how Alexander would extract it from him. "I want no hint of gossip or speculation to touch her until it is a fait accompli."

"Very well." She subjected him to her scrutiny a moment longer, then began to laugh. And laugh and laugh.

Alexander's brow twitched in annoyance. "I find nothing amusing."

"I do. Good lord, Alexander, how many women have thrown themselves at you? All in vain, like battering the most fortified castle in the world. And one red-haired girl with freckles brings you down with feathers and a twist of gold wire. This is delicious."

Somewhere deep inside, a man within Alexander laughed with her for the joy of it, but that man was far from the surface. "I do not like being laughed at."

"I know," she said, wiping her eyes. "You are Grand Duke Alexander, the most ruthless man in the world. I am enjoying this."

Suddenly Alexander pulled her into his arms and

kissed her. Not for sudden affection or to stop her laughing, but because he'd heard a step in the hall.

One of Lord Featherstone's guests, a portly man with
little hair left, peered at them and made a grunting noise.

"Disgusting," he said, then walked disapprovingly
away.

CHAPTER FIVE

Meagan sat rigidly at the breakfast table while Simone chattered on about the Featherstones' ball and everything Meagan had missed by going home early.

"Lily Carmichael danced with Lord Oberforce, can it be credited? And her engagement to Sir Samuel Rice only recently announced. What delicious scandal! And did you *see* what Lady Musgrave was *wearing?*"

Never had Meagan found toast soaked with fresh golden butter so unappealing, never had the breakfast chocolate, rich and hot, smelled so nauseating.

Meagan's father sat behind his newspaper, letting Simone talk. When he paused to turn the page, Meagan saw his smile and the fond twinkle in his eyes as he glanced at his wife. He enjoyed listening to her chatter, he'd told Meagan. Very soothing, like birdsong in the garden.

On a usual morning, Meagan might laugh at Simone's anecdotes, but this was not a usual morning.

Her head ached and buzzed, the chocolate tasted bitter, and she could barely swallow the toast. Pretending to be ill the night before, as Nikolai had directed, had not been difficult.

It had all worked as Nikolai predicted. He'd gotten her home and into the house without anyone seeing, and she'd followed his instructions of putting herself to bed and then calling her maid. The delay had given her a chance to wash herself, rebraid her mussed hair, put on her nightdress, and slide between the covers. By the time Rose arrived, Meagan had been shaking so much that Rose had become alarmed and brought out the laudanum.

A heavy laudanum sleep on top of the night's insanity had left her with a sticky taste in her mouth, a foul headache, and an aching throat.

"And Katie Southington was asked to dance *twice* by a baron's son," Simone continued. "Her mother is in such transports. A baron, just think, and the Southingtons barely able to buy coal for their fires. That would be a feather in Mrs. Southington's cap and possibly a nice roof over her head as well. Not that I thought much of him—he has no chin and a concave chest, as though a horse kicked him when he was a child. And with Katie's looks, their children will be horribly ugly, poor things. But then, he will be a baron when his father dies, and they are besotted with each other. No, the handsomest man in the room by far was Grand Duke Alexander. All of the mothers threw their daughters at *him* and, poor things, he took no notice of them. But *you* danced with him, Meagan. Is he just as handsome up close?"

Meagan washed down a lump of toast with a gulp of chocolate, nearly choking herself. "Yes," she gasped into her napkin. "He is handsome."

She remembered the sinewy strength of his hand on her waist, his sure power as he moved with her on the dance floor. The same power had flowed through him when he kissed her, lips moving hard on hers, his tongue tasting every curve of her mouth. The man did nothing by halves—he'd danced and made love with the same flowing strength.

Simone rattled on. "Quite a coup for me, my step-daughter dancing with the Grand Duke of Nvengaria. He favored no other young ladies. But all the ambitious mamas panted after him in vain, because he went home with Lady Anastasia, which was no surprise to me. She's a beautiful woman, so sophisticated, so cosmopolitan. I heard they were clinging to each other quite shamelessly in one of the upper halls. But they are foreign." She waved a dismissive hand.

The toast lodged in Meagan's throat good and hard, and she coughed, spraying crumbs across the white tablecloth.

Michael moved his newspaper and gazed at Meagan in concern. "Roberts," he said to the footman who'd just entered. "Fetch Miss Meagan a glass of water."

Roberts slammed down his tray, knocking over a pot of cream, and hurried from the room. Simone thumped Meagan on the back as Michael quickly rescued the cream.

"Poor darling," Simone crooned. "I am not surprised you took sick last night. Such a dreadful crush and a hot room. I am amazed we all did not swoon dead away."

Roberts brought a glass overflowing with water and sloshed it across Meagan's skirt in his haste to hand it to her. She gulped the water, dislodging the dry toast, tears leaking from her eyes.

"I'm all right," she managed. "Father, may I be excused?"

"Certainly." He got to his feet, newspaper forgotten, and helped Meagan to hers. "Are you all right, love?"

Meagan was far from all right, but if she sank into his embrace, she'd break down and possibly blurt out the whole story. That would never do. Her father was a loving, caring man, and she could not bear to witness the disappointment in his eyes when he found out what a lightskirt she was. She knew she would have to face the truth sooner or later, but at present it was too raw.

"I'll be fine. I will lie down and be right as rain."

Simone did not believe her. Suddenly solicitous, she helped Michael escort Meagan out of the dining room.

As they reached the hall, Roberts hurried to answer a banging knock at the front door, letting in cold March wind as he opened it. When he turned around, he staggered under the weight of two huge arrangements of flowers. The baskets overflowed with so many hothouse roses and peonies that it was difficult to tell where the flowers left off and Roberts began.

Simone pressed her hand to her heart. "My, my. Oh, Meagan, you must have won the affections of a very generous gentleman."

"Where should I put these, ma'am?" Roberts slurred, his face full of blossoms.

"Over there." Simone pointed to a table in the middle of the sitting room. Roberts lumbered forward, red and sweating.

"No, by the window, so everyone will see them," Simone said. "Do hurry, Roberts."

"Yes, ma'am," Roberts mumbled. He rolled across the room, a mass of flowers with legs, and heaved the baskets onto the tiny table in the window.

Meagan followed him, knowing good and well who'd sent the flowers. They were meant to grab attention and hold it, just like the Grand Duke himself. As Roberts struggled to balance the arrangements, Simone searched for a card. "It must be here. A gentleman would not send flowers without a note."

"It's in me pocket, ma'am," Roberts said. "If I can just . . ."

He held the weight of the flowers with his body, trying to poke into his pocket with his blunt fingers. Simone solved the problem by plucking a folded paper from his waistcoat and breaking the seal.

"I knew it!" She looked up, her eyes shining in happiness. "It is from *him*, Meagan. Look."

Meagan snatched the paper from Simone's outstretched fingers. The note was simple and short. In plain handwriting, he had written, "With my compliments, Alexander of Nvengaria."

Simone whirled around and around, the tapes on her cap flying. "I knew that waltz would be worth something. He saw you across the ballroom and was instantly smitten. Are you not glad that I advised you to put buttermilk on those freckles?"

"We will send them back," Meagan said.

Simone stopped whirling. "What on earth for?"

Meagan couldn't very well explain that Alexander was trying to make up for what they'd done by overwhelming her with an overpowering gift. She should, like a silly miss, gush with gratitude. But she wasn't a silly miss, panting for any word or gesture from him. Sending the flowers back would tell him so.

She groped for an explanation Simone would understand. "You said yourself he departed with Lady Anastasia. I should not accept gifts from a libertine, should I?"

Simone paused. "Oh, but Meagan . . ."

Meagan's father said from the doorway, "I agree. I am not certain I like this."

Michael's presence seemed to reinforce Simone's first impression. "Nonsense. Did not dear Penelope write us that Alexander has reformed and is now Prince Damien's right-hand man? Sent as ambassador to chum up with kings and sign treaties or whatever it is ambassadors do. So trusted now. How could he help but take a fancy to our Meagan?"

Meagan fell silent. She knew Alexander was making a gesture, and Meagan would not be able to make a gesture back with Simone so excited. Her stepmother busily moved the blossoms this way and that, Roberts still trying to keep them balanced on the too-small table. She hummed a happy tune in her throat. Michael watched, his brows lowering, but he made no move to stop her.

True, Penelope had written that Alexander was now sent on missions Damien trusted no others to do, but that did not mean Alexander was tamed. Meagan remembered the hard blue of his eyes as he had glared at her across the ballroom, the preemptory way he'd dragged her into the waltz, and his cool, clipped tones when he told her he'd get her home unseen if she obeyed his instructions to the letter.

No, Grand Duke Alexander was not tame.

"He is polite to send flowers, but it is a bit overdone," Michael said, still concerned. "Likely he does not understand that such a gesture will draw attention."

Oh, he understands, Meagan thought darkly. She had no doubt that Grand Duke Alexander knew exactly what he was doing.

"This means that he will call on you, no doubt." Simone whirled again, then stopped and looked about her in horror.

"Heavens, this sitting room is an atrocious mess. Roberts, call Jane up here and help me rearrange things. And Meagan, you cannot wear *that*. Change into your best morning gown, darling, and tell Rose to do some-

thing with your hair. All must be perfect when the
Grand Duke arrives!"

Except the Grand Duke did not arrive. Simone forced Meagan to sit with her for hours, then jumped at the sound of
every carriage until Meagan thought she'd scream. The
clock ticked through the hours while Meagan pretended
to sew and Simone fussed and Michael, with a wary
frown, went to his study. But the Grand Duke never came.

Instead, he sent a letter.

The missive arrived by carriage, brought in by a stiff
Nvengarian servant dressed in blue military-looking liv-
ery. The servant stood straight and tall, handsome and
blue-eyed like all Nvengarians, and argued loudly with
Roberts that he must present the letter to the honorable
Miss Tavistock's father in person.

He pushed past Roberts, went down on one knee, and
lifted a folded letter to Michael, who'd emerged from his
study at the noise. "My master, he bade me bring this to
you," he said, his accent thick.

Michael took the letter and opened it, Simone crowding
to read over his shoulder. After a moment of intense silence, Simone squealed and put her hand over her mouth.

"I knew it! I knew he was smitten with our Meagan."
She snatched the letter from Michael's hands and thrust
it at Meagan, eyes shining in triumph. "Read that."

Hands shaking, Meagan took the paper.

It was a formal and elegantly written proposal of marriage. It addressed Michael, as the father, asking his permission to pay court and outlining Alexander's extensive
lands and wealth in Nvengaria.

"Is it not beautiful?" Simone breathed over her shoulder. " '*I wish to extend the honor of inviting Miss Tavistock to
become Grand Duchess of Nvengaria and my wife.*' How ut-

terly divine. If I were a debutante I would swoon in delight. How clever of you to make him fall head over heels during your little waltz, darling."

"He must be mad," Meagan said faintly.

"To fall in love with you? Likely you were a refreshing change from all those sophisticated European women. Why should he not fall for a quaint English rose?"

Michael broke in. He was not a fool, and Meagan knew he smelled something wrong in this proposal. "We do not know for certain what his motives are, Simone."

"Of course we do; his motives are perfectly clear. He wants to marry Meagan and make her a Grand Duchess. She'll live in that beautiful mansion on Berkeley Square and no doubt have a palace of her own in Nvengaria. Think of it, my love. We'll visit Nvengaria and be invited to *two* palaces now. We must be off at once."

Michael stared at her. "Off? Off where?"

"To Berkeley Square to see Grand Duke Alexander. Meagan, darling, your hair is frightful. Rose! Quickly, you must dress Meagan's hair and get her into something presentable. Hurry now."

She thrust Meagan at Rose, who'd come up from the servants' hall to see what the fuss was about, and started to shoo them toward the stairs.

Michael stood firmly in the way. "Simone, he has extended no invitation for us to call."

Simone looked surprised. "Do not be silly. He would not have sent the carriage otherwise. He expects us to answer this letter in person."

"I want to go," Meagan interrupted.

Her father and stepmother turned in surprise, almost as if they'd forgotten her presence. "Meagan," Michael began in his kind, reasonable tone.

"No, Papa, I want to go," she said firmly. "I truly need to speak to Grand Duke Alexander." *And explain that I am not a quivering Nvengarian subject succumbing to his might.*

She recalled his words. *"I swear to you on my honor, you will not be wronged by this."* This was what he meant—a hasty marriage? And then what? His English wife hidden away in some country house like the Prince of Wales had hidden away Princess Caroline? *No, thank you, Your Grace.* Alexander and she needed to have a firm discussion.

"You see?" Simone rattled. "She wishes to go. Come along, Michael, darling, it will all be glorious and my stepdaughter will be Grand Duchess of Nvengaria. You will see."

In less than an hour's time, Meagan stood with her father and stepmother in front of the most intimidating door in London.

The Grand Duke's opulent, porticoed mansion lay in the heart of Berkeley Square, opposite lush gardens that reposed behind iron railings in the middle of the square.

Maysfield House, built seventy-five years ago by a duke and hired for the Season by Alexander, was one of the most ostentatious houses in London. The décor inside was a marvel, or so the magazines and newspapers that had discussed it claimed. Every member of the *ton* wanted to get a look at the house, but the Grand Duke's invitations were few and far between. He might be an ambassador, but without a wife to act as hostess, the *ton* pined for admission in vain.

The front door itself was enough to make Meagan turn around and run all the way back to Oxfordshire. The tall double doors with arched fanlight, shining black paint, and knocker carved like a many-toothed serpent haughtily proclaimed that the casual visitor was not welcome.

Simone never considered herself a casual visitor. She'd

ridden regally in the carriage with the Grand Duke's coat of arms emblazoned on it, making certain her face appeared in the window so any acquaintance who happened to be out and about would see her. The carriage was not the one in which Meagan had ridden home the night before, which implied the Grand Duke kept two or possibly more conveyances. Meagan had grown up in the country with a father who could afford one rather elderly barouche and count himself fortunate.

Simone waited impatiently for the servant, whose name was Gaius, to open the door to admit them to the house. Gaius seemed just as happy as Simone with the visit, and smiled broadly as he gestured them inside.

The first thing Meagan saw upon stepping into the oval entrance hall was a spiral checkerboard tile floor that stretched a long distance to a sweeping flight of stairs. The second thing was a haughty English butler whose nose was raised so high he couldn't help but look down it.

"Yes?" he said in tones of chill disapproval. "How may I help you?"

Gaius snapped his fingers, his look just as haughty. "You, inform my master the great lady has arrived."

The butler skewered him with a freezing glance. "*His Grace* does not wish to be disturbed this morning."

Gaius spluttered. "He sent me to take a letter to the honored lady, the love of his existence, the . . ."

"Yes, he sent a *letter*," the butler interrupted. "He wished the matter to be settled in writing."

"You dare keep His Grace from his beloved?" Gaius said, Nvengarian blue eyes flashing.

"It is all right," Meagan said hastily, stepping between them. She'd witnessed explosive Nvengarian tempers last year with Prince Damien's entourage and knew they could start a blood feud over who went first through a door. "We will leave."

She made to pivot out the door, but Simone blocked her way.

"Nonsense, my dear. Grand Duke Alexander will be ecstatic to see you. He wants to marry you, after all."

She pushed past Meagan and the startled butler and trotted toward the stairs that wound upward in a marble spiral. "Halloo, Grand Duke! We are here, Miss Tavistock and her family."

"Simone," Michael hissed, starting after her.

Meagan debated making a run for it.

But part of her knew that running would do no good. Alexander would simply send another efficient Nvengarian servant after her and drag her wherever he wanted her to go. He had arranged everything last night, and no doubt he had arranged everything today.

His high-handedness already sparked the rebelliousness inside her. He expected her to bow her head and accept his arrangements without question. Well, he would just have to learn that Meagan Tavistock would not be pushed about by the gale that was Grand Duke Alexander. She would not be like Nikolai, trembling before his might. She might shake a little, but she wouldn't let him know that.

Above them a door banged, and Nikolai appeared on the first landing. "Ah, you have come. Miss Tavistock and honorable father and mother, please to follow me?"

Gaius gloated, and the butler gave him a weary look. Meagan suddenly wanted to pat the butler sympathetically and fix him a cup of tea. Living with all these Nvengarians must be trying.

Simone had already made it to the top of the stairs, Michael just behind her. "What a beautiful house," she exclaimed, running her hand along the carved railing. "Just think, Meagan will live here, and I shall visit every day."

If the prospect dismayed Nikolai, he made no sign. He waited for Meagan to reach the top of the stairs and gave her an inquiring look. His friendly sympathy made her want to burst into tears, but she bravely held them in and whispered, "I am fine. Thank you, Nikolai."

Her father shot her a sharp glance, clearly wondering how she knew Nikolai's name. Meagan blushed but kept her eyes averted as she slipped past him.

The upper hall encircled the lower one in a ringed gallery supported by fantastic marble pillars and arches. Carved and painted double doors led off of this balcony into rooms described in detail in the magazines—the Asia Hall, the India sitting room, the Marble Salon, and others.

The study Nikolai led them to was high-ceilinged and decorated in shades of dark red, lit by tall windows that overlooked the square. Bookshelves covered the walls and the cavernous room ended in a desk placed before an enormous and ornate fireplace.

Behind this desk sat Alexander, Grand Duke of Nvengaria.

It was an audience they'd come to have with him, no less. He rose to his feet as they entered, every inch the Grand Duke with his dark coat, medals, and blue and gold sash of office stretched across his chest. He wore no gloves today, and the rubies on his fingers reflected the red of his earring.

Meagan swallowed the lump in her throat. She'd managed not to think of his blue eyes and broad shoulders all morning, letting worry drive away the memory of Alexander the man. But as she entered the room, the memories returned thick and fast.

Alexander's ragged voice as he whispered endearments in Nvengarian, his kisses that possessed her, his hands firm on her body. Alexander holding her on his lap, his eyelids heavy, his long hair brushing her skin. Alexander inside her, making her feel wild and wicked and free for the first time in her life.

Her face warmed under her bonnet and her fingers went ice cold. From the look in Alexander's hard blue eyes, he remembered every moment of their encounter too, and was less than happy about it.

Gaius dashed to armchairs placed about the room and dragged three into a line before Alexander's desk. He gestured Meagan to the first chair with a flourish. "Honored lady, please to sit."

Alexander said nothing, neither inviting them nor rejecting them. He simply waited for them to obey his servant.

Gaius gestured again. "You must sit. An honored lady cannot stand."

To make him happy—or at least quiet—Meagan moved to the chair and plopped into it. Gaius beamed and turned to seat Michael and Simone.

Simone readily took her chair and smiled at Gaius, who'd set a stool under her feet. "We are frightfully honored, Your Grace. Fancy you choosing our daughter above all ladies to marry. Of course she is quite charming, so it is no surprise to me. I have always praised Meagan for her unusual looks."

In truth, Simone had constantly suggested different remedies to remove Meagan's freckles and dressing her hair in ways to not draw attention to the redness of it. *And you could try a bit of slimming, darling, not that you are not adorable, but . . .*

Michael remained standing.

"You have come to accept my offer?" Alexander began, addressing Michael. Meagan noticed that though he seemed to look at all of them at once, Alexander in fact never let his gaze rest directly on Meagan.

"We have," Simone said.

"We have not," Michael corrected her. "We have come to see what prompted you to make it. You must have a shortage of marriageable ladies in Nvengaria, Your Grace, as your countrymen keep snatching up English girls to wife, particularly from my family."

Alexander's brows rose, his cool poise not in the least dented. Meagan remembered Nikolai's tale of how Alexander had destroyed half a city on a whim, and looking into his hard eyes this afternoon, she well believed it.

"Your speech is not quite flattering to your daughter, Mr. Tavistock," he said.

"To the contrary, my daughter is the most important thing in the world to me, which is why I must ask why you want to marry her. There are plenty of marriageable and important young ladies in London this Season if you simply need a wife. Why has your interest lighted on Meagan?"

Meagan chewed her lip. Michael was never one to stand in awe of the aristocracy—which was where Meagan had learned her bit of rebelliousness. Michael judged men on their deeds and their character, not their birth. Alexander, it was evident, was used to being obeyed without question. And now this unimportant Englishman dared look him in the eye and request him to explain himself.

"You will of course be well compensated," Alexander said. "And I will not require you to provide a dowry."

"Oh, lud," Meagan murmured. If he thought Michael would twitter at the prospect of riches and say, "Of course, Your Grace, you honor me," he read Michael very wrong.

"She is my daughter, sir," Michael said stiffly. "Not cattle."

"Michael. Darling," Simone murmured. "Do not spoil it."

Alexander moved a few papers on his desk. "I have already put the documents in order: special license, settlements, provision for money and jewels for Miss Tavistock during her lifetime, arrangements for a staff of her own." His gaze flicked back to Michael. "I assure you, she would be well provided for."

"I have no doubt she would be. If Prince Damien is any indication, you Nvengarians are thorough." Michael cleared his throat. "But though I do not like to give credence to gossip, the stories I hear of you give me pause. You did your best to assassinate Penelope and Damien last year, and now I hear our own king is terrified of you and will do anything you tell him. Your name is prominent on the guest lists of the most important social affairs, and you dine often with the Duke of Wellington and every other leader in the House of Lords. My wife reads the society papers avidly, and tells me."

Simone gave a nod, proud to be such a good source of information.

Michael went on, "She also tells me of your less savory activities, such as your mistress. I dislike to bring up such a topic in front of my daughter, but I wish Meagan to realize exactly what kind of man she would marry. I do not believe in hiding the truth from her."

"Nor do I," Alexander said without missing a beat.

Meagan shifted in the chair, uncomfortably warm in the deep red room. Alexander would have prepared answers for every single question a worried father could throw at him. He was that kind of man.

"If Meagan marries me, she need have no qualms about my fidelity," Alexander answered calmly.

Michael flushed. "But it still begs the question, why

have you singled out our unimportant family? There must be many prominent ladies scattered about Europe who will benefit Nvengaria in a political marriage."

Again, Alexander would not look directly at Meagan but merely skimmed his gaze over her and fixed it again on Michael. "When I met Miss Tavistock I made my choice."

And that should be enough, his tone implied.

"Forgive me for being a concerned father," Michael said dryly.

"That you are has earned my respect."

Michael drew a breath and tried another tack. "And where would Meagan live? In Nvengaria?"

"She will live in London for now, here in Maysfield House. She will be given the title of Grand Duchess of Nvengaria and all the privileges and wealth that accompany the rank, which are considerable, I assure you— houses and properties in Nvengaria and the Grand Duchess's jewels, which are worth a fortune."

Michael watched him a moment, ignoring Simone, who had slid to the edge of her seat during his mention of jewels and properties.

"Your offer flatters my daughter, Your Grace, that is true," Michael said. "But marrying you would put her among strangers, and you would not stay in London forever. Also, she would be much in the public eye, as you are, and she is not used to that."

"She will be instructed," Alexander said.

Michael inclined his head. "I grant you have provided for everything. But I must ask again, why? We have few connections and, truth be told, we are not overly burdened with wealth."

Alexander's eyes, chips of blue ice, moved almost to Meagan, then back to Michael.

Meagan sprang to her feet, unable to bear it. "This is easily settled, Father. I will refuse his suit and we will go home."

"Oh, no, you will not," Simone broke in fiercely. "His Grace is making a kind, and may I say it, very generous offer the likes of which we will not see again. As your father says, we are not important, so he must be offering for only one reason." She turned her wide smile on Alexander. "You fell in love with her, did you not, Your Grace? Love strikes when one least expects it."

Alexander's expression did not change. "That is true, Mrs. Tavistock. I fell in love."

"You see?"

"Did you?" Michael asked, sounding amazed. "I am sorry, but according to my wife, Meagan met you last night and you danced one dance. Based on that, you are prepared to offer her jewels, money, houses, property, and a title?"

Alexander's brows drew together the slightest bit. Meagan held her breath, waiting for him to summon his servant to throw them into the street.

"Father," she blurted. "May I speak to Alexander, I mean, His Grace, alone for a moment? Please?"

Alexander's eyes flickered, and Michael turned to her in perplexity. Meagan knew that all Alexander had to do was explain that he'd compromised Meagan and his argument would be clinched. Then she'd die of mortification right here on his elegant red rug.

Simone saved the day by getting quickly to her feet. "Of course. Come along, Michael. It is obvious they need to work things out between them, and parents will be in the way."

Her eyes bore the intensity of a woman determined to get what she wanted. She saw the prospect of her step-daughter married to a Grand Duke, and she would push for it like a jockey pushed his horse to win the race. In Simone's mind, Meagan had but one choice.

"Please, Papa," Meagan said.

Michael took on a look of resignation. "Very well." He laid his hand on Meagan's shoulder and said in a low voice, "Remember, you can refuse him. I will still love you and stand by you, I promise you that."

He would break her heart. Meagan blinked to keep tears from forming.

Gaius took his cue and ushered Michael and Simone out the door, leaving her, at last, alone with Alexander.

Chapter Six

Something had happened to Alexander the moment Meagan walked into the room. The previous night and all this morning he'd forced himself to be logical and cold, to put plans in motion and not think. But in his dreams he relived holding her in his arms, pressing inside of her, the taste and feel and scent of her around him.

He'd woken in the night thoroughly aroused, his cock swollen and tight. The primitive man inside him wanted to charge across London and find her and kiss her and take her. He'd been able, as he washed and dressed for the day, to tamp down the beast, hiding it behind the coolly neutral tasks of contacting his solicitor and making arrangements.

But as soon as Meagan walked into the room, the cool man departed and the predator returned. He caught her scent all the way across the room, strong like roses, light like lemon. The sinuous movement of her body under her thin silk dress sent heat through his blood. He'd remained behind the desk because he'd not be very convincing as the coolly efficient Grand Duke with the obvious erection in his breeches.

"Why do you not want to look at me, Alexander?" Meagan broke through his thoughts, her voice melodious. "It would be so much easier to speak to you, you know, if you were not staring at the moldings on the other side of the room."

He pulled his gaze from the closed door and forced it to Meagan. "Because when I look at you, I feel the spell. I cannot control it or myself when you are in the room."

"Oh." She bit her lip, drawing his attention to the moist redness of it. A bead of sweat trickled down his spine. "Then perhaps we both should study the paintings on the ceiling."

She looked up at the gaudy representations of gods and goddesses high above them, a red curl dripping to her slim neck. He wanted to go to her and kiss that neck, drawing his tongue along it and tasting the curl.

"Meagan." He couldn't help saying her name, wanting to feel it on his lips. "Marrying me is the best way to put things right."

"Best for whom? I presume you mean for me, but would it be?"

She was angry and upset, and like her father, she would not grovel on the carpet, happy that Alexander wanted to bestow such an honor. She took his breath away.

"I do not understand you," he said.

"No?" Her chest lifted with agitated breath. "I could hie off to Scotland or some such place and live out my life, unseen by society, and no one will ever know what happened between us. But if you marry me, it will be a great scandal. People will talk about it for years, the lofty Grand Duke and the plain English miss who tricked him into marrying her."

She was worried about gossip? The Grand Duke could

turn gossip to his advantage or create whatever gossip he pleased. He could play upon the English *ton* like a musician played a pianoforte.

"You need care nothing for that," he said. "The Nvengarians will think it a grand romance, and their opinion is the only one that matters."

She raised her brows. "Well, you ought to worry about what English people think if you want to be an ambassador. That is what ambassadors do, is it not, care about the customs of other people's countries?"

"You are schooled in the way of ambassadors? That will be useful, when you are Grand Duchess."

"When I am Grand Duchess?" She gave him an incredulous look. "You are certainly presumptuous, Your Grace. It would have been more pleasant if you'd asked me, *before* you sent my father that letter."

He made a conciliatory gesture. "I admit that I mistook both your character and that of your father."

In all his life, Alexander had never mistaken a person's character. He'd been able to manipulate men from the lowest born to the highest by simply knowing which of their strings to pull. Anyone else in the world, having been ushered into this room, would have already agreed to sign whatever Alexander wanted him to sign or do whatever he wanted him to do. But this young Englishwoman with red hair only looked at him in complete bafflement. He was trying to save her life, and she did not want the likes of him to save it.

"Even so, it is the best solution to our predicament," he continued. "If you give your consent, I have obtained the license and we will proceed as soon as I send for a vicar."

She stared at him in shock. "You mean you want me to marry you *right now*?"

"The more quickly it is done, the easier things will be."

Her eyes were wide, gold sparks swimming in the

brown. "Good heavens, Alexander, what did you write in your diary this morning? 'Eat breakfast, write letters, marry Miss Tavistock, meet with the cabinet'?"

"Not quite."

"No, but very close, I imagine."

She perplexed him. Every woman of Alexander's acquaintance shivered when he looked at her, either in fear of what he would do or in anticipation of him taking her to bed.

Meagan neither shivered nor looked particularly amorous. As she had done last night, she assessed Alexander the man, seeing past the trappings that surrounded him. Very few females bothered to move aside the curtain and look directly at him, but Meagan was busily tearing the curtain to shreds.

She turned to pace the carpet, walking through a sunbeam that made her hair glisten. He suddenly envisioned lifting her to the desk, laying her down on the polished wood to see her red hair spread like a curtain against the mahogany.

He leaned his hands on the carved back of his chair to stop himself. "I told you last night that I would put things right."

One side of her mouth quirked. "I imagined you meant you'd marry me off to one of your friends, some minor gentleman of increasing years who needed a wife."

His indignation flared. "Is that what men do in England? Pass their lovers to convenient friends?"

She flicked a glance at him at the word *lover*. "I believe it is common practice."

"It is not common practice in Nvengaria. I gave you my word, and I will not desert you. We were both caught by the love spell, and we will make the best of it. We may be married in name only if you wish."

That should suit her if she wanted to keep well away from him, though he was not certain how he'd keep himself away from *her*. The love spell kept reminding him of how it felt to be inside her, what her voice sounded like when she said his name in broken passion.

"You are certainly a romantic, Your Grace. I must say, it is all over London that you left with Lady Anastasia last evening and that she came here with you. I know I should die of shame before I repeat such a thing, especially to you, but I am rather blunt. I think it only fair you know this before you decide to marry me."

He smoothed his hand along the mahogany carving. Was she jealous, then? He had the words to soothe that too.

"Anastasia and I are not lovers. We have been in the past but are not at present. I asked her to accompany me home last night to focus gossip on her rather than on you. I wanted no speculation to form when you disappeared so soon after our waltz, and I could not be certain that no one noticed us leave for the terrace or go to the anteroom. Lady Anastasia spent the night at my house, but in a guest room, far from me."

"Oh." Her flush rose, a pretty color that slid under her décolletage. "Actually, that was clever."

"I am pleased you approve."

"Do not mock me. I had a terrible night, and the day has not been much better."

"A terrible night?" Alexander smiled a chill smile. "I believe I shared that terrible night. I dreamed of nothing but you. You are haunting me and being alone in a room with you is not helping."

"Did you dream of me?" The flush deepened. "I dreamed of you, too. We must still be under the influence of the spell."

"Yes." He thought he could guess what kind of erotic

dreams she'd had because he'd had them too. "I want you to tell me who gave you the talisman, and what they told you it would do. I have many enemies, and they would not hesitate to use you to get to me. So, please, do not shield anyone. It is important that I know."

To his surprise, her lips twitched as though he amused her. Perhaps that was what he found so fascinating—she looked at the world in an entirely different manner than he did. He scented danger and shadows everywhere; she walked in sunlight.

"Something is funny?" he asked.

"It is all so silly. It has nothing to do with enemies. I got the talisman from Black Annie, but by mistake."

Alexander examined his memory for the name but could not place it. "Black Annie? I do not think I know . . ."

Meagan waved her hand as though it were of no importance. "She has a house just off the Strand. All the ladies go to her for potions and the like. She is harmless, I suppose."

"You suppose. But you are not certain?"

Meagan fluttered her hand again, as though trying to erase her words. "I am annoyed with her, but over another matter. The talisman was not even meant for me. It was meant for my friend Deirdre Braithwaite, who wanted . . . well, she wanted . . ." Her face went red. "You are Grand Duke of Nvengaria, after all, and quite handsome, I must say."

"She wished to couple with me? To slake her lust?"

Meagan's cheeks burned redder. "You like to put things as bluntly as I do, but I suppose that's easiest. Being blunt, that is. No one can mistake your meaning that way."

"I believe you are wrong."

"About you being blunt? No, indeed, thus far, you are the most blunt man of my acquaintance."

She made him want to laugh, even through his impatience, and she could not know how precious that was to him. "I meant about the talisman," he said. "Talismans like this one cannot be transferred from person to person. They are made for one man and one woman specifically. Your Black Annie made it for you to give to me."

She shook her head, red curls dancing. "But she did not. My friend got a lock of your hair and paid Black Annie to make it for her."

"Did your friend ever touch the talisman?"

Meagan's look turned thoughtful. "No. Black Annie had me put my finger on it to hold the wire she tied, and a drop of my blood got on it."

Alexander nodded grimly. "Your friend may have instructed her, but this Black Annie made it with you in mind. Witches can be deceitful. It is part of their trade."

Meagan smiled suddenly, dimples appearing. "Oh, goodness, I've just thought. Deirdre paid such a sum of money for it, and if Black Annie meant it for me all along . . . But why on earth should she?"

"I do not know, but I will question her."

Meagan lifted her brows, as though wondering exactly how he'd go about this questioning.

He dug his hands harder into the chair back. "Meagan, you must marry me. I have seen what your countrymen do to a woman who is ruined. Her family hides her, if they do not outright disown her. Men assume she is fair game and proposition her. She is treated as a whore when she may only be guilty of trusting a blackguard. In Nvengaria we would not dream of doing this. We do not punish a woman for what a man has done, and if he dishonors her and she shoots him, it is regarded as justifiable and she is praised for her bravery."

"Good lord." She put her fingers to her lips, touching the pad of the lower one, and her eyes took on a thoughtful gleam. "I hadn't thought of shooting you."

"You looked quite unhappy to see me today. I would not have been surprised had you brought a pistol with you."

"I am unhappy because you are a whirlwind." She began to pace, her hands curling. "You put visions into my head of making love to you in some luxurious marble bath. And then you sweep me away from the dance floor to the anteroom, and today you sweep me here and ask me to marry you. You like to sweep, Alexander, and I cannot move quickly enough out of your way."

"The marble room is the bath chamber in my house," he said. "I had the same vision."

"I thought you did." Her face turned red again, blending to her fiery hair. "How embarrassing."

"I did not find it embarrassing. I found it arousing and frustrating. I am not marrying you simply to satisfy propriety. I told you that we could marry in name only, but that is not quite true. I want you. If this spell will have me lusting after you night and day, I want you in my house so I can conveniently have at you."

Her eyes widened. Clearly, she was unused to gentlemen expressing lusts so boldly. Alexander was not used to women who did *not* expect that. He saw turbulent waters ahead.

"And what happens when the spell is broken?" she asked.

"We will see what happens. Until then, I refuse to die of longing. Nvengarians are not Englishmen. We act on our passions, we are lovers with our wives, and we are not ashamed of what is between us." He leaned forward, his need soaring. "I do not want you ashamed of what you feel or what you want from me. I want to know what you need, no lies and no evasions. You tell me your needs, and I will fulfill them. That is my promise to you—my duty—as your husband."

She stopped pacing. "Nvengarians are rather breath-taking, Your Grace."

"*Alexander.* There will be no formality between us."

"But you are quick to give commands. Do you expect me to salute you, in private? I will in public, of course."

His smile was raw. "I am used to giving commands. It is my way. You may obey or tell me to rot in hell as you like."

"But husbands expect their wives to obey them," she said. "It is part of the vows."

"Not in Nvengaria. If a man is a fool, his wife is obli-gated to *dis*obey him. Who would follow a fool's orders?"

"And she can shoot him, presumably."

"Only in certain circumstances. I will teach you to use a pistol, so that if circumstances arise that you must shoot me, you will do it cleanly, through the heart, no lingering deaths."

She blanched. "I could never shoot you."

"You could. I see it in you. You have a heart of steel, my love, and a temper as well."

"How can you know that? I only met you last night."

Alexander released the chair and walked around the desk toward her. To his joy, she did not back away. "Be-cause you are standing here, alone with me, firing words back at me. I ravished you, I took your virginity, and yet I did not find you today sunk in illness or hysteria. You came here and faced me with the truth. You are strong." He cupped her chin. "I have never met a woman so strong as you."

"Lady Anastasia seems quite capable," she said faintly.

"She used to be strong, but the death of her husband robbed her of her heart. She is—broken."

"Oh, poor woman."

Alexander traced her lower lip with his thumb. "She was married to a Nvengarian, and when he died she nearly died with him. She works to take vengeance on those who caused his death, and she will use who she must to reach that goal. She has a good heart, but her grief has blinded her."

"You know much about people," she said, her mouth moving against his thumb.

"I have been forced to. I took Anastasia to my bed several times in the past, but she only went there to further her own agenda."

Meagan's eyes flickered at his admission. "And why were you there?"

"To further *my* agenda. There was never love between us, nor will there ever be. But we have cultivated the myth of an affair because it suits our purposes. I tell you this so that when other people whisper titillating gossip about us, you are prepared for it."

"I see."

She clearly did not. He would have to teach her everything, from the ground up. "We have laid down layers of lies, Anastasia and I. It is necessary to deceive whom we need to deceive. You, as my wife, will know the truth, but when you hear the lies from others, you must not correct them. Can you do that?"

"You mean, instead of wanting me to still wagging tongues, you want me to help you keep them wagging?"

"About certain things, yes."

"Oh dear. I know so very little about intrigue."

Alexander's world, on the other hand, was all about intrigue. "I will teach you. I will teach you so much." He slid his fingers across her cheek and brushed back a lock of her hair. "Are you willing to learn?"

"You will give me intrigue lessons?"

"You will have lessons in many things." He leaned down and trailed the tip of his tongue over her cheekbone. "I will teach you to receive all the pleasure I can give you and how to pleasure me. How we can enjoy pleasure together."

"Like last night?" she breathed.

"Last night was clumsy. I was not myself, and I rushed things. What we will have will be slow and practiced. There are cults in Nvengaria that teach the art of pleasuring. It is an amazing control of mind and body. I spent a year in one of these cults as part of my training for the duties of Grand Duke. Now I will be teacher."

A shiver ran through her body, and he lightly kissed her skin. "Husbands and wives teach each other," he murmured. "Are you willing to learn from me?"

"What could I possibly teach you?" she asked softly.

"Goodness. And courage. You have so much, and I have so little."

She closed her eyes, tilting her head back, letting his lips brush her face. "I do not feel particularly filled with goodness."

"You are. You do not fear me. Nor do you hate me."

"It is the love spell," she nearly whispered. "Nothing we can do about it."

"You are forgiving." He seamed her lips with his tongue. "I taste it in you."

She turned her head to meet his kiss. No, the spell had not dwindled. The pull of Meagan's kiss made him want to stay here with her and to hell with assassins and spies and Nvengarian intrigue. He curled his tongue into her mouth, and she made a little noise in her throat and laced her fingers around his neck.

Meagan Tavistock might be unnerved by him and his abrupt proposal, but she wanted him. He felt the threads of the love spell wrapping him, urging him to let his hand drift to the swell of her breast, to cup her buttocks and pull her to him.

He felt his Nvengarian blood heat, the urges of his ancestry running true in him. He'd never experienced these urges with his wife—she'd had her own lovers, and they'd never shared deep passion. They'd made love like friends or casual lovers, and after she'd become pregnant with little Alex, Sephronia and Alexander had only slept together on rare occasions. He'd fulfilled his physical needs on women he trusted, but he'd never fallen in love.

Meagan was different. His body knew what passion was, and for the first time, it responded to its primal call. Alexander's control was legendary, but he had the feeling that Meagan could stir the spark that released the beast. It dwelled in a space inside him, circling, waiting.

He kissed the corner of her mouth, then licked the freckles that crossed her nose. He found them adorably attractive.

The polished desk became more and more enticing. He could lift her to it, lay her back on its clean expanse, skim her skirts up her legs, and find the heat waiting between them. His erection pushed upward, ready.

He would have done it had not the door swung open behind him, and the breathless voice of Simone Tavistock filled the room.

"You see? I knew they would work everything out."

Meagan jumped, trying to press Alexander away, but he refused to free her. Sliding his arm around her waist, he turned to face the invasion of her stepmother and Michael Tavistock.

Alexander made a half bow. "Mrs. Tavistock. I am still waiting for Meagan's final answer."

Simone's wide smile beamed. "Well, of course she will. She is kissing you, is she not? And to think, I worried about her prospects just yesterday." Simone pressed her hands together and stepped toward her husband.

"This is so delightful. I believe I shall swoon. Do catch me, Michael darling."

"No." Michael Tavistock put firm hands on his wife's arms.

She sent him a startled look, then gave a decided nod. "You are quite right. There is no time for swooning; there is so much to do." She bent a steely eye on Alexander. "You told us you've obtained a special license, but a hasty wedding will never do, Your Grace. The banns, St. George's, Hanover Square, a proper wedding breakfast, and all the trimmings. Prince Damien swept my daughter away from me and cheated me out of a grand church wedding, but you, Your Grace, will not."

CHAPTER SEVEN

The denizens of the pub in Wapping, within smelling distance of the river, had become used to the two foreigners who wandered in most nights and spoke together in the corner. The publican tolerated them because they bought his best ale and paid an exorbitant price for it without question. The sailors and fishermen who frequented the tavern had at first regarded them in askance, but as the two in the corner only gabbled in German and left everyone else alone, the regulars grew used to them and finally ignored them.

One of the men was called Otto von Hohenzahl. Fifty years old, he had gray hair, an athletic build, and a round pink face, obtained from a lifetime of enjoying hearty beer and warm red wine. He spoke German in a thick Austrian dialect of the region just outside Vienna to his younger, dark-haired companion.

"Alexander was to have met with me last night, he and

his Lady Anastasia. She kept the appointment, but he did not. So where was he, eh?"

The slimmer man at his side slurped his ale, which he admitted was not bad, although not up to Austrian standards. "A funny thing, *mein Herr*. He was with a woman."

Von Hohenzahl traced the rim of his tankard. "Not Lady Anastasia. She was speaking to me, trying to pry secrets from my lips."

The younger man smirked. "No, he was with a red-haired English girl. A *fraulein*. A miss."

"*Wirklich?*" Von Hohenzahl's lips twitched into a dark smile. "The rogue. Or was she paid?"

"No, *mein Herr*, this is very interesting. Her name is Meagan Tavistock, and she has a connection to Princess Penelope of Nvengaria. Her father married Princess Penelope's mother. This must be some kind of game the Nvengarians are playing."

Von Hohenzahl looked at him sharply. "What game, I wonder? But it does not matter. I want Alexander. I will have him, I swear it." He clenched a gloved fist as though enclosing Grand Duke Alexander inside. He was determined to use Alexander to reach Nvengaria and have it—not for Prince Metternich, but for himself. With Alexander under his control, he would have the power to walk in and overthrow Damien. He would be given the credit of bringing the Nvengarians to heel, he who'd been shunted into minor positions despite the fact that he came from an old and wealthy Austrian family. Alexander was a formidable man, but von Hohenzahl knew the secret that would put Alexander in harness. "You have been watching him," he continued. "Have you witnessed any change?"

The younger Austrian shook his head. "Not yet. But I have not seen what goes on *inside* his house. It is impossible to get a spy in there."

Von Hohenzahl nodded, not angry. "I know this.

Alexander is fanatically careful. But soon, Peterli, soon he will be in my hand and all his care will mean nothing." He smiled, his eyes glittering. "What will Alexander say when he discovers that my secret weapon against the Nvengarians is Alexander himself?"

"I will enjoy finding out." Peterli chuckled.

"And my master, Metternich, will be pleased when I hand him the keys to the kingdom of Nvengaria. Perhaps he will make me a count."

"Your master will reward you well, that is certain." Peterli cast his gaze toward the bar where a young woman was sending them an impish grin. "Now, perhaps we should reward ourselves this night."

Von Hohenzahl followed his colleague's gaze and snorted. "Not here. The ladies are too dirty. I will take you to a house where the ladies are clean and friendly, and you may have as many as you like at once."

Peterli laughed, eyes twinkling. "You are generous, *mein Herr.* Please, take me to this house."

Von Hohenzahl tossed the publican an extra coin, and he and Peterli bundled themselves into greatcoats and left the inn.

From the shadows of another corner, Myn emerged, his large blue eyes thoughtful. The regulars at this public house tolerated Myn more than they did the Austrian gentlemen because Myn, while odd-looking with his waist-length black hair and tall, muscular body, drank ale quietly and disturbed no one. They'd come to accept Myn, who was quiet and calm, and they also sensed it would be unwise to disturb him.

And so, the men in the taproom that night had done nothing to betray his presence to the Austrian gentlemen.

Myn set down his ale and walked quietly out after them. He did not speak German, but he had recognized the name Alexander and a smattering of German words taught to him by his old friend Dimitri of Nvengaria. Myn also had an excellent memory for words and phrases, and he would store these up and have someone translate for him.

Princess Penelope had asked Myn to look after Grand Duke Alexander and keep him from harm, and Myn would obey her, no matter how many people he had to hurt to do it.

Simone Tavistock got her way. To Meagan's surprise, Alexander withdrew his suggestion that he and Meagan marry immediately, and promised Simone that they would have a grand society wedding.

But a month later, caught in a whirlwind of planning, Meagan began to wish Alexander had insisted she marry him immediately.

First, the jewels began arriving. The morning after Meagan had agreed to wed Alexander—although *agreed* was not the word she liked to use—a box arrived. Rose and Simone leaned over Meagan as she opened it at the dressing table to reveal a chain of large square-cut rubies bound together with a heavy strand of gold. The rubies glittered dull red against the black velvet of the box, the necklace obviously old and obviously valuable.

Simone had to sit down and wave her hand in front of her face. "Oh miss, oh miss," Rose breathed over and over.

A card inserted into the box simply said, "For Meagan. Alexander of Nvengaria."

Each day brought another box. Alexander sent large diamond earrings to drip beneath Meagan's curls, an emerald diadem, more diamonds for her throat, and a strand for her wrists. The rings came together, ten lined up in a box. Four were gold, six heavy Nvengarian silver. All bore round or square jewels, diamonds, rubies, emeralds, sapphires.

This card read, "The Grand Duchess's rings. Alexander."

Meagan touched them gently, realizing that the rings had adorned the hands of the previous Grand Duchess, Sephronia of Nvengaria. Penelope had written about Sephronia in her gossipy letters long before Meagan had met Alexander. Sephronia had been a beautiful woman, adored and admired even while her husband had been feared. She'd been a beautiful society hostess whose balls and fêtes had been perfect down to the last detail. Nvengaria would never see her like again, it was claimed.

Meagan shut the box in trepidation. Now the rings would rest on Meagan's hands, and Nvengarians would expect Meagan to host the best balls and fêtes in the land. She groaned and lamented she'd ever let Deirdre talk her into going along to Black Annie's.

The ring Alexander sent for the Nvengarian betrothal ceremony, however, he purchased himself. The package arrived straight from the jeweler's with their emblem stamped on the box. He'd bought her a simple silver ring fixed with two diamonds.

Another gentleman might have written a flowery declaration that he chose it because the diamonds reminded him of her eyes, but the note simply read, "For the betrothal ceremony. Alexander."

Meagan gently laid the handwritten card in the little box where she kept all the others, and lifted the ring to her lips.

Meagan wore the ring, along with a new gown sewn in haste by the seamstresses Alexander had sent to her, for the Nvengarian betrothal ceremony held in Alexander's overwhelming house. Alexander's entourage was smaller than Prince Damien's had been, but no less enthusiastic. His Nvengarian servants wore dark blue military-style uniforms with medals and highly polished boots, and all had the unruly black hair, brilliant blue eyes, and swarthy skin of Nvengarians.

The men formed a circle around Meagan and Alexander as they went through the ancient ceremony in the red-ceilinged ballroom, their booted feet keeping up a stamping rhythm. On the outside of the circle were Meagan's father and Simone, a few close family friends, and Egan MacDonald, the Scotsman she'd met last summer at Penelope's betrothal ceremony and wedding.

Egan remembered her. "So this is the English lassie who's taken down the grand Alexander," he said when he saw her. He swept her up into a bear hug, which Meagan returned.

Egan was replete in his garish plaids and kilt and high leather boots, his wild dark hair caught in a tail at the nape of his neck. His eyes twinkled, but they held a wary light, and he swayed with too much Scots whisky and Nvengarian wine. "And here I thought ye'd set your cap for me."

"But you love another, Egan McDonald," Meagan said teasingly.

Egan started. "Eh? Why do ye say so?"

Meagan hesitated, realizing she'd touched a nerve. "It is in your eyes. You think of her often, do you not?"

Egan grasped her elbow with an iron grip and lowered his head to hers. "You keep that to yourself, lass, all right? Never make mention of Egan McDonald and his unrequited love again."

His words were light and scented with whisky, but she sensed pain and deep anger in them.

"Of course I would not," she said. "I would never gossip about a private matter of yours."

His grip eased, but his voice still grated. "No, that ye wouldna. And for your kindness, I'll give ye a bit of advice—tread lightly around him. I know why ye want to marry him, he's told me, but he's a ruthless cur, and there's something not quite right about him."

Meagan blushed. "He told you?"

"Aye." His handsome face darkened. "And had I known beforehand, I'd have plunged a knife into his heart, but a wedding's a better thing than bloodshed. He's a dangerous man, lass. If ye ever need help, just call on Egan McDonald. I owe it to Princess Penelope to look after ye. She's a great lady, is Penelope."

"I know." Tears stung Meagan's eyes. One of her deepest regrets was that Penelope was not here to see her married. The two wrote often, but that was not the same as sitting with Penelope in her bedchamber while she poured out her heart.

She blinked back tears and turned her head to see Alexander standing at her elbow. He hadn't been there before, she was certain of it. The man moved like a cat, graceful and predatory, and often so silently that she never knew it until it was too late.

She could not tell whether he'd heard Egan's declarations. His eyes were neutral, his mouth straight. "It is time, Meagan."

Meagan felt the touch of the love spell as he put his fingers on her arm and guided her to where his servants were forming a circle. It was always there when he touched her, threads of magic that drew her to him. His tall body at her side made her feel protected, even with Egan's warning dancing through her head.

As the ritual began, Alexander's men encircled them, and the tall man called Myn held the tray with the ceremonial knife, cord, and goblet of bloodred Nvengarian wine.

Meagan glanced at Myn as she stepped to where

Alexander directed. He had blue eyes, rather larger than most men's, and he wore his linen shirt, breeches, and boots as though they were uncomfortable, as though they trapped him. His face, while masculine and handsome, was slightly pointed, and he gazed back at her in unblinking calm.

She knew where she'd seen that look before, in a small boy who could shape-shift into a demon on a moment's notice. The boy-demon had been sent to murder Prince Damien last year and had ended up giving Penelope his undying devotion.

Meagan grasped Alexander's cuff. "He's a logosh," she whispered.

"Yes," Alexander said smoothly, as though shape-shifting demons were an everyday occurrence. He gave Myn a cool nod. "Please begin."

In a deep, melodious voice, Myn spoke the ceremony that would bind Meagan to Alexander forever in the Nvengarian way. He spoke only Nvengarian, and Nikolai translated for the English guests.

One person notably absent from the gathering was Lady Anastasia. It would look odd were she to be present, Alexander had explained when she asked him.

Alexander's six-year-old son, on the other hand, was very much present, standing with Egan McDonald. Meagan had been nervous about meeting young Alex, but he'd given her his allover assessment and sensed with a child's keen perception that she was as out of place in Alexander's world as he was. He'd bowed formally, then flung his arms about her legs.

Now he joined in the foot stomping with Alexander's men, which grew louder and louder in a wild beat as Myn held up the knife and gave it to Alexander. Alexander slashed the knife across his own palm, then quickly across Meagan's, too quickly for pain. Myn bound their cut hands together with plain cord. Alexander lifted the goblet and drank, then held it steady while Meagan sipped.

They were betrothed. The Nvengarians cheered, voices rocking the garish ballroom. The men grabbed the hands of the guests and began to dance in a wild and chaotic circle. Alexander, his hand still tied to Meagan's, leaned down and brushed her lips with his.

Fire began with the kiss, and Meagan laced her hand behind Alexander's neck.

"Mine," he breathed against her mouth, and the word held finality.

It was traditional for the betrothed couple to make love afterward, but Meagan went home with her father and stepmother instead. Mayfair was not ready for the permissive sexual customs of Nvengarians, Michael said, and Alexander did not argue with him.

Alexander seemed to understand when he should concede to English notions and when he could be Nvengarian. In the game of smooth give and take, Alexander was master.

His eyes told Meagan a different story. When he bowed and kissed her hand in the echoing foyer of his house, the heat in his eyes nearly undid her.

"I will see you at the wedding ceremony in four weeks," he said; plain words, but his voice went rough, and he brushed his finger across her lips. Four weeks would be forever to wait to see him again.

As it turned out, Meagan did not have to wait four weeks. The morning after the banns were first read, an official notice appeared in the *Times* announcing the betrothal of Miss Meagan Tavistock and the Grand Duke of Nvengaria.

Mayfair went into an uproar. Invitations suddenly

bombarded the Tavistock house from every hostess in town, from duchesses to baronesses and everyone in between who wanted to see to whom the most fascinating man in England had betrothed himself.

Half of the ladies of the *ton* said they always knew Meagan Tavistock was a sweet and pretty girl and they were not surprised that the Grand Duke, wealthy, powerful, and handsome, had chosen her to be his bride. The other half hissed that Miss Tavistock was nobody and didn't deserve such a match, that her stepmother was an ambitious harpy who'd thrown Meagan at the Grand Duke. They spread still darker rumors that Meagan and Simone practiced black magic and had ensnared Alexander with witchery.

Meagan had little doubt as to who had started the last rumors after she encountered Deirdre Braithwaite at the Duchess of Cranshaw's at-home party the night after the betrothal announcement.

Deirdre pushed through the crowded staircase hall, her silk gown dangerously low on her breasts, her chest glittering with dozens of diamonds. In spite of the rather interested crush, Deirdre planted herself in front of Meagan and slapped her across the face.

"How dare you?" she cried. "You stole that talisman and used it yourself. You were in collusion with the witch all the time, weren't you?"

Deirdre could not hit very hard, but the fact that she'd done so in front of so many people astonished Meagan.

"You insisted I keep it, I believe," Meagan countered.

"So you admit you used it. Bitch—"

Deirdre broke off abruptly, not so much because of the happy stares of the other guests, but because four muscular Nvengarians dressed in blue uniforms suddenly surrounded her.

Two seized Deirdre under the elbows and turned her

around, and the other two closed in on either side of
Meagan. As the two men bore the shrieking Deirdre
through the crowd, she screamed over her shoulder,
"That's fifty guineas you owe me!"

One of the Nvengarians who remained beside Meagan, a man with a nose that had once been broken and
several nasty scars on his cheeks, said in a gravelly voice,
"You are fine, yes?"

"Yes." Meagan put her hand to her face where Deirdre
had slapped her, the sting already gone. "She's harmless,
really."

"Grand Duke Alexander, he says we stay with you.
Keep you from hurt."

"Oh, he did, did he?"

The man grinned, as though he approved of her defiance. "We stay with you all day, all night. Many bad people could hurt you, and so hurt Alexander."

"I see."

Meagan did, with a chill that disturbed her. Alexander
was an important and powerful man, and the games he
played were dangerous. She remembered how she'd
walked with Penelope last year in the fine weather to a
peaceful village square, and how an assassin had come
out of the crowd to attack Damien and then Penelope.
Meagan remembered diving in panic behind the public
well, stones scraping her hands and face, remembered
how the Nvengarian men had so eagerly surrounded
and killed the man who'd tried to harm their beloved
Penelope. The sudden violence on such a beautiful day
had frightened her and stayed with her a long time.

"I am Dominic," the burly man said. "You call me
when danger comes."

The flock of Mayfair ladies and gentlemen stared and
whispered and openly gawked. Meagan noted that they
did not draw too near, however, with the two Nvengari-

ans flanking her. Her first instinct was to flee from the scrutiny that unnerved her, but she lifted her chin. She would not run. She'd not give Deirdre the satisfaction.

She spent the rest of the evening at her stepmother's elbow, her bodyguards watching at what they thought was a discreet distance. The attention she received from the hostess and all the other guests nearly wore through her defiance, but Simone lapped up every minute of it.

"We truly are important, now," Simone crowed on the way home. "The ladies who wanted to snub me didn't dare with those Nvengarians breathing down their necks. We are *in*, my dear."

Oh, yes, in, Meagan thought sourly. *What a delightful place to be.*

Dominic and his men followed her everywhere. They slept in shifts, two on, two off, lived in the Tavistock house, and accompanied Meagan every time she stepped out the door. She was used to going about escorted by her footman, but the silent menace of Nvengarian bodyguards striding along on each side of her was much different from the presence of Roberts, who stumbled often and dropped packages every few feet.

Meagan had always gone where she pleased, not particularly noticed by anyone. Now, not only did ladies and gentlemen of the *ton* stare at her unusual entourage, but the newspapers decided to take an interest in her. Dominic and his men had to push back the nosy journalists who flocked to the Tavistock house, waiting every day for Meagan to come out. Unfortunately, the more Dominic threatened and manhandled the journalists, the more persistent they became.

In higher places, the leaders of society squared off,

sharply divided in opinion about the soon-to-be Grand Duchess of Nvengaria. The Duchess of Cranshaw, a girl-hood friend to Simone, led the supporters of Meagan, declaring her to be adorable and just right to soften up the Grand Duke. Lady Featherstone fell in with this crowd, pleased to boast that *her* ball had brought them together.

The opposition was led by the Duchess of Gower, a woman of thirty who headed a very fashionable set of ladies, married and widowed, who enjoyed the most handsome men of London as their lovers. No one spoke of their conquests out loud, of course, but Simone kept Meagan informed of every rumor. Deirdre Braithwaite was a firm member of this crowd.

The Duchess of Gower had hoped to land Alexander in her net, Simone said, and was enraged that he'd gotten himself engaged to a nobody like Meagan Tavistock. The duchess had even made a wager she'd have Alexander a week after his wedding, proclaiming he'd quickly tire of his washed-out redheaded wife.

Meagan endured Simone's tales without screaming, but only just.

"I have always hated the Duchess of Gower," Simone concluded with vicious glee. "I am pleased you have tweaked her tail, my dear. She is so proud of her beauty, but you will easily outshine her once Alexander has fitted you out with the best frocks and jewels in London. She fights dirty, but do not worry, with the Duchess of Cranshaw on your side, and me, we will send her home weeping. After all, you will be Grand Duchess of Nvengaria and many times more important than she."

Meagan groaned and buried her face in her hands. "May we move to Northumbria? Or the Yorkshire Dales? Those are sufficiently remote."

"Do not be so silly," Simone said. "Everything will be delightful." She laughed, clearly in transports.

After sessions like these, Meagan was ready to send Alexander a polite note and call the whole thing off.

But then she'd dream of him. Every night when she dropped off to sleep in her small four-poster bed, Alexander invaded her dreams. They were so real she could feel his touch on her skin, smell his breath as he leaned to kiss her, and taste him—his skin, his lips, his fingers—as he brushed them over her.

He'd come to her and strip the covers from the bed and the nightrail from her body. He'd already be naked, skin smooth over hard muscles, moonlight kissing his body. He'd climb upon the bed, his warm body covering hers, his voice low and beautiful. He'd speak Nvengarian, but she'd understand every word. "Love," he'd whisper, "I want you. I want you so much, I'm starving for you. Touch me."

She would run her fingers over his hot skin, tracing the perfect muscles of his back and shoulders. He'd let out a half sigh, half moan, his blue eyes dark. He'd taste her skin and tease her thighs with his arousal, making her want him deep inside her as he had been the night of the Featherstone's ball.

"Please," she'd beg, arching her hips to him.

"No, love. We wait."

"Why?"

"The time must be right." His hot breath would tickle the curls at her temple. "Soon."

She'd writhe in frustration, because it was a *dream*, for heaven's sake, and why could she not at least have fulfillment there? Alexander would laugh and trail kisses down her throat and between her breasts. He'd press his mouth over the space between her navel and her female places, then flick his tongue over the nub between her thighs.

She'd scream and gasp, then wake to find her nightrail raked over her legs and her fingers pressed tightly to her opening, her hand wet.

The dream never came twice in one night. She only ever had one a night, try as she might to conjure the vision of him again.

"Bloody love spell," she'd groan, punching her pillows. She no longer carried any skepticism about Black Annie and her power. Only magic could have made her life this bizarre.

CHAPTER EIGHT

Two weeks after the betrothal ritual, Meagan walked with Simone and the Nvengarian bodyguards along Oxford Street so that Simone could shop for gloves and hats and ribbons and lace by the dozens.

"I will need such things when I begin attending the important balls you give," she said. "The stepmother of the Grand Duchess must be well fitted out."

Meagan's father did not stop these shopping expeditions for two reasons. The first was that Simone was never happier than when decorating herself and imagining the envy of her friends over said decorations. The second was that Simone, as fluttery as she was, had a masterful grasp of economy. She could stretch a shilling farther than a Lloyd's of London clerk, and her bargaining skills were legendary. She knew exactly how much money she could spend and exactly how to get as much finery out of it without compromising quality. A rare gift,

Meagan always thought, although she never told Simone, who would not understand the compliment.

Ahead of them a door that led to the shop of an exclusive modiste opened and a lady emerged. She wore a full-length dark blue velvet cloak that shimmered as she moved, and beneath it a pale green gown, unadorned but at the same time breathtakingly elegant. Meagan recognized the sculpted face and lovely black hair of Lady Anastasia Dimitri.

Meagan started forward, eager to greet her, but Simone pinched her elbow. "Meagan, are you mad? A lady does not greet a courtesan, especially not her betrothed's mistress."

"But she is not his . . ." She stopped, remembering Alexander's explanation that he had woven "layers of lies" to keep gossips from realizing the truth about his relationship with Anastasia. She rearranged her words. "She is not a courtesan. She is the widow of a Nvengarian count. It seems rude not to speak to her after I met her at Lady Featherstone's ball."

Simone considered, finger to her lips. She so clearly wanted to talk to Lady Anastasia, a highly intriguing woman, but at the same time wanted to preserve propriety.

"Ah, she is coming this way," Simone said, relieved. "We can not cut her if she greets us first."

Lady Anastasia moved to them as gracefully as a swan gliding across a pond. Before the avid stares of the journalists held back by Dominic, she stopped and extended a long-fingered hand.

"Mrs. Tavistock, how fine to see you," she said, her Austrian tones giving her an exotic sound. "And Miss Tavistock. May I take it that you shop for the marriage?" She gave Meagan the barest wink.

Too many people with too many eager ears existed for

Meagan to do anything but respond politely. She imagined the journalists on the edge of the circle taking furious notes. *"Miss T— chats cordially with Lady A— on an Oxford Street outing,"* their stories would say. *"Could they perhaps be speaking of gloves?"*

Meagan knew the newspapers would be filled with innuendo, because just this morning she'd read an article that described Grand Duke Alexander sitting with Lady Anastasia at the opera the previous night and dancing later with her at the Duchess of Gower's ball. Miss Tavistock had been nowhere in sight. *"Home with a cold?"* the journalist had snickered.

In fact, Meagan had attended a rather dreary poetry reading at the Duchess of Cranshaw's, poorly attended because everyone else was at the Duchess of Gower's ball watching Alexander parade with his supposed mistress. But while Simone could be giddy, she insisted Meagan be an exact stickler for propriety concerning the Grand Duke; hence Meagan went to only respectable gatherings. Nothing—*nothing*—would jeopardize Simone's plans for the most perfect wedding of the Season.

"Yes, we are shopping for the wedding," Meagan answered. "And for after."

Lady Anastasia sent Meagan a smile that said she knew the lay of the land. "His Grace, he speaks of nothing but the wedding. He wants everything to be perfect, the right flowers, the right candles, the right jewels to give you. His servants, they go mad."

"Oh, perhaps he ought not to do that," Meagan ventured.

"Nonsense. They are all excited that they will have a mistress again. They await your arrival with happiness. And little Alex, he says you are beautiful."

"Such a sweet child," Simone gushed, and Meagan looked at her in surprise. Simone only liked children if they were spotlessly clean, quiet, and seated on the other side of a room.

"He misses his mama," Lady Anastasia said. She sent Meagan a pointed look. "You will be good for him."

"I feel as though I've stepped off a cliff," Meagan said, exhaling. "And am waiting to hit the ground."

Lady Anastasia laughed, her eyes crinkling. "Ah, I remember how it was when I was a bride . . ."

She stopped abruptly, and for an instant Meagan saw in Anastasia's eyes a grief that surpassed all hurts Meagan herself had ever felt. The grief was bottomless, like the deepest well and just as cold. Meagan realized in that moment that Anastasia Dimitri was a shell of a woman, lovely and smiling on the outside, empty on the inside. She remembered how Alexander had described her. *She is broken.*

Meagan's heart ached in sympathy. She took Anastasia's hand and squeezed it, wanting to express what she felt, unable to do so in the street teeming with people and the journalists watching and her stepmother hovering.

Anastasia returned the squeeze, her eyes flashing gratitude. She saw that Meagan understood, and she was touched by it.

"Ah, I nearly forgot," Anastasia said, releasing Meagan's hand. "Shall you be attending Lady Talbot's garden fête? She is opening her famous gardens for display for her charity work, as I believe she does each year. The king goes to this, I understand, as well as the Duchess of Gower."

Simone nodded proudly. "We have received an invitation, of course. But the damp, the Duchess of Gower . . ." She wrinkled her nose. "We may simply send a donation and stay home to not catch cold."

Lady Anastasia held Meagan's gaze with hers. "The Grand Duke, he also attends this year. The king wishes him to see the famous English gardens."

Meagan said nothing, suddenly picturing herself coming across Alexander on a deserted garden lane. Perhaps he would stop so close to her that she could feel his body heat, and perhaps he'd yank her behind a tall stand of yews and kiss her.

She had not seen him in a week and then only at a distance in Hyde Park. She and Simone and Michael had been in their landau, and Alexander had been on horseback across the park. Meagan had stared hungrily at his taut, tall body as he easily sat his horse's swift canter.

I want him, she'd thought. She wanted his easy grace in bed beside her, wanted him to touch her with the same firm hands that held the reins so competently. She watched his hips move back and forth with the horse and wanted his hips moving against her.

She'd had a swift vision of herself on hands and knees in a tumbled bed, him behind her. He'd press his stiff erection against her opening, which was wet for him. "Take me, love," he'd say, then slide in, stiff and unyielding, daring her to beg him to stop.

The landau had bumped over a rock, and Meagan had gasped, falling back to the seat. Across the green, Alexander's horse had stumbled. Alexander righted it within a step, then scanned the stream of landaus until his gaze lighted on Meagan. She knew in that quick glance that he'd had the same vision as she. The love spell was determined to drive them insane.

Simone's voice scattered Meagan's thoughts, and she returned to her present surroundings, blushing.

"Of course we will go," Simone said, as though she hadn't said exactly the opposite a few moments ago. "If His Grace will be there, he will want to speak to us and escort Meagan about. And the king is a friend. He attended my daughter's wedding, when he was still Prince Regent, you know."

Since Penelope's wedding, the Prince Regent, now George IV, hadn't bothered to acknowledge the Tavistocks with so much as a note, but Simone was the sort of person who could seize on an incident and build it into a mighty event that was forever important.

"I do know," Anastasia said. "Excellent, then I will see you at the garden fête. I will attend as well." She held out her hand to Simone again, then Meagan. When she pressed Meagan's hand, she lowered her eyelid in a tiny wink.

Meagan smiled back, understanding the signal. Whatever the *ton* thought, whatever Simone thought, Anastasia was on her side.

Lady Anastasia Dimitri returned that night to the hotel where she'd taken several luxurious rooms, and closed the doors on London with a relieved sigh. While the rest of the *ton* enjoyed themselves tonight at balls and soirees, discussing the upcoming wedding of Grand Duke Alexander and Miss Meagan Tavistock, Anastasia had been trying to pry secrets from Otto von Hohenzahl.

Tiring. She instructed the English girl she'd hired when she arrived in London to undress her, settle her into a dressing gown, and brush out her hair. The abigail worked efficiently and quietly, which was why Anastasia liked her.

With all Anastasia's experience and proficiency, she still could not decide whether von Hohenzahl had any useful knowledge or was a complete waste of time. Von Hohenzahl was a typical Austrian ex-military colonel who liked to talk of his former glories and keep several beautiful women on his string. His keen brown eyes and not-so-subtle innuendo made Anastasia know he wanted her to join that string.

Anastasia had gone to bed with men before to obtain

knowledge, but something about von Hohenzahl kept her on edge. He had said nothing, done nothing, to indicate he could be dangerous, and he did hint that his interest was merely to have a woman—Anastasia—that Metternich, the Austrian emperor, wanted. Anastasia was usually good at reading men, and her indecisiveness bothered her.

Outwardly, she showed nothing of her thoughts. She was a master at keeping her countenance smooth, expression blank, mouth lifted in a vacant smile, while concentrating on several trains of thought at once.

The maid finished brushing Anastasia's hair and plaited it for the night. Then the maid shook out the bedcovers for Anastasia to crawl under.

"Good night," Anastasia said, letting her accent be heavy. "Thank you, and may you have, how do you say, dreams most pleasant."

The maid curtseyed, even better than Anastasia at being blank-faced. "Good night, my lady."

Anastasia closed her eyes as the maid continued her duty of brushing gowns and tidying the rooms. She had learned to delve into sleep quickly when she was safe, closing off her thoughts and even her dreams. She had learned this skill from a master Austrian spy after Dimitri's death and had used it to keep grief from consuming her.

Tonight she briefly amused herself by remembering her encounter with Meagan Tavistock and her stepmother on Oxford Street. Though Miss Tavistock tried to hide it, she was quite taken with Alexander. She also had enough mettle to withstand him and the scrutiny of the entire *ton;* Anastasia sensed that. Alexander did not quite know what he was in for, and this made Anastasia chuckle with glee.

She fell asleep to the rather soothing sounds of the maid busy in the outer room, but hours later she jumped awake. The bedchamber was pitch black, the moon obscured by clouds, the candles spent, but she knew that she was not alone.

Silently, Anastasia put her hand under the pillow next to her and drew out the knife she kept hidden there. She heard no sound, not even a shift of breath, but she knew someone lurked in the shadows beyond the bed curtains. Not her maid—the abigail always smelled a bit like fresh linens—but someone who carried a scent of musk and the outdoors.

Not Alexander, who would have politely informed her beforehand if he wanted her killed. Von Hohenzahl? Bile rose in her throat at the thought of being raped by him. But von Hohenzahl was usually wreathed in cigar smoke, and she smelled none of that.

It would be stupid to call out, "Who is there?" but screaming would not do. The owners of the hotel would not like guests being murdered in their beds, especially wealthy foreign countesses whose patronage gave the hotel a certain cachet.

She drew a deep, quick breath, but before she could make a sound, a man moved faster than thought to the head of her bed and clamped his hand over her mouth.

Anastasia struggled, bringing up the knife, but he grabbed her wrist, twisting it painfully until the knife fell from her nerveless fingers. Dimitri had taught her to fight, and her years of covert activities had honed her skills. But this man was strong and fast, and he knew how to counter every move she tried.

At last she stopped, dropping limp to the featherbed, his hand still clamped to her mouth. He shoved his face to hers, a strange, rather pointed face with large blue eyes that seemed to glow. He had long hair almost to his waist, the blackness of it fading into the darkness. He said in heavy Nvengarian, "Dimitri said you would help."

Anastasia went utterly still.

He studied her with odd blue eyes whose irises seemed to be too large. She remembered seeing this man once at Alexander's house in Berkeley Square. She'd emerged from the sitting room on the second floor and had glimpsed him on the ground floor, but by the time she had descended the stairs he was nowhere in sight. Alexander had never mentioned him, and Anastasia had learned long ago that if Alexander did not volunteer information, you could not pry it from him with an axe. She'd forgotten the incident until now.

She nodded slowly to indicate that if he removed his hand she would not scream. He lifted his hand away, but remained wary.

"What do you know of Dimitri?" she asked him.

"Dimitri said you would help."

"Yes, we have established that." Anastasia pushed herself to a sitting position against the pillows, her heart beating swiftly. "How do you know Dimitri?"

"He was friend to me once," the man answered. "I taught him much."

Tears sprang to her eyes as they always did when she thought of her husband, Dimitri, so senselessly dead on a battlefield in Spain long ago. The Austrian commanders had left him to be slaughtered, and for that she hated every person connected with Metternich and the Austrian army. Hated them and had determined to make them pay.

Her fiery, handsome Nvengarian Dimitri, who had seduced a young and prim Austrian debutante called Anastasia and taught her to live life to its fullest, was dead. Dimitri had been struck down far too young, and

Anastasia had honed her grief into a weapon, determined to take revenge against those who had taken Dimitri's life.

"He was your friend," Anastasia repeated, stunned. "When?"

"Long ago. He came to the mountains to hunt."

Anastasia thought about her life in Nvengaria, where she'd been deliriously happy for too short a time. "Yes, he liked the mountains. But he never told me about you."

The man said nothing, only tilted his head, studying her.

"Why did he tell you I could help you?" she asked.

He reached out and touched her face, his fingers strong. "He said you had great beauty."

Anastasia's lips trembled. The man feathered his fingertips along her cheekbone, then across her throat.

"Please do not touch me," she said quickly.

"You let others touch you. Ones you hate. I see the hatred seeping from you, but they do not know."

He stroked the hollow of her throat with his thumb, and darkness stirred between her thighs. "How do you know this? How do you know me?"

"I watch you."

She backed away from his touch. "You cannot have. I am most careful and am never followed."

A small smile quirked his mouth. "I watch you. I watch where you go, the ones who speak to you. I watch you sleep. You never see me."

"You lie," Anastasia countered, panic rising. "I sensed you here tonight. I always know when someone is spying on me."

"Tonight, I wanted you to wake." He touched her face again, fingers featherlight.

"Who are you?" she whispered. "Are you one of Alexander's men?"

"I am Myn." He withdrew his touch, and Anastasia shivered. "I belong to no one and not Alexander. I belong—to Nvengaria."

What a strange way to put it. His words sent a wave of homesickness over her. "Yes. I, too, belong there."

Myn shook his head, long hair moving. "You are of the outer lands."

"No, I am Nvengarian. I might have been born in Austria, but I am of Nvengaria in my heart."

He placed one hand between her breasts. "There is nothing in your heart. It is empty."

His large hand warmed her skin through the nightrail. Anastasia had let men touch her, Myn was correct about that, but she always had to fight nausea when she did it. She did what was necessary in her quest to keep the Austrians away from Nvengaria, and hated the men who pawed at her, thinking her a brainless courtesan.

Myn's touch was different, neither possessive nor triumphant. His hand remained still, the callused palm between her breasts, warmth moving from her heart to the rest of her body.

She leaned slowly back on the pillows, trying to let him know that she no longer wanted him to pull away. "Why do you say Nvengaria is not in my heart? I love it. I loved it the moment Dimitri took me to it."

"Because you are not there."

Tears filled her eyes. "I am protecting it."

"I protect Nvengaria. I and my people. You are of the outer lands."

She sat up straight. "How dare you tell me what I love and what I do not? Get out of my rooms."

Myn made a faint gesture. Instantly, the candles in the room sprang to life, flickering light illuminating his tall body and hard honed muscles under a thin linen shirt.

He climbed to sit on the end of her bed, leaning on the bedpost and crossing his feet in scarred boots.

He said, "Dimitri, he loved Nvengaria. And you."

Anastasia hugged her arms to her chest, shaking in rage. "I do not want to talk to you any longer."

"I need you to talk to me. I do not understand your language, and you must tell me what something means."

She looked up again, unnerved by his sudden change of subject. She understood he would not obey her wishes and that he was far too strong for her to fight. She'd finally confronted a man she could not control. "Something in German?"

He gave a nod. "Two men, they were speaking. I did not understand." His gaze took on a faraway look, and he began to repeat, slowly and carefully, his pronunciation precise, a conversation in a Viennese dialect, to which Anastasia listened in amazement.

CHAPTER NINE

Simone was pleased that Alexander sent his carriage for them the day of the garden fête, but disappointed that he did not escort them himself.

"A fiancé ought to escort his bride-to-be and future in-laws about town," Simone said as they rolled away to Surrey in the quiet and comfortable chaise. "It is what fiancés do. Sir Hilton Trask took me and my mother absolutely everywhere when we were engaged. Of course, after the wedding, I rarely saw the wretched man."

Michael slid his arm around her shoulders. He always made a comforting gesture when Simone spoke of the hurts her first husband had given her. "The Grand Duke is busy, my love. He is a diplomat and must attend many meetings."

"Yes, but I wish we could be seen more with him. I want the Duchess of Gower to be pea green with envy. It will ruin her complexion. Would that not be delightful?"

Michael only reiterated that a man in the Grand

Duke's position had little time for pleasure, but Meagan knew good and well why Alexander avoided her. The love spell wanted them in each other's arms and cared nothing for how it got them there. If the incident in Hyde Park were any indication, the spell would flog them with erotic visions until Alexander carried her off to act them out.

Her dreams had her constantly on edge, rendering her nights sleepless and her body aching. She wondered, once the bishop pronounced them man and wife at the altar, whether Alexander would simply throw her over his shoulder, run with her to his carriage, and consummate the marriage right there.

When her imagination began to show her explicitly how this could be done, she pinched her leg, hard. She'd found pinching herself somewhat effective in stopping the visions. Her leg was already blue with bruises.

She was relieved when the carriage rolled to a stop in the Talbots' drive, diverting her from her imaginings.

Lord Talbot, an earl of large means, had purchased a ruin of a house from an impoverished lord, the gardens of which had been designed by Capability Brown. Lord Talbot had spent a huge sum to restore the gardens and make them the best in England, outdoing even those at Chatsworth and Blenheim. Every spring the Talbots hosted a fête and allowed the *ton* to tramp through the garden for an exorbitant price. The proceeds went to Lady Talbot's charities, of which she ran many. The Talbots were wealthy but also generous.

The Talbots were always lucky in their weather, and a soft arch of April sky extended to the horizon. Everyone who was anyone was there, Simone pointed out ad nauseam as they waited in the long line of carriages to descend.

"Is that not the Duke of York? Is that not Princess Esterhazy?" She bounced from one side of the carriage to the other, peering out of the windows, while Meagan sat motionless, both longing and fearing to see Alexander. She wondered also what the gossips would make of their meeting—or their non-meeting—if Alexander decided to save his sanity and avoid her.

However, by the time the three of them descended the carriage, Meagan wondered if she'd even be able to find Alexander in all the crush.

As usual, Dominic and another bodyguard pressed close to Meagan, shooting dangerous glances at anyone who approached her. Every lord, lady, heiress, and heir of the Upper Ten Thousand had descended upon the Talbots, whether because they felt generous toward Lady Talbot's charities or because they wanted to witness the fireworks between ladies of the *ton* over the upcoming marriage of Grand Duke Alexander, Meagan could scarcely guess.

Lady Talbot professed delight to see them, but then, she was *delighted* to see everyone. A tall, thin woman with a birdlike stoop and a mountainous headdress, she enjoyed her fellow man—and woman—and wanted a chat with everybody.

"Lucky Miss Tavistock," she said, grasping Meagan's hand. Her eyes were watery blue and kind. "Grand Duke Alexander is by far the handsomest man in London. Gave us all a shock when he announced he'd marry you, of all people. He must have fallen wildly in love indeed, my dear, most likely with your pretty eyes. They are quite lovely."

Meagan thanked her and curtseyed. Lady Talbot turned to her next guests, oozing sincerity as she proclaimed how *delighted* she was to see them.

"I've heard that Lord Talbot has some fascinating wa-

ter gardens," Michael remarked as they drifted among
the crowd, the hot sun beating down on Meagan's and
Simone's parasols. "Shall we view them?"

Simone gave him an amazed look, wondering how
anyone at a garden party could possibly be interested in
the garden. "Darling, I must circulate and speak to people. It has been a long time since I've been seen at a very
important event. You and Meagan run along. I know you
both like that sort of thing."

Instead of growing annoyed, Michael grasped Simone's hand. "You gad about to your heart's content,
love. Meagan and I will look at boring fountains and yew
borders."

Simone smiled as though dazzled, then released his
hand and hurried off toward a clump of ladies, calling
out to them as she went.

Meagan took her father's arm and let him lead her toward the heart of the garden, Dominic following close
behind. People milled everywhere, but Meagan saw no
sign of Alexander. Her heart thumped in disappointment, then sped up again every time she saw a tall man
with a blue coat.

The crowd thinned as she and Michael approached the
walk where Lord Talbot had his fantastic fountains. Like
Simone, most of the guests were more interested in the
wine, tea, refreshments, and gossip than in the actual
gardens.

Meagan tightened her grip on her father's arm. She
hadn't had much chance to spend time alone with him of
late, as Simone's frantic preparations kept Meagan busy
every waking moment. Michael had not been happy
with Alexander's abrupt proposal, but as the weeks
passed, he'd had grown more sanguine toward the idea
of Meagan marrying him.

Alexander had plainly shown that he intended to take care of Meagan and play by English rules. The sums he'd settled on Meagan for her widow's portion and pin money had been staggering. Michael did not like ostentation, but at the same time Alexander's generosity mollified him.

"Father, why did you fall in love with Simone?" Meagan asked abruptly as they walked.

Many people in the *ton* had asked that very question. Michael slanted her a look as though amused at her exasperated tone.

"Your stepmama can be frivolous, but she has a good and loving heart. Her first husband did not treat her well. Sir Hilton had no patience with people who did not think exactly like him."

Meagan knew the truth of this, having met Sir Hilton. "You married her because you thought she deserved kindness?"

Michael studied the first fountain, water streaming from the mouths of three fish into a bowl. "Partly. Also, she makes me laugh, we are compatible, and we were both lonely."

He contemplated the fountain a moment, then gave a little laugh and shook his head. "No, that explanation is too simple. Love happens when you least expect it, and it is difficult to explain why one loves one person and not another. I love Simone, she loves me, and we accept each other the way we are. That is a rare thing to find. So many people want to remake the other in the image of who they want them to be."

Meagan nodded, wondering if he was trying to give her a warning about her upcoming marriage. "You loved Mama, too," she said. "Why did you fall in love with her?"

A faraway look entered Michael's eyes. "Your mother and I were both very young, and she was the most beautiful creature I'd ever beheld. You look much like her."

Meagan warmed at the compliment. She had a framed sketch of her mother, done not long before her mother's death, a simple picture of a young woman with kind eyes and a sweet smile. She kept it on a table in her bedroom so she could look at it often.

"But what made you notice her in particular?" Meagan went on. "There must have been dozens of debutantes paraded before you when you were a young man."

"Not as many as you would think, my love. I had no fortune, only a modest income."

Meagan looked him up and down, brows raised. "Nonsense. A handsome man with a modest income interests a young lady far more than an ugly man with a fortune. The debutantes likely threw themselves at you."

Michael laughed. "You were not there, daughter, so you can know nothing of the sort. I never met your mother in the endless social rounds, but one day while I visited the art collection of the Duke of Devonshire, I found her observing Greek statuary. When I saw her, I simply knew. An old school friend introduced us, and we were engaged within the week."

Meagan had heard the story many times and thought it terribly romantic, but Black Annie's claim now made her view the tale in a different light. Had the smiling young woman he'd met in the Duke of Devonshire's gallery asked Black Annie to help turn handsome Mr. Tavistock's gaze upon her?

The questions bothered Meagan in light of her own constant visions of Alexander, coupled with Alexander's speculation that Black Annie had cast the spell on Meagan on purpose. She longed to visit Black Annie and shake some answers out of her, but Simone had kept Meagan constantly at her side, and the one letter Meagan had managed to post to Black Annie had not been answered.

Her father walked on, interested in fountains and assuming the conversation to be finished.

How delightful, Meagan thought, *to be six-and-forty and not worried about anything but how hydraulics work.*

Dominic, who had been wandering his usual discreet distance behind them, now moved forward and spoke to Meagan. "You look for His Grace, do you not?" he asked. "He is there."

He pointed one broad finger down a path perpendicular to theirs, and Meagan lifted her gaze and saw Alexander.

His broad, tall body arrested her attention, so much so that it was a moment before she realized he was surrounded by people, most of them female, including Lady Anastasia. Meagan saw the Duchess of Gower sidle next to Alexander, and her heart sank.

"Oh, lord," she murmured.

"There are some you do not like?" Dominic flexed his bulky hands. "I can perhaps send them away or make them afraid of speaking bad to you?"

"No," Meagan said in alarm. The last journalist who had come too close to Meagan had found himself raised over Dominic's head, with Dominic smiling and asking how far the man thought he could be thrown. While Meagan did not really think Dominic would hurt a woman, she could not be certain. "It is all right, Dominic. I will endure it."

"They must be taught to not be bad to you," Dominic said. "You will be an important lady. You will be worshipped."

"Worshipped," Meagan repeated faintly. "How interesting."

"The first wife of the Grand Duke, she was beloved. She had ballads sung and poetry written about her the length and breadth of the kingdom. A similar thing will happen to you."

"You may cease reassuring me now, Dominic."

Dominic bowed. "I will be but a step behind you, my lady."

Meagan adjusted her parasol and pretended to be interested in the nearest fountain until she realized it depicted a goddess with water spurting from very ample nipples.

She blushed and turned away in time to see the Duchess of Gower firmly take Alexander's arm. In a graceful move, Lady Anastasia Dimitri took Alexander's other arm and sent Meagan a knowing look.

The few gentlemen of the group piled behind Alexander and all the ladies, some studying Meagan and Michael through quizzing glasses, others showing relief that another male had come to even the balance of all these blasted females.

Michael nodded at Alexander and extended his hand. Meagan made a polite curtsey, wishing all but Alexander and her father would evaporate. She had at one time or other over the last weeks been introduced to these people, so she had no excuse for not speaking to them.

Alexander wore his military-style coat as usual, his athletic build emphasized by the sash of office pulled snug against his chest. It encircled his hip just where a lady might want to put her hand. . . .

Meagan snapped her gaze upward, taking in the medals that clinked as Alexander released her father's hand and turned to her. Looking at his face nearly melted her; it was strong, clean, and square-jawed, a brush of dark stubble on his chin and jaw. The breeze stirred his black hair, revealing the glittering ruby in his earlobe.

She waited, holding her breath, for the inevitable erotic visions and exhaled slowly when they did not come. Perhaps the love spell was taking pity on them, giving them a respite while she and Alexander had to stand in the middle of a crowd.

Alexander let his gaze rove her face, dip to her neck, touch her bosom. He began to reach his gloved hand for hers, then he curled his fingers and brought his hand back to his side. "Meagan."

Wise, he was very wise not to touch her. She responded with another curtsey and murmured, "Alexander."

She saw shock and disapproval on the faces of several ladies. Most married women addressed their husbands as *Mr.* or *my lord*, in public at the very least. Christian names were for intimacy, for sisters and brothers, for old and dear friends, or for lovers. Meagan sent Alexander a small smile, appreciating that he'd let her shock her enemies.

The Duchess of Gower, her fingers pasted to the crook of Alexander's arm, bared her teeth. "*His Grace* was telling us all about the unusual gardens of Nvengaria. How they're allowed to grow almost wild and how good gardeners are valued as much as princes."

Alexander paid as much attention to her as he would an insignificant insect on his sleeve. Any moment now, he'd simply brush her away.

Lady Anastasia answered. "Yes, the gardens at the palace at Nvengaria are magnificent beyond compare. You are fortunate you will be able to see them, Miss Tavistock. You will come to love them, as Princess Penelope does."

Lady Anastasia knew how to fence, Meagan thought.

She wished she could laugh at the look on the duchess's face as Lady Anastasia reminded everyone that Meagan would have privileges the duchess would not, and that Meagan's closest friend was married to the famous Prince Damien.

Not to be outdone, the Duchess of Gower took up the gauntlet. "Of course, foreign gardens can be nothing to what we have in England. Chatsworth, now, the Duke of Devonshire's house, has the most magnificent gardens in the world."

Lady Anastasia smiled warmly. "Yes, Miss Tavistock, they are modeled on the gardens at Versailles. When you have seen both, you may decide which you like better."

Highly entertained, Meagan and the rest of the party turned their heads back to the duchess to see how she would respond.

All except Alexander. His gaze was fixed on Meagan, and he showed not even polite interest in the chatter.

Before the Duchess of Gower could think of her next retort, he removed her hand from his arm and stepped forward. "I will take my fiancée to see the rest of the water gardens," he said abruptly.

The duchess choked and turned brilliant red. Lady Anastasia smiled. "An excellent idea, Your Grace. Some of the fountains are quite clever."

"Too clever," the duchess said, trying to recover. "Not fit to be seen by a young lady."

Alexander sent her a long look, his cool silence more effective than any retort. Alexander only had to gaze at a person with those steady blue eyes that missed nothing, and the recipient flinched and worried. The Duchess of Gower gaped a moment, then shut her mouth with a snap.

The first match to Lady Anastasia, Meagan thought. The duchess had skewered herself. Some victories were sweet.

"Dominic," Alexander said. Dominic came forward, alert. Alexander made a sharp gesture, and Dominic, understanding, stepped behind them, ready to keep anyone from following. Lady Anastasia took Michael's arm, inquiring in her flattering, accented voice if he would walk with her back to the main gardens.

Alexander did not extend his arm to Meagan, nor did he reach for her hand. *Better that way*, Meagan thought, as she shouldered her parasol and turned to walk beside him.

CHAPTER TEN

Alexander led Meagan around the fountain of the large-breasted woman whose nipples still gushed water, conscious of her beside him even when he kept his gaze far from her. They ducked beneath the low-hanging branch of a tree and strolled down an empty path that led away from the main gardens.

"She is Hera," Alexander said after they'd walked in absolute silence for a few minutes.

Meagan blinked. "Who is?"

"The woman in the fountain. Hera, the mother goddess. It is a symbol of fertility."

The Duchess of Gower would have tittered at the announcement, believing Alexander hinted at a sexual liaison. Meagan simply looked thoughtful.

"Well, she certainly looked to be fertilizing a good many. Are there truly naughty fountains back here as the Duchess of Gower suggested?"

She was so serene, the yellow parasol throwing sun-dappled shadow over her skin, the fine straw bonnet framing her face rather than hiding it. She further protected her skin with a light lawn fichu, a thin cloth wrapped around her shoulders and tucked into her sash. He saw the talent of his hand-picked dressmakers in her white and blue walking dress, which subtly hugged her figure.

The picture of a young English miss asking eagerly about naughty fountains made certain parts of him stand to attention.

"Yes," he answered. "Lord Talbot showed them to me earlier."

"Naughtier than Hera?"

Alexander nodded. "Decidedly. He has statuary performing the sexual act in many and varied positions. The water seems superfluous."

Meagan pressed her fingers to her mouth. "I ought to be shocked, but it makes me want to laugh."

He liked the way her eyes sparkled, her lips curving in guilty glee. Looking away, he slid his hand through hers.

His entire body focused on the warm touch of her fingers. He knew then that the love spell hadn't given in, despite the lack of erotic visions. It was merely biding its time.

He said, "I like that you laugh when it is appropriate and do not stoop to trading insults with bitches of women."

"Well, Lady Anastasia was doing so nicely. I hated to interrupt her."

"Lady Anastasia knows how to play the game."

"Did your first Grand Duchess know how to play the game?" Meagan asked suddenly.

Alexander stopped. They stood in the shadow of a tall tree that overhung the path, and shadows brushed the face she turned up to him.

"She was a master at it," he said. "None could touch her, not even Anastasia."

Meagan gave him a wry look. "And the Grand Duchess was honored by poets the length and breadth of Nvengaria, Dominic told me."

"She was."

"Ah, well, I suppose I will be master of the game too, after many long and painful years of lessons." She looked as though she faced a series of daunting mountain ranges to be scaled.

He traced her cheek. "I do not want you in the game. I like you like this, unsullied, unspoiled. The game, it will eat you alive. Leave it to me."

Her eyes closed a little, the love spell touching her too. "I would adore leaving it in your oh-so-capable hands. I would be a dutiful housewife and stay home to mend your shirts, except that I'll be expected to go out to soirees and balls and things, not to mention hosting them. I will have to face the Duchess of Gower and Deirdre Braithwaite again and again. So I will need to learn something of the game."

"The duchess, she is a boorish woman. She wishes me to bed her, and she is angry because I show no interest."

Meagan's cheeks colored beneath his fingers. "As I observed before, you are ever so blunt, Alexander. I suppose I should be happy that you are truthful about your affairs."

He shrugged. "I have no desire to have affairs. I did not even wish to marry again."

"Oh." Her slender throat moved in a swallow. "Perhaps not *that* blunt."

He realized he had hurt her without meaning to. Alexander, who could bring any woman he chose into his bed by crooking his finger—literally—was losing his finesse.

"Affairs are a distraction," he explained. "I took mistresses when I was married to Sephronia because when I had physical needs she was busy with her own lovers."

Her color rose. "Well, that was not very sporting of her."

"I have shocked you. I ask your pardon. I am not used to speaking to English girls."

"No, no, I think you are enjoying yourself trying to shock me. I am not used to speaking to Nvengarian Grand Dukes. Even Damien was easier to talk to than you are."

"Damien works to be charming." He made a small shrug. "I am more forthright."

"Yes," Meagan said fervently. "You are certainly forthright."

"You wish, perhaps, I were more like Damien? This would be better for you?"

He waited, every muscle tightening, as she tilted her head to one side and considered him. For some reason her answer had become damned important, and he had no idea why.

Meagan studied his face. Alexander was handsome, almost unbearably so, but he had a sharpness that kept him from ordinary attractiveness. Animals were beautiful like him, not men.

She remembered Prince Damien's eyes, how blue they'd been and how watchful. Alexander had the same watchfulness, but with differences. Damien hid his scrutiny behind smiles and teasing, while Alexander did not bother. You knew Alexander watched you; you felt his gaze slice you open and dissect what was inside.

Behind his watchfulness lurked a man who knew he had to be careful all the time and wished he did not. Alexander possessed warmth and an intense passion she'd glimpsed when the love spell opened him to her. Meagan had the feeling that no one else in the world, not even his wife, had ever seen that passion, the piercing flame of emotion he kept locked away from everyone.

Meagan rested her palm against his gold and blue sash of office, feeling its stiff threads. "I do not want you to be more like Damien. I like you as you are."

His gaze softened the tiniest bit, imperceptible if she hadn't been looking for it. "You please me."

"Remember, it might be the love spell making me say such things. I properly should be terrified of you. Everyone enjoys telling me how dangerous you are."

"Yes, I am quite dangerous."

He said it neutrally, a simple and undisputed fact.

She cleared her throat. "For instance, Nikolai told me that you once ordered half a city in Nvengaria flattened. Did he exaggerate?"

"Yes."

Alexander turned abruptly and began walking again. Meagan stared after him a moment, watching his lithe body move, then she hoisted her parasol and hurried after him in exasperation.

"You do know that your answers are short as well as blunt," she said when she caught up to him. "Quite cryptic. Maddening, really."

"It was only a section of the city," he said without looking at her. The sun burnished his swarthy face and made his dark hair glisten. "Not half. Narato, the capital."

He spoke with no defensiveness and no regret in his tone. Meagan remembered what Nikolai had said about people fleeing and barges filling the river, trying to escape Alexander's wrath.

"Goodness, did you wake up one morning and decide, *What a nice day, I think I will flatten half my city?* I beg your pardon, I mean a section of it."

He continued walking, shadows from the high yew hedge dappling his face and his black hair. They had left the crowds far behind, and the long paths were shadowed with thick trees and hidden fountains splashing cool moisture into the air. "Nikolai enjoys the story."

"Nvengarians are dramatic people, I grant," Meagan answered.

"Slavers."

Meagan trotted a few steps to keep up with his long-legged stride. "Pardon? Did you say slavers?"

He nodded. "Slavery and the slave trade has long been forbidden in Nvengaria. With the old Imperial Prince dead and Prince Damien off on a quest, a group of slavers tried to set up shop in Narato, kidnapping free black women and Gypsy girls along the way to fill their bawdy houses. They peddled opium as well, which they brought in through the lands of the Ottomans. I told them to free the young women and leave. They did not listen."

His tone was so matter-of-fact that Meagan shivered. Slave traders and opium men were dangerous, but what fools they'd been not to be afraid of Alexander.

"You arrested them?" she ventured.

"I sent in the army." He stopped walking, his eyes hard and opaque. "I told my men to do their worst and raze the area they had infested. The young women were to be freed to either return home or stay in Nvengaria as they chose. The slavers were executed."

"Oh."

"It is important for you to understand. If I had arrested them they might have escaped justice, gone elsewhere to continue what they did. Others would have moved in to take their places. I had to end the problem with a final stroke and leave nothing standing for others to take."

"So the people fleeing on barges . . . ?"

"Innocents who lived in the area. I arranged for them to get out before the army struck. They knew to heed me."

Meagan imagined most Nvengarians knew that if Alexander said he was sending in the army, then he was sending in the army. "Nikolai needs to modify his story," she said.

"Nikolai is Damien's man."

"Which means he leaves out the part about your compassion to the young women? I suppose having such a ruthless reputation is useful for terrifying people like the new king of England."

Alexander stopped, his expression guarded. "Yes, it can be useful."

"You are Damien's man too, are you not? You work for him now."

"I work for the good of Nvengaria. Prince Damien has proved himself to be good for Nvengaria."

"Is marrying me good for Nvengaria?" she asked hesitantly. "A nobody English miss caught in a love spell?"

His lips turned up in the corners, an almost-smile. "I do not give a damn. Marrying you is good for *me*. As I said, the Nvengarians will find it very romantic. I imagine the ballads will begin the moment word arrives that we are betrothed." His tone softened. "The very menacing Grand Duke smitten with a red-haired lady with beautiful eyes."

Meagan's face warmed. "It is good of you to flatter me."

"It is not flattery. It is truth."

"The love spell . . ."

He reached for her, his voice going low. "Makes me pleased that I have brought you here alone far from the crowd. Because the things I wish to say to you are not the sweet sentiments of an English groom for his bride."

She found it hard to breathe all of a sudden. "Things like what?" she asked faintly. "Do tell."

He captured her hand and peeled back her glove. "I believe I will show you instead."

"That sounds dangerous."

"Immensely dangerous." He lowered his lips to her wrist. Hot fires stirred inside her, the love spell flaring to life.

To her disappointment, he released her hand after one kiss, but the look in his eyes made her heart speed.

He slowly removed his own gloves, tucking them neatly into his waistband. "Since you believe me a compassionate man, I will give you a chance to flee back to your father."

An innocent miss should have a fit of the vapors when a man, even her fiancé, implied such things to her, but Meagan reasoned that if she had the vapors now, she would miss whatever it was he wanted to show her.

"I would like to stay, please."

Alexander took her parasol and reticule from her and placed them on a nearby stone bench. "The next time I offer to let you run, I urge you to consider it."

"Why?" Her mouth was dry.

"For your own good."

"You sound like Dominic."

"He is wise."

He untied the ribbons of her bonnet, lifted it from her head, and placed it next to the parasol. Then he gently unwound her fine lawn fichu from her shoulders and folded it into a thin strip. "Place your hands behind your back."

Meagan felt a frisson of worry, or perhaps it was only heightened excitement and anticipation.

"Why do you want me to?" she asked.

"It is a game."

"A Nvengarian game?"

"I believe it is played more places than Nvengaria. I will not hurt you, Meagan. Do you believe me?"

"Yes." She did, with her whole heart and body.

He stepped behind her and waited. "If I ever do hurt

you, if I cause you any pain in any way, even the slightest bit, you tell me. Do you promise? You say 'Stop, Alexander,' just like that. Promise me."

It seemed to be important to him. "Very well, I promise."

"Good. Now, shall we play?"

Meagan slowly eased her hands behind her back and clasped them together. Alexander wound the lawn fichu around her wrists, gently tying the ends. It was not tight and did not hurt, but she could not move her wrists apart.

She gave a little laugh as he walked back in front of her. "Will you now walk off and leave me to try to get free on my own? Is that the game?"

For answer Alexander cradled her face between his palms and kissed her.

Meagan suddenly understood why the love spell had not plunged them into visions. It did not need to, with them alone in the gardens, a spring breeze touching them, birdsong mixing with the sweet patter of fountains. They could touch each other and kiss to their heart's content, no need for the love spell to drive them insane.

Alexander scooped her against his tall, warm body, and she melted into the kiss. The velvet heat of his tongue moved against hers, swirling fires through her mouth. She'd never had more than chaste pecks from inexperienced swains, and now Alexander invaded her with a man's kiss, showing her what kissing truly meant. Not affection, but deep longing and so much need.

Alexander eased the kiss to an end. Then, to her surprise, he sank to his knees, his hands sliding down her torso and the curve of her hips as he went. She felt his fingers on her calves, and he began to move the skirt of her walking dress upward.

"I have imagined you bare to the sun," he said, touching her thighs with his naked fingers. "The sun on your skin, beautiful on your body."

"Perhaps it should be high summer when we do this," Meagan tried to jest. The spring air was cool, although under the heat of Alexander's breath and touch, the coolness did not seem to matter.

"Yes," he said, utterly serious.

"Nvengarians are mad," Meagan said with a half laugh.

"We are a passionate people," he corrected. "We only pretend we are civilized."

"If we are discovered here, this could be quite embarrassing."

He pressed a kiss to the twist of hair between her thighs. "No one will pass Dominic."

"The Duchess of Gower is a determined lady."

"No one will pass Dominic," Alexander repeated.

"Very well, I grant that Dominic is a pillar of strength. But . . ."

She broke off and gasped as Alexander slid his tongue over the curls, then flicked boldly inside her.

He kissed her as he had kissed her mouth, strokes of fire, deep and deliberate. The delightful friction made her rise on her toes, trying to move her hands apart, frustrated that she could not.

"Alexander, you are a very cruel man," she gasped. "No wonder the love spell works."

He parted her legs, his hands warm on her thighs, his ruby and silver rings cool bands amid the heat. She struggled not to cry out as the wonderful feeling went on and on, knowing that somewhere in the garden, held back by Dominic and the screen of trees and yew hedges, the ladies and gentlemen of the *ton* waited and speculated.

This feeling of his tongue on her was different from when he had been inside her. Then, she'd been stretched and sweetly aching—this was hot joy flying through every limb.

He murmured something into her flesh, and she felt the burn of his whiskers on her thighs. Meagan wanted him to tell her what he'd said, but she couldn't speak. She was wicked and bad and not a lady, and she loved it.

No wonder women and men pursued one another with such wild ferocity. No wonder they paid Black Annie enormous sums to make ensnaring love spells. The reward was this—a feeling of utter bliss, and though it lasted only a moment, it was worth the heartache of pursuit.

She fought her bonds, wanting to touch him and hold him, the need making what he did still more exciting.

As she struggled, a streak of rapture shot through her, and she nearly screamed out loud. He did not stop, his fingers hard on her flesh, his tongue a point of madness.

She rode on the wave of darkness, her eyes squeezed shut, arching to his mouth. She wanted more and more, and she could not break her bonds. . . .

What a wanton she'd become. Her wantonness should have bothered her more, but here with him, she felt no shame. The magic of Alexander took it all away.

A cry escaped her mouth, one she tried to suppress.

"Yes," he said against her. "Feel it."

"Alexander, what have you done to me?"

"Pleasured you," he said, and then, heartbreakingly, he pressed a last, long kiss to her female mound and rose to his feet.

Her rapture abated, but her heart still pounded, her body streaked with shivering delight. She was marrying him, happy thought. They could do this again and again throughout the long nights of their life.

Alexander straightened her skirts with a gentle hand, but his eyes were anything but gentle. They were filled with fierce possession and wicked glee, just as they'd been at the betrothal ceremony when he'd pressed their blood-streaked hands together.

"You are a bad man, Alexander," she said.

He nodded, feral smile in place. "Dangerous, I thought we agreed." He loosened the cloth that bound her hands and draped the fichu about her shoulders again.

"Dangerous to my sanity," she answered. "I am falling for you."

"It is the love spell. Love spells make one obsessed."

"Are you obsessed?"

Alexander held her face in his hands, his rings cool on her skin. "I am obsessed with you. I find I will do anything to be near you."

"You have stayed away from me for nearly two weeks," she pointed out. Her body felt tight and flushed, hovering between satiation and craving more of him.

"I know. I have been in hell. I want to be with you every minute I am awake. I want to hold you when I sleep and make love to you upon waking. I want nothing else but you. That is why we must break the spell. It distracts me from everything but you."

She loved his touch. "I would agree it is inconvenient."

"I must do so much. I spend every day with the damn king or his ministers, making their treaties favor Nvengaria. I am so good at it that I remain in London, talking and cajoling and keeping the English king under my thumb, instead of returning to Nvengaria, where I long to be. Nvengaria is an astonishing place. I want to show it to you—because that would mean I was home."

The ache in his eyes stung Meagan's heart. She did not

experience homesickness very often herself, always having her father nearby and knowing that they'd never stray too far from Oxfordshire. But sometimes, in the gray bustle of London, she thought of the green hills of home and the quiet peace of the woods and walks along the river with longing.

Alexander was thousands of miles from Nvengaria, in a strange and alien place to him. According to Penelope's letters, Alexander had rarely left Nvengaria before this. He must miss it dreadfully.

Meagan ran her fingers through his sun-warmed hair. She realized there were two Alexanders: the one who had people scrambling to do what he wanted at the snap of his fingers; and the passionate Alexander who loved his home with all his heart.

"I am certain Damien will let you return if you tell him how much you long to."

Alexander barked a laugh. "You are far too innocent, Meagan. Far too innocent to be bound to a man like me."

"Well, you cannot call off the wedding now," she said. "My reputation would be in tatters."

He growled and pulled her tight against him, no longer the controlled, suave man who'd calmly walked her away from the crowd. He snaked his hand through her hair and pulled her head back for another deep kiss.

His eyes were open, glittering and intensely blue. He pulled away from her mouth, as though he could not keep still, and kissed her face and lips and eyes. He muttered in Nvengarian, a question in his voice.

"What are you saying?" she begged him. "Teach me, so I may understand you."

He closed his eyes, tightening his body, his muscles hardening under her fingers. He seemed to retreat in on himself, his eyes taut, mouth a hard line.

She touched her palm to his face, alarmed to find it un-naturally hot. "Alexander, what is the matter? You are frightening me."

He pulled his eyes open, pupils so wide they were al-most black. "You should be frightened of me." The words were English, but harshly accented, as though he struggled to remember the language. "You should not be with me, not now. But I want this marriage. I need it."

He lifted her hand and pressed a kiss to her palm, his lips burning like a brand. He said nothing, but she felt it, this strong, strong man wanting to hold on to her and wishing he didn't want it.

Meagan determined, as he drew his tongue across her fingers, that she would find out absolutely everything about him. She would discover all there was to discover about him, beginning with why Black Annie had de-cided that she should create a love spell to bind Meagan to him forever.

When Alexander came to himself in the middle of the night, he was standing in the center of his bedroom with his clothes in shreds. Myn stood by the window, watch-ing calmly, his arms folded over his chest.

"Hell," Alexander snarled in Nvengarian.

Myn said nothing.

Alexander pulled off the tattered remains of his shirt. Nikolai had been undressing him after Alexander had returned from another tedious ball where the Duchess of Gower had tried to pump him for information of what he and Meagan had done in the gardens that afternoon.

It was none of the fool woman's business if Alexander was ravishing his beloved in the sunshine. He and Mea-gan were betrothed and they could enjoy each other's bodies as they pleased.

Meagan stunned him. She'd looked at him with understanding when he'd confessed how much he missed Nvengaria and told him not to worry, everything would be all right. No woman in his life had ever tried to reassure him, to comfort him.

He'd spent the rest of the day in wonder at the sensation. He'd had to master himself when the spell had encouraged him to carry her off to his carriage and make love to her all the way back to London. His blood had boiled hot all day, angry at him for trying to follow the damn English rules. When he finally was able to play by Nvengarian rules, he would let nothing stop him.

"Where is Nikolai?" he growled at Myn. "What happened to him?"

"He has not taken much hurt. He will recover."

Alexander stared into Myn's inscrutable face. "I attacked him?"

"When you changed."

Alexander stopped, his shirt falling from frozen fingers. "When I *changed?*"

Myn regarded him with unblinking blue eyes. He looked so human, and then he did not. "It has begun."

Alexander kicked the shirt aside and strode across the room, barely feeling the chill air licking his hot skin. "What the hell do you mean? And why did you come with me to England? You disappear for days at a time, and I have no control over you."

Myn simply watched him. "You like control."

"It is how I have survived."

"You are like her."

Alexander swung on him. "Like whom? Your cryptic conversation would make me insane, except I already am going insane."

"You are like the one you call Anastasia. She likes control and when she does not have it, she does not know what to do."

Alexander had no desire to talk about Anastasia. She'd been avoiding him, missing appointments, and that never boded well. She'd walked with him at the garden party today, but her purpose had been to antagonize the Duchess of Gower and lead him to Meagan. Anastasia was quite pleased he'd marry Meagan; she was almost giddy with it. But he hadn't spoken to her privately in days.

"Anastasia is nothing like me," he said. "She is driven by vengeance."

"As are you. When your father died, you wished to kill the men who murdered him."

The memories assailed him, the picture as vivid as the day he'd stood in the courtyard with the firing squad and watched his father be shot. The old Imperial Prince had grabbed a musket from one of his soldiers and shot Alexander's father, formerly his best friend, in the chest, laughing while he did it.

"Of course I did," Alexander answered. "I wanted every one of them to die for shooting my father. The soldiers were following orders, but I still wanted them to pay."

Myn nodded. "But you were young and too weak. You knew you had to bide your time until you were strong. You had to wait much time for your vengeance, but you had it."

"In the end, yes, I did." Alexander had tasted triumph when the old prince, half insane, had placed his hands in Alexander's and said, "I will do whatever you say, whatever you want. The people think I am Imperial Prince but I am your slave."

The revenge had not tasted as sweet as Alexander could have wished, because the Imperial Prince by that time had no idea what he did for more than an hour at a time. But Alexander himself had helped the insanity take hold of Damien's father. He had guaranteed it.

"And now you live for Nvengaria," Myn said.

"Yes. Why do you question that?"

Myn went silent, his eyes enigmatic.

Alexander moved to the window and looked out at the moonlit garden far below. He had the strange desire to be out there under the moonlight, but not in the garden. In the open, running, for some strange reason *hunting*.

"Yes," Myn said in a low voice, right behind him. "Let it take you."

"Let what take me?"

Alexander did not turn. He quivered with rage and uncertainty, and the damn love spell kept turning in his brain, making him think of Meagan lying asleep in her bedroom on the other side of Mayfair. Her flushed face in repose on her pillow, her glorious hair a riot against her white sheets. Two more weeks. He would never wait two more weeks.

"The love spell is calling the change," Myn said. "It has opened you to it."

Alexander turned around, slowly and carefully. "If you do not tell me what you mean, I swear to you I will put you in chains and throw you into the deepest dungeon. I will *find* a dungeon, no matter how hard I have to look. In fact, I will build one especially for you."

Myn smiled slightly. "You are right to be angry. Your father, he never told you. You are like her."

"Whom?" he demanded. "Anastasia?"

"Your mother."

Alexander stopped. He remembered his mother as a vague presence in his earliest years, a touch on his back as he drifted to sleep, a voice singing softly. He'd never really known her. She'd died of a fever when he was only five years old.

"You knew my mother?" Alexander looked Myn up

and down. "You cannot be older than I am. At least you do not appear to be."

"I knew her because she returned to her people before she died. She gave me attentions because I reminded her of the small child she'd left behind. You."

Alexander stared at him, letting the words sink in one at a time. "Her people," he repeated. "What people? My father and I were her people."

Myn shook his head, his black hair moving on his shoulders. "Your mother was of my people, Alexander of Nvengaria. She was logosh."

CHAPTER ELEVEN

Alexander waited in the church, expecting to feel the cool readiness he'd experienced at his first wedding, but today his mouth was dry and his face pale like he was an untried youth fearing his bride would jilt him at the last minute.

In the month since he had met Meagan at Lady Featherstone's ball, his whole life had changed. And as if the love spell had not wreaked enough havoc, Myn's announcement had shaken to the core everything Alexander believed. The fact that his mother had been a shape-shifting logosh, one of the wild peoples of the mountains, was difficult to accept.

Myn had tried in the past few weeks to teach Alexander how to shift and accept it, but the lessons hadn't worked. Alexander hadn't experienced the memory lapses or the changes since the night after the garden party with Meagan. He suspected that the love spell had something to do with it. Meagan was ripping open that part of him and letting the beast free.

Now Meagan, in a gown of yellow silk, walked toward him on her father's arm, orange blossoms in her hair and the diamonds he'd given her around her neck. She might destroy him, but he refused to call off the wedding. He had made a promise, he had ruined her, and he would do his duty by her. If he never saw her again after to-night, so be it. She deserved some compensation for blundering into the path of the Mad, Bad Duke.

The wedding had been hastily arranged, but it was still one of the grandest occasions of the Season. The entire *ton* turned out, including the Dukes of York and Clarence, their brother the king, the Duke of Wellington, the Duke of Devonshire, and many other nobles greater and lesser. With them were the ambassadors from France, Hanover, Prussia, Austria, Spain, America, and other corners of the globe. Nvengaria was a tiny country, but so many wanted to court it.

Myn attended the wedding, standing well in the back, watching with the stillness of an animal. Myn seemed perfectly satisfied that Alexander would marry Meagan, had said cryptically that it was meant to be.

As for Meagan, he was dying for her. The detached part of him wanted to keep her at a distance, but his body and soul craved her.

She halted next to him and sent him a sideways glance, her face serene. The feel of her next to him, the scent of her mixed with the orange blossoms, and her soft touch on his arm nearly undid him.

Alexander needed to be sharply focused and ruthless, calm and clearheaded. He needed to keep the beast at bay, and that was impossible when his dreams, waking and sleeping, were filled with Meagan, with touching her, tasting her, kissing her, riding her.

Black Annie needed to end the love spell before it was too late, but the damn witch was slippery. His men had never succeeded in tracking her down, not even when they became fixtures at the end of the cul-de-sac on which she lived. He'd never before been unable to put his hands on a person when he wanted to, and Black Annie's elusiveness enraged him.

Alexander realized that the bishop, mitered and garbed in golden robes, was staring at him, awaiting his response. Alexander cleared his throat and said, "I will."

Meagan raised a brow as though wondering what had his attention wandering. He'd explain to her later, in detail, exactly what he'd been thinking. Then again, maybe he shouldn't. Damn the love spell and damn Myn. Meagan deserved to know, and yet . . .

Give me tonight. Give me tonight with her, and I will tell her. Then she can decide whether she wants to go as far away as she can from me. But I need this night.

The bishop was staring at him again while Meagan fixed him with a watchful gaze. Alexander had no idea what the man had just said.

"Dreamin' of the wedding night, are ye?" Egan McDonald whispered loud enough for the first pews to hear.

Amid the tittering, Alexander said, "I beg your pardon. Please repeat the words."

Meagan gave him a tight smile. "That is what you are supposed to do, Alexander."

More titters. Alexander placed his hand over Meagan's and held it tight, while the bishop droned again what he was to say, and Alexander repeated it.

"I, Alexander Octavien Laurent Maximilien, take thee, Meagan Elizabeth Tavistock, to be my wedded wife, to have and to hold from this day forward . . . and thereto I plight thee my troth."

His beautiful bride didn't tremble at all when he slid

the wedding ring, diamonds and emeralds on a band of silver, onto her finger. His hands, however, were shaking and slick with sweat while he promised to worship her with his body. She noticed and slanted him a look of concern.

Could she know what beautiful eyes she had? Brown and shining, flecked with gold, like the sun-dappled water of a pond.

With some relief, the bishop concluded, "I pronounce that they be man and wife together, in the name of the Father, and of the Son, and of the Holy Ghost. Amen."

Alexander leaned down and touched Meagan's ripe, red lips with his own. It was done.

The wedding breakfast proceeded at Maysfield House for all the dukes and duchesses, ambassadors and their wives, not to mention Michael Tavistock and Simone, who mostly behaved herself, for which Meagan was thankful. The banqueting went on and on, the highest-placed people in the *ton* seeing no reason to abandon the food and drink and festivities too soon.

So many toasts were drunk to the bride and groom that Meagan was dizzy with champagne, and she spoke to so many people she quickly lost track of to whom she said what. The first Grand Duchess, she thought darkly, likely had been able to address each person by name and make them feel special. Meagan, in the end, could only babble incoherently and hope her utterances made sense.

She barely saw Alexander, who was being the cool Grand Duke and left her side soon after the meal. As she watched him speaking to the Russian ambassador, she wondered how many treaties favorable to Nvengaria would appear in the morning.

At long last, as the afternoon wore into evening, the guests began to depart. They would return home and change clothes and descend later on the town in the usual social whirl to gossip about the wedding.

Michael and Simone were the last to leave. Meagan kissed her stepmother's cheek and squeezed her hands, relieved that the happily chattering Simone was going home. But when Michael gathered Meagan in his arms, Meagan's tears began to flow.

Michael held her tight, the warm smell of his plain cashmere suit making her heart ache. "You be happy, my girl," he said, his voice thick.

"Yes, Papa."

Behind Michael, Simone sniffled and dabbed her eyes delicately with a lace handkerchief. "Oh dear, I was going to be so brave. But we are only streets away, and in the summer, you and Alexander will come to Oxfordshire. We will have a house party the envy of all of England. I've already begun the arrangements."

Michael pulled away from Meagan, a wry smile on his face. She shared the smile, but she already missed them.

Alexander's stiff English butler, Montmorency, stood at the open door, his nose in the air, his shoulders back. The Tavistock barouche waited outside the entrance, Roberts holding the door. Roberts scratched his left calf with the toe of his right shoe, leaving smears on his white stocking.

Dear, bumbling Roberts nearly unleashed Meagan's tears again. Her simple home life was receding like the last wave of a tide, and no matter how much she wanted to be with Alexander, she knew she was losing something irreplaceable.

She forced a cheerful smile and waved her parents out the door, telling Roberts to be careful riding home on the back of the barouche. The doors slammed, the carriage jumped forward, Roberts hanging on for dear life, and they were gone.

Montmorency shut the front door, enclosing Meagan in the echoing black and white rotunda of the front hall. She shivered, rubbing her hands on the sleeves of the dark green silk gown Meagan's new lady's maid had helped her don after removing her wedding finery. Her first matronly colors—no more pale cream and white for Meagan.

While the house had been filled with guests and bustling servants it had not seemed too large, but now the walls stretched up and up to the dome far above, and the quiet of so much empty air seemed to press in on her.

"Your Grace," Nikolai said behind her.

Meagan whirled. "Goodness, Nikolai, you move like a cat."

"I beg your pardon," Nikolai said, not looking one bit sorry. "His Grace wishes you to formally meet your staff."

"Now?" Evening shadows pierced the hall, and Meagan had been looking forward to retiring to her new chamber, throwing herself across the elaborate tester bed, and falling fast asleep. Her nerves were stretched raw.

"His Grace wastes no moment of any day." Nikolai kept his face straight, but she'd already learned that the valet's choice of words spoke volumes. "This way, please."

Meagan let go of her dream of a good sleep and followed Nikolai across the tiles and into the staircase hall. Her dress made a pleasing swishing noise, her slippers echoing on the marble floor.

"You no longer need to show guests to the door, Your Grace," Nikolai said as they began their climb up the wide staircase with its elaborate, scrolled-iron banisters. "One of the English servants can see to that."

He pronounced the word "English" with a slight

sneer, and gave a backward glance at Montmorency, who was walking toward the servants' stairs below them. The butler's back became stiffer.

Meagan spoke in a brisk tone. "In any case, they were not guests; they were my parents. 'Tis a different thing."

"If you say so, Your Grace."

"I do say so. Lead on, Nikolai. I am certain His Grace does not like to be kept waiting twenty seconds longer than he must."

Nikolai's lips twitched. "As you say, Your Grace. He is in the Asia Hall."

"Is that the room with pillars carved like palm trees?"

"No, Your Grace, that is the India sitting room. The Asia Hall has the Chinese furniture. You will soon learn to distinguish them."

"Only if I do not grow weary on all these stairs," Meagan said, struggling to keep up with Nikolai's long-legged stride. "The staff must be wonderfully fit."

"Another reason you do not need to see people to the front door, Your Grace." Nikolai waited on the landing for her to catch up. "You need only move between the first and second floors, that is all, except for large ceremonial occasions such as balls. You never need to descend, unless you are going out."

Meagan looked up the line of the staircase, which rose two more floors above them. "And what is up there?"

"The third floor houses small Alex's nursery and his nanny and tutors. Above that are the servants' rooms, and you need never climb there."

"I see." Meagan smoothed her hand on the railing. At home, she used to dash up to Rose's attic room to fetch forgotten things while Rose attended to Simone's toilette. As a girl in Oxfordshire, Meagan had often sneaked up to the maid's rooms to play card games in the middle of the night.

The third-floor landing looked elegant and lonely. Alexander's son had attended the wedding but been whisked away when they returned to the festivities here. Meagan had kissed his sticky cheek before he was carried away under the sneer of the French ambassador's wife.

"This way, Your Grace," Nikolai said, sounding anxious.

Meagan reluctantly turned and followed Nikolai around the gallery to double doors halfway along. With the exception of her bedchamber and Alexander's study, this was the first she'd see of the house's grand rooms.

The Asia Hall was decorated in hues of bright yellow, Chinese red, and lacquer black. Yellow silk with a red fan pattern covered the walls, the U-arm black lacquer chairs were upholstered in scarlet, and the cabinetry and tables were japanned or inlayed with mother-of-pearl. Windows draped in Chinese red faced the street, which lent fog-shrouded light to the candlelit room.

At least a dozen people, both Nvengarian and English, stood in a semicircle in the middle of the room. Dominic anchored one end, and a thin woman in dull gray with a long nose and intelligent eyes anchored the other. Nikolai took his place next to Dominic.

Alexander waited in front of them, standing straight. Although he'd changed his military coat with the medals for a plainer one, still blue, he'd retained his sash of office. She wondered if he wore the sash to remind his English staff who he was, or to remind himself.

He waited with his usual inscrutable coolness and no hint of the distraction she'd sensed in him at the altar. He was once more Grand Duke Alexander, in command of himself and everyone around him.

When she reached his side, he slid a hand to her waist and gave a nod toward the assembled staff. As one they bowed or curtseyed, then eyed Meagan with frank interest. Some she'd already met—Mrs. Caldwell the housekeeper, Dominic her bodyguard, the lady's maid Susan, Nikolai, Gaius, and a few of the Nvengarian footmen who'd served guests this afternoon.

Alexander began without preliminary. "These are your personal staff and will report to you. Some have been culled from my own staff, and others are new. They will assist you in your various duties and help you become familiar with your role as hostess."

Mrs. Caldwell on the end curtseyed. "Your Grace," she said, her words as tight as the gray bun on her head. "You will report your needs to me, and I will see that your wishes are carried out. I will also assist in planning the menus for all your meals and making arrangements for social activities in the house. Mr. Edwards . . ." She pointed at a trim, rather nondescript man at her side. "He will be your secretary, assisting with your correspondence and any written communications you require. You have met Susan, your lady's maid. She is French."

Susan curtsied again. Though she tried to keep a haughty demeanor as befitted a lady's maid, her brown eyes held eager excitement and her mouth kept curving into a smile.

Mrs. Caldwell continued. "The footmen in the middle are Brutus, Gaius, and— Oh, I can never remember the other one."

"Marcus," Nikolai said helpfully.

"Marcus. Outlandish names for servants, but they are Nvengarian. They speak very little English, except Gaius, who speaks some, but you can make yourself understood with gestures. They are to fetch and carry for you anything you need."

The three Nvengarians flourished grand bows in Meagan's direction. Meagan remembered Prince Damien's very enthusiastic footmen and smiled. "I speak very little Nvengarian and must learn it. I believe we'll struggle along together."

Nikolai spoke rapidly behind her, translating. The three footmen, black-haired and blue-eyed and very young, laughed and bowed again. One said something to his fellows, setting them off, and Nikolai laughed behind him. A word from Alexander silenced them all, but she noted the Nvengarians did not look abashed.

Next was another maid who would help Susan with Meagan's clothes and gloves and ribbons. The two girls eyed each other jealously. Next came an English coachman whose employment would be to drive Meagan in the carriage Alexander had provided, and an English groom, who would take care of her horses and ride out with her. Nikolai, in addition to his valet duties, would help Meagan understand and follow Nvengarian protocol.

Mrs. Caldwell stepped back to her place, the introductions at an end.

The entire line swiveled eyes to Meagan and waited expectantly. Alexander watched her too. She realized after a moment that they wanted her to make a speech.

"Oh, um, well." Meagan resisted twisting her fingers together like a girl. "It is nice to meet you, and I hope we get along swimmingly."

They waited, leaning the slightest bit toward her, then blinked when they realized nothing more was coming.

One of the Nvengarian footmen shot his fist into the air and gave a rousing shout. The other two footmen and Nikolai and Dominic joined in the answering shout. They did this five times, loud male voices reverberating from the gilded ceiling. The groom and coachman joined in enthusiastically, but Susan put her hands over her ears, and Mrs. Caldwell openly grimaced.

The first footman thumped his fist to his chest and declared something in a ringing voice. The second and third footmen followed suit.

"What are they saying?"

"That they are proud and honored to serve you," Alexander said. "That they would die for you."

She looked up in alarm. "Die for me?"

Alexander gave her a quiet nod. "As is their duty, and their right."

Nikolai broke in. "We would all gladly die for you." Beyond him, Dominic nodded silently. "We would lay our bleeding bodies at your feet to show you how much you are honored and adored."

Mrs. Caldwell looked pained. Alexander traced distracting patterns at the base of Meagan's spine.

"Oh," Meagan said. "Oh, dear."

Supper commenced soon after that, a quiet, simple supper, Mrs. Caldwell explained, showing Meagan the menu. Reading course after course, Meagan wondered what on earth the woman considered an elaborate meal.

She was also expected to change her clothing yet again. She had thought the green silk to be plenty fine for a supper dress, but both Susan and Mrs. Caldwell looked horrified and said it would not do at all. Susan and the other maid bustled her into a shimmering silver silk with a fine black net overdress, and Susan wove a rope of pearls studded with diamonds through Meagan's hair.

Meagan asked directions to the dining room, which fortunately was simply called "The Dining Room," and entered to find Alexander waiting for her.

The room was as vast as any other in the house and just as intimidating. Four thick marble pillars soared to the ceiling, and enormous paintings depicted men in Roman dress battling other men in Roman dress. Horses reared and fell in an abundance of horseflesh and blood.

The long dining table stretched beneath the paintings, loaded with silver dishes that matched the silver on the equally enormous sideboard. Eight chairs marched down each side of the table, and gilded armchairs stood at either end.

Alexander, resplendent once more in military coat, medals, and sash, the ruby in his ear winking fire, escorted her to the chair at the far end of the table. The Nvengarian footmen she'd met earlier waited there, and three similarly dressed Nvengarians waited at Alexander's end.

Alexander pulled out the chair. Meagan sank into it, and two of the Nvengarians shoved it to the table, while the third presented her a napkin over his arm. Alexander let his fingers drift over the back of Meagan's bared neck, then returned to the other side of the table, where his footmen presented a chair and napkin to him.

Meagan stared in some dismay at the array of cutlery spread before her. Three plates were stacked on top of each other, with several crystal goblets lined up beside them. One of the footmen carefully placed the first course on the top plate, a thin cutlet of fish in some buttery sauce. The footman on the other side, Gaius, lifted one of the forks and handed it to her.

The haughty Montmorency entered, bearing bottles of wine. He handed a bottle to one of Meagan's footmen, who sloshed a huge amount into the largest of her goblets. At precisely the same time, Alexander's footman served wine at his end of the table.

Alexander calmly began eating as though the machinations of his servants were in no way unusual. Meagan plucked up a tiny piece of sole with her fork and raised it to her lips. She did not much like fish, but she could hardly scorn the first offering of the very first meal in her new husband's house.

When she placed the bite of fish into her mouth, a wonderful explosion of flavor burst over her tongue, buttery, savory, salty, and smooth, delicate herbs just setting off the velvet touch of the butter. She closed her eyes and chewed, amazed at the sensations. She'd never tasted such food.

She opened her eyes to see Gaius hovering at her elbow with a huge grin, holding out the goblet of wine. Meagan took the glass from him and sipped, experiencing another savoring moment. The mellow sweetness of the wine nicely offset the fish, the flavors melding perfectly.

"Oh, my," she said, setting down the goblet. "This food is excellent. Montmorency, please tell Cook."

The butler raised his brows the slightest bit. "His Grace's French *chef* will be pleased to hear the first course is a success."

Meagan's face heated. She glanced at Alexander to see what he made of her gaffe, but her husband, far away behind silver serving dishes and candlesticks and crystal, had his attention on his food.

The soup came next, a clear broth served steaming hot in a porcelain bowl. Gaius lifted one of the many spoons and handed it to her with an encouraging smile. All three footmen waited with eager gazes for her to take her first mouthful. The soup, too, was excellent, but Meagan refrained from making any excited statements about it.

It was the most bizarre meal she'd ever had in her life. She and Alexander might have been in different rooms. Each set of servants carried out their tasks without speaking to the others, the only go-between being the butler, who handed out bottles of wine.

At home in Portman Square and Oxfordshire, supper was a lively meal, filled with Simone's chatter as she related the gossip of the day. Michael would listen with a fond smile; then he and Meagan would discuss things he'd read in his books that he thought would interest her. The table in the Tavistock dining room seated six at most, and that was in a pinch, with everyone's elbows squeezing each other's.

The vastness of Alexander's dining table could have been a desert, the empty chairs marching down each side giving the impression that only ghosts ate there. She imagined skeletal fingers reaching for the fruit bowl and shivered.

As soon as she set down her soup spoon, Gaius whisked the bowl away. In the delay between the removal of the soup and the serving of the meat, Meagan cleared her throat.

"I did not see Lady Anastasia at the wedding," she said into the silence.

Every head in the room lifted, every pair of Nvengarian eyes fixed on her. The butler stopped in the act of handing the next bottle of wine to Alexander's footman.

Alexander's eyes, bluest of all, pinned her down the length of the table. "What did you say?"

Meagan cleared her throat again. "I said, I did not see Lady Anastasia at the wedding."

Alexander fingered his wineglass, tracing the facets of crystal. "No, she thought it better she stayed away."

"Pity, I would have liked to speak to her."

He shook his head. "You should not speak with her."

"Because everyone believes she is your mistress?" *You see, I can be blunt as well.*

But her speech hadn't shocked Alexander. She'd only succeeded in shocking Montmorency, if the choking noises coming from him were any indication.

Alexander lifted the goblet to his lips, taking a swallow of wine. He passed his tongue over his lower lip as he set it down. "Yes."

"All this intrigue is so difficult." Meagan sighed.

Alexander raised his eyes again. "I beg your pardon?"

"I said, all this— Oh, never mind. This is ridiculous. I cannot even see you, let alone conduct a conversation. Gaius." She held up her hand, stopping him from setting down a plate of roast beef. "Put my food over there. I am going to sit next to His Grace." She pointed at the empty space before the chair on Alexander's right. Gaius stared in the direction and stared back at her, mouth open.

"I want to move," she repeated, raising her voice. She started to stand, but the other two footmen, Marcus and Brutus, pushed her back down.

Alexander growled a few words in Nvengarian. The footmen serving him broke away and headed down the table to Meagan. The butler backed against the sideboard as they went by, holding his bottle of wine against his chest.

"Wait a moment," Meagan said as all six footmen bore down on her. "For heaven's sake—"

She broke off with a squeak as two of the footmen lifted the chair with her still in it and half galloped with it down the length of the table. Marcus moved the chair next to Alexander out of the way, and the other two set her gently down in the place she'd requested. Gaius led the others in bringing every piece of porcelain, crystal, and silver from the end of the table to swiftly place them in front of her.

Before she could even draw a breath, Gaius laid the meat in sauce, undisturbed from its journey, in front of her.

"Well." She glanced at Alexander, who had calmly continued his meal throughout the move. "Perhaps tomorrow night we might save trouble by setting my place here from the beginning."

Alexander lifted his goblet and sipped more of the Nvengarian wine, his throat moving as he swallowed. "We will dine out tomorrow. There is a ball at the house of the French ambassador."

"Oh."

"Mrs. Caldwell will provide you with a schedule."

"A schedule."

"She and Mr. Edwards have been tasked to tell you which clothes to wear and to make certain that you get into your carriage and arrive on time."

Meagan poked tiny holes in her slab of roast. "My carriage? Will we not go together?"

He shook his head. "Not always. My tasks might not permit me to return home before my evening obligations. I have rooms at my club to use when necessary. And sometimes, we will attend different events. When two functions coincide, you will represent me at one while I attend the other."

"Represent you?" She swallowed.

"I will instruct you in what you need to do."

"Alexander—"

His gaze lingered on the pearls and diamonds in her hair, then slid to where the net and silver dress skimmed her bosom. "You will do well."

She let out a breath. "I vow, if you had told me all this before the wedding, I might have fled screaming into the night."

"I would have come after you and brought you back." His voice held dark tones.

He would have, she understood that. She shivered a little under his gaze, which held an undercurrent of determination. He wanted her, the look said, and he'd go to any lengths to have her. He was like one of the new steam machines—he determined his course and plunged on without stopping. Steam engines would take over the world, her father predicted. Alexander could, too.

"You ought to have married Lady Anastasia," she said. "She must understand all this."

"I did not want to marry Lady Anastasia. I wanted to marry you."

He did not look at her, but his voice carried conviction. She blushed and busied herself cutting a bite of meat.

It too was delicious, the velvety sauce spiced with just a hint of pepper.

"Is there any salt?" She glanced about for a caster or bowl, but there were so many silver pieces on the table she could not tell what was what. She glanced at her three footmen, who were poised, ready to get what she wanted, but they obviously did not understand her.

"Alexander," she hissed, "what is salt in Nvengarian?"

"*Pesch*," he answered, cutting his meat.

She looked at the footmen and gestured at the silver dishes. "*Pesch*," she repeated. "I want *pesch*."

The footmen froze. They exchanged an amazed glance, then their heads swiveled on stiff necks to look first at Alexander, then at Meagan.

Alexander stopped eating and raised his blue eyes to her. The moment hovered.

Then a snort burst from Gaius's mouth. Before Meagan could ask what he meant by it, all the footmen were roaring with laughter. They hung on to each other and whooped.

Meagan's face heated. "Did I say it wrong?"

"Not exactly." Alexander's voice was calm but mirth danced in his eyes. "But you asked them for a penis."

CHAPTER TWELVE

Meagan gasped in horror. "I most certainly did *not*."

"I told you to say *pesch*," Alexander said. "You said *pesche*."

She stared at him. "I cannot hear the difference. You are making this up."

He took another quiet sip of wine. "Nvengarian has many nuances that are difficult for the English to grasp."

"Which you might have mentioned before I attempted it, you horrible man." She glared at the footmen who were holding their stomachs, tears leaking from their eyes. "Stop that!"

Alexander touched her hand, his fingertips warm. "In Nvengaria, we laugh only at those we hold in great affection. Fear and reticence is not a compliment."

She wondered suddenly if it bothered him that so many men feared him. Perhaps his footmen laughing at his wife's blunder was a good sign.

"Well, you will have to teach me better pronunciation if I am to be the Grand Duchess," she said. "What happens when I am at a banquet for Prince Damien and accidentally ask someone to pass me a—you know?"

Alexander's hot blue gaze fixed on her. "I imagine most gentlemen at the table would be willing to oblige you."

Her entire body warmed, his touch stirring the tendrils of the love spell. "You should not say such things. I am certain they would simply make a joke of your silly wife."

He leaned closer, medals clinking. The footmen had recovered themselves somewhat, but they still smirked and broke into the occasional chuckle. Meagan felt the tethers of the spell close on her, and from the dark look in Alexander's eyes, he did as well.

"The last thing any Nvengarian gentleman will do is laugh," he said. "I am certain you will have plenty of choices for your paramours. That is something else we need to discuss. I believe you will intend to be discreet, but there are rules to follow that you may not know of."

She stared back at him, her forkful of spicy meat hovering above her plate. "I have no idea what you mean. What are you saying?"

Alexander's expression was perfectly serious. "I mean that you will have many candidates for your lovers, but you must be careful whom you choose. Also you will need to be instructed in the use of contraceptives. My position in the Nvengarian government is such that I must not let another man's child under my roof. It would be too dangerous."

He *was* perfectly serious. Meagan laid down her fork, her body stilling in shock. The Nvengarian footmen continued to hover, waiting to whisk away plates and serve more food and wine. They didn't understand enough

English to follow along, and Montmorency, thank heavens, was too far away and absorbed in his bottles of wine to hear.

"Alexander, are you saying you expect me to *cuckold* you?" she hissed. "That I will take lovers and break my vows and behave like—like Deirdre Braithwaite?"

Alexander answered in the neutral, reasonable tone that made Meagan's hands curl into fists. "I am a powerful and wealthy man, and you are a beautiful woman. It is inevitable that gentlemen will dance attendance upon you and natural that you will single out one or more for your attentions. It is the sort of thing that happens in the circle you have entered."

Meagan recalled his blunt admissions that his first wife had taken lovers and that he'd done so himself from time to time for physical relief. He was calmly assuming that Meagan would do the same.

His quiet words brought the emotions that had been curdling inside her all day into sudden boiling rage. She turned to the butler, her eyes burning.

"Montmorency," she said in a clear voice. "Take the footmen out. I wish to speak to His Grace in private."

Alexander did the brow lift again, but he gave Montmorency a nod when the butler looked at him questioningly. Montmorency clapped his hands and said loudly to the Nvengarians, "Come along, you lot."

The Nvengarians gave him blank stares, and Alexander, blast him, did not translate. Montmorency repeated his command in a louder voice, pointing at the door.

The footmen, understanding the gist, began to argue. Gaius furiously waved the bottle in his hands, sending an arc of wine over the polished table. The other five shouted at Montmorency, pounding fists on the table, sending the silver dancing.

Alexander returned to eating, as though a roomful of

screaming, angry footman and a trembling, red-faced
butler was nothing unusual. No wonder people were
afraid of him, Meagan thought, fuming. He could shut
out everything, a cool look in his eyes, as though the
emotional frenzy of his fellow man could not touch him.

His withdrawal made Meagan more furious than ever.
Without stopping to think, she snatched up his full goblet of wine, lifted it high, and poured it into his lap.

Alexander leapt to his feet, his cutlery crashing to his
plate, and the footmen abruptly ceased shouting.
Alexander's thigh sported a decidedly wet stain that
spread rapidly across his crotch. After one frozen moment, the footmen abandoned their argument to swoop
upon him, white cloths fluttering like flags of surrender.
They swarmed around him, arms and elbows waving
wildly as they tried to wipe him down.

Meagan watched with a twinge of satisfaction. The
man who so coolly spoke of living separate lives and of
her taking lovers now glared at her in fury above the
heads of his mob of footmen.

"Gaius!" Meagan shouted. Her voice broke through the
frenzy, and Gaius actually turned to her, blue eyes round.

Meagan knew something about directing servants.
One had to take a firm hand with Roberts or else fires did
not get laid or boots polished or food lugged home from
the markets. Gaius understood English much better than
the others, so she singled him out as her point of contact.

"Gaius," she repeated, pointing a rigid finger at the
door. "Go!"

Gaius looked from her to Alexander. Alexander was
lost behind his footmen, but she heard his growls in
Nvengarian mixed with the footmen's babble. Meagan
turned her commanding gaze to a glare.

"*Now*," she said.

She imagined thoughts warring in Gaius's head,

whether to stay and assist Alexander, his master, or to avoid the anger of his new mistress. Meagan met his gaze, and something in her eyes must have triggered a decision to do things her way.

He rounded on the other five footmen, shouted something in harsh Nvengarian, and swept his arm toward the door. The others drew apart reluctantly, revealing Alexander in his chair, dabbing at the stain on his trousers.

"You must go too, Montmorency," she said, putting a note of icy hauteur in her voice. "We will ring if we need you."

Montmorency gave her a grateful look as though *these* sorts of commands he understood. He drew his butler's persona about him, though his lips trembled and his cheeks were white. "Very good, Your Grace."

Gaius led them out, the footmen still arguing at the tops of their voices. Montmorency followed, then the shouting cut off abruptly as Montmorency swung the door shut.

Meagan drew a breath and turned around. Alexander was glaring at her, his color high, his blue eyes livid. Any moment he'd lash out at her, giving her a lecture on the dignity of her position, instructing her that a Grand Duchess of Nvengaria did not pour wine into her husband's lap. Especially not in front of servants who would spread the story far and wide.

His dark blue trousers bore a wet patch from his knee to the join of his legs, and the cloth dangling from his hand was stained a dull red that nearly matched the redness of his face. His sash of office had twisted from his footmen's exuberance and his medals hung askew.

Meagan pressed her hand to her mouth, barely containing her giggles. "Oh, Alexander," she gasped. "You look so funny."

He threw the cloth down and came at her. His look

was fierce, mouth drawn, and at the last moment, she decided her best course of action was to run.

Too late. Alexander's strong hands closed over her arms, and he hauled her to him. She landed against his chest, his impossibly tall body arching her backward, and he dragged her mouth to his for a brutal kiss.

Alexander put all his strength into the kiss, tasting her laughter and the heady, buttery flavor of the sauces she'd eaten. It was a raw, possessive kiss, meant to tell her who was Grand Duke around this house.

The love spell had swamped him the moment she'd turned from the door, her face pink with anger, her starry eyes surpassing the jewels in her tiara. When she'd dissolved into helpless laughter, pressing a plump hand over her mouth, he knew he'd never seen anything more beautiful in his life.

Under him, her mouth became malleable, softening to him. She was learning to kiss well, to taste him without shame. He moved his mouth to her neck, loving the scent of her.

His very elegant first wife would never have dreamed of pouring a goblet of wine into his lap, let alone laughing at him when he tried to mop up. Sephronia had always been conscious of her poise, calculating every word before she spoke and every action before she performed it. Meagan's spontaneity was refreshing.

"You soothe me," he murmured.

"Then how can you think I would betray you?" She pulled away from him and gave him a disappointed look, her lips forming a near pout. "I would never take a lover, never. How could you think that of me?"

He smoothed a lock of hair from her face. "Because when the love spell is broken, you will not want to be married to me. Perhaps you will feel cheated and angry."

He knew the truth of this. The day Meagan realized she was trapped in a marriage she did not want, she would look for a handsome gentleman to whom she could pour out her troubles. That was the way of marriages of convenience.

Alexander hoped the love spell would be over by then, because the thought of Meagan crying on another man's shoulder, possibly in his bed, rampaged jealousy through him. He wanted to set guards around her and say, "Mine, and mine alone."

If Meagan spoke the Nvengarian word she had tonight, completely wrong and in that seductive accent of hers, the passionate men of his country would fall at her feet, literally. Duels would be fought over her. Meagan would soon recognize her power, and she'd learn to use it.

He would not blame her. The stupid English treated her like a nonentity. She would at first be surprised at the attention she commanded and then grow to like it. She needed to learn that her power could easily be turned against her, that discretion would be her only defense.

He kissed the tips of her fingers. "I know you do not wish to speak of it, but you must promise me that you will be open about the gentlemen who court you. If one of them tries to create difficulties, I must know immediately. It will stop problems that could become disasters."

She raised her gaze, but the look in her eyes was far from compliant. "Even if I hated you, Alexander, I would not break my vows. This is my honor you are speaking of. Perhaps things are different in Nvengaria, but in England, our word, once given, means something to us."

Alexander thought of the dozens of Englishmen he'd met who spoke of honor in one breath and broke their words with another. Certain things seemed to be sacrosanct, such as paying a gambling debt to one's fellows even if it meant the family went hungry, or never touching a young, unmarried miss, although a gentleman could tumble her married sisters to his heart's content. Married women took lovers, but they'd never dare admit it in public, yet a man could speak frankly about visiting his mistress and not be considered odd. Nvengarians were much more open and honest about their affairs.

"I admit English customs confuse me," he said. "As closely as I have studied them, the nuances are strange. For instance, the Duchess of Gower has two gentlemen lovers who service her at the same time. No one is shocked as long as it is not talked about."

Meagan's mouth formed a pink O. "Two? Oh, my, I wager my stepmother did not know *that.*" Her eyes took on the feral gleam of a woman who knew gossip another woman didn't. "Goodness. I wonder what on earth they do."

The love spell chose that moment to slam him into another vision. The dining room dissolved and he knelt on a bed with Meagan against his chest, her legs wrapped around him. He was inside her, rocking her back and forth on his hips, his greedy, eager arousal stretching into her.

Behind her knelt another man, his face obscured by darkness. His hands were between Alexander and Meagan, holding Meagan's breasts while he kissed her neck. Alexander had no idea who the other man was and was too far gone to care. The heat of their bodies, the scent of sex, and the intense feeling of losing himself in Meagan blotted out the rest of the world.

And then he was standing, cold and out of breath, back in the dining room, his hands hard on Meagan's shoulders. She stared at him in shock, eyes wide, red lips parted, and he knew she'd had the vision too.

"Oh," she said. "So that is what they do."

Alexander scraped her close, binding her flat against

his body. "I do not want another man touching you. Not ever. Not *ever*. You are mine, Meagan, and I will keep every man away from you, even if I have to fight them all."

She lifted her face, her eyes dusky. He smelled desire on her like night flowers. "But you just said I should calmly discuss my lovers with you."

She was smiling. She knew what was in his heart, damn her. She saw straight through him, something no one, not even Sephronia, had ever done.

"To hell with what I said." He lifted her into his arms, and she looked quite pleased about that. "I will murder any man who touches you."

She pressed a warm kiss to his cheek. "Now *that* is much more satisfying."

He knew he should leave her and let the love spell play out, and not risk stirring the beast lurking below his surface. But he wanted her and he'd been keeping himself from her and she was warm in his arms.

He carried her to the table, sweeping away silver and crystal with his strong arm, not caring when things shattered on the floor. She smiled, her eyes half closed as he set her down, not worried in the least about what he would do.

"You are the only woman who has ever dared laugh at me," he breathed, skimming her skirt up her legs.

"It was rude, but I could not help myself. Poor Alexander." She giggled again.

"I love it when you laugh. You can pour wine on me anytime, if it makes you look like that."

She threaded her fingers around his neck. "You are sweet."

"And no woman has ever dared call me *sweet*."

"Then you have not met the right women. You are the sweetest man in the world, Alexander."

Alexander began to laugh. He remembered the looks

on the faces of the English king and several cabinet ministers yesterday when they'd tried to slide in a clause to a treaty that said Nvengaria would sell England its gold at a ridiculously low price. When he'd spied it among the tiny print and made his feelings known, he doubted fat George would have called him the sweetest man in the world.

"The love spell has rendered you a little bit mad, I think," he said.

"I know that. But you *are* sweet. You could have had your way with me and simply left me to my ruin."

"Instead I married you so I could have my way with you any time I liked."

"Mmm, that sounds nice."

He loosened the top of her silk bodice, the black net of which shimmered against her long, beautiful body, and licked from her breasts to the hollow of her throat.

She tasted like heady wine and the salt of warm skin. He'd always made love to women to sate basic needs and to pleasure them, but he'd never been elaborate. Return pleasure for pleasure, but go no deeper.

Now he wanted to do everything he'd ever thought about or read about, the wilder the better. He'd learned many ways of pleasuring when he'd studied in the cult of Eros as a young man and had only used a fraction of them. He wanted to try every single technique on Meagan and have her try a few on him. He wanted to explore new positions—for instance, on the edge of a dining room table.

The love spell made his beautiful wife perfectly willing. She kissed him happily as he pulled her skirts up to bare her hips and the beautiful warmth between her thighs. She sighed as his fingers found her mound, already swollen for him, her honey flowing over his hands.

"Remember what I said in the gardens?" he murmured. "That if I ever hurt you, you say 'Stop, Alexander.' And I will stop."

"I remember. And then you made me feel the most amazing things."

"I want to make you feel amazing things again and again. Every day and every night for the rest of our lives so that you will never want to take a paramour."

"What about when the love spell wears off? Will you want to pleasure me every day then?"

Alexander rubbed his thumbs over her nub until she dragged in a sharp breath. "How could I not?" he asked. He kissed the fiery line of her hair. "How could I not want you?"

"Exactly why I shall never take a lover."

He'd never let her take a lover, even if he had to shoot every man who came near her.

He hastily undid the buttons holding his trousers over his very hard erection. "Do you remember our vision of the bath chamber?"

"Oh yes," Meagan breathed. "Do you mean the one against the pillar or the one on the bench?"

"Both. I want to do both with you. How fortunate the eccentric builder of this house had hot water pumped from a cistern to the bath chamber."

"Quite fortunate."

"And do you recall the one we had while riding in the park?" His staff tumbled out, swollen and ready as he thought of the vision she'd plunged him into. "Another I'd be pleased to act out, and then perhaps you can ride me."

A pink blush stole over her cheeks. "I am not certain how to do that."

"I will teach you. I will teach you so many things, my Grand Duchess."

He eased her thighs apart and positioned himself in the lovely place between her legs that was open and ready for him. She went rigid, but with longing that was obvious as she wriggled her hips toward him.

"What about the vision of the second man?" she whispered. "The one we had a few minutes ago."

"Nvengarian husbands sometimes bring in a third party for their wives," he answered. "Or the wives bring one for their husbands." He kissed her and lifted her buttocks to slide himself into her. "But we'll keep to two in our bed, Meagan. We will have plenty to do with just the two of us."

Whether she heard and understood, he didn't know. Her head fell back as he penetrated her, her eyes dimming as want took over her body.

Rain pattered on the long windows at the end of the room; candle flames hissed as they met liquid wax. Meagan closed her eyes, her lips parting in desire, ringlets of red hair spilling down her neck.

Everything about her made him want her with animal-like insanity. The way her hair curled about her forehead, the cool tips of her fingers on his cheekbones, the glow in her brown eyes of a woman wanting a man.

He ought to go slowly. Their other encounters had been quick and harsh, his lust too strong to quench. She deserved gentleness.

But she awoke such a fierceness in him. He was losing the iron control under which he'd held himself since the day his father died. He'd always believed that love and trust meant betrayal. Alexander had turned a smooth face to the world and suppressed the rage deep inside.

Meagan, with her soft smile, her gentle brown eyes that could suddenly flash with mischief, the no-nonsense way she talked, was steadily prying away the boulder under which the real Alexander hid.

He drew her mouth up to his and kissed her with hard thoroughness. Her desire smelled good, and it tasted good in her mouth. Either his sense of smell and taste had sharpened or she projected her needs to him, maybe both.

He should have let her go to her room and have her maid slowly undress her and put her to bed. He could slide between the sheets later and strip off her nightrail or leave it on to preserve her modesty. That was how husbands went to their wives in England.

In Nvengaria, woman and man played many games with each other, but none involved tamely coming together for the act itself. He did not want the *act*. He wanted Meagan, whole and his, her clothes in shreds, her naked body warm in his arms. Whether they were under the covers on the bed or on the window seat made no difference to him.

Her eyelids heavy now, cheeks flushed, she clung to him. He kissed her flesh, nibbled her and suckled her neck, loving the smell and feel of her. His medals pressed her breasts, the sash of office rubbing her skin, imprinting her as his own. *Mine*, his thoughts snarled in Nvengarian. *All mine*.

She watched him with soft eyes, parting his coat, her fingers tracing the interlaced tattoo ringing his biceps. He'd gotten the tattoo from a man he'd met in Greece during his Grand Tour, who'd learned the art from a Chinese man. The strange, smooth design had some significance that the Greek had tried to explain and Alexander did not understand. "Two lives," the man had said. "Duality. I chose it because I sensed this in you."

Alexander had gotten the tattoo as part of his hidden defiance against the old Imperial Prince. No one saw it but himself and his valet, and his lovers, who thought it made him dashing. Sephronia had never mentioned it.

Meagan traced the patterns with the tips of her fingers, her featherlight touch erotic.

Nestled inside her, his erection began to pound, the intensity of her closing around him driving him into mindlessness. *This is what it is like to come home.*

The animal in him took over and poetry went to hell. He drove into her, loving the cries of pleasure that escaped her mouth. He would make her his, make her belong to him, damn the spell, damn Nvengarian customs, damn that he was Grand Duke.

He wanted it to be her and him, man and woman. "You and me," he croaked in Nvengarian. "This is you and me."

She didn't understand him. God, when she'd turned her innocent eyes on his footmen and said that very naughty word, he thought he'd fling her to the floor and take her right there. She thought he'd taught her the word wrong to make her a laughingstock, but he'd truly forgotten how much trouble the English had with pronunciation. Any nuance was lost on them.

It had never been so adorable before.

He'd told her the literal translation of the word, not the erotic connotation. She'd done the equivalent of a proper English lady asking to suck on a cock. No wonder his footmen had stopped in shock.

He had not been exaggerating when he told her that every man at Prince Damien's dinner table would climb over each other to accept her offer. But Alexander would fight them off, with sword and pistol if need be. Meagan was *his.*

He leaned on his fists and drove into her, fast and hard. Their hips met, the table creaking, the remaining silver dishes rattling to the floor. He wanted to crawl inside her, to have her part of him forever.

I don't want this frenzy with you, he said silently, unable to form words at all now. *I want it to be slow and good and loving. I want to love you. I want it to be real.*

The wildness of it danced fire on the edge of his vision. He heard his own groans of pleasure, his voice hoarse and rasping. She screamed, her brown eyes wide. He should stop, he should be gentle. He'd promised her when he'd begged her to marry him that he would attend to her every need and fulfill her thoroughly, not give her this mindless sexing.

But he could not stop. Something else controlled his body, and he gave in to it. *Need her, want her.* Never stop.

His climax hit him. His muscles bunched, and his seed shot inside her, and she moaned with release, her hips lifting to meet his.

He dragged her to him and collapsed into a chair, holding her close. He pressed his face into her neck, not wanting to look at her. Meagan was slowly delving into the darkest parts of his mind and unearthing things he could not afford to have disturbed.

He felt her shift as she cuddled close and kissed his cheek, tracing the pattern of the tattoo with light fingers. "I love you," she whispered. She gave him another kiss, then rested her head on his shoulder. "I know it is the love spell making me tell you that, but it feels good to say it." She gave his biceps a little squeeze, her voice bearing a smile. "I love you, Alexander."

At her low words, another frenzy hit him. Alexander set her on her feet and dragged off his coat to put over her torn bodice, then scooped her into his arms and made his way to her bedchamber. There he stripped her and himself and made love to her in the deep featherbed until they both fell into dark slumber.

CHAPTER THIRTEEN

Alexander woke in the garden, naked, blood streaming from deep scratches on his chest. Nikolai and Dominic stood several paces from him, watching him warily.

This time the panic did not come, because he knew what was happening to him. "*The logosh is a part of you,*" Myn had said. "*You must embrace it or it will devour you.*"

He could feel the beast wanting to get out and not knowing how.

"Sir?" Nikolai said, a waver in his voice. "We should get you back inside. Her Grace might wake."

The last thing Alexander remembered was Meagan snuggling down beside him after their last wild bout of lovemaking. She'd murmured "good night," and rested her head on his shoulder, arm around his waist. Trusting.

"What did I do? Did I hurt her?"

"No, Your Grace," Nikolai said. "You came down from your wife's chamber and ran outside."

"What else?"

"You didn't have any clothes on, for one," Dominic added. The big man's face was grim. "You said strange words and you scraped at yourself as you ran. And your eyes . . ."

"What about my eyes?" he rasped.

"They—glowed," Nikolai said. "Your Grace. They got bluer and kind of wider."

"I see." Alexander tried to gather his usual control about him like a shielding mantle, but he could not quite master it.

Dominic nodded. "I saw it too."

Alexander exhaled, raising his head to the darkness. Clouds layered the sky, but he could feel the moon behind them glowing silver and bright.

"Who else saw?" he demanded, the cool tones of Alexander the Grand Duke returning.

"No one, sir," Dominic replied. "Everyone else had gone to bed. We followed you out."

"And the Grand Duchess?"

Nikolai shook his head. "I looked in on her, sir. She did not wake."

"Thank God for that." Alexander rubbed his hands over his arms, his blood cooling. "I want both of you to keep these incidents quiet, do you understand?"

"Of course, sir." Nikolai sounded shocked Alexander would even ask. Dominic gave a stoic nod.

"I know you are loyal," Alexander said. "But there are those who would exploit the knowledge to gain power over me or Nvengaria."

Both men nodded. They understood about spies and intrigue. From what Myn had told him, von Hohenzahl and a flunky had met in a tavern in Wapping to discuss Alexander, though they'd been maddeningly vague about why they wanted him. They'd said he was their "secret weapon" against Nvengaria, which made Alexander fear that von Hohenzahl already knew the Grand Duke was part logosh.

How can he know? Alexander wondered. He had no answer to that. Von Hohenzahl had even sent men to watch Alexander's house. The men were easy to spot and Alexander let them watch, instructing his own men to follow them. Von Hohenzahl was wasting his money.

More troubling was Anastasia's behavior. Myn had gone to her to translate the conversation he'd overheard. Myn had then reported it to Alexander, but Anastasia had not mentioned one word of it, and he was not certain why. She played her own games and was not always on Alexander's side.

"Where is Myn?" he asked abruptly. "I want to talk to him."

"Disappeared again, sir," Dominic answered. "I last saw him this morning, after you came back from getting married. No one's seen him since."

"Damn."

Nikolai gave a little cough. "Are you ready to go back, sir? I'll fetch water to wash you up."

"Yes." Alexander clenched his hands. "I will sleep in my chamber, not my wife's."

With regret, he thought of her bed, a warm nest with Meagan in it. She'd smell of her perfume and lovemaking, and he wanted to sink back into her warmth and lose himself. But the thought that his logosh side might emerge and hurt her bothered him.

"Let us be quiet about it. See that she does not wake. And when Myn returns, send him to me immediately. Even if I am asleep."

"Yes, sir," Nikolai said.

The two men flanked him as they walked back to the house, Alexander stepping inside with regret. It had felt so right to be out in the darkness. A small part of the garden that remembered its wildness called to him, urging him to remember his wildness, too. Myn had told him that the memory lapses occurred when the logosh in him tried to take over, while the Alexander part of him tried to regain control by blotting out the memory of shifting.

They moved through the silent house, Nikolai catching up a candelabra to light their way upstairs. Alexander found he didn't need the light. He could clearly see every molding, every garish gilding in his lavish hired house even without the flame from Nikolai's candles dancing on them.

Dominic returned to his duties of guarding the house and Nikolai escorted Alexander to the bath chamber and left him to soak.

Sitting up to his neck in the steaming water, Alexander recalled the first vision he'd had of Meagan, the two of them naked and wet and enjoying each other against one of the monstrous marble pillars. How wonderful it would be to open his eyes and see her sliding into the bath with him, her red hair curling with the steam, her smile wide and welcoming.

His erection began to lift. He'd never get enough of her, never. The love spell was killing him, and yet he never wanted it to leave. To lose her now would be one of the most difficult things he'd ever faced.

He heard a soft step and opened his eyes, but it was not Meagan. Myn stood on the other side of the steaming bath, his rough clothes a startling contrast to the very formal wear of Alexander's servants.

Myn said nothing, his blue eyes nearly glowing in the steam-filled room. Alexander hauled himself out of the bath and reached for his dressing gown.

"Myn, I want you to teach me. Teach me about being logosh. Teach me how not to hurt Alex and Meagan."

Myn regarded him silently for a moment or two, those eyes missing nothing. Then he gave the faintest nod. "Yes."

Meagan decided, in the morning, that something had to be done about the garden. She viewed it from her window as Susan laced her into another gown, this one a dark golden silk.

Like the house, the garden was ostentatious, attempting to imitate a huge formal French garden in one-tenth of the space. The result was short, tight walks of yew hedges, ridiculous topiary, and an actual maze in the middle of the garden with four turns in it.

"Would it not look more inviting with roses and a small lawn and one path and benches along the way?" Meagan said as Susan clasped a string of emeralds around her neck. "One could not have a garden party as it is now, because half the guests would be hidden behind shrubbery, the other half lost in the toy maze." She smiled. "I will have to consult His Grace, of course. I will discuss it with him at breakfast."

Although she already missed home, she looked forward to her first breakfast with Alexander. She'd speak to him about redoing the garden while he ate his toast and drank his coffee and looked over his newspaper. She could smile at him, sending him a secret reminder of the passion they'd shared the night before, while the oblivious servants refilled their cups and took away plates.

She understood now why ladies wanted to be married. The cozy sharing of a life with someone was much to be desired.

"His Grace breakfasted some time ago," Mrs. Caldwell said, entering the room. "He is now on his way to Carleton House."

"Oh." Meagan's domestic vision burst into dribbles of disappointment. "Why did no one wake me? It is only gone nine. I certainly could have risen to take breakfast with him."

"He instructed that you were not to be disturbed," Mrs. Caldwell said. "But if you desire to know when he will leave each morning, I have brought you his schedule for the week."

She handed Meagan a sheaf of papers covered with tiny writing. "Goodness," Meagan said, scanning the columns of dates, times, and places. "We shall never have a meal together at this rate."

"His Grace is quite busy," Mrs. Caldwell said, but with a note of sympathy. "If you like, I will instruct his secretary to compare his schedule with yours and overlap some time."

The cozy scenes of husband and wife enjoying each other's company faded and vanished. But Meagan was determined to have some of it. "We can at least begin our day with breakfast together. Please make sure I am awake and ready to meet him each morning."

"Very good, Your Grace." Mrs. Caldwell gave a decided nod, as though she approved of Meagan asserting her wishes. "Your own breakfast awaits you in the dining room, and I am afraid you have quite a lot of correspondence already. Mr. Edwards will go over it with you along with your appointments for the day."

Meagan exhaled, feeling the weight of being Grand Duchess descend on her. "I suppose we'd better get on with it, then. Lead the way."

She blushed as she entered the formal dining room, remembering how Alexander had sent a rain of silver to the floor as he'd lifted her to the table to make love to her. The servants must have known exactly what had transpired when they came in to clean up. She'd told

Alexander she loved him, but she wasn't sure what he'd made of that. Ignored her, she hoped.

The table held almost as much silver and porcelain this morning as it had last night, even though she was eating alone, and a light breakfast at that. An overflowing pile of folded cream-colored letters lay to the right of her place, and Mr. Edwards, with a plain cup of coffee before him, had already begun sorting them and making notations in a book.

Gaius, Marcus, and Brutus waited eagerly to serve her. As they had the night before, they pulled out her chair and offered her a napkin with a dramatic flourish.

She discovered that Mr. Edwards had already scheduled her to pay calls on the wives of other ambassadors this morning. A garden party and a dinner had already been set up in her honor this afternoon, and she'd attend both. Then a ride through Hyde Park in her new carriage—she could invite a friend to ride with her, preferably someone highborn such as Lady Featherstone or the Duchess of Cranshaw.

After Hyde Park, Meagan would make ready to attend supper at the French ambassador's house and meet Alexander there.

"I feel a bit sick to my stomach," Meagan said, setting down her cup of chocolate. "Perhaps I am coming on with a cold and should not leave the house today."

Mr. Edwards gave her a smile that hinted at a bit of kindness, and told her she would do just fine. "I will coach you how to greet each of the ladies and what to say to them—or I should say, what *not* to say to them. There is always the safe topic of the weather."

"The weather. Yes." Thank God for England's weather. House parties would end in disaster if not for the refuge of discussions about the weather.

"What about Alex?" Meagan asked as Mr. Edwards

went on opening correspondence and making notes. She'd seen nothing of the boy since he was led upstairs by his nanny yesterday, and she'd not heard a peep from the floor where he lived. In her experience, quietness in a boy of six was not usual.

Mr. Edwards gave her a blank look. "Alex?"

"Yes, Alex. His Grace's son and heir. Alexander does see him from time to time, does he not?"

Mr. Edwards's expression cleared. "Ah, you wish to see his young grace's schedule. I have it here." He rifled through his books and pulled out a sheet of paper. "Here we are."

"Alex has his own schedule?"

"His Grace wishes his son to have the most rigorous education possible, as young Alex will be Grand Duke one day."

Meagan ran her eye down the list of subjects Alex would be taught this morning: history, Latin, politics, French, geography, and English grammar.

"Good heavens."

At least he was allowed to leave the house on occasion, if only for lessons in riding and fencing. However, the entry "walk in Hyde Park" at eleven o'clock had been marked through.

"Because of the rain," Mr. Edwards explained as Meagan returned the paper.

The rain looked fairly light to Meagan, barely spattering the windows, but the day was gray and heavy and the rain could turn to torrents. "It seems much for a boy of six. And I noticed no entries for seeing his father."

"His Grace makes time to talk with his son several times a week and check his progress," Mr. Edwards said. "His Grace is . . ."

"An important man. Yes, so many people have told me."

Meagan then and there determined to have a talk with Alexander about young Alex. Alexander would no doubt raise his brows in cool surprise that she thought he was anything but an exemplary father, but she knew Alexander loved his son. She saw it in his eyes. Why, then, did he ignore him so much?

She took a bite of buttered toast. "I note there is no entry for chatting with his stepmother, either."

"Ah, no, I see there is not. I will consult the Grand Duke about scheduling you an appointment if you wish."

"No need. I will consult the Grand Duke myself."

Mr. Edwards gave her a hesitant look. "His Grace is rather busy."

"Make me an appointment with him, then," Meagan said, exasperated. She threw down the toast. "I believe I am finished with breakfast."

"Very good, Your Grace. Perhaps, then, you will start on your correspondence."

He picked up a stack of at least a hundred letters and piled them high in front of Meagan's plate. Her eyes rounded, her mouth went dry, and her sturdy resolution to keep her new duties from controlling her began to crumble.

Breathing a tiny sigh, she put out her hand and picked up the first one.

"You are an interesting man, Herr Alexander. I have been looking forward to this meeting."

Otto von Hohenzahl clasped Alexander's hand, narrow rings on each of his fingers. His handshake was firm, his eyes clear blue and ingenuous. Von Hohenzahl was a tall man with graying hair, a trim physique, and a round red face. He smelled of cheroot and beneath that a touch of acrid perfume.

Decadent, Alexander thought. A hedonist who likes his

pleasures—wine, food, cheroots, women. Alexander also added *intelligent* as he sensed von Hohenzahl sizing him up in return.

"I must congratulate you on your nuptials," von Hohenzahl said, releasing Alexander's hand and smiling a sly smile. "So surprising it was, to learn that the Grand Duke had taken a young English miss with no title or fortune as his bride."

Alexander shrugged. "I fell in love."

"*Mein freund*," von Hohenzahl laughed, "is that any reason to *marry* a woman?"

"I believe it is." Alexander let his voice cool. Von Hohenzahl shot him a startled look, then smoothly let his laughter die.

"Ah, well, it is your second marriage. In a second marriage a man can be indulgent if he has used his first marriage well. You have a son and heir; why not enjoy yourself?"

"Yes." Alexander did not want to sit in the proffered chair in von Hohenzahl's surprisingly tasteful sitting room. The Austrian had taken a townhouse in Curzon Street furnished for the Season, as he'd explained when Alexander arrived.

There was nothing wrong with the house or the sitting room, which was decorated in hues of yellow, but Alexander's senses, heightened since his logosh side had begun pushing its way to the fore, smelled something unsavory behind the fresh paint and the slight dust in the carpet. He could not place it, but he did not like it, and he decided to be very, very careful.

"I have a busy afternoon ahead," he said. "Many appointments that will not wait."

"A pity," von Hohenzahl answered. "I would have liked to have a long conversation. But no matter. We will proceed more quickly if we switch into a language we both know?" He said the last in Nvengarian.

Alexander's senses came even more alert. "Not many Austrians know Nvengarian."

"Except the fair Lady Anastasia, eh? I envy you her, my friend. But I am puzzled—you say you married for love, and yet Lady Anastasia, she too you love, if rumor is correct?" He smiled suddenly. "Ah, but you Nvengarians, you never let that stop you. You love a wife, you love a mistress, why not have them both? And if the two ladies like each other—well, all the better."

A growl rose in Alexander's throat. The man was correct that Nvengarians did not have the same restrictions on their beds that the English put on theirs, but what a Nvengarian did with his paramours or his wife was his own business. To make rude hints or to mock him or his ladies was grounds for a duel, usually a deadly one involving knives or swords. No clean twenty paces and one shot each. Duels in Nvengaria were fast, bloody, and permanent.

Von Hohenzahl seated himself and removed a cheroot from a box on an octagonal table. "I admit to curiosity about the practice. While one is busy with the first lady, what does the other do? Or do you have one on each side? Or perhaps the ladies entertain each other while you are in audience?"

For an instant, Alexander wanted nothing more than to take his knife and decorate von Hohenzahl's elegant ivory waistcoat in his own blood. Alexander's fingers moved to his pocket where a fine steel knife with an ornamented blade rested, a pretty thing but deadly. He took a few steps toward the man, red flickering on the edges of his vision.

He imagined himself very clearly cutting deep creases

in the man's chest, the glee he'd feel doing it, the taste of the man's blood on his fingers.

It was so real that he heard von Hohenzahl's screams and his own animal-like snarls. Then the vision fell away, and he was standing in the middle of the carpet, his hands in tight fists, the only sounds in the room the clock ticking on the mantel and a slight sucking sound as von Hohenzahl tipped a candle toward himself to light his cheroot.

Alexander deliberately moved back, legs stiff and shaking, to the nearest sofa and made himself sit down. Von Hohenzahl glanced at him through a cloud of smoke, and Alexander swore he saw a gleam of satisfaction in the man's eyes.

Von Hohenzahl had been goading him, wanting Alexander to lose control. The realization that von Hohenzahl knew he was logosh jolted more anger through him. Someone had betrayed him—no one knew what he was except Myn, Nikolai, and Dominic.

"I have many appointments," Alexander said in the coldest tone he could muster. "What do you want to offer me?"

"A chance to stop Metternich," von Hohenzahl said. "He longs to add Nvengaria to Austrian domains, as you know. After all, Austria has every bit of land leading up to your border under its protection, and Prince Metternich ever asks the question, why do you resist?"

"Because our independence is precious to us," Alexander answered at once. "We will fight to the last man for it—preferably *his* last man, which he will discover if he tries to breach our mountain passes."

"Precisely what I have told him." Von Hohenzahl grinned and sucked on the cheroot. "But you see, my friend, I have found a way into Nvengaria. Your passes are small and defensible, that is true, but with cunning, they can be breached."

"What way?" Alexander asked in a hard voice.

"Now, that all depends on you. I will promise you that I have not shared my research and speculations with Metternich. He has a way of taking things useful to him and discarding the person who helped him. I tire of being overlooked."

"So you are willing to sell the information to me? Because I will reward you better?"

"You are blunt, Your Grace."

"My wife has remarked upon the same thing. I truly am busy and wish you would reach the point."

"*Natürlich.*" Von Hohenzahl smiled. "I am a businessman and would like to make a profit, but I am not a traitor to my own country. I would do nothing against the Austrian empire. On the other hand, I feel no obligation to give them information so that Metternich can control still more territory. Nvengaria is not a threat."

"No," Alexander agreed. Nvengarians did not want to expand. They were happy where they were, and Alexander's and Damien's jobs were to keep the rest of the world out.

"I will share the information with you, as a friend, so that you can take precautions," von Hohenzahl said. "That is what friends do, you know, help each other."

Alexander felt a twinge of disgust. "What are you asking of me? Money?"

"No, no, Your Grace, do not be so boorish. That is for the English, so uncultured. Have you tasted their wine? It is wretched. And their women's dress—ach, my wife would faint at such tawdriness. I am happy she chose to stay in Vienna where things are civilized."

"You have not answered my question."

"I beg your pardon; I did not mean to be evasive." Von Hohenzahl sat on the edge of his chair, letting the cheroot dangle from his fingers. "What I want in return for this information that could spell Nvengaria's end—is you."

CHAPTER FOURTEEN

Alexander stilled. Von Hohenzahl watched him like a cat regarding a mouse hole.

"In what sense?" Alexander asked, voice calm.

"What are you willing to give up for me? Your life? Your service? Your role as Grand Duke?"

Alexander got to his feet. "You know nothing," he growled. "You are a grasping little man with nothing to give me. I would never pledge myself to the likes of you."

Von Hohenzahl rose. "You would. You are key to Nvengaria, Your Grace. Not Prince Damien with his prophecy and his long-lost princess. The kingdom would have fallen apart under the old Imperial Prince if not for you. I know that. I watched. You made sure Damien had a kingdom to return to, and what did he do for you?" He smirked. "Tossed you out to watch over the boorish English as far across Europe as he could throw you. All your devotion and all your work, and your reward is exile. We are much alike, you and I."

Alexander subjected von Hohenzahl to his chill Grand Duke stare. "I have nothing in common with you. You are nothing but a petty official in Metternich's cabinet."

Von Hohenzahl chuckled, not offended. "While you are the second most powerful man in Nvengaria. And yet, my friend, you need me, if you want to be restored."

"I will not move against Prince Damien. He rules by right, and if I must remain behind the scenes I will do it. I want *Nvengaria* to prosper, not my own glory. That is why you and I have nothing in common." Alexander made a show of pulling his watch from his pocket and studying it. "As you clearly have nothing to offer me, I will depart. My next appointment is an important one."

Von Hohenzahl lost his smile and his eyes gleamed in a way Alexander did not like. "Pledge yourself to me, Your Grace. It will be easier for you if you come to me willingly now. Later, it will not be so easy."

Alexander speared him with a look. "If you threaten me, I ensure you will regret it."

"I make no threats, Your Grace. I only state the truth. The danger will be less if you follow me, not only to yourself, but to your pretty new wife. And your son. He is merely six years old, I believe. So very young to be in danger."

The need for blood rose inside Alexander again. Every Nvengarian had blood lust, a trait never stamped out in the eight hundred years since his people lived in mountain tribes. He'd felt his native stirrings before, but this was different. He wanted to give in to the logosh inside him, a beast that would take control and rip von Hohenzahl apart before he could so much as scream.

Alexander saw in his mind exactly how he could do it, and knew he'd have the strength.

But Alexander the Grand Duke had been in charge longer than the logosh. He fought to cool himself, knowing that the game of politics he played was much more important than his need to hurt von Hohenzahl. Von Hohenzahl was an amateur in the game, that much was certain. Alexander would take care of him.

He gathered his control about himself once more, using the meditation techniques Myn had taught him. "Twice since my arrival, you have tried to provoke me to rage," he said to von Hohenzahl. "I must wonder why."

"That you will discover, in time," the Austrian answered. "You will remember this conversation and regret that you did not take my offer."

"I spit on your offer," Alexander said and strode out of the room.

Outside, Alexander summoned his own bodyguard, a man called Julius, to ride with him in the carriage. "Watch von Hohenzahl," Alexander instructed. "I want a report on where he goes, whom he speaks to, what he does. And if I tell you to question him, employ whatever method you think would be useful. Hurt no others, but if you need to torture him a bit, I will not mind."

Julius, a huge man with glittering blue eyes and a friendly grin, nodded. "Yes, Your Grace."

Alexander's heart pounded as he reviewed the interview with von Hohenzahl. He thought of Meagan and the pleasing way she'd snuggled against him in bed last night. He pictured some Austrian thug with his hands around her slender throat, and rage twisted through him.

"Tell Dominic to put as many men to guard the Grand Duchess and my son as it takes," he said. "No one is to approach them without my clearance. No one. Do you understand?"

Julius looked concerned, but asked no questions, as usual. "Yes, Your Grace."

Alexander made himself sit back and look out the win-

dow at the passing sights of Mayfair. He wished he had
the power to scry in stones like the mages did in Nvengaria, so he could watch Meagan no matter where she
was. As much as he hated the thought, he needed to stay
away from her. That damn love spell was too distracting,
and who knew how he'd hurt her if he shifted to logosh
in her presence. But at the same time he disliked not
knowing exactly where she was and what she was doing
at that precise moment.

"Fishing?" Young Alex's tutor stared at Alex's schedule
as though the word had somehow crept onto it without
his notice. "The Grand Duke said nothing about fishing,
Your Grace."

The tutor, a youngish man with thin limbs and a sallow complexion, was Nvengarian but spoke English expertly and looked as though he'd never lifted his nose
from a book in his life. He'd gaped in astonishment to
see the new Grand Duchess sashay into the schoolroom
on the third floor late that afternoon and begin asking
about Alex's curriculum.

"His Grace's ideas on education are a bit lacking,"
Meagan said. She gave Alex a sly wink, and the boy
looked back at her, wide-eyed.

The tutor gasped. "His Grace—lacking?"

Meagan studied the schedule she held in her hand.
"Latin on such a perfect fishing day should be outlawed.
You have canceled his ride in the park, and Alex needs
some sort of fresh air. Fishing is perfect."

"But it is raining," the tutor pointed out, looking triumphant. Meagan could hardly dispute the rain.

"It has lightened, and the fish will be biting. At home
in Oxfordshire, my father and I would have had our
poles out and dangling over the river long before this.
Alex's father is busy, so I will take him."

"Take him?" the tutor exclaimed. "You?"

Alex followed their speeches, his head going back and forth as each spoke.

"Yes, of course, me," Meagan retorted. "I am his step-mama. I can certainly take my own stepson to Hyde Park for a bit of fishing."

"Hyde Park? His Grace will never allow it. Not as far as Hyde Park."

"It is not all that far, and we will go in the carriage," Meagan said. "He was to have riding lessons in Hyde Park in any case."

The tutor played his trump card. "His Grace will be very angry."

Alex winced, hope dying on his face.

Meagan tried to picture Alexander shouting at her for presuming to interrupt his son's lessons, but when she thought of Alexander, all she could envision was him crushing kisses to her lips after she'd poured wine all over him and lifting her to the table and making wild love to her.

The dratted love spell would not let her remember anything but the way his eyes went dark when she raised on tiptoes to kiss him, the gentleness of his touch when they lay down to sleep. She could not think of him without wanting to touch him, to feel his strength under her fingers, to taste his lips on hers.

It was so very, very distracting. She'd tried to pay Black Annie a surprise visit earlier today, much to her servants' distress because the journey to the Strand was not on her schedule. The visit had proved fruitless, Black Annie having conveniently stepped out just before Meagan arrived. The cherubic maid said she'd no idea when Black Annie would return, and Meagan had gone away to keep her other appointments.

Meagan had then spent hours undergoing the scrutiny

of other ambassadors' wives at the Duchess of Cranshaw's garden party. Except for the fact that Meagan's stepmother had once been married to a baronet and that her best friend was now Princess Penelope of Nvengaria, Meagan had nothing in common with them, and they made certain she knew it.

Only the Duchess of Cranshaw's support and the fact that Meagan held the title of Grand Duchess kept her from rushing home in fury and distress. But she was a diplomat's wife now, which meant she could not say what she thought and walk away in a huff. A diplomat's wife had to be, well, diplomatic. She supposed she'd learn to take their rebuffs, which were couched in the politest possible terms. Insufferable women.

Many of them regarded faraway, tiny Nvengaria as insignificant, which made her very angry on Alexander's behalf. Perhaps Nvengaria was not as large as France, but its people had a huge, indomitable spirit. She'd told the Parisian ambassador's wife so, earning herself a long stare through a lorgnette.

She'd returned to Alexander's ostentatious house, angry at it for mocking her simple upbringing in a happy family. She'd changed into a walking dress and marched to the third floor, demanding Nikolai to show her the way to the nursery.

Now she lifted her chin and faced down the tutor. "I will explain to His Grace. You will not be blamed."

"You do not know His Grace," he muttered.

Meagan ignored him. "Alex, would you like to go fishing with me?"

Alex slammed his Latin grammar shut and sprang from his seat. "Yes!"

Meagan held out her hand. She was surprised at the rush of feeling she had when he wrapped his small fingers around hers. She grinned and squeezed his hand. "Then let us go find some fishing poles."

She did not, in fact, take him all the way to Hyde Park. She decided, after one look at the horde of journalists gathered outside the house, that they needed to be more private, so she led Alex to the park in the center of Berkeley Square.

The park was a huge oval that ran the length of fifteen or more houses. Inside its wrought-iron fence were trees and greens and walks for the residents of the square, who alone possessed keys.

Dominic and his men surrounded them as Meagan and Alex walked across the busy square. The journalists struggled to keep up, even more passersby joined to see what was happening, and quite a large crowd followed them to the gates of the park.

Once inside, Meagan and Alex had a small respite, except for the Berkeley Square residents who'd decided to see what they were up to. The journalists hung over the gates, taking down every move the eccentric new Grand Duchess of Nvengaria made, and passersby climbed up next to the journalists, avidly curious.

"Why have we come here?" Alex asked. "There are no lakes or rivers."

"No." Meagan stopped on the path. "But there are puddles." She pointed to a wide, flat sheet of water, made by this morning's torrential rain. "A perfect place to learn."

Alex eyed it doubtfully. "Will there be any fish?"

"One never knows," Meagan said. "Here, I will show you how to fix your hook."

Alex was an excellent pupil. He had never fished before, he said solemnly, though he had read about it. She took up a brand new pole that Nikolai had been hastily dispatched to obtain and showed Alex how to string the pole and how to put a wriggling worm on the hook. Then she showed him how to stand right at the edge of the water and flick his wrist gently to lower his hook to entice the fish.

Alex, his black hair wet with rain, copied her movements precisely. He was like Alexander, she realized. Alexander liked to show perfection to the world, no flaw or chink in the wall surrounding him. The love spell had surmounted that wall, letting Meagan alone see the real man. Others feared him only because they could not see his heart.

Or perhaps, she thought with a sigh, the love spell had rendered her overly sentimental.

The journalists called questions from the fence. Some of them shouted rather questionable remarks about a lady holding a long pole, which thankfully Alex did not understand. Dominic, however, glowered at them and told them what he would do to them if they didn't take themselves off. Since Englishmen of the lower classes were not easily cowed, they shouted right back at him, hinting at what they did to foreigners what thought they were better than them.

Oh lud, Meagan thought, pretending to focus on the fishing. Tomorrow the *Times* could very well read, *Her Grace the Grand Duchess of Nvengaria Incites a Riot in Berkeley Square Over the Question of How Well She Grips a Pole.*

The shouting died away and things fell eerily silent. Meagan knew before she looked up, before she heard his boots crunching gravel on the path, exactly who approached.

Alexander walked toward them in a dark blue greatcoat, his head hatless, as was custom for Nvengarians, black hair sparkling with droplets of rain. He did not smile at her and his blue eyes were as watchful as ever.

Alex raised his head and saw his father. "Hallo, Papa."

He waved as Alexander neared them. "Stepmama is teaching me to fish."

Alexander stopped, taking in Meagan, the puddle, the fishing poles, and the lines disappearing into the water. Meagan expected his eyes to grow chill, for him to instruct Dominic to escort his wife and son back to the house at once.

He watched for a long time, the breeze stirring his dark hair and the tails of his long coat. His black boots were finely polished, the tops splashed with mud from his walk across the green.

When he spoke to Alex, his voice was neutral, almost gentle. "Have you caught anything?"

"Not yet," Alex answered, his gaze on the water. "But you must give them time, Stepmama says. She says we're bound to catch something sooner or later."

"Does she?" Alexander stepped behind Alex and looked critically at the pole. "You hold it well. A light touch, that is good."

"Stepmama taught me," Alex said.

Alexander flicked his gaze to Meagan, his eyes unreadable, then reached down and made a small adjustment to the pole with his black-gloved hand. "I did much fishing when I was a boy. Damien and I used to sneak away from our tutors to a lake in the woods."

"Truly?" Alex exclaimed in delight.

"Only we knew where the lake was, or so we believed. I imagine our bodyguards followed us at a discreet distance."

"Did your papa go fishing with you?" Alex asked.

Alexander waited a beat too long to answer. "He was very busy."

"Like you," Alex said. "You are a very important man."

Alexander released the pole, but he remained staring at it, not looking at Alex or Meagan. Suddenly, he turned around and gestured for Dominic. Dominic trotted over. "Your Grace?"

"Send for a fishing pole for me."

Dominic blinked. "Your Grace?"

"A fishing pole. Swiftly, Dominic."

Dominic turned and galloped toward another body-guard, bellowing in Nvengarian. The others took up the cry, calling to Alexander's servants who waited outside the fence, who in turn bellowed to the servants nearer the house.

A pole was brought while the three waited, Alexander silent, Meagan anxious, Alex oblivious. Alexander looked over the pole Dominic handed him, pronounced it fine, stripped off his gloves, and baited it himself.

They fished quietly, the three of them at the edge of the puddle, while the bodyguards, the journalists, the passersby, the nannies and children in the park, and the curious residents of Berkeley Square watched the eccen-tric Grand Duke and his family.

They remained there until the wind turned cold and Alexander announced that they should go inside. Mea-gan nodded, her hands already numb, and returned her pole to Dominic, who'd come to collect them.

Alexander lifted young Alex to his shoulder, strangely subdued as they walked along the path and through the gates.

The crowd parted before them like water from the bows of a ship as they exited the park. Dominic and the others held back the tide, and they walked across the square and back into the echoing foyer of Maysfield House.

Alexander set Alex down and steered him toward the stairs. "When you want to fish again, I will arrange an expedition to a lake in the country, where you will find many fish."

Alex smiled happily. "Will you come too, Papa? And teach me?"

"We will all go. I will arrange it."

Alex whooped and turned in a circle. He caught the hand of one of the footmen, who pulled the boy playfully up the stairs.

"If you attend to your lessons," Alexander said, as though remembering to be an admonishing father.

"Yes, Papa." Alex beamed at him with an angelic expression, then told the footman he'd race him up the stairs. The footman obliged, slowing his steps so that Alex could patter ahead.

Alexander rested one arm on the railing and watched his son, his expression somber. That, coupled with his lack of annoyance at Meagan for taking Alex out of his schoolroom, worried her.

"Alexander?"

He swung to her, eyes glittering, and the love spell flared. He gripped her shoulders and kissed her, pressing her against the newel post. The kiss was possessive, his fingers biting into her flesh.

With effort, he wrenched himself away from her, and they stared at each other, breathing hard.

"You must ready yourself for the ambassador's supper ball," he said.

"Oh, yes." She bit her lip, thinking of the French ambassador's wife, in no hurry to meet the woman again. "I suppose I must. If I am not well dressed, the ceiling might fall in."

Alexander smiled, true mirth flickering in his eyes. Then the mirth died abruptly, and he slid his fingers across her cheek. "Come upstairs with me," he said in a low voice. "I need you."

Meagan closed her eyes. She ought to point out that

they had little time and should not be late to the ambassador's ball, but she opened her eyes and nodded.

Alexander took her hand and ran lightly with her up the stairs then down the corridor to his bedchamber, which, if anything, was larger and more sumptuous than hers. He abruptly told Nikolai to find something else to do, then he undressed her and took her twice in his deep featherbed, his strong body pinning her fast.

He made love silently, frantically, as though he could not get enough of her, then held her close, breathing like a man who'd swum far and fast against a very strong current.

"I am still waiting for you to shout at me." Meagan straightened her velvet cloak and looked across the carriage at her husband as they bumped their way through crowded Mayfair streets to Grosvenor Square.

He turned from the window, which he could not possibly see out of because the glass reflected the bright carriage lamps inside.

"Shout?" he inquired in his low voice. "Why should I shout at you?"

"For the fishing. For having the gall to rush into Alex's nursery and muck about. For changing the precious schedule."

He turned to the window again. "I am not unhappy that you wanted to see Alex. Sephronia never did."

Meagan's heart gave a quick beat. "Did she not?"

"She never spoke to Alex. I had not expected you would wish to, either."

"Good lord, why ever not?" she asked indignantly. "He was her son. And so like you." She stopped when he shot her an ironic glance. "I beg your pardon. I suppose I should not speak ill of her."

Alexander rested his hands on his thighs, broad fingers in black gloves. "Sephronia loved Alex, in her own way. She was proud of him, but she did not enjoy children."

"Not even her own? I beg your pardon again, but I cannot fathom that she not only did not want to be with him, why she did not want to be with *you*." She held up her hand. "I know, I am not Nvengarian and do not understand, but she should not have done it."

His expression did not change. "It was a political marriage and one of mutual convenience. Sephronia did her duty."

He spoke matter-of-factly, but how had it been for him to know his wife preferred to find pleasure elsewhere, showing so clearly she did not love him? Likely he'd calmly gone about his business and said nothing, but how had it *felt*?

"How could she not be happy to stay with you night after night?" Meagan blurted. "Was she blind?"

He smiled faintly, his row of medals glinting beneath his greatcoat. "You flatter me."

"I have eyes, Alexander. I vow, you are the handsomest man I've ever seen, and that includes his magnificent Highness, Prince Damien of Nvengaria. All Nvengarians are handsome." She pressed one hand to her bosom, where she'd hoped the décolletage of her gown would cover her freckles, but it was not to be. "But you, Alexander—you quite take my breath away."

He was silent a moment. "I wish you could mean that."

"I do mean it. I've just said."

One hand on his thigh curled into a fist. "When the love spell is gone, perhaps you will not."

"The love spell cannot change what you look like, silly. I believed you handsome months ago when I saw your portrait in the newspapers. Grand Duke Alexander of Nvengaria, ambassador from the court of Prince Damien. I could not believe any man could be quite so handsome—I thought perhaps the newspaper drawings were exaggerated. Of course, at the time, I was quite angry with you for trying to assassinate Damien last summer, but I am no longer. *That* I blame on the love spell."

She loved the way his mouth lifted in one corner, the promise of laughter held back. "Damien and I have—how do you English say?—repaired our fences."

"Mended your fences. Penelope says so in her letters. I will believe it better when I see you and Damien face-to-face."

"I think I will be so pleased to be home in Nvengaria that I might embrace him."

"Let us not expect miracles." She shivered, remembering how he'd pinned her hands above her head in his bed not an hour ago, murmuring Nvengarian phrases she still did not understand. "They call you the Mad, Bad Duke, you know. No one is ever sure what you will do next."

His brows drew together. "That is an English joke of some kind, is it not? The Mad, Bad Duke."

"I suppose it is a joke. It was said of Lord Byron that he was mad, bad, and dangerous to know. Lady Carolyn Lamb said that about him—she behaved quite scandalously, you know. I suppose whoever started that name is implying you are dangerous." She drew a breath. "Which is true."

His eyes flickered. "I met Byron—he traveled briefly to Nvengaria before he went to Greece. I thought him portly and full of himself."

Meagan suppressed a giggle. "Apparently, he was quite the ladies' man. All the women chased him."

Alexander looked skeptical. "They read his poetry,

perhaps, and wove romantic stories about the man who wrote it. I also heard he preferred young men."

"I have no idea. Papa would never let me read Lord Byron's poems." She shot him an impish grin. "But I did anyway, under the covers at night. Papa said they were lewd."

"She walks in beauty, like the night," Alexander said softly.

Meagan stopped. The words, spoken in his low, silken voice, caught at her heart. "What did you say?"

"It is a poem of his. Very apt, I think." The darkness in his eyes held her. The love spell chose that moment to remind her of how his tongue had felt when he licked her between her breasts in his bed.

His gaze skimmed the silk gown that bared her shoulders and the soft mound of her bosom, and the diamonds that rested against her white skin. Alexander leaned forward and drew his gloved fingers along her neck, caressing the line of freckles.

"Alexander," she said longingly.

The carriage slowed, then jerked to a halt.

"Ah," Alexander said, disappointment in his voice, "we are here."

CHAPTER FIFTEEN

An hour later, Alexander pretended to listen to a Prussian count complain about everything English and let his thoughts be pulled to Meagan.

He knew, though she stood all the way across the vast room and not in his direct line of sight, that she'd raised a wineglass to her lips and smiled over it, that her apricot-colored gown clung to her shoulders and breasts like a stream of water, that her warm red hair swept upward to reveal her long, kissable neck, with the faint smattering of freckles that embarrassed her.

He wanted to taste them again, to run his tongue over the uneven line of line of faint dots, the most beautiful thing he'd ever seen.

How did I live before I knew this woman?

He ought to stay away from her. Encounters like the one this afternoon had their merits—he'd made love to her quickly, and then she'd hurried from the room, throwing a smile over her shoulder as she'd gone. If he did not linger too long with her, perhaps everything would be all right. But he wanted to bury himself in her and not come out. When he was with her, love spell or no, he was complete. In his entire life, he had never felt so whole.

He wanted to be next to her now, his arm around her, letting every man in the room know she was under his protection.

He half turned to watch just as three gentlemen joined the small group of ladies to whom she chatted, obviously demanding introduction. His blood burned. He'd known it would happen, that once Meagan's beauty was revealed to the gentlemen of the *ton*, they'd be smitten. She had not taken very seriously his discussion that she would be approached by men who wanted a paramour and that she had to be careful whom she chose.

"Ah," the Prussian ambassador said, interrupting him. "There is Lady Anastasia Dimitri. You would never find such beauty in an English woman. The pure Germanic strain is best, I have always thought."

Alexander looked across the ballroom to where Anastasia had entered on the arm of the French ambassador. She spoke perfect French and, by the look of things, had entranced the ambassador.

"Excuse me," he said and began moving across the room to her. Heads turned as he went, people anticipating a scandal and readying themselves to enjoy it.

Alexander stepped in front of Anastasia and bowed. "My lady." He took her hand and pressed a kiss to it, then nodded to the ambassador. The Frenchman inclined his head with poor grace.

"There is a waltz beginning," Alexander said, "and none dance it better than Lady Anastasia Dimitri."

The French ambassador understood the message and

stiffly handed Anastasia over. He moved off to look after his other guests, and Alexander took Anastasia to the middle of the floor and pulled her into a waltz.

"Alexander." Anastasia laughed as they began to whirl. She continued in Nvengarian. "You have just fed the *ton* delicious scandal. Taking your mistress out for a waltz not only in front of your wife but before you have danced with her. They will feed on it for some time."

"Good. I do not need them chattering about my real purpose."

"Your wife might disagree." She shot a look at Meagan, who followed Alexander's movements on the floor with a rather wistful expression on her face.

"I have explained things to Meagan, and she understands. She is intelligent."

Her brows arched. "High praise from a man who does not suffer fools gladly."

"My wife is no fool." He felt a surge of pride, which was not lost on Anastasia. But though she had a teasing twinkle in her eye, he sensed her watching him carefully, thoughts whirling behind the words she spoke. "But then, neither are you. Please explain to me why you did not come to me with the conversation Myn overheard and asked you of."

He felt her miss a step of the rhythm. "Myn obviously told you. I thought you did not need to hear it from me."

"I pay you, Anastasia, precisely to learn about conversations like the one von Hohenzahl had in a tavern in Wapping. Myn needed you to translate the Viennese dialect, which I do not know. I waited for you to speak to me of it, and you never did. You have avoided me for weeks."

"Because I did not think it important." Her eyes were worried.

"I think it vastly important, and so do you. Smile at me, people are watching."

Her face was strained, but she forced her lips into a smile.

"That is better," he said.

He found this role so much easier to play, the Grand Duke unraveling intrigues surrounding Nvengaria, rather than the man under a love spell wondering what had happened to him. "Now tell me what game you are playing or I will waltz you out to the terrace and throw you over the balustrade."

Anastasia's bosom rose with her breath. She knew he was capable of carrying out the threat. "Good lord, Alexander, he called you his secret weapon against Nvengaria. I needed time to think on that, to discover whether you were in league with von Hohenzahl to take your revenge on Damien. You met with von Hohenzahl today, I know." Her smile hardened. "If you have any intention of betraying Nvengaria, I will stop you even if I have to kill you. And you know I will do *that*."

"I'd expect no less of you. I've already told von Hohenzahl to go to the devil. If you believe I would do one thing to jeopardize Nvengaria, you do not know me. I would remove Damien only if I thought it was best for Nvengaria. Neither you nor von Hohenzahl understand my motives."

"Can you blame me? No one understands you, Alexander." She spoke in exasperation and also fear.

He smiled. "Meagan does."

Anastasia stared at him, then her gaze softened. "You truly care for her."

He shrugged. "It is the love spell. Which is why I do not waltz with her. If I did, I would take her off and ravish her. Best that I keep the length of the room between us."

Anastasia glanced at Meagan again. "She certainly looks at you with affection. She is a sweet girl, Alexander. Do not hurt her, I beg you."

"I have no intention of hurting her."

She gave him a sharp look. "If you are toying with her, using her to further your own schemes, I will never forgive you. She isn't one of us, and she does not understand our world."

"I do not want her to understand it." Alexander swung Anastasia in the waltz so he could keep his gaze trained on Meagan. His wife chatted easily with the gentlemen around her, and his blood heated with jealousy. "I want her as she is, innocent and trusting."

"Then she will never last if you take her to Nvengaria."

"You were innocent and trusting in Nvengaria," Alexander said. "You never lost your innocent wonder, I remember. Not until Dimitri died."

Her eyes clouded. "I do not want to speak of Dimitri. Let us return to von Hohenzahl. What do you intend to do?"

He sensed the grief in her as usual when her husband was mentioned, but he sensed something new too, a sharp worry he hadn't seen before.

"I want you to help me against von Hohenzahl," he said. "Pretend to be a loyal Austrian, help me make certain he is nothing more than a nuisance."

She made a moue of distaste. "He is unsavory, and he has made it clear that he wants me. I have done things I am ashamed of to gain information, but von Hohenzahl disgusts me."

"Even so, he has made threats against Meagan and Alex, and I want him rendered impotent."

Anastasia gave a short laugh. "Interesting choice of words, Alexander. I—"

She broke off, her face draining of color as her gaze fixed on something behind him. Alexander turned in the dance, but he saw nothing behind them but the long row of windows leading out to a terrace and ladies and gentlemen of the *ton* standing nearby.

"What is it?" he asked.

"Did you set him on me? He has been following me everywhere." She glared, her brown eyes shining with anger.

"I cannot answer if I do not know who you mean."

She snapped her hands from him, breaking the dance. "Myn, your pet logosh. What does he want from me? Oh, I cannot stay."

She whirled, diamonds flashing in her hair, and fled the ballroom, leaving Alexander standing alone in the middle of the floor in front of the entertained *ton*. Alexander growled under his breath, then growled again when he saw Meagan hurry out of the room after Anastasia.

Scurrilous gossip would make much of this. Hiding a sigh, he strode after them.

Dominic, like the good bodyguard he was, had followed Meagan, and Alexander followed the man's bulk to a small sitting room at the end of a hall.

Inside, Anastasia sat on a sofa, her arms drawn about her body, rocking and shaking. Meagan hovered over her worriedly, her handkerchief held out in offering. Alexander closed the door against the interested stares of people who'd crowded the hall behind him.

"What do you think you are doing?" he began.

Anastasia looked up and shrieked. Meagan too gasped, and Alexander swung around to see Myn calmly stepping through a window in his logosh form. Dominic tensed but made no move.

Myn's demon form shrank and melded into that of a wolf, huge and gray, his eyes still logosh blue. He padded to Alexander and rose to become human again in a hum of magic. He wore nothing on his large body, which in no way seemed to worry him.

Meagan's mouth hung open, but Anastasia regarded Myn in near terror.

Alexander felt the magic in himself respond, his body wanting to change. He fought it. Now was not the time, not here in an anteroom in the French ambassador's house.

"Has something happened?" he asked the logosh.

"The one you call von Hohenzahl awaits you," Myn said in Nvengarian. "He has ordered men to capture your wife or you, he said he did not care which. They wait in the streets between here and your own house."

Dominic growled. "Let me take them, Your Grace. I and my men will rout them." He smiled a feral grin. "It will be a pleasure."

Nvengarians loved a good fight. Alexander shook his head. "If you round up these men, von Hohenzahl will simply hire more. I will confront him and cut off the problem at the head."

Dominic's eyes glinted. "Even better, sir."

"What is he saying?" Meagan asked, brown eyes round. "Alexander, I don't understand."

"Intrigue," he answered her in English. "Nvengarian and Austrian intrigue. Dominic will take you home and he and his men will stay with you, while I visit von Hohenzahl. Anastasia, I want you with me. I will leave you at your hotel."

Anastasia's eyes were haunted, but she forced a smile. "If you run off with your mistress while your wife goes home alone, people will talk."

"Good. While their minds are filled with tittle-tattle, we can go about our business undisturbed." In Nvengarian he said, "Myn, I need you too."

Meagan rose swiftly and put her hand on Alexander's arm. "You are going to do something dangerous, aren't you?"

"More dangerous to von Hohenzahl, I assure you."

Her fingers closed over him, the love spell sliding around them both. Damn von Hohenzahl. If not for him, Alexander could ride home with Meagan alone and lift her into his arms in the carriage. He'd experiment with how much they could do in a moving conveyance in the middle of Mayfair.

He slid his arm around Meagan's waist and pulled her close, leaning down to kiss her. Never mind the other three staring at them, Dominic in glee, Anastasia wistfully, Myn neutral. He wanted Meagan and her taste and her scent, damn intrigue and damn all Austrians who couldn't stick to gossiping in coffeehouses in Vienna.

The door swung open behind him, the draft breaking his bliss. A deep voice and a Scottish burr filled the room. " 'Tis a wee commotion you're causing out here, Your Dukeness. Everything all right?"

Reluctantly, Alexander eased away from Meagan. Her eyelids were heavy, lips parted in longing, the love spell affecting her as much as him.

"Egan McDonald," he said to the Scotsman who filled the doorway. Egan's kilt, his brogue, and his wild hair showed that he was fully playing the Mad Highlander tonight. "Perfect."

"Tell me, lass, what it is about Nvengarian men," Egan said, a teasing twinkle in his eyes as he and Meagan entered Maysfield House, "that makes their brides so sad to be shunted off to the likes of Egan McDonald? First Princess Penelope, now the Grand Duchess. A man's got his pride, ye know."

Meagan let Gaius take her cloak and led Egan to the India sitting room and called for tea.

"I beg your pardon, Egan," she said. "Please forgive my rudeness. I am worried about Alexander is all."

Alexander, before he'd kissed her and departed with his entourage, had beckoned Egan to him. "Guard her well," she'd heard Alexander say in a low voice. "Stay with her until I return."

"Ye needn't worry about him running to another woman, lass," Egan said, sitting in a particularly ugly armchair and stretching out his brawny legs. "Especially not Anastasia. I gather ye know why he works with her. But even if he did not, 'tis not his way to pursue a bit of muslin. He's a cold man, is Alexander."

"No, he is not."

Meagan clamped her mouth shut as Egan raised his brows and Gaius trotted in with a tray of tea and some whisky for Egan. Meagan felt some small affection for Gaius because he reminded her much of Roberts, the bumbling Tavistock footman, although Gaius did not drop things nearly so much.

Egan motioned for Gaius to leave the decanter of whiskey. The young man moved it to a table next to Egan and departed, and Egan poured himself a large measure.

"Ye've cracked his shell, have ye?" Egan lifted his glass in salute. "Good on ye, lassie."

"Alexander does not have a shell." She thought of the warm passion she'd glimpsed in her husband's eyes, not only when they were making love or under the love spell, but when he glanced at her from across the ballroom tonight or glared at her after she'd poured wine in his lap. "He is a man of deep feeling. Others have made him bury it, that is all."

"Well, ye'd know best." Egan took another gulp of whisky and winced. "Och, this stuff doesna agree with me as when I was younger. I saw Alexander staring daggers at the smitten gentlemen around ye, so ye might be right. He's letting the feelings out for ye, any rate."

"Do you know what he is doing tonight, Egan?" Meagan poured tea from the silver pot, her hand unsteady. "He has not given me precise information about his intrigues."

Egan shook his head. "The only people who know what he's up to is himself and Lady Anastasia and that logosh."

Meagan bit her lip, thinking of how Myn had suddenly appeared and how unnerving it had been to watch him change shape. Why the logosh would turn up at a ball to find Alexander, she did not know, but it worried her. They'd spoken mostly in Nvengarian, which meant everyone in the room but she had understood what was going on. "He is in danger, isn't he?"

"Grand Duke Alexander of Nvengaria?" Egan raised his brows. "He's been in danger since the day he was born, love. You canno' be high-placed in Nvengaria without assassins gathering in the shadows. The position of Grand Duke is inherited, but when the line is gone, the Council of Dukes elect the next lucky sod. The plotting that goes on would curl me hair, were it not already." He grinned.

"You know so much about Nvengaria. I know so little, except what Penelope writes, and I have the feeling she gilds the truth. She likes to put a bright tint on things."

Egan crossed his booted feet, settling himself comfortably. "I lived there a time, with a Nvengarian family. Cousins of Prince Damien, as a matter of fact. They were distant enough relatives that the intrigues of the court didn't touch them, and they kept themselves apart from the old Imperial Prince. Safer, that was."

"I wish Alexander was not so important," Meagan

said softly. "But then, if he were an ordinary Nvengarian he'd have stayed in Nvengaria, and I never would have met him."

Egan slanted her a curious glance. "Then ye would have been spared all this muck."

"I know, but I wouldn't know Alexander." She fingered the diamonds at her throat, his latest present to her.

Egan chuckled. "Lassie, I believe ye are in love."

"It is a love spell. You are an old friend, I don't mind you knowing. A woman called Black Annie put a love spell on us, and I do not know why. For her amusement, it seems."

"A love spell. Och, how Nvengarian."

"Black Annie is English."

"Yes, but someone must have paid this witch to do the spell, probably to confound Alexander. He's a powerful man and there's more than one who'd like to see him fall."

Meagan felt a twinge of worry. "I know. But why me? Why not some important man's wife? That would be much more of a scandal and hindrance than making him fall for a country gentleman's daughter."

"Donna ask me, lass. The ways of Nvengarians are a mystery, doesna matter that I lived there. Young Zarabeth could confound a saint, and then she had to up and marry one of the Council of Dukes. A bloody idiot from all I hear."

Meagan's curiosity piqued, Egan's tone and scowl diverting her from her own troubles. "Zarabeth?"

"Daughter of the family I lived with. She could scold like the veriest fishwife, devil take her."

His eyes softened, and Meagan sensed his thoughts drift back to Nvengaria and the scolding young woman who had married someone else.

"Egan," she said.

He snapped his head up as though realizing he'd given himself away. He met Meagan's measured gaze and smiled ruefully. "Keep it to yourself, lass. Egan McDonald, the Mad Highlander, is a fool."

"Is she why you never married?"

Egan drained his glass of whisky and poured another. "Me, marry? The Mad Highlander, the great war hero, the wild bachelor? Why, ladies would be cryin' their eyes out. . . ." He trailed off, catching her look. "All right, ye've caught me. What is it about ye and your friend Penelope that makes me enter the confessional?"

"Did Zarabeth turn you down?" Meagan asked.

"I never asked her. She was too young, I thought, and we parted not on the best of terms. As I said, she could scold." His voice dropped. "And then I learn she's married. What's a bold, brash Scotsman to do?"

"Perhaps you will find someone else," Meagan suggested gently.

"Doubtful, lass. And donna get that matchmaking glint in your eye. I had me chance, and 'tis done. I truly donna mind hordes of ladies chasing me up and down Mayfair, so put it out of your head that I am miserable, and tend to your own troubles."

Meagan couldn't help smiling. Egan was red and uncomfortable and reaching for more whisky. She'd keep her thoughts to herself, but there had to be someone. . . .

She laughed a little. "Do you know, the Duchesses of Cranshaw and Gower have made me promise that I will give a ball, my first as Grand Duchess of Nvengaria. I am terrified. The Duchess of Gower wants me to trip, and the Duchess of Cranshaw wants me to blossom so she can rub it in the face of the Duchess of Gower. They are squeezing me in two."

Egan looked grateful she'd changed the subject. "A grand idea. When the *ton* learns ye can host a fine entertainment, they will turn a favorable eye on ye. Your star will rise."

"But good lord, Egan, I know nothing about it."

"That is why ye have staff. Leave it to that nice Mrs. Caldwell." He shivered. "She can look at a man and make him feel like a guilty schoolboy what's not finished his rice pudding."

"She has been very kind to me. She knows the running of this house backward and forward."

"See that? She will have the ball arranged in a trice, and ye have dozens of servants to do all the work. All ye need do is stand at the top of the ballroom stairs and shake hands until your fingers go numb."

"I hope you are right."

Egan leaned back in his chair and studied the brightly colored and rather unconvincing tigers and lions and gods cavorting on the ceiling. "Good lord, that's enough to make a man nauseated. Or give him nightmares. How do ye live in this ornamented house?"

Meagan jumped to her feet. "I cannot sit still. Would you like me to give you a tour? Montmorency leads people around on Wednesdays for a shilling. This will save you the cost."

Egan grinned. "Lead on. I will gawk as much as ye like."

Meagan hoped that wandering through the many rooms of the mansion would still her worry about Alexander, but that was not to be. She took Egan to the ballroom with its curved red ceilings and huge gold and crystal chandeliers. They visited the Asia Hall and the anteroom done in glittering gold and white, and the huge dining room with its black marble columns and paintings of bloody battle on the walls.

"Nice thing to look at while you're eating," Egan remarked.

Meagan laughed. "Precisely what I thought upon first viewing them." Her smile died and her eyes widened as the paintings reminded her of Alexander's battles. "I wish he would have let me stay with him tonight. I hate not knowing what is happening to him."

Egan sent her a sympathetic smile. "Aye, lass, I know. But Alexander is a resourceful man, and experienced, and he's got that logosh and bloodthirsty Nvengarians around him. 'Twill be all right." His smile turned to a grin. "Let me regale you with stories of my crazy family in Scotland. I'll make ye laugh, and he'll be home before ye ken it."

Yet even as he began his stories Meagan knew they couldn't distract her from Alexander.

Otto von Hohenzahl looked fearfully down at the Nvengarians who had him pinned to the wall of his study. Alexander watched him from across the room, Myn beside him. The logosh now wore his usual linen shirt and rough breeches, clothes he had stashed in Alexander's carriage.

Myn's appearance at Alexander's side had caused von Hohenzahl to go sheet white and gibber in fear.

"I find it curious," Alexander began, "that you know what a logosh is. Not many do."

Von Hohenzahl spoke thick German, his dialect almost indecipherable. "He can kill all of us in this room."

"I know." Alexander spoke Nvengarian, refusing to switch languages for von Hohenzahl's benefit. "Perhaps I will leave him alone with you, to find out what he does."

"No!" Above his pristine cravat, von Hohenzahl's eyes bulged.

"Then cease threatening my family. If your men come anywhere near them, I will let Myn do whatever he likes with you. That might mean ripping out your throat or telling you Nvengarian fairy tales. I will let him choose."

"You see," von Hohenzahl bleated. "I was right."

Alexander growled. "Right about what? Be clear."

"The logosh will follow you. You can lead them, Your Grace. That is your key to taking over Nvengaria, not negotiating with Damien."

His eyes gleamed with ambition, and Alexander felt disgust. The man must truly think he could dance into Nvengaria with Alexander at his side, have Alexander create an army of logosh to sweep down on Damien and boot him off the throne. Was this the "secret weapon" he'd been raving about? He was a fool if so. The logosh served Princess Penelope and her alone.

"You assume I have any interest in taking over Nvengaria," he said, voice cool. "Certainly not if it means letting an Austrian get his clutches on it."

"Nvengaria will never stand up to Austria," von Hohenzahl said desperately. "We are too strong. We will win through in the end and be the most powerful empire in the world."

"Spare me your pseudo patriotism. You care for your own glory, not Austria's. You would double-cross Prince Metternich in a heartbeat if you thought you could. You want Nvengaria for yourself, to prove to Metternich you can take it."

"If you kill me, another will spring up to take my place," von Hohenzahl said.

"If I kill you, it will be to make you be quiet."

Julius held up his wicked-looking knife. "May I cut his throat, Your Grace? Please?"

Von Hohenzahl's eyes widened at the bloodlust in Julius's smile.

"No, Julius. London is a civilized place, more or less. I would not like to lose you to their justice system." Alexander walked closer to von Hohenzahl and looked up at him. "From now on you have a new master—me. You dislike Metternich because he steals your ideas and ignores you. Now you will work for me against him."

"I cannot," von Hohenzahl said, face white.

"If you do not, you will die and no one will be able to tell how. I have many more problems to take care of than you, and a new wife to tend to. I would like one less distraction while I get to know her."

"Metternich will kill me," von Hohenzahl bleated.

"He might. But if he doesn't, I certainly will. The choice is yours."

He instructed his guards to release the diplomat. The two men who held von Hohenzahl looked disappointed, but they eased off and lowered the man to his feet. The Austrian swallowed and adjusted his cravat.

Alexander studied him coldly. "Give me your loyalty and I might be lenient. But I will watch you, and if you take one step too far, if you make one more threat to my family, you will pay a high price."

"What about the Austrian woman?"

Alexander allowed no flicker of emotion to cross his face. "You speak of Lady Anastasia Dimitri?"

"Yes," he panted. "Lady Anastasia. She is up to something. She is hand in glove with Metternich, and she means to bring down Nvengaria. Allow me to break her for you, to show you my loyalty."

Alexander regarded him in disgust. The man switched loyalties too quickly, and such a person was not to be trusted. The idea that Anastasia would work with Metternich was ludicrous, and von Hohenzahl was either lying or he was a fool. Alexander heard the lust in von Hohenzahl's voice, the hope that he could have Anastasia to himself.

He felt a tingle of anger next to him—he *felt* the anger, but it was not his own—and turned to see Myn, blue eyes glowing, growling in his throat. The growl was soft but menace-filled and von Hohenzahl blanched.

"Myn looks after Lady Anastasia," Alexander said calmly. "No need to trouble yourself."

Von Hohenzahl whitened, unable to look away from Myn.

"You will make an appointment with me tomorrow," Alexander continued, "at which time you will outline whatever you were scheming with Metternich about Nvengaria. You will be watched."

Julius and his men nodded avidly, smiling. The most bloodthirsty thugs in London would have backed down to Julius's smile.

Von Hohenzahl swallowed. "Nvengarians," he muttered.

Alexander bathed him in a cold stare. "You will get more mercy from Nvengarians than you would the Austrians. Unless of course you betray me."

Von Hohenzahl removed a white handkerchief and dabbed his face. "Yes, yes, of course. I am pleased now that the man I hired to take your wife today was unsuccessful. She is too well-guarded. You are to be commended."

Alexander's cold shattered and fell like a broken shell. "To take my wife?"

"Today, as she ventured to the green in Berkeley Square. I heard reports that she was fishing in a puddle, but journalists often get things wrong. Or perhaps I did not understand their atrocious English."

"You hired someone to kidnap my wife?"

Von Hohenzahl did not seem to hear the fury in Alexander's voice. "I needed her, but it went wrong. My man was unable to get near her, and I dismissed him."

The beast reared inside Alexander, blotting out reason and civility. His vision swam and darkness hit him like a wave. The last thing he heard was a hideous snarl coming from his own throat.

CHAPTER SIXTEEN

Alexander was standing in another room, his coat torn and ruined, his breath coming fast, blood on his hands. Myn stood in front of him as calm as ever, Julius behind him with a dagger out.

"What happened?" Alexander demanded. "Did I kill him?"

"No." Myn cocked his head and regarded Alexander with his odd-shaped blue eyes.

Julius shook his head. "No, but the Austrian man's breeches are no longer dry. You would have killed him, but for Myn holding you back." He tried to speak stoically, a bodyguard startled by nothing, but his knuckles on his knife were white. Nvengarians sometimes displayed berserker rage, which was clearly what Julius thought had happened.

"Did I change?" he asked Myn.

"No."

"Stop being so damn cryptic. What did I do?"

"You almost changed," Myn said. "You stopped yourself."

"Not on purpose. I remember nothing."

Myn shrugged.

Alexander clenched his hands, bloody and raw, trying to calm the tremors rushing through his body. "I cannot control it. I have to control it." He looked up at Myn, who regarded him silently. "Teach me more. Teach me how to change and how to remember when I do."

Myn regarded him a moment longer, then gave a nod.

Julius, who obviously did not understand what they were talking about, looked worried. "Your Grace? What do we do with Herr von Hohenzahl?"

"Watch him." Alexander tried to snap back to his Grand Duke persona. "Put as many men on him as you can spare, but do not let one guard stray from the Grand Duchess. I will need a new coat, and then you return home and tell my wife I will be late."

"Late," Meagan repeated as Julius, Alexander's bodyguard, stood stone-faced in the India sitting room, to which she and Egan had returned. "Did he say how late?"

"No, Your Grace. He is with the logosh, Myn."

"I see."

She did not, really, but Julius seemed to want an answer. Egan McDonald, lounging in his chair with the whisky, shot her a look of sympathy. "Looks like ye'll have to put up with me company a little longer, lass."

"Why aren't you with him, Julius?" Meagan asked. "I thought you were his personal bodyguard."

Julius looked uncomfortable, or as uncomfortable as a brick wall could look. "He sent me home, Your Grace."

"Why? A rather curious thing for him to do—he is always going on about how dangerous it is to be Grand Duke."

Julius said nothing, but Meagan read in his eyes that he did not like that Alexander had sent him away either.

"Egan . . ."

Egan quickly held up his hands. "Doona ask me, lassie. Doona ask me to trot about dark and rainy London to find your husband."

Meagan blinked. "I know you are not dearest friends with him, but . . ."

"What I think of him isna the point. He instructed me to look after ye. If I run after him and God help me, find him, he'll peel the skin from me bones for leaving ye alone."

Meagan glanced at Julius, who nodded grimly. "You are to be guarded at all costs," Julius said. "You and His Grace's son. The logosh is with His Grace, and he's stronger than anything I've ever seen."

"True," Meagan said. "But is Alexander safe *from* Myn?"

The worry in Julius's eyes grew, meaning he had no idea. Meagan rubbed her knuckles, not liking the chill in the pit of her stomach. Something was wrong.

"And doona get that look," Egan said. He pointed a broad finger at her. "*You* willna trot around London looking for Alexander under every bush. I imagine our dear Grand Duke sent home his guards not only to protect ye but to keep ye home." He got to his feet, his kilt swaying as he steadied himself against the whisky he'd consumed. His gaze lit on the chessboard in the corner. "Stay here and play chess with me. See if ye can trounce a drunk Scotsman."

"I will," Meagan promised darkly. "My father taught me to play."

"Well, then."

He glided unsteadily to the table with the chessboard and pieces and sat down. Meagan closed her mouth on hot words as she went to join him, to Julius and Dominic's immense relief.

She'd have things to say to Alexander later, she decided. Many, many things.

"Where are we?" Alexander asked.

Myn shrugged. "Woods."

They were a long way from London. He could tell by the tang in the air and the absence of the fetid scent of the city. Myn had brought him here, the logosh able to move through distances like a bird flew through air. Alexander remembered none of the journey and didn't know if he'd become a logosh during the transition. He did not think so, because his clothes were firmly on him, his spare coat unripped.

Nikolai always sent a spare suit and several shirts with Alexander wherever he went. One never knew if some clumsy servant would spill wine or candle wax on the Grand Duke, who must appear pristine at all times. Alexander admitted that Nikolai's preparedness didn't hurt Alexander's reputation for perfection.

Of course, the only person in London who'd spilled wine on him since he arrived was Meagan.

His body craved her. He remembered making love to her before they readied themselves for the ball, how satisfying it was to bury himself in her. Not just in the technical sense, but surrendering to the taste and scent and feel of her. As inconvenient as the love spell was, it had given him something he'd never had—complete happiness in being with a woman.

He'd never, ever been able to lose himself in someone else, never been able to trust that the woman he was with wouldn't somehow betray him. His affairs had been casual in the extreme with widows or courtesans, never in-

nocents and never lasting more than a night. He always
made sure that some enemy would not and could not use
the ladies he chose, either before or after their liaison
with Alexander.

A few of the women had written books about their encounters with him that sold very well. Alexander always
combed the manuscripts beforehand and expurgated
anything dangerous, and no one had dared stop him.
His reputation as a lover had risen, and the ladies gained
prestige of a sort and were strangely grateful to him. Being singled out by the Grand Duke could make a lady's
career.

The moment Meagan Tavistock looked at him had
changed everything.

Which was why he'd asked Myn to help him. He
wanted to go to Meagan without hurting her, and he
couldn't trust himself not to. He needed control. He
didn't mind that he'd attacked von Hohenzahl and
scared the piss out of the man, but he did not want to risk
his lack of control with Meagan. He wanted her with
such intensity that the frenzy could trigger his change.

Myn gazed pointedly at Alexander's suit before starting to remove his own clothes, unembarrassed.

Alexander toed off his boots, then unhooked the cords
of his coat. "Nikolai will never forgive me for hanging
my clothes on a tree," he said dryly.

Myn either did not comprehend or did not care. Without a word, the logosh stripped off his breeches and shirt,
tossed them into a pile and walked away into shadows.

*What would the London newspapers make of Grand Duke
Alexander nude in the woods with one of his entourage?*
Alexander smiled a little as he undressed, imagining
what joy they'd get from such a story. He'd simply have
to make damn certain no one saw him.

He hesitated a moment, his skin bare to the night, before collecting his clothes and following Myn. Walking barefoot in the woods in the dark was a risky practice, but somehow his body knew how to avoid the rocks and sharp twigs that littered the forest floor.

He could see, too. The moonlight was faint, riding in and out of thin clouds, but even when the silver orb obscured itself, Alexander's heightened senses could make out the outline of every tree and leaf, the gleam of animal eyes in the shadows, and the outline of Myn walking ahead of him to a small clearing.

He laid down his clothes on a dry spot, then put his hands on his hips and scanned the clearing, sensing the heartbeat and rapid breathing of each rabbit and mouse and shrew in the underbrush. Did animals feel like this? Did wolves know every breath their prey took?

"How do I control the change?" he asked. "I want to do it at will, not wake up wondering what the hell happened to me."

"You cannot."

"What?"

Myn was staring across the clearing as though he too sensed the small lives in the underbrush. "You cannot control your logosh side. It controls you."

"I have been controlling it for thirty-two years. Even in the worst times of my life, it has not risen up to plague me. Not until now."

"Because of the love spell."

"The love spell triggered it." Alexander flexed his arms, wanting to run for some reason, not in panic, but for the pure joy of it. *To run, to hunt.* "I thought so."

"The love spell tore down the walls you had built between yourself and what you are. You did not control the logosh in you; you pushed it aside. Once the man you hated and feared most in your life was dead and Nvengaria was safe, the walls you built started to break. And then the love spell destroyed them."

"That is the longest speech I have ever heard you make. But you are wrong. I did control it."

"No." Myn's eyes grew still more blue. "The beast inside will kill you if you do not surrender to it. Logosh is what you are."

"I am only half logosh."

"Then it will be harder for you."

Alexander balled his fists. "I do not want to hurt Meagan. Do you understand that? I cannot hurt her."

"Then surrender."

The air around Myn shimmered, and his form changed. He became a demon, one of the dark, hideously strong beings who had invaded the throne room the day Prince Damien and Penelope returned from Nvengaria. They had nearly killed Alexander, and Penelope herself had brought Alexander back from the dead.

Since that day the logosh had devoted themselves to Princess Penelope, following an old tale that told of a princess who had befriended a logosh and so won the devotion of his tribe. Alexander understood that devotion, knowing he owed Penelope his life.

Alexander's heart beat faster, dark tingling beginning in his spine. "I never wanted to be a demon."

It is what you are. Myn did not speak words, and Alexander was not reading his mind. He simply knew what Myn meant.

Myn shimmered again and his form flowed into that of the wolf he'd been at the ball. *You are the demon, but you may show what form you wish to the world.*

But first, Alexander thought, he must become the demon.

Surrender was not a word with which Alexander was

comfortable. He'd surrendered to Prince Damien, but only conditionally, because he believed that Penelope could keep Damien under control. He hadn't really surrendered to the love spell. It had simply taken him over.

He remembered Myn's teachings on meditation. Stretching out his hands, he studied his fists, marking each sinew and hair that curved over his fingers. His hands were brown, darker than an Englishman's, his ancestry showing in the burnish of his skin. The Magyars, warriors of Eastern Europe, had come from the Russian Steppes in ancient times to settle in the Danube Valley, spilling north into Nvengaria and intermarrying with a few Turkish tribes that had migrated there. The Nvengarians' darker skin and wild ways came from them.

He loved to look at Meagan's hand on his, her pale fingers stroking his as though she found every part of him fascinating.

For Meagan, for her safety, he surrendered.

The world did not look much different for a moment, and then everything changed. Shadows sharpened as though the moon had come out, but it had not. He saw colors he never knew existed, exact shades between green and blue, a color beyond purple he could not identify.

Every blade of grass, every leaf, every grain of earth was sharp and whole. He definitely heard the heartbeats of animals now, heard their quick fear as they sensed a predator among them. He heard the steady beat of Myn's heart, the heat of the other logosh's blood, and could pinpoint with precision where Myn was.

Alexander's hands changed. Hard with muscle, demon skin covered them, but it was not unpleasant as he had feared. It looked right, as though Alexander had finally broken through.

But Meagan would fear this shape. He knew how the

boy logosh, Wulf, had come to England in pursuit of Penelope and how he'd terrorized the household, including Meagan. He did not want Meagan to look at him in fear.

Another shape, then—Myn had said he could present any face to the world he wanted. He already knew the Alexander shape, but when he needed to change he would choose something less frightening to the average Englishwoman, less frightening to Meagan.

He had it. He'd always admired the creatures, and a few of them inhabited the high mountains north of Nvengaria.

Alexander concentrated. He studied his hands again, nearly jumping when they began to be covered with smooth, silky black hair. His fingers grew shorter and rounded into claws, and then he felt the compulsion to drop to all fours.

When he landed, the look of the world changed again, going black and white but sharper still, with shadows convex and concave rather than in straight lines. He rumbled in his throat, a growl emerging that sent the more sensible rabbits dashing for safer hiding places.

Alexander put one paw in front of the other, feeling the strength in sleek sinews, shoulders bearing the weight of his long back. He licked his mouth, tongue tasting sharp whiskers and the strange sensation of fur.

He broke into a trot without realizing it, following the scent pattern of Myn's wolf form, the trail of smells sharper than that of sight. The moon came out as he moved into the woods, highlighting the empty clearing where he'd been, the breeze stirring his abandoned clothes and the sash of the Grand Duke of Nvengaria.

Alexander did not return home until dawn. Egan McDonald, with Scots stubbornness, refused to leave, no matter how many times Meagan won at chess.

"I have taken a hundred guineas from you," she said as he laid down his king yet again. Early light brushed the edges of the curtains, sliding between cracks to touch the near-guttered candles.

"A glutton for punishment I am." Egan retrieved the chess pieces and set them up. "Again?"

"Good heavens, no." Meagan rose, impatiently shaking out her apricot skirts, tired of the lovely dress. "Haven't you things to do? Mad Highlander things?"

He looked up at her, holding the white queen between broad fingers. "If I go off to do Mad Highlander things, will ye go to bed?"

"No."

"Then I stay. And anyway, Alexander—"

"I know, ordered you to look after me. Blast him."

"Meagan, he is a—"

She held up her hand. "If you say he is a very important man, I believe I shall scream."

"Let me finish a sentence, woman. I was going to say he is an unpredictable man. Ye can never be sure what he's going to do. When I arrived in Nvengaria with Damien and Penelope last summer, Alexander was calm as anything, ushering us into the throne room and behaving like a caring host. And of course he meant to execute Damien as soon as he possibly could, and me too perhaps. Whatever Alexander's gone off to do, unless he wants us to know what it is, ye never will."

"I intend to ask him."

"Good luck, love. I admire the man, and he's proved a boon to Damien and Penelope, but no man holds his cards closer to his chest than Alexander of Nvengaria. He's got the new king trembling in his Bath chair every time he comes near."

"Are you afraid of him?" Meagan asked.

"I haven't decided. I'm happy he's found a sweet thing

like ye to be his bride, but sometimes I feel that cold stare on me—"

He broke off and swung around. Meagan looked up and started to see Alexander leaning on the doorframe, bathing Egan in a good example of his cold stare. How long he'd been there she had no idea.

Her heart missed a beat in relief. She dropped the chess piece she'd been righting and skimmed across the room to him. His coat was unbuttoned, his sash of office held in his hands, his shirt unlaced to show a brown *V* of throat and chest.

"Alexander." She threw her arms around his neck and buried her face in his shoulder. He smelled of fresh air and woods and green things.

She felt his broad hand on her back. His grip tightened for a moment, and then he gently released her.

"McDonald," he said.

Egan held both hands up in a gesture of surrender. "Donna be giving me that look, Your Dukeness. I was merely keeping your wife company—er, entertaining her—er—damn it, man, we played chess all night and she beat me like I was wet behind the ears. Lost a fair hundred to her."

"Which you do not have to pay," Meagan said quickly. "It was kind of you."

"A man pays his debts of honor, even the Mad Highlander," Egan said with a self-deprecating smile. "I'll send the money around with my batman. The lazy sot needs something to do."

He swept Meagan a bow, then moved sideways past Alexander to the hall. The two men never took their eyes off each other.

Once Egan had made his way around the gallery and quickly down the stairs, Alexander closed the door.

She wanted his kisses, needed them, but she also

wanted to scold. "Where did you go? Did you kill von Hohenzahl?"

For answer, Alexander pulled her into his arms. His lips heated hers, and for a moment she didn't mind that he didn't answer her question.

When he eased away, he frowned as though he did not remember who she meant. "Von Hohenzahl? No. He is a fool. He thought I had weakened, but I have only become stronger. I think he will no longer be a threat, at least not immediately."

"Then where?" She wished she understood his cryptic words. What had made him stronger? Marriage to her? Surely not. "Or is this something a wife, especially not the Grand Duchess, should ask?"

He looked different somehow, softer about the eyes, as though he'd discovered something that made him thoughtful. "I will tell you soon. It is a good secret, love, I promise you that."

"Layers of lies," she said, remembering what he'd told her the day he'd proposed to her—if she could call his demand for her to drop everything and become his wife a proposal.

He shook his head. "This has nothing to do with Anastasia."

"The *ton* is gossiping like mad, you know, watching you hie off with her and shunting me to Egan."

He moved into the sitting room, his gait restless, and paused to absently right the chess pieces. "You have heard this? I thought you went nowhere after you departed the French ambassador's house."

"Well, I *imagine* the *ton* is gossiping like mad. When my stepmother comes to visit tomorrow, she will tell me everything."

He turned, the black king in his hand, his stance more relaxed than she'd ever seen it. "I left Anastasia at her hotel before I approached von Hohenzahl. I promise you that."

Meagan gave a little laugh. "Do you know, if any other gentleman protested he hadn't the remotest interest in a beautiful woman with a perfect face and lovely eyes, I would call him a liar. But you, I believe."

"I am grateful for your trust."

She went to him, the love spell not wanting her to keep even a room's distance between them. "It is not trust. It is that I have learned how your mind works. You compartmentalize everything, especially people." She drew a line with her finger on the chessboard, along a row of squares. "Here are the ones you cannot trust." She made a second line. "Here are the ones you *can* trust until they prove otherwise. Here are the ones useful for *this*, there are the ones useful for *that*."

She made neat columns with her forefinger, dividing the board into even rows. "Everything and every person goes into a compartment. Somewhere, perhaps in a box of her own, you have your wife." She placed the white queen in a black square. "She charms others for you, she informs you of what she learns from them, and every once in a while, she provides you with a son." Her voice grew soft as she set the black queen in a white square. "Sometimes she is named Sephronia, sometimes Meagan."

She felt the weight of his silence and found his eyes focused hard on her, his gaze hot with whatever fire he usually kept dampened.

Meagan sometimes thought she did not fear Alexander because he always had half his mind on something else. But now as he focused the full of his attention on her, she realized the power he had, and not only because he held the title of Grand Duke.

Here was a man who had firmly ruled Nvengaria from behind the throne and had nearly succeeded in taking over. Here was a man who had razed part of his own city to rid it of corruption. If he ever seemed tame, it was because he wanted to turn that face to others in order to disarm them. Behind the civility was a ruthless man descended from barbarian tribes, and Meagan had awakened him.

"I did not marry you because I wanted another wife," he said. "The last thing I wanted was another wife. I married you because I hurt you, and I did not want to leave you in the dust of my passing. I married you because I wanted you." He swept his hand across the chessboard, erasing her imaginary lines and sending the chess pieces to the floor. "I want to send it all away, every bit of it, and have you and nothing else. That is what I want."

Meagan twined her fingers together. He made her feel selfish but at the same time frustrated. She certainly had not wanted to marry someone as formidable as he and live in this gaudy house and smile at ambassadors' wives and duchesses who were eaten through with jealousy.

"You made me Grand Duchess as though if I slipped on the title, I would become as powerful as you," she said. "But it isn't like putting on fancy dress. It's only me behind the mask, a plain miss from Oxfordshire. I am in the box, Alexander, whether you meant to put me there or not."

He softly touched her hair. "But it *is* fancy dress, as you say. You put on the mask of Grand Duchess, and everyone sees that. In time, they forget about the miss from Oxfordshire and see only a woman poised and beautiful and powerful—as powerful as you want to make them think you are."

"Beautiful," she mused. "Poised. Words never before applied to me. I do not know if I can play the role, dearest husband. I do not have the devious mind you do.

While you are putting people into their compartments, you are busy devising five different schemes in which you could use them." She pointed her finger at him. "And do not tell me otherwise. I have watched you do it."

"I do what I must."

She laughed. "That is not normal, Alexander. Most of us meet people and wonder what their thoughts are about the latest play at Covent Garden or if they'd enjoy a game of whist. Not *'How can he aid me in manipulating the English cabinet?'* or *'How can I use her to spy on the Prussians?'*"

He closed his hand softly around her accusing finger. "I am Grand Duke of Nvengaria. It is my business to watch all the time, to decide whom to trust and whom to use. It is what I am."

"The trouble is you never stop being Grand Duke. You tell me to put on the mask, but you never take yours off."

"Because I cannot." He brought her finger to his mouth and flicked his tongue over the tip. "I can never remove the mask. I learned to wear it when I watched a man I trusted murder my father and then expect me to kiss his cheek and embrace him. I had to be Grand Duke then; I could not have been Alexander, because I would have died in that moment. Every day, had I been only Alexander and done what Alexander wanted, the Imperial Prince would have tortured me, likely very slowly, until I begged to die. I had to live—to avenge my father—and I had to be Grand Duke every day of my life for that."

The sadness in his voice hurt her. She imagined him at thirteen years old, forcing a look of blank coolness as he watched his father's execution. She saw in him determination that no matter what happened, his own son would never witness what Alexander had witnessed.

"Tell me what to do," she said, her voice low. "I will do anything you want, be anyone you want to keep Alex from that. I promise."

He looked at her for a long time, his sash of office, the reminder of who he was, crumpled in his hand. "When I met you I had no idea who you were, or where to, as you say, compartmentalize you. I did not lie when I said that I did not want to marry, but I also did not lie when I said I needed to marry you. I need you to let me be Alexander the man, not the Grand Duke."

"It might just be the love spell, you know," she said softy, "devising a reason for you to want to stay with me."

He drew his knuckle along her cheek, the sash of office brushing her skin. "Why do you think I have not found a means to break the spell? My men could have found Black Annie by now if I'd truly wanted them to. They could have questioned her and even quietly murdered her—I have the means to command that. But the spell, it is giving me something I never had. I am not in such a hurry to give it back."

"I do not want to break it, either," she answered. "Although it can be most inconvenient. It is difficult to stand and speak politely to the Duchess of Gower while I imagine holding you. And I do not mean holding you in my arms, I mean holding a specific bit of you, in my hands."

His smile heated her blood. "Is that what you thought at the ball tonight? And I imagined you were pleased at the attention of the gentlemen."

She blinked. "Indeed, no, they could not believe I had a single thought in my head beyond the state of the weather. I have been well trained to talk about the weather, but one soon has enough of it."

"I promise you, my wife, that I will never make you speak about the weather." He skimmed fingertips across her lips. "Now, about what you wanted to hold in your hands . . ." Alexander tilted her head back, pulling her to his mouth.

He seemed different somehow. As Meagan kissed him, she thought the taste of his lips had changed. She realized after a few heartbeats that he was warm, his skin, his mouth, his breath. Not the heated frenzy of the love spell or the cool rigidity of the Grand Duke.

Alexander the man.

She pulled back a little. "What happened to you tonight?"

He smiled, feral and wild, the Nvengarian in him evident. "Something wonderful. I have conquered it."

"Conquered what?" She ran her hands up inside his open coat, finding the solid warmth of his chest. "You madden me, Alexander."

He kissed her forehead, then her lips again. "Wait here for ten minutes exactly, then go into the garden."

She started. "The garden? It is still dark outside. And cold and damp, I wager."

His smile was more of a grin, a thing she'd never seen on Alexander. "You may wear boots and wrap up warmly. I have something to show you, my duchess."

CHAPTER SEVENTEEN

Ten minutes after Alexander left her in the sitting room, Meagan entered the garden behind the house. The sky was still dark, it being the small hours of the morning. She'd hastily found her boots and a warm mantle for herself, not liking to wake her maids. The household would be stirring soon, and she had the feeling that Alexander did not want his servants to know his secrets.

Meagan had not been wrong about the cold. The spring wind was crisp, the paths wet with last night's rain. She pulled a fold of her mantle over her nose and tried not to sneeze.

"Meet me in the garden," she muttered. "Where in the garden exactly? I wonder if other women have husbands as trying as mine."

She stepped down onto the main path and began to walk toward the maze, a high hedge that enclosed its four turns. She'd have to bring Alex out to play hide and seek in it.

She found no sign of Alexander. It was still too dark to see the path properly, the gray light of dawn being swallowed by lowering clouds. She could not even see footprints indicating the direction he'd gone.

"Alexander?" she called softly. "It really is quite cold out here."

No answer. The wind rustled the yew hedges and stirred the leaves of the apple trees hung with rose vines. The garden was a mad place, with sharply sculpted flower beds placed against hedges with tiny paths in between. The designer must have been released from Bedlam solely to plan this garden.

She reached the maze and peeked inside but could see nothing in the darkness. "Alexander?"

Something rustled deep within the maze. Annoyance touched her. Why on earth should he want to meet her in the middle of the maze? The India sitting room, as bizarre as it was with columns carved like palm trees and tigers stalking the ceiling, was at least warm and dry.

"Nvengarians," she said through chattering teeth as she entered the maze.

Halfway to the middle, she found Alexander's clothes discarded on a wrought-iron bench, his boots carefully placed to not absorb too much mud. She touched the still-warm coat.

Why should he throw off his clothes in the middle of the garden on a blustery morning? Her heart gave a painful beat. He hadn't run mad, had he? Perhaps that was what had changed about him, that he'd given into madness in his brain.

"Oh, Alexander," she whispered. She hurried through the last turns of the maze, eyes widening against the dark.

Something brushed her thigh, something warm and dark and sleek. Stifling a scream, Meagan jumped against the hedge, its branches scraping her back.

Facing her was a panther, a huge black beast, its eyes a luminous blue glow in the darkness.

Meagan froze in shock. The panther watched her, its tail brushing the leaves behind it. She smelled warm fur and felt the heat of its body and its breath scalding her hand.

Thoughts careened through her head. Was this what Alexander had wanted to show her? Perhaps he'd brought the beast here as a pet for her—it was the sort of overblown gift Alexander would give her.

Was it tame? She thought of Alexander's clothes lying on the bench. What the devil was going on?

"You didn't eat Alexander, did you?" she whispered, half jesting. What wildcat politely waited for his dinner to undress?

The panther reared to its hind feet. Meagan screamed, but there was nowhere to go but into the hedge firmly behind her. The cat's huge paws pinned her shoulders and its wide, rough tongue licked her from chin to forehead.

Before she could squeal in protest, the panther shimmered, and then Alexander was pressing her against the hedge, the length of his naked body covering hers. He was laughing.

She gaped. "Alexander, what—"

He closed his eyes, and his body shimmered again. Then he was the panther, playfully butting her face. She tried to twist away, and he dropped to all fours and twined his long body around hers.

"What is happening? Tell me at once."

Alexander rose up, human once more, and gathered her against his body, which was plenty warm. "I have discovered what I am. Myn showed me. I am logosh, Meagan."

"But—" She pushed against his shoulders, trying to take in what he was saying. "Logosh are demons."

"We can show any face to the human world we choose. I thought you would be less frightened if you saw the panther first."

"Except I was frightened of the panther. Why are you suddenly logosh?" she asked, dazed. "Surely you would have noticed before."

He laughed, his voice rumbling like the panther's growl. "My mother was logosh, but I never knew."

"Your mother?"

"Myn told me she fell in love with my father and left her people for him. She kept the secret of her true self from all but him." He paused thoughtfully. "My father probably reasoned that if the Imperial Prince had known I was logosh, he might have exploited me in some horrible way. He was a monster. And my father was executed too abruptly to have time to give me the information." He smiled. "No fear that the demon in me would come forth because the human side of me was so cold and controlled. Myn showed me what to do, how I can live with both sides so I can be with you."

She touched his face, which was rough with unshaved beard. "Does anyone else know?"

"Outside the family, no, although Myn has likely told Anastasia by now."

Meagan's stunned mind tried to process the information, her body not certain it shouldn't be terrified. "This means that Alex is logosh too."

"A bit more diluted, but yes. I will explain it to him."

She wondered whether the small boy would be frightened or fascinated. Probably a little of both.

"You seem happy about this," she said.

He smiled and rubbed his hands over her arms, as though trying to warm her. "It explains much about what I feel inside me. Myn taught me not to fear it. It seems such a relief to give into it and be—what I am."

She laughed shakily. "You are explaining to me that I have married a demon."

"Half demon. Logosh are magical creatures, not evil ones."

"Myn unnerves me something fierce."

He traced her cheek. "I will teach you not to be afraid. I will teach you so much, Meagan."

Meagan bit her lip, trying to still her trembling. She did not want to show him her fear. She wanted—well, she was not even sure she had not fallen asleep and was dreaming all this.

"I am still getting used to being married to a Grand Duke. And now a logosh Grand Duke."

"I will help you. I promise you, love."

He spoke so persuasively, the powerful Grand Duke reasonably telling his subject that the ordeal she faced would be harmless.

The wind blew across the top of the maze, dipping down into the hedges. Meagan shivered. "Did you have to tell me out here in the garden? Couldn't we have had this discussion in a nice warm bedchamber?"

His eyes flickered, the blue almost glowing. "An excellent idea."

Now she felt the tendrils of the love spell spill over her. She touched his face, tracing his warm lips. The idea of being with him and this sudden, newfound wildness, the danger, made her shiver in longing. "Perhaps we should go up now. It will be several hours before we're awakened for breakfast."

He kissed her fingers. "A *most* excellent idea."

The kiss on her lips promised heat and excitement to come. Meagan pulled away with great reluctance. "Remember to put on your clothes first, darling," she said. "Lest Mrs. Caldwell catch sight of you and faint dead away."

* * *

This lovemaking was the best he'd had since taking Meagan the first time. Alexander knelt behind her on the bed, his thighs spread around her while she leaned against him. She'd twisted her red hair into a simple knot, the better for him to reach her very kissable neck.

Her apricot silk dress lay in a crumple on the floor, his sash of office a slash of gold and blue across it. Candles flickering around the bed bathed them in a golden glow, Alexander having shut the curtains against the coming morning.

He drew his hands up to cup her breasts, his body alive to the scent and feel of her. His erection nestled between her thighs, not in her, just brushing her opening as he kissed and touched her. His long dark hair grazed her cheek, and her eyes half closed in pleasure.

He wanted this, slowly pleasuring her until they both were more than ready for fulfillment. He'd promised her he'd teach her everything about sensual lovemaking if only she'd marry him and ease the need inside him.

If Black Annie hadn't made the ridiculous love spell, Alexander would never have met Meagan. He might have had her pointed out to him or even introduced as Princess Penelope's dearest friend, but he'd never have touched her or kissed her. Unwed English maidens weren't for Nvengarian sexual techniques. He should have busied himself with courtesans used to such things and left Meagan Tavistock strictly alone.

Unthinkable.

Slow touching. That's what he'd learned in the cult of Eros in the mountains of Nvengaria, slow touching without eroticism, deliberately avoiding intimate places until the body was on fire with longing.

He'd been twenty years old when he'd gone to the temple to study, which had been part of his training to take up the mantle of Grand Duke. The first month had been nothing but meditation, calming the mind and learning awareness of every part of the body.

The second month had been spent with two women who'd taught him the art of massage and soothing by touch. Not until he'd been at the temple eight weeks had the actual sexual training commenced.

Alexander skimmed his hands up Meagan's arms, fingertips just brushing her skin. She half turned in his grasp, seeking his lips, but he moved his head so she could not kiss him. She made a frustrated noise.

"Not yet, love," he said. "I will tell you when."

"I am feeling quite desperate," she answered.

"As am I. But we wait."

She whimpered, and he smiled in satisfaction. For half an hour since they'd come to her bedroom and nearly torn off their clothing, he'd been stroking her skin, touching nothing more intimate than her breasts and then only fleetingly.

His erection stretched hard with longing, but he'd learned how to placate it and keep it ready but not over-eager. He'd always been able to control his urges until the damn love spell overpowered him. But what Myn had taught him tonight reminded him of the control he'd learned in the temple, which worked to help calm the love spell without masking it.

Make it wait. Make it want.

He trailed his fingers down Meagan's thighs, pressing a little, feeling her strong muscles beneath soft skin. Across her abdomen now, stroking a slow hand over her navel. He massaged, fingers kneading, barely touching the swirl of hair above her mons. At the same time, he nibbled the shell of her ear, sharp little nips to arouse her.

"You are beautiful," he whispered.

She shivered. His command of English stayed with

him, no longer scattered as it had been when the love spell had first taken him.

"My heart," he murmured as he continued to nibble her ear.

"Alexander, I want to make love."

Her breathing was coming fast, her skin flushed with need. He chuckled. "I know you do. But not yet."

"Why not?"

"We need to wait. You will like it better for the waiting."

"We did not wait before."

Alexander flicked her earlobe with his tongue. "Because the frenzy caught us before I had a chance to teach you. There are so many facets of pleasure to explore that we could spend years learning them."

"Years?"

"Do not sound so alarmed. You will love every moment of it."

She bit her lip. He leaned down and licked it, catching her sharp teeth as well.

He'd never been with a woman he'd felt so comfortable with. No, *comfortable* was the wrong word. Comfort implied the end of excitement, and Meagan excited him in countless ways. He wanted to spend days in bed with her, exploring and learning and teaching.

He'd pleasured women during his affairs, but the pleasure had been calculated and precise—he'd brought the women to ecstasy while he remained in complete control. Losing control, even briefly in orgasm, was dangerous for a Grand Duke, and Alexander had never said one word, or spoken one endearment, or even cried out a name in his bed that might be held against him when he returned to sanity.

With his first wife, he hadn't had to be quite as tediously careful, but he and Sephronia had always known they were in bed for one reason—to get a child to carry on the line. Once that had been done, Sephronia and Alexander had gone their separate ways. In public they appeared together—they had made an efficient team—but in private they rarely saw each other.

Now he had a woman with whom he did not have to guard his every word, an innocent girl he was free to love as much as he wanted. He didn't need to get a child on her, although he would not mind another son or daughter to carry on his shoulders.

He could do with Meagan things he'd longed to try but could not because there'd been no woman he could trust.

He lightly massaged her shoulders, bending to nibble his way across them, leaving light teeth marks in her skin.

Meagan giggled. "That tickles. Am I supposed to laugh?"

"Laugh as much as you want. I love to hear you laugh."

"What is that for?" She pointed at a tiny brush he'd retrieved from his desk before he came in and a small ceramic pot that rested on the night table.

"I will show you."

"Show me what?"

"Do not worry. It will wash off."

Her eyes widened in alarm. Alexander reached for the pot and brush, the interlaced tattoo on his bicep flexing in the candlelight. As she watched, curious and uneasy, he opened the pot and dipped the pointed brush in the ink.

He steadied his hand on Meagan's back as he began to trace on her shoulder a thin design similar to his interlaced tattoo.

She shivered at the strange sensation of cold ink on her skin, but held very still. "Did the first Grand Duchess like to be painted on?"

"I have no idea. You are the first lady I have thus adorned."

"Why are you adorning me, exactly?"

He swirled the ink on her shoulder, drawing it down her shoulder blade to her spine. It pleased him to make precise designs, the black standing out starkly on her smooth skin.

"I want to. It is an ancient custom in the Orient for lovers to decorate each other's bodies."

"Truly? I wager Englishmen and women do not do this decorating."

"I do not know. I have never asked them." Alexander blew on the ink to dry it. "You are lovely."

"I want to see."

Alexander returned ink and brush to the night table and left the bed to bring a small mirror from her dressing table. Meagan craned her head to train the mirror on her shoulder and the intricate, interlaced design he'd produced.

"It's pretty. Do women in Nvengaria wear tattoos?"

"Not very many, I should think, unless they have been in the East. As I said, it will wash off."

She lowered the mirror and peeked at him over her shoulder. "Now I wish to paint on you."

Alexander smiled. He brought her the brush and ink and held very still while she began to copy the tattoo on his right bicep to his left. The brush slid across his skin, the trickle of ink cool on his flesh. The fine point of the brush tickled as she drew it along the inside of his arm, flicking short strokes through the longer lines. Her brow furrowed as she studied her work, her breath warm on his skin.

His blood stirred as tendrils of her long hair lightly touched his thighs. He studied her bowed head, the curls on top mussed, and he carefully leaned and pressed a kiss to it. She made a slight noise of impatience, then the brush's tip traced around his arm again in one long, cool stroke. The light sensations coupled with her so near slid warmth through his body.

"There," she said, finishing. "I like it very much. But I think my maid will be quite puzzled when she washes my back tomorrow."

He gently removed the brush and ink and replaced them on the table, enjoying that he had to lean over her to do so. "Then I will wash it for you and spare her the astonishment."

She slanted him a warm smile. "I believe I would like that."

"I believe I will too."

"Can we make love now? I feel quite ready."

He grinned. "Not yet, Lady Impatience. Lie down on your back."

Meagan touched her shoulder. "Is the ink dry yet? It might smear."

"It does not matter. I will have Mrs. Caldwell purchase new bedding if it does."

Obediently, Meagan lay down on the covers, strands of red hair splaying across the linens.

A pulse of energy shot through him, pressing aside the calm he'd held up to this point.

No.

He drew a breath and began a meditation, resting one hand on Meagan's abdomen to steady himself.

"Are you all right?" Her soft voice held concern.

"Yes." He closed his eyes, lightning flickering on the edges of his vision. "I will be."

He brought to mind the techniques of calming and centering Myn had taught him, the ball of light he'd learned to visualize in his hands. His energy, his strength, his calm.

The lightning went away. He drew a long breath. He could control, he could steady himself, he could stay with her.

He smoothed his hand over her abdomen, drawing his fingers to the soft curls between her thighs. His teachers had described a woman's opening as a flower, petals spreading and swelling at a man's touch.

Liquid pooled inside her flower, hot on his fingers, her nectar waiting for him. Beautiful.

The scent of her could drive him wild. His senses had heightened since he'd given in to the change, and her scent now covered him completely. He could lose himself in her.

He leaned down and licked her opening, drawing his tongue carefully over each sweet fold. She arched beneath him, a groan escaping her mouth.

She was more than ready for him. When he flicked his tongue over her nub, she thrust herself up to his mouth, fingers gripping his shoulders. He needed only a few more licks before he brought her to sweet climax.

He caught the climax in his mouth, his strong hand holding her down. She writhed and arched against him, her cries of pleasure ringing through the chamber.

Alexander held her all the way until she was spent, her body shining in perspiration. Gently, he disengaged her frantic clutches and looked up at her, his smile triumphant.

"You are a cruel, cruel man, Alexander," she gasped.

"I know."

He braced himself over her, sliding his hand down to bend her knee and press it to her chest. In that position, she was wide open to him, and so wet and slick from her climax that he slid easily and quickly inside her.

CHAPTER EIGHTEEN

Meagan's body was already on fire from his touch and his mouth, and now his hardness stretched and pressed her with incredible sensation.

His blue eyes glittered in elation that bordered on madness. His skin was roasting hot, his tattoo sharp on his dark skin, the tattoo she'd drawn gleaming with still-damp ink. She traced the patterns of both, loving how his biceps flexed beneath her touch.

He moved slowly inside her, drawing almost all the way out before pressing back in again. The weight of his large body pushed her into the mattress, his skin heating her sensitized breasts.

She arched against him, meeting him slow thrust for slow thrust. He turned his head and closed his eyes, the ends of his hair brushing her face. His eyelashes curled thick and black against his cheek.

His thrusts were like fire, so deep inside her she screamed with it. In and out, hips rocking, the bed creaking a rhythm beneath her. He slid callused hands up her arms and pinned her wrists to the pillows.

He gritted his teeth, jaw tightening, and growled.

"Alexander?" Her throat was raw.

He opened his eyes, blue fury blazing from him. "Damnation."

He said the word in Nvengarian, but she'd heard it enough from the servants to understand it.

"Damnation," he repeated in English, sweat beading on his forehead. "Not now. Not now."

"Please," she moaned.

She moved her hips against his, needing the wild friction inside her. His hands on her wrists were like iron manacles pinning her while he rode her.

His face held anything but pleasure. It was granite-hard, as though he struggled to force himself back into the persona of the Grand Duke.

"No," Meagan begged. "Stay here with me. Be Alexander."

He kept riding her, mouth set in a grim line, pinning Meagan so hard she could not move. Candlelight gleamed on the sweat on his body, muscles flowed as they flexed with his strength.

He was losing control, she could see that, and fighting hard to retain it. But he pressed her open so wide, his stiffness so deep inside her that she groaned with it.

Her leg hurt where it bent against her, pinned by his body, and her wrists burned like fire. But it wasn't pain, it was—exciting, and she wanted to let him do anything to her he wanted.

She started to come. She twisted her hips, wanting him deeper and deeper inside her. The delicious feeling nearly pulled her apart.

"Yes, love," she screamed. "Please."

He met her scream with a deep snarl, his mouth covering hers, teeth closing hard on her lip.

Then all at once he withdrew from her and landed to sit on the side of the bed. He was shaking, his breathing hoarse, and he held on to his body, every muscle tight.

Meagan rose weakly on her elbows, her body feeling both spent and heavenly. She put her hand on his arm and found his skin fever-hot.

"It is you," he said. "I cannot control it with you."

Hurt pricked her heart. "Then do not."

When he finally looked at her the bleakness in his eyes was vast.

"Do not control myself?" He lifted her hand and showed her the bruises on her wrist. "Did you enjoy this? Do you want more?"

"It did not hurt me."

"No? What if I did worse? Would you still look at me with love in your eyes?" He pushed her hand away.

"You are a gentle man." She lightly touched his arm again.

"I am not *gentle*. I do not know what I am. I am this beast, this logosh. I thought—I was so proud, thinking I'd learned to control it, thinking that being logosh will make me more powerful than ever." His eyes darkened as he studied her. "That is all I want, Meagan. Power over everyone so no one can hurt me."

"You are the second most powerful man in Nvengaria," Meagan pointed out. "Believe me, I am constantly reminded by everyone I see."

"It is a sham. It is false." He touched his chest, shadowed muscles sliding. "That is me making others believe I am powerful, to keep them at a distance. I was ice-cold when I told the old Imperial Prince to give me control of the kingdom. All I wanted to do was plunge a knife through his rotten heart. I wanted to peel his skin from his body for taking a real life away from me."

"But you have your life now. He's dead and gone." Meagan stroked his arm, distressed she did not know how to comfort him. "You have me and Alex, and Damien and you are friends again, and Nvengaria is at peace. You can live now. Starting right this minute."

She knew she babbled platitudes, but the look in his eyes unnerved her.

He stared at her, then laughed, though his expression changed little. "You are an amazing woman, Meagan Tavistock. You should be terrified of me, and instead you pat my hand and say '*It is all right, everything will be better.*'"

"I cannot bring myself to be afraid of you. I've seen your kindness."

"Sorcery has touched your brain." He gently stroked her temple. "Without the love spell, you'd be shaking in your shoes to be near me."

"Good heavens, Alexander, I've seen the way other women look at you, and believe me, it is not in fear. The Duchess of Gower in particular can't keep her eyes off you. And look at the lengths to which Deirdre was willing to go to get into your bed. They certainly hate me for having the gall to marry you."

"But it *is* fear, Meagan. It is part of why they want to be with me. To feel the danger, and the fear."

"That seems rather silly." She had to admit that the power of him, his strength tamed for her, was incredibly exciting, but she did not want him to think she was anything like Deirdre Braithwaite. "Much better to be laughing with you than shaking in my shoes. Besides, my shoes are all the way over there."

He put one hand over his face. "Damn you, Meagan, for being so adorable."

Boldly she slid her hand across his abdomen, feeling

the smooth muscles. Even more boldly, she let her fingers trace the ridges below his navel to find the hard, hot erection still swollen and stiff for her.

His fingers clamped her wrist nearly as hard as they'd pinned her to the bed. "Meagan."

"Let me," she begged. "Let me touch you."

He stared at her, his blue eyes hard and filled with stone stubbornness, which she realized masked fear. Very slowly, he peeled his hand from her wrist.

Without asking again for permission, she stroked all the way up his very long staff to the firm flange at the end.

"God help me," he said, his jaw hardening.

Meagan leaned her head against his chest, letting her fingers explore the fascinating part of him that made her feel so wonderful. The tip was soft like velvet, but firm and blunt, the shaft so very hot. She cupped her hand over it, stroking her fingers down the side, liking the sleek firmness of it.

Alexander leaned back on his elbows, his cock pressing upward into her hand, his eyes closing as though he was in pain.

"Am I hurting you?" she asked worriedly.

"No. Dear God, do not stop."

He guided her fingers along him, from tip to base, then released her to do what she willed. She lightly stroked all over him, then dipped her hand down to the firm, tight balls that lifted to her.

"Ah, God," he said, then trailed off into Nvengarian phrases.

She smiled. "Good. When you start speaking Nvengarian, I know I'm pleasing you as much as you please me."

He opened his eyes, the blue glowing, and growled something at her. She did not understand him, so she decided to take no notice.

"You always make me feel wonderful," she said. "I

know I am likely not very skilled, but I would like it if you felt nearly as wonderful."

His fingers threaded her hair, his breathing hoarse. She took that as a good sign and continued stroking him. Once she got used to touching his staff and the interesting flange, she lowered her head farther and touched it with her tongue.

She just brushed the tip, her tongue finding the tiny slit there. He tasted warm and dark and a little salty.

She wanted to taste more of him, but he groaned and hauled her up to him, taking her mouth in a bruising kiss.

She tried to protest. "I was not finished."

"You are."

He nearly threw her to the mattress, and she squealed at his abruptness. The smile had left his face, and she understood suddenly what he meant when he said she should be afraid.

No gentleness this time. He entered her with a fierce possessiveness that rendered her unable to breathe. He pinned her wrists again, not seeming to care that his body overpowered hers.

She was screaming with climax very soon after he began, but he went on and on, the heavy bed thumping into the wall.

As soon as he hit his own climax he ripped away from her and got off the bed just before his body rippled into the powerful demon that was the logosh. His eyes, enlarged, blazed blue.

Meagan screamed and scrambled against the headboard, dragging the pillows in front of her.

Alexander's body shimmered, and he was himself again, breathing hard, his skin coated in sweat. "I cannot control it. I cannot. Damn it."

"Be the panther again. You said you could be any shape for the rest of the world."

He shook his head. "Do you not understand? I cannot control it around you—the Goddamned love spell will not let me . . ."

"Let me touch you again. You liked it when I touched you."

She reached for him, and he backed quickly from the bed. "Stay away from me. The best thing is for you to stay away from me."

Her heart twisted. "I do not want to."

He pressed his eyes closed and balled his fists. His chest rose with a long breath, as though he was trying to calm himself, but he shook hard.

"Come back to bed," Meagan begged. "We do not have to make love. We will rest, and talk, and be with each other."

He opened his eyes and looked at her, some of the chill returning to his gaze. "I cannot simply talk to you. The love spell wants me to have you. And if I have you, I cannot control the logosh."

"We can try."

He was silent a long time, and she closed her mouth over her pleas. He took long, deep breaths, his skin covered with perspiration as he struggled to pull the chill mantle of Grand Duke Alexander around him again, just as Nikolai might bind him into his coat and sash of office.

"There is no need for us to be together," he said. "I no longer have the necessity to sire an heir."

"No longer have the necessity?" Meagan repeated, incredulous. "What do you mean, that you think of this for necessity?"

His gaze warmed the slightest bit. "I come to you for pleasure, Meagan. But it is best we do it no longer."

He cooled, his eyes becoming closer to the chips of ice they'd been when she'd first seen him weeks ago in the ballroom at Lady Featherstone's. He snatched up his trousers and slid them over his legs. "I will speak to Mrs. Caldwell and Nikolai about our future living arrangements."

"Future living arrangements . . ."

He lifted his shirt from the pile and put it on, turning away at the same time. "This is driving me mad, and seeing you makes it worse. I will not risk hurting you simply to sate my own pleasure."

Tears stung her eyes. "What am I to do?"

"You have your duties," the Grand Duke said to her. "For now, that will have to do."

He turned abruptly and strode to open the heavy door and step into the shadows of the hall. She saw him lift his hair out of the way of the shirt before he shut the door and was gone.

Meagan sat back on the bed alone, her heart aching. He was trying to shut her out as certainly and firmly as he'd closed the door. She knew the love spell drove him mad—it drove her mad too. But they should find the answer together; they should think of a way to conquer the logosh together. Her father and mother and now her father and Simone had always done things as a family, and she knew no other way.

Living arrangements? What the devil did he mean? Would he be so cruel as to send her away? And where would he send her? All the way to Nvengaria? Or back to Oxfordshire with her father?

Hurt laced her and she pressed her face to her bent knees. He'd never wanted this marriage; he'd been tricked as thoroughly as Meagan had. He'd tried giving in to the love spell, and now he was going to banish it by closing her off from him.

Meagan lifted his sash of office from the floor and held it against her bare body. The stiff gold threads scratched her skin as she kissed it and pressed it to her face.

She cried for a while, releasing the pain, and then she sat lost in thought. Alexander might want to avoid her or send her away, but Meagan had never been one to bow her head in obedience, at least not without a fight. Her father had taught her that if a request was not reasonable, she should question it, not follow blindly.

She hugged the sash and remembered his lessons, letting ideas trickle through her head. She wiped her eyes, her hardheaded confidence returning.

The Grand Duke might have stood up to the old Imperial Prince of Nvengaria, he might have stood up to slavers and opium sellers in his home city, he might have stood up to von Hohenzahl and his thugs, but he had never stood up to Meagan Tavistock when she undertook a campaign to make a person see reason.

Poor Alexander, Meagan thought, trying to bury the worst of the hurt deep inside her. He would not know what hit him.

She kissed the sash of office and smiled a shaky smile.

Meagan began her campaign the next day—or rather, later that morning when Susan ventured in to rouse her.

Meagan opened heavy eyelids and screwed them shut again at the broad sunshine coming in through the windows. She'd fallen asleep twined in the sash, which now lay twisted beside her on the pillows. After her long night and the hard lovemaking this morning, her head throbbed and her eyes were sandy.

"I have just ze zing for you," Susan said. She removed the sash with a knowing smile and helped Meagan don a dressing gown. "A fine beverage that will pick up your spirits something wonderful."

The beverage, whatever it was, was truly remarkable. It looked rather greeny-purple when Susan brought it to her, and Meagan sipped it doubtfully, but within a second or two, fire sparked through Meagan's every limb and her eyes opened fully.

"Merciful heavens! What is this?"

Susan winked one brown eye. "A family secret. My mother, she was something of a potion mixer."

Meagan did indeed feel refreshed and ready to face the world. Susan bathed and dressed her in a dark blue morning gown, looping her hair into becoming braids pinned under a small lace cap.

Mrs. Caldwell entered the room just as Susan put the finishing touches on Meagan's costume. "Breakfast is ready, Your Grace," the housekeeper said briskly. "In the dining room."

Meagan smiled, beginning step number one of her campaign.

"The dining room is rather large and dark for a morning meal, Mrs. Caldwell. Have it served in the little morning room at the back of the house. The windows light it nicely and the view of the garden is pleasant."

Mrs. Caldwell raised her brows but gave a nod. "As you wish, Your Grace. In that case, breakfast will commence in the morning room in a quarter of an hour."

Susan giggled as Mrs. Caldwell bustled out. Meagan pretended to be cool and collected, but her heart raced, her nerves tingling with her audacity.

The morning room was much more intimate than the enormous dining room. She and Alexander would have to sit quite close together at the little table she'd seen in there when she explored the house yesterday. They would eat and have conversation like husband and wife, discussing what they would do that day. She would ask nothing more of him today, just the breakfast as a couple.

Twenty minutes later, Meagan seated herself in the sunlit room and spread her napkin across her lap. Gaius, Marcus, and Brutus began their dance of serving her food and drink, bumping into each other as they went to and fro in the small room. Meagan waited serenely, pretending not to notice.

Once Meagan's plate was covered with eggs and slices of ham and buttered toast, the footmen stood back and beamed at her, waiting for her to begin. Alexander's place across the little table remained stubbornly empty.

Her heart sinking a little, Meagan scooped up her first bite. The food was scrumptious, as were all the meals served in Alexander's house, but Meagan scarcely tasted it.

"Has His Grace breakfasted already?" she asked. "I believe I instructed Mrs. Caldwell that I was to be awakened so that His Grace and I would take our morning meal at the same time."

Brutus and Marcus, not understanding, looked bewildered and anxious. Gaius, the only English speaker, straightened importantly. "His Grace does take breakfast the same time as you today."

Meagan stared at the empty place across the table. "Does he? Is he invisible?"

Gaius frowned a moment, then grinned when he understood. "No, not invisible. He eats in the dining room."

"But I instructed Mrs. Caldwell to set up breakfast in this room."

Gaius nodded fervently. Marcus and Brutus copied him, clearly having no idea what was being said. "Yes, breakfast to be served to *Her* Grace in the morning room. *His* Grace ordered that he would eat in the dining room."

Meagan threw down her napkin, smearing eggs onto the tablecloth. "Oh, for heaven's sake."

The three footmen jumped out of the way as she leapt to her feet and strode past them, her skirts swishing.

Meagan's heart pounded as she hurried around the

gallery to the double doors of the fearsome dining room. They stood closed, barring her way, the heavy walnut panels telling her to scuttle back to her place in the morning room and leave well enough alone. She set her mouth, thrust the doors open, and strode inside.

Sitting calm as he pleased at the head of the table was Alexander, restored to Grand Duke finery. His sash of office, untwisted and showing no signs of being in bed with Meagan, rested in a perfect angle across his chest.

"Alexander," she said in indignation.

He looked up at her, eyes cool but with a spark of answering determination in their depths. "Good morning, Your Grace."

She approached the table, confidence in her campaign weakening under his stare. "I meant that *both* of us should breakfast in the morning room. Together."

He lifted one dark brow. "Did you? I am afraid the staff misunderstood."

She planted her hands on her hips. "Oh, did they?"

"I believe they did."

She studied him, his hair tamed once more into its sleek queue, the ruby earring in place, his hand steady as he held his fork at his plate.

He returned her look, not challenging but watchful. She could bite her lip, turn around, and run away, but she was not yet ready to surrender.

She beamed a sudden and sunny smile on him and leaned down and kissed his forehead. "Well, no matter. Do have a lovely day, Your Grace. Enjoy frightening the king."

His body stiffened at her kiss, but the hot look in his eyes when she straightened up told her everything. He wanted her. Holding himself in his Grand Duke persona at that moment was taking all his strength.

"Today I will begin plans for a grand ball to be held here," she continued. "The duchesses are correct; I should begin my duties as society hostess. I will have my stepmama help me; she will so enjoy that. I will ask Mrs. Caldwell to keep you informed of the arrangements, and Nikolai will add it to your schedule."

"Meagan," Alexander said under his breath, his tone warning.

Meagan backed up a step and made a quick curtsey. "Ta ta, Your Grace. I look forward to seeing you when our schedules next coincide."

Making herself turn around and not look back at him, she sped from the room, her slippers whispering, and did not stop until she'd returned to the morning room, followed by the startled but steadfast Gaius, Marcus, and Brutus.

She dropped into her chair, blowing out her breath. Step one complete.

She found then that she was shaking too hard to eat and had to ask Susan to mix her another draught of the healing elixir.

Meagan began her preparations for the ball at once. Mrs. Caldwell was pleased at the prospect of opening the house to the public and helping Meagan be a hostess for the *ton* to admire.

Meagan brought Simone in to help for several reasons. First, Meagan knew her stepmother would be hurt beyond measure if she were not at least consulted about the ball, and Meagan did not want to begin her married life by shutting out her family. Second, Simone was a walking *Debrett's Peerage*. She knew everything about everyone who was anyone.

Next Meagan consulted with Mr. Edwards to compare

her schedule with Alexander's. She made a few revisions in both, much to Mr. Edwards's distress. "We need not mention these to His Grace," she said, smiling.

The secretary tried to protest, but Mrs. Caldwell unexpectedly came to Meagan's aid. "I find the changes excellent, Your Grace. His Grace will be happy to spend more time on family matters."

For all her briskness, Mrs. Caldwell was a romantic at heart. She'd had a happy marriage that produced three daughters who were now happily wed themselves.

Mrs. Caldwell highly approved of Meagan spending time with young Alex, and showed her a newspaper drawing of Meagan, Alexander, and little Alex standing on the green in the middle of Berkeley Square, solemnly fishing from a puddle.

"*The eccentric Nvengarian First Family,*" the journalist had written, then went on to speculate what they did behind the closed doors of the opulent mansion.

"Absolute rubbish," Mrs. Caldwell said, her smile broad. "Every father in the *ton* will be plagued by his son to take him fishing in puddles. You are an Original, my dear."

"Is that good?" Meagan asked in trepidation.

"They will admire and envy you for it, believe me, Your Grace. You will be famous."

Meagan tried to be glad rather than worried.

Her scheme continued that afternoon when her schedule originally said she would ride in Hyde Park in a landau at the most fashionable hour. She'd changed it to driving a pony phaeton with Alex by her side at a much earlier hour. Her four hulking bodyguards rode nearby as usual, making her conspicuous in the extreme, but that couldn't be helped.

She pleased Alex by letting him drive a little bit of the way, showing him how to hold the reins between his fingers. Alex proved competent with horses already, having been trained to ride, he said, when he was three years old. Someday, he declared, he'd ride as well as the upright man on the black stallion who cantered slowly toward them.

Meagan's heart missed a beat as she watched the tall body of the approaching rider, his firm legs guiding the horse, his hands quiet on the reins.

"Papa!" Alex waved, losing hold of the reins, which Meagan rescued before the horses could take advantage and run—or more likely, stop and refuse to budge.

She wondered whether Alexander would simply turn his horse and ride the other way, pretending not to see his son waving madly at him. The park was by no means empty. Early afternoon riders were exercising mounts or enjoying quiet drives before the rest of the *ton* would descend on the Rotten Row and crowd them out.

Alexander must have decided not to give them something to gossip about. He continued to ride toward the phaeton without missing a beat. Meagan's hands were slick with sweat inside her gloves by the time he slowed the horse and turned it to walk beside them. The bodyguards, both his and Meagan's, dropped behind to give them some privacy.

Alexander was a handsome man on a horse. His riding breeches hugged taut thighs, black boots encased his firm calves, and gloves outlined the sinews of his hands like a second skin. He rode hatless, as did all Nvengarians, his black hair shining in the spring sunshine.

He bowed slightly in the saddle, his eyes cool. "Your Grace. Alex."

"Good afternoon, husband," Meagan said brightly. "How pleasant to find you here at this hour."

"Yes, an amazing coincidence." He eyed her steadily, black lashes barely flickering.

Alex, unaware of any nuances, leaned toward him. "Hallo, Papa. Stepmama is letting me drive the horses. She says they are too quiet and should be taught to move their lazy fat bums."

Meagan fixed a smile on her lips. "Perhaps the mares are a bit too gentle for me."

Alexander gave her a polite nod, just as he would to a guest who complained of a lack of fresh linens. "I beg your pardon, I had heard you were timid with horses."

"Indeed, I am skittish of stallions such as yours, or those named Lucifer or Thunderbolt. But I do believe a few snails passed Alex and me on the way down the lane."

Alexander inclined his head, still the polite host. "I will see that some swifter horses are made available to you."

"Thank you, that would be kind."

Meagan spoke through a stiff smile that hurt her face. She'd hoped to provoke him into some kind of reaction, but his expression remained neutral. A man playing cards with him would never have a chance.

Of course Alexander had perfected the stone-faced expression years and years ago, as Egan McDonald had told her, while Meagan had never had cause to hide her emotions. He was master of the game indeed.

"Horses are afraid of Myn," Alex announced. He leaned over Meagan to pass his hand along the black horse's coat. "Because Myn is logosh."

"The horses know he is a demon," Alexander agreed.

"Whereas horses are never afraid of your father," Meagan said, shooting Alexander a significant glance.

Alexander, damn him, didn't take the bait. He patted his horse's neck absently, waiting for the next thing Meagan would throw at him.

Young Alex paid no attention. "Papa, may I ride with you?"

Meagan saw Alexander's expression soften the slightest bit. "Of course you may. Hold out your hands."

Alex obediently raised his arms high, and Alexander leaned over to scoop him out of the phaeton. Alexander's coat brushed Meagan's cheek, the scent of Alexander and fresh spring air washing over her.

She wished it could be her perched in front of Alexander while he wrapped his arms around her waist. She bit her lip, wanting him so much, the love spell flaring at the one brief touch.

Alexander helped Alex close his hands correctly over the reins, and then he gave a nod to Meagan and nudged the horse into a slow trot.

Meagan watched them ride away, thinking perhaps it was better she stayed behind so she could see Alexander's tall back and tight backside competently swaying with the horse's movement.

She thought about the letter she'd written that morning, another one of her steps toward making Alexander see reason. This spring Penelope had sent her a plain-looking pad of drawing paper, explaining that it was magic. Whatever Meagan wrote on it would reach Penelope in faraway Nvengaria in a matter of minutes. Penelope had a pad of such paper in her study and she could return the message. Prince Damien's advisor, a small man called Sasha, had been working for months to perfect the spell.

Meagan had not used the paper, not certain she believed in Sasha's magic, but she thought it could not hurt to try. She penned the letter swiftly and left it where her efficient secretary would not find it.

In the letter, Meagan had explained to Penelope that she wanted to be a good Nvengarian wife and asked that Penelope give her some guidance. Nvengarian wives,

Penelope had told her, were exceptionally skilled at pleasuring their husbands in bed. Entire volumes had been
written on the different ways a woman could make sure
her husband had everything he wanted in the way of
sexual gratification.

Penelope had once written her a funny letter about
this, and then the tone of the letter changed as she wrote
that many of the techniques worked very well.

Meagan gazed across the green at Alexander, feeling
an odd catch in her heart as she watched him steady Alex
in the saddle. Alexander loved his son, that was evident,
with a fierceness that made everyone's fear of him seem
foolish. Alexander was a passionate and deeply caring
man, and it showed as he leaned protectively over Alex.

When father and son returned to the phaeton, Meagan
smiled at Alexander, a true smile, not a challenging one.
He handed Alex back into the phaeton with only a sharp
look for Meagan, then bowed to them both and rode off,
Alex waving. Meagan watched Alexander's graceful
body as he cantered away and couldn't stop watching
until he disappeared to the other side of the park.

She arrived home to find that the words she'd written
on the paper had vanished, and a letter from Penelope
rested in their place.

CHAPTER NINETEEN

"Nikolai!" Alexander shouted into the dressing room.

"Your Grace?"

Alexander stood in the doorway to his bedroom at three in the morning several days later. Nikolai had just tied him into a dressing gown, and Alexander had entered his bedroom, already dreading his sleep but knowing he needed it.

Dreams of Meagan made his nights hell. In the dreams he'd begin by seducing her slowly, making her smile in a way that meant she loved his touch. Then the dreams turned ugly. He lost control time and again, ravishing her and hurting her until she screamed for him to stop. But he wouldn't stop. He was killing her and the wildness in him couldn't be tamed.

So he slept fitfully and stayed far away from her during the days, making certain he took his meals out. He knew his disappearing from the house angered her, but it was far better she was annoyed with him than physically hurt by him.

Nikolai appeared in the doorway to the bedroom looking bewildered but also a touch guilty.

"What is *this?*" Alexander demanded, gesturing to the bed.

The down covers were folded back as usual, but rose petals had been strewn all over the linens. A half-blown red rose stood in a vase next to the bed, and a handkerchief lay spread on one of the pillows.

"Um," Nikolai said. "Someone has decorated, sir."

Alexander barely held on to his temper. "This is seduction number twenty-eight in Adolpho of Nvengaria's *Book of Seductions*."

Nikolai considered. "Yes, Your Grace, I believe it is."

The book had been required reading at the temple. It could have been subtitled *Three Hundred Twenty Ways to Please Your Nvengarian Mate in Bed*.

"Who gave my wife Adolpho's *Book of Seductions?*" he demanded.

"I really don't know, Your Grace." Nikolai looked relieved that he did not know.

"More to the point, why was she allowed into my bedchamber to prepare it? I gave strict instructions that she was not to enter here."

The guilt in Nikolai's eyes grew. "I let her in, sir."

Alexander absently loosened his dressing gown, his eyes on the waiting bed. "Explain to me why you did."

"She looked at me, sir."

Alexander bent a steely gaze on him. "She *looked* at you?"

"The Grand Duchess, she has a way of looking, sir. You find yourself backing down, and you don't know why. It seems absolutely wrong to disobey her."

Alexander relented. "Yes, I know. I've seen the look."

Sweet stubbornness, red hair and freckles. She was so damned hard to resist.

"Shall I clear it away, Your Grace?" Nikolai asked.

Alexander heard blatant reluctance in his tone. Nikolai was a romantic, as most Nvengarians were, and no doubt longed to see his master and mistress on the best of terms. Nvengarian servants were always pleased to come across their employers kissing madly in the halls.

Alexander opened his mouth to snap at him to take it all away, then stopped. "No, leave it. She's gone to so much trouble."

"Two hours she was in here, Your Grace."

Alexander sent him a chill stare. "That will be all, Nikolai."

"Yes, Your Grace." He hastily withdrew, leaving Alexander alone with his rose-strewn bed.

Seduction number twenty-eight. Flower petals on the sheets, the room candlelit and cozy, a single red rose to signify the heart. A handkerchief just touched with the scent she usually wore.

Number twenty-eight wasn't meant for physical lovemaking between husband and wife. It was meant to bathe the senses of the husband and remind him of the wife when she was absent.

He will contemplate nothing but her when awake and dream of her when he sleeps.

As though Alexander needed impetus to dream of her. Did she believe him made of stone?

He stripped off his dressing gown, then his nightshirt. Kicking off his slippers, he walked naked to the bed and stood looking down at it. He imagined Meagan tucked up in her own bed across the house, her red curls tangled on the pillow, a satisfied smile on her face.

Slowly he lifted the covers and slid between them, feeling the silk of the rose petals drift against his skin.

He nestled down in the pillows and touched the handkerchief she'd left on the pillow. She'd scented it with the light, spicy perfume she preferred.

He blew out the candles near his bed and closed his eyes, the unusual smells and textures cradling his body.

His dreams of her that night were very erotic and in no way brutal or frightening.

The preparations for the Grand Duke and Duchess's ball swept Meagan into a new world. Thank heaven, she thought again and again, for Mrs. Caldwell and Simone, not to mention the eager helpfulness of her footmen, Gaius, Marcus, and Brutus.

Mrs. Caldwell knew exactly what florists and food suppliers to bully, Simone knew exactly who should be invited and who to snub, and Gaius, Marcus, and Brutus happily ran all over London and carried things up and down flights of stairs and around and about the house without complaint.

Being mistress of a grand house, Meagan discovered, was all about making choices. Mrs. Caldwell or Mr. Edwards presented her with lists of musicians, types of flowers, colors of bunting to drape in the ballroom, and menus of food and wine, and Meagan chose what she wanted.

At home in her father's house, Meagan's choices had been pathetically simple. Roberts would stumble into a room sometime in the afternoon and blurt, "Cook wants to know if we should have mutton stew or what's left of yesterday's roast for dinner."

In Alexander's house, Mrs. Caldwell laid down long menus in French, most listing dishes Meagan had never heard of. Simone, fortunately, knew what most of them were and what wines Meagan should order as well.

"My first husband could be a horrible, penny-pinching miser when it suited him, but he knew a great deal about food and wine. It was only *me*, my dear, he admonished to practice the greatest economies. His chef could throw about the most expensive ingredients imaginable, but I had to account for every penny spent on every inch of ribbon, can you credit it? When he died I purchased a pair of *extravagantly* expensive gloves and wore them to the funeral."

Nikolai also advised Meagan, declaring that the ball should be "very Nvengarian."

"What does that mean, exactly?" Meagan asked in trepidation.

Nikolai stood stiffly in her private sitting room, his hands behind his back, the afternoon sunlight catching his dark hair. "We should show these English people how a ball is done. Have all the Nvengarians in the house perform the traditional sword dance. It is very exciting."

Anything to do with Nvengarians and swords tended to be exciting, but perhaps not in the way a Mayfair hostess would want it to be. "Sword dance?" she repeated. "How many are skewered during this sword dance?"

Nikolai laughed, eyes sparkling. "Only the bad dancers are skewered, and only if they make a mistake. The sword dance takes much skill and to see it performed is the greatest pleasure."

"It sounds—um—lovely."

"We all are trained in the art of the sword dance from childhood, even His Grace. But you and His Grace will perform the traditional dance of the married couple, of course, the dance of the lord and lady."

"I'm afraid I don't know this dance."

"No matter. His Grace will teach you." His expression took on a faraway look. "I well remember the balls of my former master and mistress. Guests would come from miles around, every baron and count and duke in the land. A hundred and one men would perform the Nvengarian sword dance, and the maidens would dance together, and the married couples would twirl, all in colors like butterflies. Ah, it was a sight to see."

"This was the philandering baron whose wife later took a knife to him?" Meagan asked.

"Yes." Nikolai nodded. "He was not a good man, but he did know how to host a ball."

"Ah," Meagan said. "Well, I shall try to live up to it. Thank you, Nikolai."

Egan McDonald, it turned out, had to teach Meagan the traditional Nvengarian lord and lady's dance because Alexander proved elusive. Whenever Meagan tried to schedule time with him to talk about the ball, Mr. Edwards explained that His Grace had too many appointments or Alexander would abruptly leave London on an errand to a diplomat's country house.

Mr. Edwards never looked happy relating this news, his plain English face unable to conceal his embarrassment. Meagan had a few times overheard him and Mrs. Caldwell agreeing that Alexander was neglecting his wife rather shamefully and they hadn't thought that was Nvengarian custom.

Meagan's heart squeezed whenever she thought of Alexander. He had not shouted at her about seduction number twenty-eight, but nor had he acknowledged it. Nikolai had told her that Alexander had slept in the bed, but he'd put on his clothes and left the house the next day without a word.

Meagan had planned to carry on with seduction number forty-three of the book Penelope was copying out for her on the magic paper, but at Alexander's lack of reaction, she hesitated.

When Egan McDonald paid a call, handsomely dressed in a black coat, loud plaid kilt, boots and lawn shirt, she told him of the dance dilemma.

"That's easy, lass," Egan said, grinning at her. "I learned dancing when I lived in Nvengaria. I'll teach ye."

They went up to the ballroom, which was flooded with sunshine, the weather this week being soft and warm. "And where is your husband today?" Egan asked as they entered.

Meagan knew exactly where he was because she'd memorized the schedule Mr. Edwards had presented to her this morning. "Off wooing another diplomat." She sighed.

"Wooing and Alexander donna go together. More like bullying said diplomat into doing what he wants."

"He doesn't bully me," Meagan answered glumly. "He barely speaks to me."

Egan gave her a sharp glance. "Doesna he, now? Maybe I'll have to have a talk with our Alexander."

"No. Egan, please do not. Forget I said anything. I am just maudlin and have a headache and am out of sorts."

Egan raised his brows, but to her relief he dropped the matter. She certainly didn't want Alexander believing she'd recruited Egan to admonish him.

"Now then," Egan said, and began his dancing instructions.

The dance started with the couple standing side by side and facing opposite directions. "Your arm goes around the front of my waist like so, and my arm goes around yours." His strong hand rested on her hip. "Then we reach up and clasp each other's other hand, like so."

Meagan curved her arm over her head and met Egan's fingertips. "Goodness, this is a most intimate dance. Rather like the waltz."

"Aye, it is intimate as ye say. And 'tis only how it begins."

Meagan's thoughts whirled back to the night she'd met Alexander. She remembered feeling his gaze all the way across Lady Featherstone's ballroom and then the warmth of his hand on her side as he swept her into the dance. She'd been terrified of him and intrigued by him and so much in lust with him she thought she'd collapse at his feet.

She was still intrigued and her lust had in no way diminished, but she was no longer afraid of Grand Duke Alexander. Her glimpses into his heart had told her he was a man who loved with a tenderness he did not like to show.

"Penny for your thoughts," Egan said teasingly.

Meagan realized she'd been staring into the distance, remembering the strength in Alexander's hands when he'd pulled her out to the terrace, the heat of his lips when he'd first kissed her.

Her face flamed. "I beg your pardon."

"Donna worry, Meagan. Alexander is a cold man, but he'll not resist you for long. A warm-haired bonny lass like you will wear him down."

His voice was kind, and Meagan forced a smile. "Do not mind me. As I said, I have a headache. Lead on."

Egan did not believe her, but he ceased asking questions.

The dance was intricate. The couple moved clockwise with a shuffling step, then each spun around, clasped each other's waist again and moved counterclockwise. Then they parted, held each other's hands, and pivoted this way and that. They came together again in the same stance as in the beginning, but stood closer, hip to hip.

"Ye go on like that in the same steps, until man and lady are right close together. Alexander can show ye how close. And then ye go through the steps again, this time faster."

He swung her around. After a few tries, she got the hang of turning and grabbing his waist just as he grabbed hers, their hands meeting exactly. They sped up, and Meagan laughed with the exuberance of it.

They turned swiftly, Egan's kilts flying as much as her skirts, and she saw Alexander standing still as a statue just inside the ballroom's double doors.

She stumbled to a halt. Egan swung around once and stopped beside her.

Alexander never moved, but the blue of his eyes glittered.

"Afternoon, Your Grace," Egan said cheerfully. "I was just teaching Her Grace some steps to a Nvengarian dance."

"So Mrs. Caldwell informed me." Alexander did not move, remaining fixed in place as though he'd been nailed there.

Egan bowed to Meagan and lifted her hand. "Perhaps ye'd take over? This dance is best done between man and wife."

Meagan held her breath. She longed to dance with Alexander, longed to feel his hands on her waist, his hip pressed to hers. Surely he'd seethe that Egan had the temerity to dance the lord and lady's dance with Meagan. He'd rush to her, glare at Egan and snatch Meagan's hand, maybe growling protectively.

Instead, Alexander made a stiff nod. "No. You carry on."

Disappointment hit her like a kick to the stomach, and on the flood of pain came anger. She wanted to storm across the room to her stone-faced husband and kick him in the shins. If Egan hadn't been standing next to her, she would have.

Instead she swept Egan a haughty curtsey. "Thank you very much, Egan. *You* have been most helpful."

She held her head high and marched across the ballroom, past Alexander, and out the double doors. Alexander turned to mark her passing, and she saw the flash of fury spark through his eyes. That was all the emotion he betrayed, and she knew she had to be content with it.

Alexander became aware of Egan McDonald at his side, grinning hugely.

"Never took ye for bein' obtuse, Alexander," Egan said. "Your wife wanted to dance with you, not me, as handsome and charming as I am."

Alexander gave him a brief, chill smile. "I know."

"Are ye a fool? She's a lovely lass, agog to be with you. If you're not careful, some blade will snatch her up to be his bit on the side."

"I know," he repeated, his tone hard.

"Then what ails ye, man? Run to her. Finish the bloody dance."

"Did you give her a copy of Adolpho's book?" Alexander asked abruptly.

Egan stopped, his inane smile fading. "Adolpho's book?" He looked blank for a moment, and another delighted grin spread across his face. "The *Book of Seductions*? Ye poor fool. No, 'twas not I, but I wish I'd thought of it."

Alexander believed him. Egan's surprise and then glee were genuine.

"I am puzzled as to where she could have laid her hands on a copy," he said. "I own one, but left it in Nvengaria."

"'Tis a good question," Egan mused. "I doubt English booksellers have heard of it. Is it not only available in Nvengarian? How has she translated it?"

"I do not know." Alexander felt something tighten inside him. "But I intend to find out."

"Adolpho's *Book of Seductions*?" Anastasia hid a delighted gasp with her fan.

She and Alexander stood in a supper room in the Prussian ambassador's house. Meagan's schedule had sent her to a ball in her honor at the Duchess of Cranshaw's, and Alexander had come to the ambassador's house alone. Anastasia had arrived with an Austrian count, no doubt one she was pumping for information of some kind.

"Yes. Is the question so difficult?" Alexander asked churlishly. "Did you obtain or translate a copy for her?"

"Goodness, no, Alexander." She smiled, her eyes taking on a faraway look. "I remember when Dimitri gave me a copy after he first met me, telling me it was a book that would help me improve my Nvengarian. The devil. I was quite shocked. I laugh now to think what an innocent I was."

Alexander noticed to his surprise that Anastasia spoke of Dimitri without the usual flash of pain in her eyes. There was fondness, affection, and love, but her bitter grief was absent tonight. He wondered what had happened to engender such a change.

She rapidly waved her fan in front of her face. "I thought you would be pleased that Meagan has done such a thing. She is no wilting weed and has obviously decided to embrace being a Nvengarian wife in all its facets. Congratulations are in order, dear Alexander."

Alexander did not answer. His friends did not understand what Meagan's determined attempt at seduction might cost him, or her, and he could not explain.

Part of him wondered whether some clever person,

knowing Meagan was the only woman in the world who could unleash the beast inside him, had passed her a copy of the book.

"I will feel more comfortable when I find out who gave it to her," he said.

"The matter is simple." Anastasia bathed him in a winsome smile. "Ask her."

Alexander made an exasperated noise and moved off to speak to another irritating ambassador who was trying to run him down.

Anastasia sat in front of her dressing table later that night, a silk peignoir across her bare shoulders, her dark hair crackling as her abigail brushed it out.

She thought of Alexander's dilemma and smiled. Bravo for Meagan for not laying herself down before the ruthless Alexander and letting him step on her. Sephronia had handled being married to Alexander by being every inch the Grand Duchess and staying out of his way. Meagan seemed bound and determined to be his *wife*.

Adolpho's *Book of Seductions* was required reading for Nvengarian girls when they came of age, but the book was extremely racy by English standards. She also wondered where Meagan had come by it and decided that Meagan had more facets to her than met the eye.

Anastasia's maid finished her hair and stood back deferentially, ready to tuck her mistress into bed for the night. Anastasia shook her head, remaining in the chair.

"That is all, thank you so much. I will sit up and read a book."

The well-trained abigail nodded. "Yes, my lady. Take care you don't catch a chill."

She poked the fire high and threw on another shovelful of coal, ensuring that Anastasia would be well warmed, before dusting off her hands and departing the room.

Anastasia smiled as she went. The woman had taken it upon herself to become Anastasia's nursemaid these days, being of a mind that every lady should have a husband to look after her, no matter she was a widow and vastly wealthy. Anastasia felt the abigail's pity, and it amused her.

She lost her smile as she lifted the brush and pulled it through her hair.

Dimitri had liked to brush Anastasia's hair. He'd stood behind her and carefully stroked the hairbrush through her tresses, the feeling of the brush on her scalp sensual and intimate. Then Dimitri would lean down and kiss her, and things would turn exciting from there.

Dimitri had been the most exciting man Anastasia had ever met. He'd sometimes tired her desperately with his excitement.

Now where had that disloyal thought come from? She frowned at her reflection.

Dimitri had taken shy little Anastasia away from her prim and proper Austrian home and showed her a world of incredible delights. Nvengaria's soaring sharp mountains and deep valleys had amazed her after living her entire life on the flat plain of Vienna. She had never even seen the magnificent Alps in her own country until Dimitri had showed them to her.

Dimitri had taught her how to live outrageously and love outrageously, how to find her wild side and set it free. Her pious Austrian family had been shocked and horrified by her swift marriage to him, but the Nvegarians loved her.

Dimitri had taught Anastasia to ride like a hellion, shoot pistols as well as any man, dance for three days and still be able to host another grand dinner party. They had been wild and reckless and young, and Anastasia had been so, so happy.

He had died the same way he'd lived, brave, defiant, risking everything. He'd often told her that his greatest fear had been dying in a bed, old and diseased, while grown children hovered round, waiting for their inheritance.

Well, he'd avoided that fate on both counts. Dimitri had died in a blaze of glory in the Peninsular War, and Anastasia had never conceived a child.

Dimitri had left her a large estate and all the money he'd accumulated through his grand speculations. But she had no child, nothing of him, and that had hurt her for a very long time.

Her thoughts of Dimitri were interrupted by a soft knock on the door. The sound was so faint that at first she hadn't thought she'd truly heard it.

She lowered the hairbrush. "Come in," she said softly.

The door slowly opened and Myn, dressed in rough breeches, boots, and linen shirt, entered the room. His hair hung in long black tangles to his waist, his blue eyes fixed on her.

"I thought you'd come tonight," Anastasia said without turning around. "But I must say I never thought you'd knock first."

Myn closed the door and came to her, watching her in the mirror. "I learn human ways."

Her heart beat faster. The nearness of him, the fresh, outdoor scent of him did things to her senses. Sudden warmth pooled at the base of her spine as he picked up the hairbrush.

She closed her eyes as he slid the brush through her hair. With his other hand, he loosened the ties that held her peignoir closed and dipped his fingers inside to touch her bare body.

CHAPTER TWENTY

Alexander hunted. He ran through the woods, the muscles of his long, lean cat's body rippling, his breath coming fast and hot. He was far from civilization, where cultivated fields had given way to woods and bleak moors.

He needed to run and run and run.

His logosh instincts had wanted him to kill innocent Egan McDonald for daring to dance with Meagan that day. He'd decided to travel a long way into the countryside where he could run the instincts into the ground.

It should have been Alexander taking Meagan into his arms and spinning her gently, not Egan. But then, the love spell coupled with the logosh inside him could not have borne dancing with her. Alexander would have carried her off, or ravished her in the ballroom under Egan's nose, he was not certain which.

Alexander craved her and he needed her, and he needed to avoid her. Hence he'd taken himself as far away from London as he could and changed.

He liked the shape of the panther, liked the sleek black fur that helped him be unseen in the dark, the heightened senses of smell and hearing and his strange new sense of sight. The creatures of the forest gave him a wide berth, but he could sense them waiting in the dark, huddled in panic.

No need to worry, he thought with a touch of grim humor. He wasn't a true panther but a human who liked his meat cooked and served on a plate with sauce. A good bottle of wine with it didn't hurt either.

Alexander wondered as he ran if returning to Nvengaria without Meagan would break the love spell. Or perhaps he could send Meagan and Alex back to Nvengaria without him, if his duties did not permit him to leave England. Princess Penelope would no doubt be happy to see her best friend.

But then his heart burned at the thought of being so far away from his son and his new wife. When Alexander had surrendered to Damien last year, his one fear had been that Damien would separate him from Alex as punishment. Damien had looked surprised at that assumption, a good sign that Damien was not the monster his father had been.

Alexander caught a scent along one path and loped onto a flat expanse of moor. A wolf sat under the moonlight, a breeze ruffling its fur.

"There are no wolves in England," Alexander told him. He did not actually speak—he had learned to convey ideas without words.

"Or panthers," Myn said.

"No. We ought to be careful lest an eager farmer shoots us or captures us for a menagerie."

Myn looked at him with his light blue eyes, no humor in his expression. "As you say."

"You have been with Anastasia," Alexander said. He caught the unmistakable scent of Anastasia's floral perfume even over Myn's wolfness.

As a human Alexander would have many complicated thoughts about Myn sleeping with Anastasia, such as whether Anastasia was up to something, or whether Myn was, or how he could use their partnership to his advantage. As an animal and logosh, he saw a very straightforward picture—Myn wanted Anastasia and Anastasia needed Myn.

"She has been deeply hurt," Alexander said.

"Yes. Dimitri was my friend, but he was not good for her."

"No." Alexander saw everything with startling animal clarity. "He made Anastasia fly too high and fall too far."

"He should have loved her better."

Alexander stretched himself on the ground, uncramping the muscles of his cat's body. "When you were with Anastasia, how did you keep the logosh at bay?"

"I did not." He turned his wise wolf's face to Alexander. "The logosh is not evil or harmful. We are strong and dangerous, but that is only part of us. We love our mates and our children with tenderness."

"You have had your entire life to practice being logosh," Alexander pointed out, "while I have only known of it several weeks."

"It is part of you," Myn said. "You must let it be part of you. You cannot keep it separate."

"The last thing in the world I want is to hurt Meagan."

"Then let her help you. Every Nvengarian has violence inside him, as does every logosh. Nvengarians embrace violence while logosh are peaceful people until necessary. Let your love for her bring you peace."

Alexander whuffed, a useful sound panthers made.

"The love is a spell that winds me to a frenzy. I want to devour her, I want . . ." He broke off. "The love spell does not care if I hurt her."

"Then you must look beyond the spell to what is truly in your heart."

"Or I should break the spell. This Black Annie must be a powerful witch to evade me all this time. I will hunt her."

"I predict you will not find her."

Alexander growled deep in his throat. "I must find her. What is in my heart is all mixed and tangled in the love spell and I don't know what I truly feel."

"You will if you look closely enough."

"Damn logosh." Alexander rolled to his feet. "The way I know I am only half logosh is because I don't speak in riddles. Only full logosh are as cryptic as you."

Myn, to his surprise, gave him a wolf's smile. "It is useful."

Alexander loped away, back to where he'd left his clothes. He'd return to the inn where he'd taken a room and ride back to London tomorrow.

"Look into my heart," he repeated with a cynical growl, not waiting to see if Myn followed. "I haven't looked in so long I know I'll not like what I find there."

The Grand Duchess of Nvengaria's first hosted ball was the talk of the *ton* for years to come, for more reasons than one.

"Not your fault, darling," Simone said days later, reading yet another newspaper story about it. "You couldn't have anticipated . . . well . . . everything."

It started fine enough. The footmen had swarmed through the house hanging drapes and looping wreaths of flowers through chandeliers and wall sconces. Mrs. Caldwell and Meagan had chosen Nvengarian red, blue, and shimmering gold, and the colors swirled through the house like the brightest of blossoms.

Both Nvengarian and English flags hung in the ballroom, the entire theme of the party being good English and Nvengarian relations. It did not hurt, Mrs. Caldwell said, that Meagan came from a blue-blooded English family of unblemished background, not rich perhaps, but she had *breeding*. And breeding of course was much more important than riches any day.

Meagan tried to believe this, knowing that half the ladies in the *ton* looked upon her as a country bumpkin in finery.

The musicians tuned in their corner of the ballroom, the butler carried bottles of wine to and fro, and the Nvengarian footmen dashed about on last-minute errands. Susan had taken one hour to dress Meagan and one hour on her hair.

The result was stunning. A silver silk dress skimmed Meagan's body, shimmering under a net of midnight blue, and a circlet of diamonds glittered in her hair. The ensemble looked so simple but was the result of countless machinations by Susan, with the assistance of Meagan's second maid and Mrs. Caldwell.

Meagan roamed the house—carefully, so as not to muss her hair, thus having to endure another hour with Susan tugging and twisting it—looking over the preparations yet again. Everything seemed fine, yet Meagan paced nervously.

"Don't worry, darling," Simone said, glittering with jewels Meagan had given her. "You will be the envy of the *ton*. You have this splendid house and a splendid husband and splendid diamonds, and the ball will be the best of the Season. Everyone talks about you, my dear."

Meagan had never been shy, liking forthright ways

that often unnerved Simone, but now her heart fluttered at Simone's words. She would never get used to being the center of attention. She also worried about the ices melting and the flowers drooping and the wrong words coming out of her mouth to the wrong person. The newspapers would either pronounce her first ball as Grand Duchess a brilliant success, or they'd print scathing reports that would make her hide under the bed for the rest of her life.

As she stood in the center of the ballroom, watching Marcus and Brutus clinging perilously to a ladder to secure a garland to a chandelier, she became aware of Alexander behind her.

She knew these days exactly when he came into a room and when he left it, whether she actually saw him or not. Half the ballroom separated them, but she knew he stood in the doorway before she even turned around.

Her hungry gaze roved his tall form and muscular body arrayed in his tight Nvengarian coat and sash of office. He had been so elusive of late, never taking meals in the house, barely speaking to her when they met in public though he showed her every politeness.

The people of the *ton* thought them madly but tastefully in love. Only Meagan knew of the nights in bed alone when Alexander did not even bother to come home.

She knew he went out with Myn, because she saw the two of them coming and going often enough. But if she ever entered a room where they spoke together, Alexander would break the conversation and leave without a word. She tried to ask Myn what was happening, but her Nvengarian was still halting and Myn pretended not to understand her.

Husbands, she thought in exasperation. *Maddening creatures.*

She started across the ballroom to him now, expecting

him to abruptly turn and depart when he saw her. If she could have run to block his exit without looking like a fool, she would have, but she had to settle for striding majestically toward him and hoping he did not run away.

Before she could reach him, Nikolai stepped into the ballroom and caught Alexander's attention.

"Your Grace, there is a problem with the sword dance."

Problem? Meagan's heart beat faster. Two hours before her first hosted ball she did not want to hear the word *problem*.

She realized Nikolai spoke English, likely for her benefit. "What problem?" she demanded as she reached them.

"One of the footmen is ill." Nikolai's expression said that he disdained such weakness.

"I know," Meagan answered. "Gaius. I believe he ate something that disagreed with him, and I told him to stay in bed."

"Humph," Nikolai said.

"He is quite ill, poor thing. Moaning piteously and very green."

"What has Gaius's illness to do with the sword dance?" Alexander interrupted. He would not look at Meagan, but she felt his attention touch her like a caress. Just the heat of his body anywhere near her was enough to drive her mad.

"There is no one to take his place, Your Grace, and it must be an odd number of dancers, as you know." Nikolai cleared his throat. "The others, they wished me to approach you to ask you to take Gaius's place. Everyone knows what an expert you are at the sword dance."

"Do not flatter me, Nikolai," Alexander said. "I am competent but not expert."

Nikolai looked worried. "If you do not agree, then we must cancel. There is no one else."

"Why not have a second person drop out?" Alexander asked. "Then you would still have your odd number."

Nikolai looked horrified. "Ask one of the men to sacrifice his part in the sword dance? That would be too devastating for him, and I certainly cannot single out one man and dismiss him. Not if I want to live to see the morning. It must be all of us or none of us."

Meagan laid her hand on Alexander's arm and nearly got lost in the warm feel of steely muscles beneath his coat sleeve. "Do help them, Alexander. They have worked so hard."

She felt the weight of his stare and looked up to find his blue gaze hard on her. Since he'd told her he was part logosh, she'd felt a honing of his attention, his stares becoming more focused and exacting. He looked at one thing at a time now, whereas before he'd had his fingers manipulating the strings of everything around him.

At this moment he looked at Meagan with the keenness of a predator. He wanted her. That was fine, because she wanted him, but she also knew he would not give in to the wanting.

His attention to Meagan closed like a shuttered lantern and refocused again on Nikolai.

"I will do it," he said. "But do not rejoice yet. If someone gets stabbed, it will be your fault."

Nikolai beamed. "Excellent, Your Grace. I will tell them the glorious news." He sprinted away, his step buoyant.

Meagan kept her hand on Alexander's arm, hoping his intense gaze would return to her. "He seems pleased. Are you really that good at the dance?"

"Competent, as I told him." Alexander's gaze still followed the path Nikolai had taken. "The dance is part of every Nvengarian male's training."

"Alexander," Meagan said softly.

At last he looked down at her, and she wanted to take a step back. The anger and impatience in his eyes could have knocked over a house. She moved her hand along the inside of his arm, knowing he'd likely pull away, but not being able to help herself.

His eyes darkened, pupils spreading to drown the blue. "Please walk away from me," he said, voice unsteady.

Meagan did not answer. She tightened her fingers around the warm cashmere of his coat.

He leaned closer, breath hot on her cheek. "I want to rip that pretty dress to shreds and put my hands all over your body. That is what I will do if you do not walk away from me. Is this what you wish?"

She slanted him a hot smile. "I do, as a matter of fact."

"In the middle of the ballroom with guests soon arriving?"

"I think I care not whether it is in the ballroom or the morning room or the bedroom."

He went rigid. "You *want* me to lose control?"

"No." Meagan stroked his arm once more, then with great reluctance released him. "I just want you."

She turned her back on him and glided away. That was what the instructions in Adolpho's book told her to do. A man could not resist a woman giving him a promising look and then abruptly leaving him. She threw a swift smile over her shoulder, following the lesson to the letter, but Alexander never moved.

He would have her tonight, Alexander determined as the guests began to stream in the door.

He as a good host waited at the top of the stairs to greet them. Meagan stood next to him, her faint spicy perfume filling his nostrils. He could smell the true scent of her under the perfume, his heightened senses letting him find the lush femaleness of her.

She'd known exactly what she was doing earlier today,

rubbing his arm and giving him that secretive look, then the little smile over her shoulder as she left him. Seduction number seventeen from Adolpho's book.

Whoever had given her that book would pay.

Then again, he would not mind reading the book *with* her, playing along with whichever seduction she chose.

And he would. His lessons with Myn had helped. Learning to let go after twenty years of holding in his true self was proving the most difficult thing he'd ever done. But letting the logosh part of him come into his life without fighting it or trying to control it was the only way, Myn had said.

Little by little, Alexander was learning to be what he was. Soon, perhaps, he would be able to be himself with Meagan. The night he'd lured her to the maze he had so complacently believed he could control everything—the logosh, himself, the lovemaking.

But that had backfired, Myn told him, because being logosh wasn't about control, it was about releasing control.

Tonight Alexander would take Meagan upstairs when they were both fatigued by the ball, and he'd undress her. They'd be tired from dancing and smiling at people and solving the little trials that cropped up when one hosted a ball. In their mutual exhaustion, he could commence with slow, quiet lovemaking that eased her to sleep and let him bathe his senses in her.

He sent her a faint smile from time to time, one only for her. When she caught the smile, color rose on her cheeks and her eyes sparkled. She knew.

But first they had to get through the tedious ball. The reception line was long because every single person Meagan had invited had turned up. Refusing an invitation to famous Maysfield House for the Grand Duchess's first at-home affair would never do.

George IV came, Bath chair and all, and three ladies

hovered around him, throwing each other jealous glances. A very elderly dowager duchess arrived, leaning heavily on a pair of walking canes and supported by her granddaughters, because, she said in a booming voice, she wouldn't miss this for the world.

Meagan had invited the most important and most tastefully elegant people of the *ton*. Not everyone had a title, but they came from the best families or were the best conversationalists or the most philanthropic in London. His heart swelled with pride at her taste and discernment. Meagan was going to gain a reputation for keeping brilliant company.

Her guest list had extended itself to the lovely Lady Stoke, wife of Viscount Stoke, who, stories went, had once been a pirate, and probably still was. The viscount looked the part—waist-length blond hair tamed into a queue, a broad-shouldered muscular body, and faint lines on his face etched by sun, weather, and harrowing experiences. He had taken well to *ton*ish life, or perhaps that was the influence of his beautiful wife on his arm and his equally beautiful black-haired daughter.

Stoke's daughter from his mysterious first marriage, with her exotic looks and deep brown eyes, was the same age as Meagan. Miss Maggie Finley had not yet married, and rumor spun that her mother had been a wild Polynesian woman. The *ton* regarded her with interest but was not certain they wanted such a foreign-looking miss among their ranks. As an outsider to English shores himself, Alexander sympathized with her.

The way Miss Finley smiled at Meagan, and the way Meagan smiled back, however, he was suddenly sure that the two of them would get along well. Alarmingly well.

Stoke's blue eyes twinkled as he shook Alexander's hand. "Your Grace, I have been interested to meet you," he rumbled, his voice like broken gravel. "I assisted your

Prince Damien across the Channel last year one step ahead of your assassins."

Alexander remembered that Damien had slipped from England before Alexander's hired men could catch up to him and Penelope, taking a pirate ship across to France.

Alexander bowed slightly. "It seems you did. In retrospect, I am grateful."

Stoke grinned and clapped him on the shoulder. "Always enjoy a challenge."

"Damien and I work together now," Alexander said.

"So I heard." Stoke's gaze was knowing. "Don't worry, Your Grace, I won't let my band of merry pirates loose in here."

"I should think not," his wife said with a look of mock horror. "Once was enough."

"But it brought me closer to you, love." Stoke spoke teasingly, but Alexander did not miss the light of affection in his eyes. Lady Stoke blushed at their private joke.

Stoke moved on, his fingers sliding to the small of his wife's back, a protective move that put him at her side. Alexander envied him his ease with his wife, longing to find that ease with Meagan.

"You are lovely, Miss Finley," Meagan was saying to the black-haired girl. Maggie Finley had coffee brown eyes that were wide and slightly slanted, high cheekbones, and creamy skin tinged brown. "You must call on me. My dearest friend has gone away, and I desperately need a girlish chat."

"Why thank you, Your Grace." Miss Finley opened her eyes wide as though she hadn't expected to be received with such enthusiasm. Alexander could have told her that Meagan's interest was genuine. Nothing she did was false.

When Miss Finley flowed off after her father and stepmother, Meagan smiled at Alexander. "Oh dear, if we become friends, we shall be known as Meagan and Maggie. People will laugh."

Her red-lipped smile and the happy sparkle in her eyes made him want to forget the rest of the ball and drag her by the hand to their private rooms and begin the gown ripping.

Not yet. The love spell and the logosh were still too strong, and he wanted to be tired enough to tamp them down. "Later, my love," he whispered into her ear.

He had not answered her comment, but Meagan understood and blushed rosy red. The warmth of the blush crept to her décolletage and beneath, drawing his eyes to the firm swell of her bosom.

The next guest was approaching, and Alexander reluctantly turned away. But before the guest, a gray-haired baron, reached them, Lady Anastasia swept in past the majordomo and grasped Alexander's gloved hand. A wash of perfume swamped him, and she smiled her most vivacious and brittle smile.

"Alexander," she said. "Your Grace, I must speak to you—in private." She flashed a smile at Meagan. "You do not mind, my dear, do you?"

CHAPTER TWENTY-ONE

The naive Meagan of six weeks ago would have been confused and jealous to watch Anastasia latch on to Alexander and drag him away to the French anteroom. The more seasoned Meagan knew that Anastasia would not so obviously take him off unless she knew a piece of intrigue that worried her. And because Lady Anastasia worried, Meagan worried.

As soon as she could, Meagan slipped away from the gray-haired baron and hurried across the landing to the French anteroom, so named because every gilded object in it had been purchased—legally or illegally—from Versailles.

She paused in the doorway. Alexander and Anastasia faced each other, heads bent, on chairs in which Louis XVI and his queen had reposed before fleeing the mob.

"Has something happened?" Meagan asked softly.

They turned to her, Alexander with his Nvengarian

blue eyes and Anastasia who looked just as foreign but in a different way.

"Close the door," Alexander instructed.

Heart speeding, Meagan eased the door shut behind her. Part of her was pleased that Alexander did not send her away by saying it was Nvengarian business, but she also knew that the truth would not be pretty.

"Von Hohenzahl still boasts he will best you, Alexander," Anastasia was saying in prettily accented English. "And that you will be his best chance to restore himself to Metternich's graces."

Alexander made a dismissive gesture. "I never believed I tamed von Hohenzahl. My men are watching him, and he does not make a move without my knowing. For instance, I know that his underling, Peterli, offered you a vast sum tonight to seduce me and hand me over to him. And that you took the money."

Anastasia flushed. "I did so to make him tell me what he plots."

"And did he?"

She looked glum. "No, he told me nothing but that I was to bring you to him."

Alexander arched a brow. "Perhaps we should consider me seduced, and you can truss me up and deliver me as promised."

Meagan strode to them. "What on earth for?"

Alexander's eyes had gone chill, the calculating, scheming Grand Duke coming to the fore. "To see what he plans, my love. Villains like to gloat of their intrigue in front of their victims. It makes them feel clever."

"And there you'll be, bound helpless in front of him." Meagan flushed. "I believe that is a flawed plan."

"I never intend to be helpless. I will have my men in place to retrieve me, and I might have a few surprises for him."

"Now who is being overly clever?" Meagan planted her hands on her hips. "You would put your life in danger, not to mention the lives of your loyal men, just so this Herr von Hohenzahl will tell you his plans?"

"My bodyguards are Nvengarian. They would be offended if I did *not* put their lives in danger."

"What of your wife and son? Are we to stay at home wringing our hands wondering whether you live or die?"

"She has a point, Alexander," Anastasia put in.

Alexander remained maddeningly calm. "I would be well looked after. The time spent wondering would be short."

Meagan leaned forward until she was eye level with Alexander. "I know Nvengarians, my dearest darling. They would delight in getting themselves killed for you, the more bloodshed the better. You might die with them, but oh, the ballads that would be sung afterward."

"Another good point," Anastasia murmured.

"I do not like loose ends," Alexander said coldly, his eyes so blue and so close to hers that the love spell started to touch her. "Von Hohenzahl is a loose end, and I will snip him. My greatest fear is that he will get behind me and use you somehow, you and Alex. You two are my weak points, and my enemies know it."

"Your weak points. How very flattering."

"Perhaps my English is faulty. I mean to say you are the key to my heart. If something happens to you, it will break me."

Meagan stopped, her body going warm, lonely, empty places inside of her suddenly filling.

"If we end the love spell, perhaps that key will go away," she said. "At least in regard to me."

He gave her a steady look that let her see straight into him. No taint of love spell, no fear of logosh, no cold

Grand Duke, just Alexander. "I no longer believe that ending the love spell will make any difference."

Their gazes caught and tangled, Alexander's eyes as blue as a summer lake.

In that moment, Meagan realized she loved him. Not with the craving lust of the spell, and not with the need of her newly awakened desires—she loved the man who'd swept into her life and carried her off to this fantastic fairy-tale house and showered her with gifts like she was a princess.

Alexander could have married her and shoved her into a garret or sent her to some lonely house far away. He could have abandoned her altogether after taking her virginity, simply walking away and leaving her to her ruin. He was a powerful man, and her family had no power at all. He would have gotten away with it.

Instead he'd defied gossip and the requirements of his position to take a nobody miss to wife. Then he'd proceeded to draw Meagan into his home and his life in ways he did not have to. He could have let her believe Anastasia was his mistress instead of telling her the truth, he could have condemned her for spoiling Alex's routine instead of joining her in the fishing expedition, and he could simply have ignored her as so many society husbands did their wives.

She'd thought he was different from the everyday English husband because he was foreign, but she realized with sudden clarity that Alexander's kindness and compassion came from within himself. Surprising he had compassion at all, really, after the horrible things he'd gone through as a child.

To the rest of the world he showed the hard, cold man who had learned to suppress his turbulent emotions to survive. To Meagan he showed glimpses of the other man, the one who so carefully lifted his son onto his high-strung horse and held him steadily while they rode. The one who avoided Meagan for fear of hurting her. The one who told her exactly what to expect from his life so she would not be blindsided by the danger and intrigue surrounding him.

In that moment when their gazes met, Meagan let herself nurse a wild hope that Alexander loved her too. He was capable of deep love, and her greatest happiness would be to have that love directed at her.

Anastasia was watching them with avid interest, in no way about to turn her head and pretend not to notice them. "I dislike to interrupt, Alexander, but you do remember von Hohenzahl, do you not?"

Alexander slowly dropped his gaze and looked away, taking the warmth with him. Meagan felt suddenly cold and rubbed her hands along her arms.

"I will take care of von Hohenzahl," he told Anastasia.

"Alexander," Anastasia began.

She was interrupted by the door opening. All three swung around, but it was only Myn who slipped into the room and closed the door behind him. His black hair hung long and loose down his back, and his intense blue eyes went directly to Anastasia and stayed there.

She flushed berry red, the fear with which she'd previously regarded Myn gone. Meagan looked at her in surprise, but noted that Alexander did not look amazed in the least. Her mind connected things, and her eyes widened.

Alexander gave a little shake of his head, as though telling her to say nothing. She frowned back at him. He'd known about Myn and Anastasia, drat him, and hadn't said a word.

Alexander rose to his feet and took Meagan's elbow.

"Anastasia, tell Myn what you just told me, but neither of you act yet. I will decide whether I should let you deliver me to him. For now, I need to be a host and keep my guests speculating on why I like to disappear into anterooms with both my wife and my mistress."

Myn remained silent, but this was usual for him. He glanced at Meagan and Alexander as Alexander guided Meagan toward the door, but his gaze moved back to Anastasia as though he could not keep it from her.

Anastasia closed her eyes, her face still red. Alexander bustled Meagan out the door, his fingers points of warmth on her arm.

"Good gracious," she whispered as they moved back to the ballroom. "I will never forgive you for not telling me, Alexander. We ladies like to know when our friends have found someone."

"I believe what she has found is a challenge," Alexander replied, in no way chastised. "It will be good for her. She's built heavy walls around her heart and hidden herself behind them."

Meagan studied his granite-hard face and the line of black whiskers on his jaw. "Well, you ought to know all about that."

His eyes were still. "Why do you think I understand her so well? We both have dealt with our grief by burying ourselves in our work."

"You don't always, you know."

"Always what?"

"Have to bury yourself. Not any longer."

He stared down at her a moment, blue eyes narrowing. Suddenly he scooped her to him, his arm hard on the small of her back. His lips came down on hers, briefly searing her, and then he was gone.

He strode back to the ballroom, away from her, nearly

colliding with Egan McDonald, who was heading toward them.

Egan watched Alexander's retreating figure in surprise. "Everything all right?"

" 'Tis as usual," Meagan said, taking his arm. "Danger, intrigue, Alexander stubbornly trying to solve all the problems of the world himself. A typical day in the household of the Grand Duke of Nvengaria."

Egan bellowed laughter, but the laugh was hollow and his brown eyes looked haunted. Meagan studied him in concern. His usually swarthy face was pale, and he had dark smudges under his eyes as though he hadn't slept much of late.

"Egan, what is it?"

He returned her look innocently. "Eh? What's what?"

She pulled him to a halt outside the ballroom. "You are not very good at pretending, at least not to me. Has something happened?"

Egan's usual good-natured smile deserted him, and for a moment she thought he'd glare at her and walk away.

"I had some news that I didna like, and I'll thank ye to not repeat it to anyone."

"I'd never betray a friend's confidence," she said indignantly.

He smiled. "Aye, you're a good sort, and Alexander doesna deserve ye, but I've always said that. Remember the Nvengarian lass I told ye about?"

"The one called Zarabeth? Oh dear, is she ill?"

"No." He shook his head, dark curls moving. "I had a letter from Damien about her husband, who turns out to be a black-hearted, good-for-nothing, be-damned . . ." He broke off, eyes filling with pain. "Beggin' your pardon for the language, but I'd like to murder the son of a bitch."

Meagan flinched at the viciousness in his tone. "Why? What has he done?"

"He's been scheming against Damien, pulling Zarabeth into it, unwittingly on her part. She's a sweet lass, never would hurt anyone." He grimaced. "Well, except for the time she nearly hit me on the head with a whisky bottle, but I deserved it. Her husband is a hard, cold man, I've been told, and Zarabeth had to choose between loyalty to him and loyalty to Damien, her cousin. She chose to tell Damien of her husband's plots, and she's holed up in Damien's palace while her husband stirs up an insurrection."

"An insurrection?" Meagan said in alarm.

"Hush, lass, that's not for general knowledge. Damien isna worried about this particular uprising and thinks it will be put down in a trice. Apparently, 'tis not the first one he's had since coming home."

"Good heavens, does Alexander know?"

"Aye, he does. Damien tells him everything. Apparently 'tis not so dire that Damien would call Alexander home."

Meagan relaxed slightly, but her annoyance stirred. She'd just been thinking so eloquently that Alexander had let her unilaterally into his life, but she realized he had not shared every secret with her, including the one about Myn and Anastasia. She would have a few things to say about that.

She patted Egan's arm, wanting to comfort him. "Damien and Penelope will take care of your Zarabeth."

"Aye, I know they will, but it kills me not to be there where I could take a knife to the blackguard."

"It's likely Damien would not let you. Zarabeth is his cousin. Damien will avenge her, and he has enough power to do so."

"Aye," Egan repeated. "But 'tis a hard thing, lass. She wouldna want me to protect her even were I there. We were friends, but we did not part on the most cordial of terms. She never even told me of her marriage."

"I am sorry."

Egan shook himself, coming out of his doldrums. "Listen to me go on. It's me own troubles, lass, donna be bothering about them." He pasted on his Mad Highlander smile and held out his hand to her. "Now, let's go have a good knees-up."

Meagan smiled back at him, trying to look reassuring, but she was troubled. An insurrection, however minor, would put her best friend Penelope in danger, no matter that Damien, and apparently Alexander, thought the matter easily solved. It was worrying being connected with such powerful men.

But the wife of a powerful man pretended not to let such things trouble her. Lifting her chin, she sailed into the ballroom with Egan, where they slid into the roles of the entertaining Mad Highlander and the lofty new Grand Duchess of Nvengaria.

Alexander saw Meagan enter with Egan, both of them smiling merrily over some shared joke, and envied the easy camaraderie Egan seemed to engender. Camaraderie was not for Alexander of Nvengaria.

All eyes turned to the new Grand Duchess, lovely in her silver and midnight gown. Egan had her possessively on his arm, but the gentlemen of London began to flow to her from all parts of the room, like moths attracted to a particularly colorful flame.

Alexander watched it happen as he had at the French ambassador's ball, the first they'd attended as man and wife. The gentlemen's attentions at first bewildered Meagan, then she found them amusing, then she blossomed under them. He watched her begin to realize her power, how she only had to flick her fingers and the young bloods would run to fetch her sherry or a macaroon.

She smiled at them, not flirting, but rewarding them when they pleased her. He watched her tell a few gentlemen to pick out this young lady or that one to dance with, and the gentlemen bowed and rushed to do the bidding of their newfound goddess.

Alexander did not miss the dark glances some of the bolder gentlemen shot Alexander as he went about his own duties as host. He had the feeling he would once again have to propose a shooting exhibition to deter too many tiresome requests for duels.

The ball wore on. Alexander noted that Michael Tavistock kept his wife reined in so she did not throw herself *too* much on the king and the royal dukes or Wellington. Alexander escorted Simone Tavistock to supper himself, letting her squeeze his arm and behave as though they'd been intimate friends all along. He understood that she was rubbing her rivals' noses in her new position, and Alexander knew all about keeping rivals on their toes.

The supper was a lavish banquet the staff had worked on for days. The tables and sideboards were heavily laden with pheasant, fish, roasts, goose, duck, ham, pullets, soups clear and cream, jellied consommés, bright greens and salads, sauces of every flavor, and bowls overflowing with apples, grapes, pears, and hothouse strawberries.

The centerpiece of the main table looked like something from a Gothic cathedral—a small square fountain with five tiers of carved wooden angels and gargoyles that rose to an apex high above the table. Water spilled down the angels and gargoyles, spinning wheels that rang soft bells, so that the whole thing was a musical accompaniment.

"Oh, how clever," Simone Tavistock said at his side. "Meagan did so well on all the arrangements, did she not?"

"Yes," he said, unable to keep the note of pride from his voice.

Simone took on a smile of delight. "She was so very well raised, dear girl, by her father all alone, but countrified, quite countrified. Of course once I became her mother I took her in hand and gave her a great dose of polish. She had a fine foundation and all it needed was my touch to bring out the best in her. Do you not think she turned out well, Your Grace?"

Alexander's gaze strayed to Meagan as she walked to the supper table on the arm of the very portly King George, slowing her steps to match his. She glanced over at him, saw him with her stepmother, and sent him a tiny smile that warmed his heart.

"Meagan is an exquisite young woman," he said. Simone preened, believing he was paying *her* a compliment.

Supper commenced and flowed predictably. Alexander had to talk to every lady but his wife, and Meagan spoke to every gentleman but her husband.

He noted that Egan and Michael Tavistock hovered close to Meagan, which gave him some relief. They'd protect her, and that pirate turned viscount looked like he'd be good in a fight as well. Alexander could trust Myn to keep an eye out for von Hohenzahl and his underling Peterli during the ball, and afterward Alexander would deal with the Austrian.

Perhaps Alexander would let Anastasia "sell" him to Peterli after all, however much Meagan protested, and then turn the tables on the Austrians, wrap them in ropes, and deliver Peterli and von Hohenzahl to their beloved Prince Metternich. That would be the end of von Hohenzahl. Metternich was a ruthless and urbane man, much like Alexander, and he did not look kindly upon bumblers.

First Alexander needed to get through the supper and then the rest of the ball without giving in to the temptation of sweeping up Meagan and carrying her upstairs to ravish her.

"Yes, of course," he said with the half attention he'd been paying the marchioness at his side. "English cricket is a quite an interesting game, I agree. Tell me more."

After supper came the exhibition dancing the Nvengarians had been practicing all week. Meagan stood with Egan McDonald as the men formed a circle in the center of the ballroom, naked steel swords in their hands. The swords were plenty sharp—as Nikolai had repeatedly mentioned.

A sigh of interest ran through the ladies in the ballroom. The men wore collarless lawn shirts open over muscular chests, thigh-hugging trousers, and knee-high boots. Biceps flexed as the Nvengarians hefted their swords.

Those with longer hair had pulled it into queues, as Alexander wore his. They formed a circle, eleven models of Nvegarian male perfection.

Meagan's gaze strayed hungrily to Alexander. Like his men, he'd dispensed with his coat and stood easily in this half undress, one brown hand on his hip, waiting for the dance to begin. His usual ruby earring glittered in his ear, matching the ruby on his hand.

"You look quite intense," Maggie Finley said next to her.

Meagan let out a small sigh. "When I made my coming out, my friend Penelope and I used to sit in ballrooms and search for tight trousers, TTs we called them, and rate them. My husband, I think, would have earned the perfect score tonight."

Miss Finley laughed in true mirth. "I must learn this game."

On Meagan's other side, Egan nudged her. "Stop ogling your husband and pay attention. They're about to start. Now this, lass, is something to see."

The Nvengarians used no music. They began by slowly clapping their swords against those of the men next to them, turning back and forth to clap first one, then the other.

Because there were eleven, one man each half turn would not touch his sword to another's. It was a different man each time, seemingly random. Meagan nearly went dizzy trying to decide how they knew which man would be out at a particular time.

The men increased their speed a tiny bit at a time, and began to accompany the sword striking with a slight stamping step that shuffled the circle slowly inward, then out again. The shuffling step caused the men's backsides to sway slightly, and the fluttering of ladies' fans increased.

The odd man out of the sword clapping began to toss his sword once, having just enough time to grasp the hilt again before striking his neighbor's blade. They went on like this for some time, their precision beautiful to watch. The tossed swords went up in a glitter of steel, first here, then there, while the rhythm of the stamping boots and the clattering swords kept a succinct time.

Meagan watched Alexander, one hand on his hip, his other hand strong on the hilt of his sword. He frowned in concentration as he clacked his sword against the blade next to him, once, twice, three times, then tossed his sword precisely when the other two men weren't there to meet him.

He performed with a polished skill that astonished

her, an easy grace she'd never encountered in anyone else. She remembered the last time they'd gone to bed before he'd begun avoiding her, when he'd showed her the arts of pleasure he'd studied in Nvengaria. Every movement that night had been as precise and polished as the dance was now. His own passion had shone from behind the moves, reflected in the intensity of his blue eyes.

Perhaps tonight she'd again lie under his long, taut body, and he'd move into her with the same intense precision. She watched the muscles of his arm flex as he tossed the sword again, catching it with ease, his strong hips moving with the dance.

"Do not swoon, Your Grace," Miss Finley whispered with good humor behind her fan. "People will talk. Believe me, I know how the *ton* can talk."

"Am I that obvious?" she whispered back.

Miss Finley grinned. "Everyone is watching the dancers, fortunately."

At that moment, Alexander shouted a word that sounded like "Hep!" and the dancers doubled their speed. The movements were exactly the same, except they now went twice as fast.

The audience gasped as the swords clacked and rang and the circle moved in and out, the blades flying high as each man tossed his in turn. After only a few moments of this, Alexander called "Hep!" again, and the dancers again doubled their speed.

The crowd murmured in admiration. The dancers shuffled together and apart, blades flashing, then the whole circle began to move first clockwise, then counterclockwise, boots flashing in intricate steps. The time for each man to throw his sword had shortened considerably, and yet they did it, catching them without missing a beat or dropping a one.

They began adding more difficult moves, spinning once as they tossed their swords, keeping in perfect rhythm with the others.

Meagan nearly screamed when Alexander flipped his body backward and landed on his feet again in time to catch his sword. A few other dancers copied his move while some spun in place, three, four times before catching the sword to the audience's stunned gasps.

And then Alexander shouted for the pace to increase again. This time the sword man out tossed his blade astonishingly high while the men on either side of him clashed swords across his body. Meagan held her breath, waiting for the blades to slash blood across her husband's clean white shirt, but the swords never touched him.

The dance whirled faster still, Nvengarian wildness taking over. Alexander shouted his command, and another dancer cried a high-pitched ululation, echoed by the others.

They began to move with lightning speed, the swords clashing and rising and falling, their booted feet crossing and uncrossing in complex steps as they went around the circle and together and apart.

Another cry split the air, and all of a sudden, each man tossed his sword high, their cries echoing to the fussy painted ceiling. The wall of deadly blades arced higher and higher, the swords reaching the apex, and spinning to come down in a rain of glittering steel.

The men caught the swords at precisely the same moment, not dropping one. The circle burst apart, dancers spinning in dizzying circles or flipping over their swords held against the floor. Their cries and stamping filled the room as each dancer grabbed a woman by the waist and swung the startled lady across the ballroom.

Nikolai grabbed Miss Finley a second before Alexander, his eyes hot and blue, snaked his arm around Meagan's waist and dragged her to the floor. Out of the corner of her eye she saw Anastasia being pulled out by Dominic, and then Alexander spun Meagan with him, his mouth set, his face wild, his arm strong around her waist.

This was not the stately Nvengarian dance Egan had taught her. This dance was crazed, Alexander's arm rock-solid against her abdomen, his sword held out to his side. Whenever they passed another whirling couple, Alexander's and the man's swords met in a ringing clash.

"You're mad," she shouted and then she started to laugh. "You are completely mad."

He grinned at her, the wild and feral Nvengarian loose at last. It was as though without his medal-bedecked coat and sash of office, he could let free the being inside him. His face shone with perspiration, as did his muscled chest bared by the open *V* of his shirt. He looked like his barbarian ancestors, the Magyars and the gypsies and the nomads in tents under the stars who lived and loved with great passion.

"I love you," she said beneath the stamping and shouting and clanging and clapping. "I love you, Alexander."

Alexander jerked her close, and there in front of their five hundred guests, he scooped her to him and kissed her.

His sword clanged Nikolai's, and the valet laughed out loud. Meagan joined the laughter, tasting the frenzy of Alexander's bruising kiss.

A loud crash sounded, even over the riot of dancing and shouting, and the two tall windows at the end of the ballroom broke and fell in sheets of shimmering glass. The night rain and wind tumbled in, along with five men carrying pistols cocked and ready.

The gunmen's gazes roved the crowd that scrambled away from them, women screaming, men shouting.

Meagan had the feeling she knew whom they searched for. With his sash of office and medal-bedecked coat gone, the assassins weren't sure which of the Nvengarians spinning around the room was Alexander.

So they decided to shoot at them all.

Alexander threw Meagan behind him as ten pistols rose and ten shots roared into the crowd. The smell of gunpowder choked her, her ears ringing from the discharge. She shrieked as her slippers slid out from under her, and she landed in a heap of silk and net on the floor.

Drifting powder filled her vision and she smelled blood mixed with acrid smoke. "Alexander!" she screamed.

In another instant, her bodyguards were there, Dominic and his men surrounding her like an impenetrable wall. She could not see past their huge bodies, and they nearly crushed her between them, the smell of sweat and wool overpowering her.

"Alexander!" she cried, pawing at Dominic's shoulder. "Let me see."

Dominic and the other bodyguards paid her no attention. Their job was to protect her and they weren't letting her out of their circle. Nikolai had once said they'd die to the last man for her, and now, facing the line of pistols, she believed it.

Another volley was fired. Dominic grunted and bent in half, and over his shoulder Meagan saw many things.

She saw one assassin go down as Nikolai and Marcus and Brutus tackled him. She saw Myn leap forward as a pistol went off, changing into his logosh form in midair. His clothes fell away in shreds and the pistol ball crashed into his side.

The man who'd fired the pistol turned white as Myn shrugged off the shot and bore down on him in all his logosh fury.

And Alexander . . .

Alexander's eyes glowed brilliant blue as he dove for one of the assassins. His shirt was red with blood, his sword stained with it, his lips curling in an animal-like snarl. The assassin threw down his spent pistol and ran from Alexander, leaping through the window to a rope dangling there, disappearing from view.

Alexander did not bother with the rope. He reached the window, sword still in hand, balanced a moment on the sill, then dove through into the windswept night.

CHAPTER TWENTY-TWO

Hours later Meagan sat upright on her bed, gazing straight in front of her. Simone hovered nearby, bathing Meagan's hands in lavender water while Mrs. Caldwell plumped pillows and kept repeating that everything would be all right after Meagan had a nice rest.

Meagan only wished they would leave her alone before she went mad. Alexander had disappeared, and his men could find no sign of him.

Her guests had fled into the night after the attack, the ball dispersing. Miss Finley had wanted to stay and help Meagan, but the Nvengarian bodyguard sent her home with her mother. The viscount had gone with them protectively, looking pleased he'd been able to participate in a good fight.

Sleep was out of the question. Meagan stubbornly refused the laudanum-laced tea Mrs. Caldwell kept trying to press on her. She could only see, over and over, Alexander spreading his arms and diving out the ballroom window, two stories above the ground. No one had seen him since.

Had Alexander changed form and chased the assassins and dispatched them? Was he dying of a gunshot wound in some dark passage in London? Or was he dead already?

The dratted Nvengarians would not let her out of the house to go look for him, not even Dominic, who'd taken a shot to his side and lay feverish in his bed in the attic.

Nikolai arrived to report on Dominic's progress as Mrs. Caldwell tried to persuade Meagan yet again to drink the tea. "He will live," Nikolai assured her, his eyes glittering. "But he is proud to have fallen for you. He would die one thousand deaths for you and think it not enough."

"I don't want him to die even one death for me," Meagan said, pushing away Mrs. Caldwell's teacup-laden hand. "Do make him stay in bed and recover."

Nikolai looked slightly disappointed at her practical order, but bowed. "I will convey Your Grace's wishes."

"And why aren't *you* out looking for my husband?" she demanded.

"Julius and the other bodyguards will find him, Your Grace, rest assured. I stay home to prepare either to heal His Grace's wounds or to lay him out for his funeral."

Meagan flinched, and Mrs. Caldwell said sharply, "Go out of here with your talk of funerals, you ridiculous young man."

Nikolai looked perplexed. "If Grand Duke Alexander has fallen in battle protecting that which is most dear to him, his funeral and monuments will be the grandest the world has ever seen."

Simone clapped her hands over her ears, upsetting the bowl of lavender water. "Do make him stop. I cannot bear it. I cannot dress all in black, it does not suit me. Oh, my poor dear Meagan."

Mrs. Caldwell slammed down the teacup and ran at Nikolai, eyes flashing, arms outstretched. "Out! Now!"

Nikolai took one startled look at a hundred and fifty pounds of angry housekeeper bearing down on him and fled.

"It is too much for me," Simone said, dabbing her eyes with a lace handkerchief. "I am sorry, my dear, I must have a lie down."

Meagan felt a flicker of relief beneath her numbness. Simone in a sick room was not conducive to good health.

"That is all right, Stepmama. Mrs. Caldwell will show you to a guest room. You will stay here tonight."

Mrs. Caldwell at last abandoned the bloody teacup. She called the maid, Susan, to come and keep an eye on Meagan while she half escorted, half dragged Simone out of the room.

Susan sat down by the bed, trying to look cheerful. "Now then, madame," she said brightly. "I shall tell you funny stories and make you feel better."

"You are kind, Susan," Meagan said. She pushed the untouched teacup toward her. "Do have some tea. Mrs. Caldwell made it and it seems a shame to waste it."

Meagan never succeeded in leaving the house. With Susan snoring softly under the influence of the laudanum-dosed tea, Meagan had dressed and crept downstairs. Her plan was to go to her father and have him take her to Bow Street where she could hire a Runner to search for Alexander.

But the bodyguards left behind to guard the house were diligent. They stood at the front door, arms folded, like a wall of muscle and blue coats, and refused to let her out. Explaining what she wanted to do, Nikolai translating, did not help. Bow Street Runners weren't

Nvengarian and would not understand. Alexander's men would find him. Meanwhile, Her Grace should go back to bed.

The bodyguards spoke in grunts and monosyllables, but from their annoyed glares she knew Nikolai translated correctly.

"In that case," she snapped. "If I am to be your prisoner, I wish to be informed of everything you find. No matter how unimportant, you tell me everything. If you do not, I will . . ." She broke off, looking at the stoic bodyguards and Nikolai as he rattled off the translation. "Well, I shall have something to say about it."

Drawing her dignity around her, she turned and swept back up the stairs, seething all the way.

When daylight broke, she donned a morning dress with a mantle and half boots and swarmed down the stairs after choking down a half cup of coffee, all she could manage.

The same bodyguards reposed at the door, blocking her way.

"Do not worry, I am not going to Bow Street," she said in a freezing voice. "I have an appointment of a different nature in mind. You may come with me, all of you. So please call my carriage, Nikolai."

The bodyguards grudgingly allowed her this much, but would not let her out the front door until the carriage arrived at the step. Four of the bodyguards piled onto the outside, then the coachman started the horses and followed Meagan's directions to Garland Close, just off the Strand.

Meagan did not really expect Black Annie to be at home. If Alexander's men could not find the elusive witch, she did not believe an unexpected call would do the trick. Therefore she was quite surprised when the cherub-faced maid opened the door and said, "Oh, yes, Your Grace, Mrs. Reese is in. Would you care to step this way?"

Black Annie kept Meagan waiting in the pleasant sitting room only a few minutes. Dressed in a neat gown of gray, she entered and curtseyed politely, but a twinkle lit her eyes.

"Your Grace, how kind of you to call on me. What can I do for you today?"

"I believe you know perfectly well why I've come," Meagan said, tight-lipped.

Black Annie gracefully slid into a seat opposite Meagan. "You look well, if I may be bold to say so, Your Grace. Much better than when I saw you with Mrs. Braithwaite. I believe married life agrees with you, although you do look a bit tired this morning. Did you not sleep well?"

"My husband has gone missing."

Meagan hadn't meant to blurt that out, but her worry consumed her.

Black Annie looked thoughtful but not worried. "Nvengarians are always surrounded by intrigue, Your Grace. He will turn up when he's finished."

"He was chasing assassins."

"Well, of course he was. Gossip of what happened at your ball is all over town. Some believed it part of the Nvengarian festivities, calling it a prank put on by lunatic foreigners."

Meagan blinked back tears. "One of my bodyguards is hurt, and my husband is missing. I'd hardly call that a prank."

Black Annie leaned forward and patted Meagan's knee, her smile motherly. "I truly am sorry, Your Grace. What may I do to help?"

After Simone's hysterics and Mrs. Caldwell's nurse-maid fussing, Black Annnie's kind-voiced concern unleashed the tears Meagan had kept dammed up all night. They spilled out, unhindered, before Meagan could stop them.

Instantly, Black Annie was at her side, gathering Meagan into her arms, her plump body comforting.

"There now, don't take on so. The Grand Duke has much experience chasing assassins, and he can defend himself. Being part logosh will help him."

Meagan lifted her head with a gasp. "How did you know about that?"

Black Annie smiled. "It is simple, my dear. I knew his mother."

"You did? But . . ." Meagan stared around the very English, very middle-class sitting room in astonishment.

"Did you not guess, Your Grace? I am half Nvengarian. My father was English, my mother from Nvengaria."

Meagan shook her head. "No, I did not know."

"Hmm, I had thought it was obvious. I was raised in London, and when my father died, my mother took me back to Nvengaria to meet her family. Because my mother was inclined to the Craft, she knew of the logosh and took me to the mountains to find them. I met Alexander's mother when she was dying, poor thing. She worried about the child she was leaving behind. She said she had a feeling that Alexander would one day end up in England—he hardly could avoid it, being Grand Duke, so that was not a very difficult prediction—and would I make sure he was all right? I promised. And last autumn, sure enough, he turned up in London."

"You knew he was logosh all along?" Meagan asked. "Why did you not tell him?"

Black Annie looked blank. "You mean he did not know?"

"No, he did not find out until recently. And that was all your fault."

Black Annie withdrew her comforting arm. "My fault? My dear, what are you talking about?"

"The love spell." Meagan rose to her feet in agitation. "The be-damned love spell you made for me, I mean, for Deirdre. Except Alexander said those sorts of spells are very specific, and that you truly made it for me and him."

"He is right. I did, yes."

"Why?"

"Why?" Black Annie looked surprised. "Because I thought you'd suit, of course."

"You thought we'd suit?" Meagan laughed, a little hysterically. "So you decided to trick me . . . but your love spell is tearing us apart. The spell released the logosh inside Alexander and now he refuses to come near me. Every time the spell flares, he is afraid he'll hurt me, so he keeps his distance, and I never see him anymore." She choked on sobs.

Black Annie watched her, puzzled. "I'm afraid I do not understand. Every time the spell flares? What do you mean?"

"I mean that every time Alexander and I are within glancing distance, the spell makes us want nothing but to be with each other—in bed, you know what I mean. We have both been trying to find you, to make you break the spell, but you have been unfindable, and I do not know what he's done with the talisman." She made a helpless gesture. "You must know a way to counteract the spell without the talisman. Please, I will pay you as much as Deirdre did—more, I can give you whatever you want if it's money you need. I seem to be very rich now. When Alexander is no longer under the influence of the spell, perhaps he will be able to control the logosh and he will cease avoiding me . . ."

"Meagan." Black Annie's gentle voice cut through her words. "You are making no sense. The spell is finished and gone. It was only temporary. It dispersed the night you consummated your marriage."

Alexander saw everything with beast's eyes, the world black and white and curved but very sharp about the edges. He smelled blood and knew the assassins lay inside the small house he'd tracked them to.

They hadn't known he'd followed, foolish, foolish men who'd left a huge trail of scent—blood, unwashed bodies, gunpowder.

Alexander the man might wonder who the men were and what their scheme was, how they'd managed to get into the garden past his guards, who they worked for, what their master wanted them to accomplish, and how he could use them to counteract the plot. Alexander the beast did not care. These men had compromised the safety of his wife, his son, his home, and for that they would pay.

He padded softly through an unkempt garden and to a window, able to smell their stench and hear their grating voices. He shimmered into his demon form, hid in the shadows near the window, and peered inside.

He saw a warm, comfortable sitting room, but the men in it looked anything but comfortable. Otto von Hohenzahl stood before the fire in a lavish dressing gown, holding a cheroot in one hand and a crystal goblet of wine in the other.

His expression as he gazed at the men before him was one of abject horror.

"You idiots!" he said in loud, clear German. "You invaded his house in front of dozens of witnesses? Why would you do such a stupid thing?"

"To avenge you," the man who seemed to be the leader said. "At least that is what Peterli told us."

"Peterli . . ." The name died on von Hohenzahl's lips. "Oh, God in heaven. Why would he do such a thing?"

A distant part of Alexander's mind remembered that, according to Myn, von Hohenzahl had been speaking to a man called Peterli in the tavern in Wapping.

"To avenge you," a new voice repeated as a younger man entered the room. He was dressed to the nines in a fine Austrian military uniform, his dark hair crisp, his eyes slightly crazed. "And keep you from being taken in by that bastard Alexander. He turned you from your higher purpose."

"Higher purpose?" von Hohenzahl spluttered.

"To bring Nvengaria under the wing of Austria, where she belongs. To teach the arrogant Nvengarians all about submission."

Von Hohenzahl's face went ashen. "You are mad, Peterli. My plan, it failed. I cannot make a move without Alexander's men watching me, and they must have followed you here tonight. I am doing what is prudent, withdrawing until he tires of me so that I can start again."

Peterli glared at him. "That is not how to make Austria great or Prince Metternich happy."

"Peterli, you are too young. You do not make Austria great by charging into balls at ambassadors' houses and shooting at people. You plan and wait and have patience. You succumb to enemies when necessary, and plot for later. That is how you live another day in this game."

"Game?" Peterli looked aghast. "I thought you were an honorable man, *mein Herr*."

"Now you sound exactly like the Nvengarians. You have utterly ruined me, Peterli. Even now, a pack of

Alexander's dogs will be hunting you—and me—and I do not think they'll wait for someone to translate that you acted without my knowledge."

"You would betray me?" Peterli said, shocked. "You would hand me over to them?"

"I would. I'll not waste twenty years of plans because of a hothead like you."

"But I *avenged* you. Alexander took away your honor."

"Peterli, you are so impossibly stupid."

Alexander smelled the young man's shift from triumph to bewildered surprise to blood-crazed fury. Peterli had come here expecting to be praised and rewarded, only to find himself slapped on the nose like a slow-witted dog.

Peterli moved fast. Before the word "stupid" had completely left von Hohenzahl's lips, Peterli had a long knife in his hand and was plunging it toward von Hohenzahl.

Von Hohenzahl was faster. He lifted a primed pistol from the table that held the expensive bottle of wine and fired it directly into Peterli's chest.

The impact sent Peterli flying backwards to the floor, a look of astonishment crossing his face before he died.

The smell of fresh kill released the beast inside Alexander. He smashed the window glass and the wooden frame and tore into the house.

In terror, von Hohenzahl aimed his pistol at Alexander, but it was already empty and harmless. Alexander ignored him and slashed heavily into a man who'd brought up a pistol ready to be fired. The others tried to flee.

Alexander slid into his panther form and sprang after the running men, tackling one and hurling him into the others before they could reach the front door. He played with one fallen man like a cat would, pinning him and swatting at him as he squirmed in terror.

He changed back into his logosh form and swung around just as von Hohenzahl tried to plunge his knife into Alexander's back. One blow of Alexander's fist sent von Hohenzahl across the sitting room to smash against the wall. A second blow dispatched another man with a gun who landed on his side, bleeding and groaning.

Alexander spun back into the room, changing into the panther as he sprang to von Hohenzahl and planted one large paw on the man's chest. Von Hohenzahl looked appropriately terrified.

"It was not me," he bleated in heavy Nvengarian. "I was true to you."

Alexander growled, giving von Hohenzahl a close-up view of his very long, very sharp teeth.

Von Hohenzahl shook all over, his body stinking of fear. "You almost succeeded," he whispered.

Before Alexander could puzzle out what he meant, a sudden swarm of men with weapons descended upon the room. A net of metallic thread landed around Alexander's snarling body and something hard crashed against his skull.

Meagan stared at Black Annie in shock. "Temporary? I do not understand. The love spell is just as strong as it was the day it began."

Black Annie looked quite pleased with herself. "He is a very attractive and captivating man, my dear. Of course you fell in love with him."

"No, it was the love spell. I saw the visions. Alexander saw them too."

"Have you had any visions since your wedding night? Or just the feelings?"

Meagan realized suddenly that she had not. She'd had one last vision in the dining room when she and Alexander shared their ridiculous supper and he'd made love to her on the table. After that, the visions had not plagued her, but she'd assumed that the love spell no longer needed them. Her own imagination could conjure plenty of ways in which she and Alexander could enjoy each other.

She looked at Black Annie in anguish. "But if you are right, then I am truly in love with him. What am I going to do?"

"Continue to love him, of course. The love spell nudged you together, but you and Alexander made it real." She smiled in triumph. "You see? I knew you'd suit."

"But how could you know? You did not know me, and I had never heard of you. What made you think Alexander and I should fall in love?"

Black Annie rose, perfectly complacent. She went to her writing table, took a carved wooden box from one of the drawers, and from that extracted a letter.

"Your temperament is very like your mother's, my dear, though you inherited your hardheaded practicality from your father. Your mother and father loved each other desperately, and before you believe it was all magic and not real, I gave them the same sort of spell I gave you and Alexander. It pushed your father into noticing your mother and took them to the altar, but their life afterward was their own doing." She pushed the letter into Meagan's hands. "If you want a full explanation, read."

Meagan was in no mood to read anything, but she took the letter and unfolded it.

The page was worn with time, covered in a crisp handwriting Meagan recognized from the few papers and books she had that once belonged to her mother. Her breath caught as she read the first words.

My dear Arabella, when you read this letter, I will be gone, dead and buried and at peace. I wanted to say good-bye to you who have been a dear friend to me, the woman who gave me the two greatest gifts of my life, my husband and my daughter.

Meagan's heart ached as her mother's voice reached from the past. Through fresh tears, Meagan read on.

I was a foolish young woman when I approached you, saucily wanting to catch the eye of the handsome Michael Tavistock. You gave me your wise smile and said you would help me. You knew me for a frivolous thing, and you gave me your gift, not because I craved it but because you knew it was good for me. When Michael met me that day at Chatsworth and could not keep his eyes—or his lips—off me, I knew that you had done what I asked. And at such a bargain!

But it is not of my own happiness that I write you to-day. My greatest sadness is that I will not live to see my daughter grow to womanhood. I will miss her debut and her first dance and her first blush of love. I will miss her wedding and the dear grandchildren she would have given me. Her father will do his best, of course, but she will need wisdom from another party when it comes time for her to make her match.

Please, Arabella, my dear friend, can you find it in your heart to make certain she finds the man who will be her truest love, who will befriend her and be kind to her and love her for everything she is? I want for my daughter the same happiness you helped me achieve, with a man who will love her as she deserves. Guide her to him as you guided me with your magic, bringing to me the greatest happiness a woman could know.

> *And my dear friend, to make you smile, I have en-*
> *closed your future fee. One bob.*

Black Annie gently took the paper from Meagan's frozen fingers and led her back to the sofa.

"This is why you gave me the talisman," she said. "Why you had me help you when you made it."

"Indeed. I watched you from afar the years you were growing up, and I confess, I sent in a spy now and then to keep an eye on you—a charwoman here, a gardener there. When Grand Duke Alexander came to London, I realized that you and he were perfect for each other. He needs a forthright young lady who will love him with an honest heart and bring him out of his shell. You need an intelligent man who will challenge you a little but also see your true worth." She smiled, dimples on her cheeks. "And it does not hurt that he is so very handsome."

Meagan thought of Alexander's body touched with firelight as he drowsed next to her, his fingers a breath on her hair. She thought of him in his shirt and tight breeches and boots last night as he danced the wild sword dance of his people.

She remembered when she'd first seen him in the ballroom at Lady Featherstone's, how his blue eyes had burned her all the way across the room. And how he'd looked in their first shared vision in the bath chamber, his hair slick with water, his eyes half closed, his lashes thick against his brown skin.

The intensity of her longing had never diminished. She wanted him as much now as she had when the love spell first gripped her in its power.

Her tears flowed again. "But I have lost him. No one knows where he is, and his men cannot find him. I love him, and I've lost him."

"Here, now." Black Annie pressed a crisp handkerchief into her hand. "Do not give in. Alexander is a resilient man, and he is logosh, and he can look after himself. He's the sort who will solve the problem and waltz home and ask for a brandy. I wager he's been in worse danger than this in his life and that he's got many tricks up his sleeve."

Meagan had to admit that Alexander could be as ruthless as a rapier and wield himself as such. Even so, it was horrible not to know where he was and if he was all right.

"You are a witch," she sniffled. "Can you not look into water or a gem or some such and see where he is? Penelope says the mages in Nvengaria do this."

"Scry for him, you mean?" Black Annie shook her head. "I can mix philters and love potions and make enchanted candles, but seeing over a distance or seeing the future takes a special talent, which I do not have. I am sorry."

Meagan shrugged, pretending the announcement did not dash her hopes. "You do have one quite interesting power," she said, wiping her nose with the handkerchief.

"And what is that, my dear?"

"You got Deirdre Braithwaite to give you fifty guineas."

Black Annie started, then she began to laugh.

But for all Black Annie's hopeful words, Alexander had not turned up by the time Meagan arrived home.

His men were still looking for him, Nikolai reported. Meagan spent a wretched day looking out of the windows, starting at every sound, and putting off callers, both the curious and the genuinely concerned. She spent a long time with Alex, who could pay no attention to his lessons through his own worry for his father.

Then, when twilight faded to darkness and clouds built up to cover the moon, Myn appeared.

He stepped out from the shadows of the darkened hall as Meagan wandered down to her own chamber. She gasped and pressed her hand to her chest. "Good lord, Myn, you must stop doing that. I'd scold you more if I weren't so happy to see you. Have you found him?"

As usual, Myn did not answer directly. He held out his large, callused hand, his blue eyes luminous in the darkness.

"Your husband," he said in slow Nvengarian. "He needs you. You must come."

CHAPTER TWENTY-THREE

Meagan half expected Myn to spirit her off by some magical means, but they used the more conventional method of a coach and four. Myn climbed into the carriage with her, which sent the horses nervously dancing, but nothing disastrous occurred.

Inside she found Julius, Alexander's chief bodyguard. Julius sported nasty abrasions on his left cheek and temple, and he looked both angry and jubilant.

"Gracious, are you all right?" she asked him.

"I fight," Julius said as the carriage pulled away. He gave her a grim smile. "I like to fight."

"Where is Alexander—I mean, His Grace?"

Julius started to speak, then shook his head. "I have not the English."

"Myn?"

Myn would not answer, and whether he understood or not, Meagan could not tell. Frustrated, she sank into the soft cushions of Alexander's carriage, wishing her Nvengarian lessons were going more quickly.

She tried to draw comfort from the fact that Myn had said *Your husband, he needs you,* not *Your husband, he is dead.* Needing her implied that Alexander was at least alive, a hopeful adjective to which Meagan clung.

They rode out of London and headed southeast as darkness thickened and rain sheeted down. For four hours they traveled country roads, neither man volunteering where they were going. Meagan knew from which streets they'd taken out of London that they rolled toward the heart of Kent, but she could tell nothing beyond that.

She huddled in the corner and tried to slow her racing thoughts. What would she find at the end of this long journey? Alexander hurt, ill, dying?

Please, God, let him be all right, she prayed with all her strength. She could not formulate more elaborate prayers, just that plea over and over.

At long last the carriage turned into a small lane, the outside lanterns throwing spangles of light against tall grass and worn gateposts.

"Where are we?"

"Alexander," Myn said.

Meagan cupped her hands against the cold glass and peered out, but she could see little. "Where?"

Myn said nothing.

I know," she sighed, sitting back down. "You have not the English."

The lane was not very long, perhaps a quarter of a mile. At the end of it, Meagan was startled to find a large country house, one left over from the period of the Tudors, with deep gables and half timbering, rambling away into the darkness. The coach pulled up in front of a wide, dark door that stood open, giving her a glimpse of a lighted flagstone hall.

"Who lives here?" she asked.

"Alexander," Myn repeated.

She had no way of knowing if he understood the question, and Julius offered no help.

Julius hauled himself out of the carriage and handed her down. Meagan hurried toward the house and nearly cried with relief when she saw the large kilted form of Egan McDonald striding out from the flagstone hall. "Egan, thank God."

"Now that's a greeting I more like to hear." Egan seized Meagan's hand and pulled her into the house, growling back over his shoulder at Myn. "About bloody time ye got here."

Myn replied in flowing Nvengarian, and Egan gave a reluctant nod. "He said he couldna travel too fast with you, and he is right. But 'tis me stuck here with His Bloody Grace, 'tisn't it? Beggin' your pardon, love."

Egan had discarded ballroom finery for an old kilt and scarred boots, linen shirt and threadbare coat slung on against the cold. Egan was lord of a vast Highland estate in Scotland and had plenty of money from what Meagan understood, but he was far from dandified. He ought to be a Highlander of old, Meagan thought, fighting with claymore and knife on the hills of Scotland for the freedom of his country.

Meagan hung on to his hand as though it were a lifeline. "Egan, you must teach me Nvengarian."

He looked at her in feigned surprise. "What, now?"

"They could not tell me what happened, and I am maddened to distraction. Where is he? Take me to him, I beg you."

Egan's tone softened. " 'Tis not that simple, lass. Myn

has the idea you are the only one who can help him, but I think he's a wee bit daft."

Meagan's heart sped. "Please tell me, Egan. If you do not, I will . . . oh, I don't know, I am tired of crying, and screaming or swooning seems ineffectual, but I will do it."

Egan put his arm around her waist, as gently as a brother, and walked her into a sitting room lit by a fire in a huge fireplace. "Come in and warm yourself, lass. You're shaking all over."

Her dazed stare swept the comfortable furnishings of the room. "I don't understand. Whose house is this?"

"Alexander's," Egan answered. "Did ye not know? He hired it to woo reluctant diplomats with fishing or walks in the very English countryside. A quiet place to ply them with wine and country air and make them do as he pleases."

It sounded like something Alexander would think of. She imagined him here, playing gracious host and watching with keen blue eyes for the right moment to move in for the kill. "And Alexander is here?"

"In a manner of speaking. Sit down, love."

Meagan balled her fists. "No. I will not sit down or be mollified until I know what has happened. Or must I begin the screaming?"

"Now, lass, me head's not up to that. What happened is this—Alexander found Herr von Hohenzahl, fancy Austrian gent, and the assassins in a house not many miles from here, arguing amongst themselves. Well, then, Alexander charges in and starts wreaking havoc in the pleasant drawing room, and von Hohenzahl calls in about a dozen men to truss up Alexander and capture him."

Meagan's eyes widened. "And Alexander is still there?"

"No." Egan's expression grew troubled. "This is von Hohenzahl's story, ye must know, and he wasn't terribly coherent with the broken jaw your dear husband gave him. Alexander went a little mad, he said. We found von Hohenzahl's house strewn with bleeding Austrian thugs, most of them groaning piteously. Alexander, by that time, was far away."

"Far away where?" Meagan demanded, eyes round.

"Far away here. He'd come to this house, maybe sensing that here was a place to rest, rather like a horse knows where its stable yard is."

"*Sensing?* What the devil do you mean? Why wouldn't he know?"

Egan chewed his lip and gave her a sideways look. "Now, promise ye willna fash yourself. The thing is, Alexander turned himself into the logosh beastie and a logosh beastie he's staying. We canna get near him. He doesn't know us or where he is, and I'd wager he doesn't know who he is himself."

In a wave of fear, Meagan pushed past Egan and out of the room. "Where is he?"

Egan stopped her with a firm hand. "In the woods still. We've got him cornered at least, but dinna go rushing out there. Myn thinks you can calm him down, but me, I'm not so sure."

"At least let me see him."

Egan hesitated. "He's in a bad way, lass."

Meagan swung on him, putting on the most imperious Grand Duchess voice she could muster. "He is my husband and the Grand Duke of Nvengaria. I want to see him *now.*"

Egan hovered another moment, wanting to argue, then he sighed. "Very well, Your Grace. Never say I didna warn ye."

He took her down the huge hall and through a door that led into the yawning darkness. His broad hand on her elbow guided her down stone steps and along a path through a well-kept garden. At the end of this they passed through a gate to uncultivated lands beyond.

Julius and Myn met them in the woods and walked along with them, Myn moving almost noiselessly through the trees. The path wound onward, Egan's steadying hand keeping Meagan from tripping over rocks and tree roots hidden by the darkness.

Meagan heard the snarling before she reached the ring of men with lanterns and swords. A huge black panther circled restlessly between them, teeth bared. Every once in a while, the panther would lunge at a man, who'd thrust his sword forward with skill, driving the animal back.

The wildcat's lips curled over its white, long teeth, blue eyes crazed in the lantern light. As she watched, the panther's form shimmered and became an upright logosh, the eyes and snarls unchanged. The form wavered again, as though he could not hold the shape, and dropped to become the sleek black panther once more.

He wasn't running away, Meagan thought. As logosh, and even as the panther, he should be able to get past these men and run as far and fast as he wanted to.

But he does not want to. He knows he belongs here.

She started forward, but Egan's strong hand held her back.

Myn growled something in Nvengarian, and Egan scowled. He replied in English, "I'm not thinking 'tis the best idea, letting her get near him when he's in this state. Beauty soothes the wild beast only in fairy tales."

An icy blast of wind made Meagan shiver, and the panther circled again, fur ruffling.

"Thank you for the compliment, Egan," she said, voice shaking. "I think no one has ever called me a beauty before."

At the sound of her voice, Alexander swung his head around, but there was no awareness or intelligence in his eyes.

"I still think 'tis a bad idea," Egan said. "Is she to put out her hand and say 'nice kitty'?"

"Do not be so silly, Egan. He might recognize me, and if he does not . . ." She stopped. If Myn could not reach Alexander through this wild state, there was nothing to say she could. "They will have to let me through."

Myn barked a command at the sword-wielding men, who did not look happy to open their ranks to let Meagan near the panther. Their job was to protect the Grand Duke and Grand Duchess, whether that meant escorting them through a London mob or keeping the logosh Grand Duke under control.

"I do hope it's you in there, Alexander," Meagan said, as she moved past the men and stood with the lantern light at her back. "I would feel silly saying these things to another logosh."

The panther's eyes met hers, devoid of all thought but the need to hunt and kill.

She drew a breath. "They believe you'll change back to Alexander simply because I wish it, you know, like a hen-pecked husband. You shall have to set them straight on that account. You never do anything I ask, not even take breakfast in the morning room with me."

She laughed nervously, but the panther ignored her. He paced away, prowling the circle, muscles rippling with his restless stride.

"Not much privacy out here, is there?" Meagan went on. "You'd think the woods would be quieter than a ball-room, but not when you're the Grand Duke and Grand

Duchess, I am afraid. We will always be surrounded by servants and bodyguards. Never a moment to ourselves."

Alexander swung toward her. He shimmered into his logosh form, and then suddenly to Alexander, tall and naked, his eyes filled with hot fury.

"Get away," he snarled, and then dropped back into the panther.

"Alexander." Meagan choked back tears. "Please don't leave me alone."

The panther ignored her. That one moment of awareness had vanished, and he continued to pace, his eyes devoid of all but animal thought.

"I heard a funny thing today," she said, wiping tears from her face. "I talked to Black Annie. She seemed surprised we'd been trying to find her, but I believe she craftily avoided us for as long as she pleased. She told me that the love spell had finished on our wedding night. That it was over. That anything we have felt since then is all our own doing. Is that not amusing?"

It wasn't in the least amusing, but she was babbling, trying to think of things that might break through his wall.

"So really," she went on, "all the times I told you I loved you, it was not the spell controlling me. I moved my own lips and spoke from my own heart. Are you not entertained?"

His distracted pacing slowed but did not stop. He moved like a caged beast, uncertain and frustrated.

"I love you, Alexander," Meagan said. "It is very frightening to feel it this much, but I cannot help it. I love you."

Alexander growled, his breath grating in his throat.

"I love you whether you are a man or a logosh or a Grand Duke. I want you in my life—I cannot live any other way. If Nikolai has to make a bed for you on the floor, so be it, and if you claw the furniture to shreds, well, the chairs in the India sitting room are hideous anyway."

Tears trickled down her face, chilling her skin in the biting wind.

Alexander shimmered to stand upright as himself, breathing hard, eyes glowing blue in the darkness. "Stop," he grated.

"I cannot stop. I love you. I will keep saying so until I die, whether you understand me or not."

Alexander stared at her, then swept his gaze around the circle at Egan and his bodyguards, who watched warily, holding swords ready.

"Go," he snarled in Nvengarian, before he dropped into panther form again and resumed his silent stalking.

Meagan chose to believe he meant the men, not her. "Please, gentlemen," she said. "Do give my husband and me some privacy."

"Not a good idea, lass," Egan said, moving protectively next to her. "He's no' right in the head at present— God knows what he'll do if ye are alone with him."

Alexander turned and saw Egan at Meagan's side. His eyes narrowed with sudden hate and he leapt, forms blurring to first the logosh and then the panther. Egan sped out of the way, swearing. Alexander came to his feet by Meagan, remaining in panther shape. He circled her, pressing his sleek body against her, glaring at Egan and the others.

Egan held up his hands. "All right, all right. I willna touch her."

Meagan put her hand to Alexander's fur, sinking her fingers in the hot softness. He rumbled deep in his belly, pressing hard against her as he circled.

"Go away, Egan," Meagan said. "Let me be with him."

"It is best," Myn said behind her. Julius and Egan looked rebellious.

"Please," Meagan said to Julius, a word she knew he understood. "Please, Julius. I can shout if I need help."

Egan scowled. "By the time we come running, lass, it might be too late."

Meagan felt the sinuous strength of Alexander against her, the protectiveness that flowed through his body as he twined about her. "He will not hurt me."

"I'm no' convinced of that." Egan gave her a serious look. "Even Alexander the man is unpredictable, love."

"I have to try."

"She is right," Myn said. "Let her."

Egan continued to project angry worry. Julius and the bodyguards did not look any happier, but at last they obeyed Myn.

Meagan rested her hand on Alexander's back as she walked slowly through the widening circle of men and swords. Alexander moved silently beside her, his great feet making no noise on the damp ground. His body was hot, warming her through her skirts.

They walked quietly past the bodyguards, past Egan, who looked like he hated himself but didn't know how to stop it, and past Myn, quiet and enigmatic.

Meagan's hand on Alexander's back, fingers threading through his fur, the two of them walked alone and unhindered to the house. They entered its welcoming warmth, and Meagan closed the door behind them.

CHAPTER TWENTY-FOUR

Alexander rose, feeling his man shape stretch his limbs and his back, his legs moving to hold him upright. He stood in the sitting room of the Elizabethan house he'd hired, a fire roaring in the huge grate, the windows shuttered against cold darkness.

Meagan was just latching the last shutter, her cloak lying in a pool of dark velvet on the floor behind her. Her hair, loosened from its knot, sent strands of red flowing down her back.

Alexander was naked, but his skin was hot. He clenched his hands, willing his body to remain in this form.

Meagan turned from the window. She studied him a moment, her sweet brown eyes roving his body, taking in the deep cuts on his arm from the fights in the ballroom and against von Hohenzahl's men. He vaguely remembered tearing loose from von Hohenzahl's net and rampaging his would-be captors, tossing them this way and that. He remembered von Hohenzahl screaming for them not to kill Alexander, and then screaming in fear when Alexander turned on him. Von Hohenzahl's blood had tasted best of all.

Alexander felt his form harden toward the blood-thirsty logosh, and he struggled against the change.

"You've been hurt," Meagan announced.

His attention riveted to her again, and his man shape solidified, which included the firm rise of his cock.

She moved toward him. "Will you promise to stay here while I fetch water to wash your wounds?"

Alexander unclenched his jaw, willing his brain to think and speak with her in English. "You should go," he said harshly. "Have Myn take you home."

"I am home. This house is yours, at least as long as you're in England, correct? In that case, I live here too." She looked at the low-beamed ceiling, the simple comfortable furniture, the whitewashed walls. "It is quite charming, not to mention a relief after Maysfield House. You were very clever to find it—a place you can bring those who won't be impressed by ostentation."

"Meagan."

"I am not leaving, Alexander, so put it out of your head."

She had to move past him to reach the door. He caught her, distracted by how her sleek hair slid over his fingers. "You are not safe with me."

To his amazement, she smiled. "I believe you will defend me against all comers. I am your wife, Alexander. I am staying."

His fingers tightened. "If you stay, I cannot guarantee I will be gentle with you."

She reached up and touched his cheek, her fingers cool points on his burning skin. "I am not afraid."

"You should be afraid. I want you. I will take you."

She caressed his cheek, her eyes soft, then withdrew. "I hope so. Now, I shan't be long."

He made himself let her go. She walked away, the delicate sway of her backside stoking the fires inside him. His rock-hard erection stood straight out from his body, a fact her roving gaze had not missed.

What had she said out in the woods? He'd barely been able to register her presence, let alone her words. He'd so wanted her there that he feared himself imagining her soft scent and melodic voice.

She told me that the love spell had finished on our wedding night. That anything we have felt since then is all our own doing.

In other words, the heart-wrenching, gut-twisting love he felt for Meagan, the longing to have her beside him every minute—holding her hand during the day and buried deep inside her at night—came from his own carnal lusts, not a spell.

No, it was too intense, it had to be magic. He'd never felt anything like it in his life.

His wife banged back into the room with a large bowl of water and an armful of towels. "Thank goodness the water was warm. Someone has kept your kitchen fire going and heated water, presumably so Julius and his men could have coffee after chasing you about. I do hope they don't catch cold out there, but I will not let them in to interfere with us."

Humor trickled through Alexander's near madness. No woman but Meagan would dream of standing up to a Nvengarian fighting man like Julius and tell him to go find something else to do. Alexander would have to give him a raise in wages.

The humor deserted him when she folded back the sleeves of her cotton dress and dipped a towel into the bowl. Her bare forearms glistened with perspiration, and a tendril of red hair fell to skim the surface of the water.

He wanted her with a fierce intensity that would not

let him hold back. He moved to her much like the panther would move, quietly and with determination, the thick wool of the carpet prickling his bare feet.

She met his gaze, unafraid, and gave him a little smile before wringing out the cloth and stroking the wet towel across the cuts on his arm. "I would not want you to take sick."

He slid his hand behind her head and threaded his fingers though her loose hair as she dabbed at the smears of blood on his interlaced tattoo. When she raised her head, he saw tears on her face.

"I was so worried about you," she said.

No woman had ever worried about him, not even Sephronia. The former Grand Duchess, stately and regal, cold like a diamond, would never have stood by him while he struggled to regain his sanity. She would never have looked at him with love in her eyes and say she'd worried for him.

Meagan, on the other hand, had come all the way out here in the dark, had stood in front of the beast in the freezing cold woods and declared her love in front of a dozen men, and now dabbed at the blood on his arm, fearing he'd take a fever.

He stroked Meagan's hair, reveling in how sleek and soft it was. No longer able to speak, he leaned down and kissed the tears from her face.

As his lips met hers, what little control he had evaporated. He heard the growl in his own throat, and her eyes widened.

Then they were on the floor, Meagan landing on top of him, the water cascading over them in a warm arc. Alexander kissed her, furrowing her hair where droplets of water glistened like jewels. She closed her eyes tight, tears still beading on her lashes, the line of freckles across her nose an endearing sight.

She pressed her fingers into his bare shoulders, indenting his flesh. The slight pain only increased his desperation.

Too many wretched garments barred the way between her and himself. Alexander found the fabric-covered buttons at the back of her bodice and impatiently pushed them at the holes. No, not fast enough. He spread his hand.

Fabric tore and buttons popped, and he fumbled with the ties that held her stays. The night he'd first made love to her, he'd been able to slowly and deliberately work the complicated laces free, but tonight his clumsy fingers tugged and pulled to no avail.

"Let me." She dropped a kiss to his lips, then rose to her knees, her thighs on either side of him, his erection pressing the tangle of her skirts. He had already snapped the laces, and she reached behind her to tug and pull them free.

The stays came off to reveal her pale chemise, her tight, dark nipples pressing the fabric. She shrugged off the remains of her bodice, then unlaced her chemise and pushed it from her shoulders. Her breasts came into view, beautiful and taut, fitting perfectly into his hands.

Every lesson he'd learned at the cult of Eros fled his conscious mind. He only knew he wanted Meagan with mindless intensity and would not be satisfied until he sated himself with her.

"Take off the dress," he commanded.

Meagan, face still stained with tears, climbed to her feet and let her chemise and gown fall from her hips, then she stepped out of the clothes and tossed them aside. She was naked except for her stockings and slippers, just as she had been at Lady Featherstone's the night the love spell had made him take her. She was even more beautiful now, pink-cheeked and starry-eyed, knowing what it was like to have him inside her and wanting it again.

He reached to her hips and dragged her down on top of him. "Ride me," he said.

Her lips curved to a smile, a woman pleased that a man wanted her so much. She slid her knees to either side of him, rubbing the lips of her opening against his waiting cock. He groaned with frustration, fingers clamping her wrists.

"Please."

The secret smile broadened. Her opening was so slick, filled with honey. Still she teased him, rubbing the folds against his flange, scraping her hard nub against his tip.

"Do not," he said between gritted teeth. "Do not, Meagan, you will regret it."

"I don't believe I will," she said softly, and then finally she eased herself straight onto him.

As soon as she tightened around his stiffness, her red lips parting with what she felt, Alexander lost the remnants of his sanity.

His mind went blank, shooting down roads of wildness he didn't understand. All he felt was the tight point where they joined, her wrists under his fingers, her soft backside resting on his thighs.

Do not hurt her, his mind warned him, but he was beyond all thought.

He thrust up into her, reveling in the hot pressure of her. He wanted to stay inside her forever, in this woman he loved, letting her scent cover him, the smell of her honey coupled with her own musk and the sweet spice of her perfume.

Love you. I love you.

When he pried open his eyes he saw her far gone in the feel of it, her eyes closed, hands clenched against the pain of his grasp on her wrists.

He was hurting her. He slowed his thrusts.

Instantly her eyes jerked open. "No," she begged. "Don't stop. Please."

Alexander released her hands and grasped her hips, pulling her harder onto him as he thrust deep inside her. He slid one hand to where they were joined and rubbed his thumb against the twist of hair and the firm nub beneath it.

Meagan screamed. She ground her hips faster and faster, her shrieks driving him to a frenzy.

He felt himself start to change. *No. No, not yet.*

"Alexander," she said, brown eyes wide.

He twined his fingers through hers and held on so hard that his nails creased her skin. "Do not let me go away. Keep me here."

She nodded, loose strands of hair brushing his chest. She held his hand firmly, never mind that he must nearly be breaking her fingers.

She leaned to him, the points of her nipples hard against his flesh. "I love you, Alexander. Stay with me."

He nodded. The logosh wanted her as much as he did, but he would stay for her. He had to.

He felt himself begin to change again, his muscles rippling. Meagan stared in shock, and then he was Alexander again. "Damn it."

"Stay with me," she breathed. "Be my husband. I love you."

"Say it again."

"Stay with me."

"No." He could barely think of words. "The other."

She skimmed her lips over his face. "I love you. I love you, Alexander."

"God help me." He climaxed, his body shuddering with release, his temperature soaring. He swore his skin burned, and then his hands became claws, raking Meagan's flesh.

"Alexander," she cried desperately. "I love you."

Exerting every ounce of strength he had, Alexander willed the claws to become fingers again, ordinary brown hands scratched from bramble in the woods.

His seed filled her and he gathered her against him, his breath raw, his heart pounding.

They lay together, breathing hard, trying to recover, every inch of Alexander's body hurting and yet satisfied.

He scraped the hair back from her forehead. "You are the most precious thing in my life. My Meagan. I love you."

She let out her breath and a little laugh came with it. "Oh good. Because I love you too."

Meagan was too exhausted to walk up the stairs to the bedrooms above. She happily let Alexander scoop her into his strong arms and carry her.

The gallery creaked with the interesting squeal of an old house, the railings dark with age. She fell in instant love with the bedroom Alexander took her to off the first landing. The chamber was small, situated in the front of the house and right over the warm sitting room. The bed had a carved headboard and a high mattress piled with pillows and thick down quilts.

"If you had brought me to this house right away," she said as Alexander set her down on the cozy comfort of the bed. "I would not have hesitated half as long when you asked me to marry you."

He raised his brows, a ghost of the cool Grand Duke returning. "I thought anything less than my overblown house in Berkeley Square would not please you."

She smiled sleepily as he climbed into the bed beside her and pulled quilts and pillows around them. "I am a country girl and I like simple pleasures."

"I will endeavor to remember." He rested his head on her pillow and slid a strong arm around her waist, his large body warming the bed better than a hot brick.

"I admit I was curious to see what was inside that house." She smiled. "And what was inside you."

"I believe you saw that clearly enough tonight."

"I wanted to see it. I want all of you—logosh and Grand Duke and Alexander and warm furry panther."

He frowned. "You are pleased that your husband is a wild beast?"

"Hmm." Downstairs after he'd lain on the carpet catching his breath, after she'd stretched herself on top of him and soaked in his warmth, he'd risen and refilled the bowl of water from the kitchen to gently clean the scratches his half-man, half-panther self had made in her thighs. The scratches were light, just drawing blood. He'd kept his incredible strength sheathed for her even then.

She ran her fingers lightly over his lips. "I believe Nvengarian women like their husbands to be beasts in the bedroom, although I assume they do not mean so literally. At least, that is what it says in Adolpho's *Book of Seductions*."

His dark brows drew together. "I have been meaning to ask, who gave you this book? I am aware of no translations of the *Book of Seductions* in English."

"Penelope is copying it out for me. Her Nvengarian is much better than mine, so she is translating and sending it to me in letters."

"Is she? Good God."

"Why? What is the matter?"

Alexander raked a hand through his hair. "You and Princess Penelope, the leader of Nvengaria, reading the *Book of Seductions* together. I thought English girls were shocked at the mere mention of men and women sharing the same bed."

Meagan grinned. "Of course we talk about seduction and bed games and men's physiques all the time. We are simply discreet. I never told you about TTs."

He looked perplexed. "TTs?"

Quickly Meagan explained her girlish game of tight trousers with Penelope, and Alexander's eyes glinted with humor. "Is that what ladies whisper behind their fans in ballrooms? And I thought Englishwomen were demure to the point of tedium."

"We learn to keep our ribald ways well hidden. Are you shocked? Did you want a shy bride?"

"I believe I told you I wanted no bride at all." His blue eyes heated. "Until I saw you, and I could not keep visions of you out of my head."

"That was the love spell."

"It was more than that. It was you with your red hair and adorable freckles and the most sensual body I'd ever seen in my life."

"You're mad. You can't really like my freckles."

"I love them." He bent his head and drew his tongue across the line of them on her collarbone. "I love every inch of you."

"Then I shall tell my stepmama to stop bleating at me to put buttermilk on them."

"You could put wine on them," Alexander murmured against her skin. "Or perhaps chocolate."

"I've never heard of those as remedies for freckles."

"No, but I would enjoy lapping such things from your skin."

Her body heated with anticipation. "We shall have to see what we can do about that. And now . . ."

"Mmm?" He softly kissed her shoulder. "I thought you were tired, my wife."

"I am exhausted and do not believe I shall remain awake more than five minutes. But will you do something for me? Just to please me?"

"Name it," Alexander said.

"Will you shift into the panther again?"

He studied her a moment, his gaze sharpening. He asked in a quiet voice, "Why?"

"Because there is no fire in the room and your fur would be warm to sleep against."

He watched her, eyes glowing with the magic inside him. "I thought you wanted me to remain Alexander."

"But you still would be Alexander. You would just have a soft coat."

He stared at her incredulously, then suddenly he began to laugh. The laughter built up from chuckles to a full-blown roar and he flopped over onto his back, his arms across his stomach.

She had never heard him laugh so, not the full surrender to mirth that shook the bed and filled the room with his gravelly voice. Tears streamed from his tightly closed eyes as he gasped for breath.

"I love you," he said, rolling over to kiss her again. "I have been fighting myself all this time, and you sum it up in one simple sentence."

"Well, 'tis true," she said.

"It is true." He kissed the tip of her nose, his smile wide. "But it took you to tell me."

"I am pleased I am so wise. Now, will you?"

He kissed her, a long satisfying kiss that made her wish she were not quite so tired. But after a sleep, perhaps . . .

"For you, my Grand Duchess, I will oblige."

Meagan raised up on her elbow as Alexander rolled over, putting his tightly muscled back to her.

She was not certain she saw it begin, but Alexander's hands curved to claws, then his arms thinned as his shoulders grew broader and heavier, his face elongating to the black harshness of the big cat. And then all of a sudden her bed was full of wild animal, a smooth black-coated panther lying next to her, its breathing loud in the darkness.

"Thank you," she said. She snuggled down next to his furred warmth, sliding one arm around his middle. "Good night, Alexander."

She heard and felt the rumble deep inside his body, and then she fell into sleep.

Lady Anastasia quickly opened her hotel room door when she heard the soft knock, sensing with her entire body who it was. Clad once again in her velvet peignoir with nothing beneath, she stood aside to let Myn enter.

"Alexander?" she asked anxiously.

"Found, and well," he said as he closed the door. "His wife is with him."

"And everything is—all right?"

"She loves him," Myn answered, his large blue eyes never changing. "She will ground him and keep him as he needs to be. And he loves her well in return."

Anastasia relaxed. "Well, I know you would not have left him if all was not settled. Thank you for looking after him. He is a difficult man, but he deserves his happiness."

"I watch him as a favor to Princess Penelope. The logosh serve the princess."

"How kind of you."

She felt brittle and nervous, and she did not know why. He'd come to make love to her again, that was certain, because why else would he come? Not to reassure her. He unnerved her and baffled her and made her long for his strong body and the intensely satisfying way he'd taken her.

She had never wanted another man since Dimitri's

death. When she'd gone to bed with men since then, she'd done so because she needed something from them, secrets or favors to further her ruthless quest against Austria.

But she wanted this man with his large blue eyes and quietness that soothed her and excited her at the same time.

Her hands trembled as she began to undo her peignoir. He moved to her and quietly covered her fingers with his. "Anastasia."

Her smile shook as much as her fingers. "What is the matter? Once, and that is all I am allowed to have? Are you punishing me because I loved Dimitri so well?"

Myn slid his arms around her waist. His very obvious erection pressing her abdomen reassured her that he wanted her. "I will return to Nvengaria soon."

A lash of pain went through her, one she'd not felt since the day she'd finally realized her husband was gone. "How soon?"

"A few days. You will come with me."

"What?" She tried to shake her head. "I cannot. I have to stay and finish my missions. I have to help Alexander."

"No." His lashes were thick and dark, like his hair. "Your time here is finished. I will take you home."

"You don't understand. I cannot go back to Nvengaria. Not now, not ever. I can't face it. I can never—" She broke off, words choking her.

"That is why you must go. You will return there to heal yourself—with me."

"Why do you want me?" she asked. "Why do you want me to go with you, to fall in love with you?"

He traced patterns on the small of her back. "I knew Dimitri well. He wanted you to live. That is all he ever wanted."

She nodded, remembering the honest vitality of Dimitri, how he'd whirled her into a waltz, then out onto a terrace for her first real kiss. He'd showed her life as hard as he could.

"I haven't been living, have I?" she realized. "For six years, I have not really lived. I may as well have remained with my staid family in the staid middle of Vienna and never gone with him."

"Nvengaria made you live," Myn said. "Let me give you back your life."

He was such a large man, and her body fit well against his. She remembered his hands on her in the night and how for the first time in a long time she'd actually *felt.*

She wrapped her arms around his neck, letting go of something that had hurt inside her for too long. "Very well. I will go with you."

He kissed her, a bruising, almost brutal kiss. "It is well," he said. "We will go. I believe you will like my family."

She stared a moment, then she laughed. "Good lord. Never say I have to meet your mother."

He smiled mysteriously and said nothing. It felt good to laugh, and good to see him smile. He kissed her again, and then to her delight, he continued unlacing her peignoir and pushed it from her bare shoulders, his hands finding the curve of her hips.

When Meagan woke to sunshine flooding the room, Alexander was Alexander again, smiling his handsome smile as he looked down at her. She returned the smile as he eased her onto her back, then he slid his body over hers and made love to her, fast and hard.

They dressed each other in clothes that Alexander kept here, a suit of subdued black for himself and a dark blue cotton gown for Meagan. He showed her a wardrobe full of dresses for her—when he had the seamstresses make her Town clothes, he'd had them sew more serviceable clothes for when he brought her to the country.

"You have kept this place a closely guarded secret," she said as he laced her into her stays.

"I wanted to surprise you. There is excellent fishing in the lake. Do you think Alex would like it?"

Meagan glanced out the window to the green downs and the sunshine glinting from clear blue water at the edge of the woods. She wished she could have seen this loveliness last night as they charged here to save Alexander. She might have been less frightened had she known what beauty he had found.

"I think he will love it." She turned when he finished and slid her arms about his waist. "As will I."

"Then we will come here as soon as I finish with one errand in Town."

She raised her brows. "What of our schedules? What of our social standing as Grand Duke and Duchess of Nvengaria?"

"Our schedules can go to hell for a few weeks. If I hadn't been so adamant about being Grand Duke every minute of every day in Nvengaria, I might have had a real first marriage."

"I don't know," Meagan said thoughtfully. "From what you tell me of Sephronia, she was in love with your position and not you. She adored being Grand Duchess, but she ought to have loved you better."

"I am difficult to love."

"No, you are not." She smiled against his lips. "Loving you is the easiest thing I have ever done."

His hand moved to the back of her stays, his fingers finding the knot that held them closed. "You should not have said that. Not if you are in a hurry to go home."

She shivered against him. "Julius will be waiting with the coach. Impatiently, I wager."

Alexander had told her that Egan, after ascertaining that everything was all right last night, had taken Julius and the others to the steward's house to get warm. They'd drunk Nvengarian wine and told tales and played cards for the remainder of the night. Myn had disappeared, but that was typical of Myn. Meagan had a feeling she knew where he'd gone.

"Julius can wait a little longer," Alexander murmured as his hand splayed open the laces of her stays. Meagan twined her arms around his neck and let him do as he pleased.

CHAPTER TWENTY-FIVE

Grand Duke Alexander met with Prince Metternich, first minister of Austria, in a room in Carleton House that Alexander had bullied the English king into letting them use. Metternich had come to England for diplomatic talks and Alexander saw no reason not to exploit the time.

Metternich was an elegant man with carefully curled hair and a strong face that held just a hint of plumpness. The two men faced each other, each seated in a gilded chair across a short space of carpet woven with huge roses. Each man had a decanter of brandy and a goblet beside him, which footmen had filled before discreetly retreating. Alexander had demanded that this meeting be strictly private.

After the preliminary dance of inquiring about the state of both men's health and that of their families, and Metternich congratulating Alexander on his recent marriage, Alexander launched himself into why he'd cornered the savior of the Austrian Empire.

"Your toady, Otto von Hohenzahl," Alexander said. "Please do not let him annoy me again."

"Ah." Metternich moved a ringed hand in a dismissive gesture as he reached for his brandy. "Von Hohenzahl has retreated to Vienna. I believe he has a country home outside the city where he tends roses with his wife."

"I know he acted against your wishes and without your knowledge," Alexander said. "But he is yours. I hope I did not startle you when I delivered my—package."

Metternich's eyes flickered. The morning after Meagan had healed him, Alexander had sent Julius and the others to wrap von Hohenzahl in cords and drop the trussed-up man outside the London house in which Metternich was staying. Alexander had tucked a note into von Hohenzahl's dressing gown pocket to explain the matter.

"A whimsical prank," Alexander continued, his voice colder than it had ever been. "But I was feeling whimsical that morning. However, if one of your servants is fool enough to endanger my wife and son's lives again, you will pay and you will pay dearly."

Metternich took a thoughtful sip of brandy. He was an intelligent man, who had not taken over the falling-apart Austrian empire and made it whole again without a great deal of strength and cunning.

"If Nvengaria were Austrian," he said smoothly, "these sorts of things would not happen. Consider it, my friend. Your little country would never have to fear the press of Russia or the Ottomans again."

"What about the Austrians?" Alexander said dryly. "We will never bow to you, we will never succumb, we will never let you in." He picked up his own glass of brandy but did not drink. "Become used to the notion."

Metternich sighed. "I really did not think you'd say '*Oh, very well*' and hand Nvengaria over to me. But I must ask, Your Grace, while we have a private moment, why not? Why on earth should you not want to be part of the larger whole, part of the empire that is the most powerful and wealthy in Europe? In other words, why are you Nvengarians so damned stubborn?"

He asked it as though he was curious about an oddity.

"Because we should lose ourselves," Alexander answered. "Because eight hundred years ago when the first leaders of our barbaric tribes made a pledge to each other to make life better for their people, we promised to never knuckle under to any outsider. We would remain Nvengarian, untouched and untouchable. We are a proud people, and we will remain so until the last one of us is dead."

"Time marches, Your Grace. The world changes."

"I know. Which is the point of me being here in England. To bring Nvengaria into the world without letting the world conquer it. Prince Damien is no foolish playboy figurehead, and never mistake him for one. He knows exactly what he is doing, and I stand right beside him."

"Watching over his shoulder, eh?"

Alexander made a conceding gesture. "As you say."

The two men studied each other, Metternich's eyes shrewd. But he nodded and dropped the subject.

For today, Alexander had won. Austria and Metternich would never give up, Alexander knew, but neither would Alexander.

They finished the brandy and rose, both men extending hands at precisely the same time, breaking apart after one brief handshake. The footmen, cued, opened the double doors for them.

"I was introduced to your wife at the king's soiree last

evening," Metternich said as they walked out of the room, side by side, at the exact same time. "She is quite a beauty. Again, I congratulate you."

Alexander's mouth softened as he remembered waking up next to Meagan in her bedroom in their Berkeley Square house that morning. He'd had a leisurely breakfast with her in the sunny morning room as had become their habit, sending for Alex to join them. It was a welcome novelty, living as a happy family.

Meagan and her courage had given him that. If she'd not charged out to the country to show him that his love for her would keep the beast from hurting her—and that she loved him, beast and all—he would never have known, at last, what happiness could be.

He hadn't really understood what Myn meant by *surrender* until Meagan had shown him. Myn had meant complete surrender, letting go of all the hurts and angers Alexander had accumulated in his life, the fear he'd learned to embrace at such a young age. The death, the vengeance, the years of watching and fear, were in the past. Meagan had made it possible for him to begin again.

"She is," Alexander answered with a cordial nod, his heart warm. "I will convey the compliment."

Metternich nodded back, and the two men parted.

"Fishing," Meagan said, "is a satisfying occupation."

She watched her husband and his son standing knee deep in water at the edge of the lake, both in tall boots, both with lines dragging on the surface. It was late June, the Season over, and sunshine sparkled on the deep blue water.

On a slight rise above them stood Alexander's Elizabethan house, splendid and old and quaint and cozy. They'd retreated here days ago for a welcome respite.

Meagan stretched out on a blanket on the grass watching Alexander give Alex solemn fishing lessons. They stood side by side, one a miniature of the other, and let their lines bob.

When Alex's line began to pull, he let out a cry of delight and followed his father's instructions to the letter to pull in a flopping silver fish.

Meagan sat up and clapped her hands. "Excellently done, Alex. We'll have Cook fry him up for supper."

Alex looked in distress at the beautiful fish dancing on the end of his line. "We are going to eat him?"

"Well, yes." Meagan laughed. "That is the point of catching fish."

Alex looked at the struggling fish a moment longer, then unhooked it from his line and tossed it back into the lake.

Alexander glanced over at Meagan, his blue eyes full of mirth. "He has a soft heart, I think."

"It is all right." Meagan placed a hand on the tiny swell of her abdomen where Alex's brother or sister grew. "We have plenty of roast from yesterday evening."

She lay back on the blanket, resting now as she needed to do more often these days. The sky arched blue above her, a few clouds drifting past to give cooling shade once in a while. A perfect English day in a perfect English summer. Her father and stepmother were wandering the gardens somewhere, enjoying Alexander's hospitality while giving him and Meagan privacy.

Alexander had invited her parents and looked surprised at Meagan's surprise that he should do so. Of course they should grow to know one other, he said. They were family.

Myn had departed soon after Meagan's rescue of Alexander, stating that Alexander no longer needed him. Anastasia had resigned as Alexander's spy and had gone to Nvengaria with Myn. She had looked both relieved and rather bewildered at the turn of events, but the haunting grief had eased from her lovely eyes.

"Your Grace!" Nikolai's voice floated down the hill and soon his lithe form loped toward them from the direction of the house.

Meagan stifled a sigh. When Nikolai came to find Alexander in person, there was usually some tedious errand Alexander had to perform, such as meet with an ambassador or soothe the English king's ruffled feathers. Some things never ceased.

Alexander looked around but did not seem alarmed. He never looked alarmed, drat him. He could be calm and cool even as a wild panther.

Nikolai came panting up, his polished boots the worse from the muddy path. "A letter, Your Grace," he said, waving a folded paper. "A letter from Nvengaria. From the Imperial Prince himself!"

Without undue haste, Alexander carefully thrust his pole in the bank and waded to shore. Alex copied his movements and followed.

"The Imperial Prince has written before, Nikolai," Alexander said. "Why is it an occasion to interrupt something as important as fishing?"

"He's never sent a letter magically, Your Grace," Nikolai panted. "It popped in on the tray in the hall—poof—sent by a spell."

Alexander reached for the paper, carefully wedged his finger under the wax, and opened it. He read for a moment, then his face lost color and he curled his fingers to his lower lip.

Meagan struggled to her feet. "Alexander, what is it? Bad news?" Her heart beat faster, wondering if Penelope or her child had taken ill or become hurt.

"No, it is nothing like that." Alexander looked up at her, his eyes intense. "Damien is recalling me. He wants me to return to Nvengaria to help him with a few problems." He tried to sound matter-of-fact as he scanned the letter again. "More important than me keeping the English king under the whip."

Meagan reached him where he stood statue-still over the letter. But his body shook, and happiness kindled in his eyes.

"You mean we are going home?" she asked.

"Yes." He lifted her suddenly and spun her around, then crushed her against him. "Home." He said the word with such longing that her heart nearly burst for him. "With you, where I belong."

Nikolai stared at them. "To Nvengaria?" he repeated as though too stunned to comprehend it. "We return to Nvengaria?"

"Yes, Nikolai," Meagan said, laughing. "His Grace has just said so."

Nikolai jumped straight into the air and punched it with his fist. He let out a ululation, then he turned a cartwheel and rushed up the path, shouting the news at the top of his lungs.

Alex ran after him, attempting the cartwheel and nearly falling in the mud. He scrambled up, brushing himself off, and sprinted after Nikolai's retreating form.

Alexander held Meagan close. "Do you mind? Leaving England? Your father and stepmother may come with us, of course. I would not separate you from those you love."

She framed his strong face between her hands. "Stepmama will adore living in a castle. Do not worry, dear Alexander, it has always been my fondest dream to travel."

"Then we will go together. As leisurely as you like,

stopping in as many places as you like. I will show you the world, my Grand Duchess."

"If I see it with you, it will be a fine thing." She kissed the bridge of his nose.

He pulled her into a darker kiss, one filled with promise and excitement, and of number one hundred twenty of Adolpho's *Book of Seductions* that they'd shared last night, the one that involved soft leather tethers.

The lesson might have commenced at once had it not been for Simone's shrill voice and her slight form racing down the hill. "Oh, my dears," she cried before she reached them. "Nvengaria. In the palace with darling Penelope and my grandson. I shall have to have entirely new gowns—gracious, there is so much to do. Fancy me and your father in a royal palace." She pressed her hands together. "Oh, the Duchess of Gower and Deirdre Braithwaite will stew in envy now!"

EPILOGUE

A wild panther roamed the woods of Nvengaria, sleek and black, his blue eyes glowing. The rare panther existed in the northern mountains of the country, but this one was a little bit different.

For one thing, a red-haired young woman walked next to him, unafraid, resting her hand on his strong shoulder. The second odd thing was that two children rode on his back, fingers sunk in his fur.

One child was a seven-year-old boy with black hair and blue eyes and an eager smile. The second black-haired boy also had Nvengarian blue eyes but was about a year and a half old. The older child steadied his young friend as they rode, with great responsibility. The woman carried a child trussed on her back, a small girl with reddish-black hair who had been born six months before.

Following the panther and the woman came the Imperial Prince and Princess of Nvengaria, both in casual clothes for walking in the woods. Behind them trailed a few Nvengarians bearing a wide picnic basket between them. Heaven forbid that Prince Damien and Princess Penelope should venture into the woods for a picnic without a full seven-course meal complete with wine, cutlery, and crystal.

"Are you certain it was up this hill?" the Prince called ahead.

His handsome face held an easy attractiveness, his lips curving to a ready smile. His eyes contained intelligence, a man who knew how to use his attractiveness and charm to his own benefit.

He addressed his question to the panther, who rumbled low in his chest.

"He is certain," the red-haired Grand Duchess of Nvengaria said over her shoulder.

"How she understands him is beyond me," Damien muttered. He closed his hand around Penelope's and helped her over a rock.

"Love," Penelope answered, giving her husband a warm smile. "It translates everything."

For a moment Damien let Penelope remain on the rock, which put them at eye level, and gave her a long kiss. "What do you translate from that?" he murmured.

"That I am looking forward to retiring to our chamber this evening."

"As am I, love." Damien kissed her again, then helped her down and caught up to the others.

The panther waited impatiently, one blue eye peering around his broad shoulder.

Damien put his hands on his hips and looked around him. "Are you sure? It has been years. A decade and more, in fact."

The panther's rumble became an irritated growl. Meagan turned wide brown eyes to Prince Damien. "Alexander never forgets anything."

Damien made a conceding gesture. "That is true. Carry on."

"Besides, his senses are ever so much keener now," Meagan said. "Alex, dear, make sure the little prince holds on tight."

The panther continued his prowl, moving carefully to not jostle the two boys on his back. The little girl Meagan carried slept on, oblivious to the summer day and the two most important men in the land cutting their way through the woods. She knew only that her mama carried her and her papa was at her side.

After another five minutes of climbing, they broke through a clearing. The panther walked ahead after giving Damien a "next time, trust me" look from his animal-blue eyes.

Meagan stood at the edge of the clearing in awe. The trees gave way to a beautiful valley containing a crystal lake, framed by soaring mountains. Wildflowers covered a meadow, rolling out a carpet of blue, red, yellow, violet, and pink at their feet.

Next to her, Penelope pressed her hands together. "It is absolutely beautiful. You used to come up here, Damien?"

"When we were boys," Damien answered, his eyes taking on a faraway look. "We'd run out here at the break of dawn, Alexander and me, to fish and pick berries and get into all sorts of trouble."

At the edge of the lake, the panther gently rolled onto his side, letting the boys slide from his back. Young Alex gave the panther a fond hug, and the little prince patted him.

Meagan hurried down the slope, her mind switching to practicalities. "Alex, dear, give your papa his clothes."

Alex solemnly held out a bundle hanging from a strap. The panther took the strap in his mouth and loped away beneath a thick stand of trees.

By the time Penelope and Damien and the entourage with the basket reached the lake, Alexander the Grand Duke of Nvengaria emerged from the woods dressed in breeches, shirt, and boots.

Meagan admired him as he strode to them. She loved it when he left the Nvengarian finery behind and wore clothes that showed off his physique. His muscled chest was shadowed in the *V* of the loose shirt, giving her a glimpse of black hair that curled across his skin. The breeches hugged his thighs in a fine way, and Meagan found it difficult to drag her gaze away.

"It seems like forever since we last came here," Damien breathed as he and Alexander strolled side by side while the ladies set up their luncheon.

"A long time, certainly," Alexander agreed. He glanced at his son and Damien's playing together in the tall grass, the older showing the younger some gentle game. "Things have come full circle."

Damien nodded. "There was a time I never thought our children would play together." He bent a glance on his wife and Alexander's, two women from England who had their heads together, giggling over something.

Alexander watched them too. He remembered what had happened the last time he'd caught Meagan and Penelope giggling together. Meagan had met him in their bedchamber that night, having once more strewn it with rose petals and scent. She'd been wearing nothing but a leather and lace corset with a collar of diamonds around her throat.

While he'd stood in stunned silence and feasted his eyes on her, Meagan had blushed deeply. "Do close the door, Alexander, before someone sees me."

The door had banged behind him instantly, and Alexander had turned the key in the lock.

"Do you not recognize seduction number two hundred twelve?" she'd asked impatiently. "Penelope and I spent all day planning this."

The lovemaking after that had been nothing short of explosive. Watching Meagan now, whispering with Penelope and throwing mysterious glances at him, made his arousal stir in anticipation.

"English roses," Damien said absently.

Alexander snapped his attention back to him. "What?"

Damien gazed at their wives, sun gleaming on Meagan's red hair and Penelope's honey-golden. "English roses brought us happiness. And friendship again?"

Alexander had not had much time to speak with Damien personally, as the ten months since he and Meagan had arrived in Nvnegaria had been consumed with either political duties or Alexander's preoccupation with the birth of his second child.

He'd become instantly besotted with his daughter, Annie, and stole as many minutes as he could to be with her and Alex and Meagan. Alex would grow up to be Grand Duke, and Annie would be a sought-after bride, but Alexander determined that they both would have childhoods, happy ones.

Alexander studied Damien, his oldest friend and a man he'd once thought was his bitterest enemy. As boys, they'd roamed these woods. As young men, they'd been pulled apart, and then hatred and fear had erected an insurmountable wall between them. At least, they'd thought it insurmountable.

"Your father is dead," Alexander said as Damien waited, eyes watchful. "He was a monster, and he made us enemies. We should not continue to let him win."

THE MAD, BAD DUKE   369

Damien's mouth relaxed into a smile. "Precisely what I was about to say. Or at least, very close." He held out his hand. "Friends?"

Alexander took Damien's callused hand, and something warm laced his heart. "Friends."

They shook firmly, then drew apart, looking back at their wives again, a favorite pastime of them both.

Damien's eyes narrowed. "They are planning something."

Both Penelope and Meagan were watching them with sly smiles, and Alexander's heartbeat sped. "Yes, they look quite conspiratorial."

"They've learned Nvengarian intrigue," Damien offered.

"God help us."

"We will need it."

"They also have Adolpho's *Book of Seductions*," Alexander reminded him.

They shared a worried glance, then Damien broke into a grin. "Damn, but we are lucky men."

"Indeed." Alexander grinned back.

"Shall we find out what they intend?" Damien asked.

"Let them reveal it in their own time," Alexander said as they started walking toward the ladies. "We can pretend we know, and drive them mad wondering how we guessed."

Damien threw back his head and laughed. Sure enough, both women looked at them, their smiles wavering.

"You are an evil man, Alexander of Nvengaria," Damien chuckled.

"I have had a lifetime of practice," he answered, and then they went to their wives and children. Meagan greeted Alexander with a kiss that warmed his blood, her eyes glinting in suppressed excitement.

As the picnic commenced, Alexander and Damien gathered wild raspberries from a patch they remembered, which had grown even bigger and richer in the years between. They were joined soon after by Myn and Anastasia, Myn as cryptic as ever, Anastasia relaxed and laughing, happiness radiating from her.

That night, Alexander reposed next to Meagan in their huge bed in the palace, tired from their day in the sunshine and games with the children. He'd become a panther again and Myn a wolf, to the boys' great delight.

When they'd at last retired to bed, Meagan had begun one of Adolpho's elaborate seductions, which involved wine and fruit and scented oils, but Alexander had swept aside the accoutrements and taken Meagan in deep, satisfying lovemaking.

Now Meagan smiled at him across the pillow, her eyelids heavy. "I love you, Alexander."

Alexander shimmered briefly into panther form and licked her face. She squealed and laughed, and he shimmered back. "Why did you do that?" Meagan gasped, wiping her face on the sheets.

"To say I love you too."

"Perhaps you could say it not so wetly."

Alexander grinned. He dabbed her face dry with the sheet, then rolled on top of her and showed her, by deed and by word, how very much he, Alexander the man, loved her.

JENNIFER ASHLEY

Penelope & Prince Charming

His blue eyes beguile. His muscular form can satisfy any fantasy—and to top it off, he's royalty! What woman would dare refuse the most sought-after lover in Europe? Miss Twice-a-Jilt Penelope Trask, that's who. And, unfortunately for Damien, marrying Penelope is the only way to inherit his kingdom. Good thing this enchantingly infuriating woman doesn't seem *completely* immune to his many charms. But wooing is difficult, and a strong desire threatens to overwhelm them every time they touch. Why hasn't anyone mentioned the road to happily-ever-after is so difficult?

Dorchester Publishing Co., Inc.
P.O. Box 6640   ___5606-2
Wayne, PA 19087-8640 $6.99 US/$8.99 CAN
Please add $2.50 for shipping and handling for the first book and $.75 for each additional book. NY and PA residents, add appropriate sales tax. No cash, stamps, or CODs. Canadian orders require $2.00 for shipping and handling and must be paid in U.S. dollars. Prices and availability subject to change. **Payment must accompany all orders.**

Name: _____

Address: _____

City: _____ State: _____ Zip: _____

E-mail: _____

I have enclosed $_____ in payment for the checked book(s).

CHECK OUT OUR WEBSITE! www.dorchesterpub.com
____ Please send me a free catalog.

JENNIFER ASHLEY
CONFESSIONS
of a
LINGERIE
ADDICT

The fixation began on New Year's Day: Silky, expensive slips from New York and Italy. Camisoles and thongs from Beverly Hills. Before, Brenda Scott would have blushed to be caught dead in them. Now, she's ditched the shy and mousy persona that got her dumped by her rich and perfect fiancé, and she is sexy. Underneath her sensible clothes, Brenda is the woman she wants to be.

After all, why can't she be wild and crazy? Nick, the sexy stranger she met on New Year's, already seems to think she is. Of course, he didn't know the old Brenda. How long before Nick strips it all away and finds the truth beneath? And would that be a bad thing?

Dorchester Publishing Co., Inc.
P.O. Box 6640   ___ 52636-0
Wayne, PA 19087-8640 $6.99 US/$8.99 CAN

Please add $2.50 for shipping and handling for the first book and $.75 for each additional book. NY and PA residents, add appropriate sales tax. No cash, stamps, or CODs. Canadian orders require an extra $2.00 for shipping and handling and must be paid in U.S. dollars. Prices and availability subject to change. **Payment must accompany all orders.**

Name: _____

Address: _____

City: _____ State:_____ Zip: _____

E-mail: _____

I have enclosed $_____ in payment for the checked book(s).

CHECK OUT OUR WEBSITE! www.dorchesterpub.com
_____ Please send me a free catalog.

Just One Sip

Katie MacAlister
Jennifer Ashley
Minda Webber

A sunbathing vamp in Vegas? Meredith Black is absolutely positive the tanned god with the gorgeous smile couldn't have possibly made her his for eternity with just one glance. But he'll sure have fun proving it.

‡ ‡ ‡

Battling a demon lord is all in a day's work for the Dark One named Sebastian. But now he must take on a horde of unhappy zombies and an obnoxious teen vampire if he wants to win the hand of the one woman who can make him whole.

‡ ‡ ‡

Talk show host Lucy Campbell has made a career of interviewing Druid witches, trolls, and an occasional goblin. But now she wants more. Only she wasn't expecting to get involved with a vampire detective who has a slight incubus problem.

Dorchester Publishing Co., Inc.
P.O. Box 6640   ___52659-X
Wayne, PA 19087-8640 $6.99 US/$8.99 CAN

Please add $2.50 for shipping and handling for the first book and $.75 for each additional book. NY and PA residents, add appropriate sales tax. No cash, stamps, or CODs. Canadian orders require an extra $2.00 for shipping and handling and must be paid in U.S. dollars. Prices and availability subject to change. **Payment must accompany all orders.**

Name: _____

Address: _____

City: _____ State: _____ Zip: _____

E-mail: _____

I have enclosed $_____ in payment for the checked book(s).

CHECK OUT OUR WEBSITE! www.dorchesterpub.com
____ Please send me a free catalog.

ATTENTION
BOOK LOVERS!

Can't get enough of your favorite **ROMANCE**?

Call **1-800-481-9191** to:

❋ order books,

❋ receive a **FREE** catalog,

❋ join our book clubs to **SAVE 30%!**

Open Mon.-Fri. 10 AM-9 PM EST

Visit **www.dorchesterpub.com**
for special offers and inside
information on the authors you love.

We accept Visa, MasterCard or Discover®.
LEISURE BOOKS ♥ LOVE SPELL